HIGH PRAISE FOR MORRIS WEST'S VATICAN TRILOGY

The Shoes of the Fisherman
"The year's most important novel, the year's best. A MASTERPIECE."
—*Chicago Tribune*

"A novelistic drama of great power and immediate concern. BRILLIANT." —*Time*

"MAGNIFICENT!"
—*New York Herald Tribune*

The Clowns of God
"Excellently written and highly provocative...in the very best Morris West tradition."
—Irving Stone, author of
The Agony and the Ecstasy

"Stunningly apocalyptic...engrossing and full of ideas...MORRIS WEST AT THE TOP OF HIS FORM!"
—*Sunday Express* (London)

Lazarus
"A superb, absorbing novel...a tense and exciting thriller!"
—*Library Journal*

OVER 60 MILLION COPIES OF MORRIS WEST'S BOOKS SOLD WORLDWIDE!

Also by Morris West

THE SHOES OF THE FISHERMAN

MORRIS WEST

ST. MARTIN'S PAPERBACKS

THE SHOES OF THE FISHERMAN

Copyright © 1963 by Morris L. West.

Cover illustration by Danilo Ducak.

All rights reserved. No part of this book may be used or reproduced in any manner whatsoever without written permission except in the case of brief quotations embodied in critical articles or reviews. For information address St. Martin's Press, 175 Fifth Avenue, New York, N.Y. 10010.

Library of Congress Catalog Card Number: 89-70343

ISBN: 0-312-92466-6

Printed in the United States of America

William Morrow and Company edition published 1963
St. Martin's Press trade paperback edition published 1989
St. Martin's Paperbacks edition/April 1991

10 9 8 7 6 5 4 3 2

AUTHOR'S NOTE

Rome is a city older than the Catholic Church. Everything that could happen has happened there, and no doubt will happen again. This is a book set in a fictional time, peopled with fictional characters, and no reference is intended to any living person, whether in the Church or out of it.

I cannot ask my friends to accept the responsibility for my opinions. So those who have helped me with this book must remain anonymous.

To those who gave me their stories, to those who placed their learning at my disposal, to those who spent upon me the charity of the Faith I offer my heartfelt thanks.

Thanks are due also to Penguin Books, Ltd., for permission to reprint three extracts from the Philip Vellacott translations of Euripides (*Alcestis, Iphigenia in Tauris, Hippolytus*).

Also to Reverend Father Pedro A. Gonzalez, O.P., for a passage from his thesis on Miguel de Unamuno, which is incorporated without quotes in the body of the text.

M.L.W.

THE SHOES OF
THE FISHERMAN

I

THE POPE was dead. The Camerlengo had announced it. The Master of Ceremonies, the notaries, the doctors, had consigned him under signature into eternity. His ring was defaced and his seals were broken. The bells had been rung throughout the city. The pontifical body had been handed to the embalmers so that it might be a seemly object for the veneration of the faithful. Now it lay, between white candles, in the Sistine Chapel, with the Noble Guard keeping a deathwatch under Michelangelo's frescoes of the *Last Judgment*.

The Pope was dead. Tomorrow the clergy of the Basilica would claim him and expose him to the public in the Chapel of the Most Holy Sacrament. On the third day they would bury him, clothed in full pontificals, with a mitre on his head, a purple veil on his face, and a red ermine blanket to warm him in the crypt. The medals he had struck and coinage he had minted would be buried with him to identify him to any who might dig him up a thousand years later. They would seal him in three coffins —one of cypress; one of lead to keep him from the damp and to carry his coat of arms, and the certificate of his death; the last of elm so that he might seem, at least, like other men who go to the grave in a wooden box.

The Pope was dead. So they would pray for him as for any other: "Enter not into judgment with thy servant, O Lord . . . Deliver him from eternal death." Then they would lower him into the vault under the high altar, where perhaps—but only perhaps—he would moulder into dust with the dust of Peter; and a mason would brick up the vault and fix, on a marble tablet with his name, his title and the date of his birth and his obit.

The Pope was dead. They would mourn him with nine days of Masses and give him nine absolutions—of which, having been greater in his life than other men, he might have greater need after his death.

Then they would forget him, because the See of Peter was vacant, the life of the Church was in syncope, and the Almighty was without a Vicar on this troubled planet.

The See of Peter was vacant. So the Cardinals of the Sacred College assumed trusteeship over the authority of the Fisherman, though they lacked the power to exercise it. The power did not reside in them but in Christ, and none could assume it but by lawful transmission and election.

The See of Peter was vacant. So they struck two medals, one for the Camerlengo, which bore a large umbrella over crossed keys. There was no one under the umbrella, and this was a sign to the most ignorant that there was no incumbent for the Chair of the Apostles, and that all that was done had only an interim character. The second medal was that of the Governor of the Conclave: he who must assemble the Cardinals of the Church and lock them inside the chambers of the conclave and keep them there until they had issued with a new Pope.

Every coin new-minted in the Vatican City, every stamp now issued, bore the words *sede vacante*, which even those without Latinity might understand as "while the Chair is vacant." The Vatican newspaper carried the same sign on its front page, and would wear a black band of mourning until the new Pontiff was named.

Every news service in the world had a representative camped on the doorstep of the Vatican press office; and from each point of the compass old men came, bent with years or infirmity, to put on the scarlet of princes and sit in conclave for the making of a new Pope.

There was Carlin the American, and Rahamani the Syrian, and Hsien the Chinese, and Hanna the Irishman from Australia. There was Councha from Brazil, and da Costa from Portugal. There was Morand from Paris, and Lavigne from Brussels, and Lambertini from Venice, and Brandon from the City of London. There were a Pole and two Germans, and a Ukrainian whom nobody knew because his name had been reserved in the breast of the last Pope and had been proclaimed only a few days before his death. In all there were eighty-five men, of whom the eldest was ninety-two and the youngest, the Ukrainian, was fifty. As each of them arrived in the city, he presented himself and his credentials to the urbane and gentle Valerio Rinaldi, who was the Cardinal Camerlengo.

Rinaldi welcomed each with a slim, dry hand and a smile of mild irony. To each he administered the oath of the conclavist: that he understood and would rigorously observe all the rules of the election as laid down in the Apostolic Constitution of 1945, that he would under pain of a reserved excommunication preserve the secret of the election, that he would not serve by his votes the interest of any secular power, that if he were elected Pope he would not surrender any temporal right of the Holy See which might be deemed necessary to its independence.

No one refused the oath; but Rinaldi, who had a sense of humor, wondered many times why it was necessary to administer it at all—unless the Church had a healthy dis-respect for the virtues of its princes. Old men were apt to be too easily wounded. So when he outlined the terms of the oath, Valerio Rinaldi laid a mild emphasis on the counsel of the Apostolic Constitution, that all the proceed-ings of the election should be conducted with "prudence, charity, and a singular calm."

His caution was not unjustified. The history of papal elections was a stormy one, at times downright turbulent. When Damasus the Spaniard was elected in the fourth century, there were massacres in the churches of the city. Leo V was imprisoned, tortured, and murdered by the Theophylacts, so that for nearly a century the Church was ruled by puppets directed by the Theophylact women, Theodora and Marozia. In the conclave of 1623 eight Car-dinals and forty of their assistants died of malaria, and there were harsh scenes and rough words over the election of the Saint, Pius X.

All in all, Rinaldi concluded—though he was wise enough to keep the conclusion to himself—it was best not to trust too much to the crusty tempers and the frustrated vanities of old men. Which brought him by a round turn to the problem of housing and feeding eighty-five of them with their servants and assistants until the election should be finished. Some of them, it seemed, would have to take over quarters from the Swiss Guard. None of them could be lodged too far from bathroom or toilet, and all had to be provided with a minimum service by way of

cooks, barbers, surgeons, physicians, valets, porters, secretaries, waiters, carpenters, plumbers, firemen (in case any
weary prelate nodded off with a cigar in his hand!). If
(God forbid!) any Cardinal were in prison or under in-
dictment, he would have to be brought to the conclave
and made to perform his functions under military guard.

This time, however, no one was in prison—except Kri-
zanic, in Yugoslavia, and he was in prison for the Faith,
which was a different matter—and the late Pope had run
an efficient administration, so that Valerio Cardinal Rinaldi even had time to spare to meet with his colleague,
Leone of the Holy Office, who was also the Dean of the
Sacred College. Leone lived up to his name. He had a
white lion's mane and a growling temper. He was, moreover, a Roman, bred-in-the-bone, dyed-in-the-wool. Rome
was for him the center of the world, and centralism was
a doctrine almost as immutable as that of the Trinity and
the Procession of the Holy Ghost. With his great eagle
beak and his jowly jaw, he looked like a senator strayed
out of Augustan times, and his pale eyes looked out on the
world with wintry disapproval.

Innovation was for him the first step toward heresy,
and he sat in the Holy Office like a grizzled watchdog,
whose hackles would rise at the first unfamiliar sound in
doctrine interpretation or practice. One of his French colleagues had said, with more wit than charity, "Leone
smells of the fire." But the general belief was that he
would plunge his own hand into the flame rather than set
his signature to the smallest deviation from orthodoxy.

Rinaldi respected him, though he had never been able
to like him, and so their intercourse had been limited to
the courtesies of their common trade. Tonight, however,

the old lion seemed in gentler mood, and was disposed to be talkative. His pale, watchful eyes were lit with a momentary amusement.

"I'm eighty-two, my friend, and I've buried three Popes. I'm beginning to feel lonely."

"If we don't get a younger man this time," said Rinaldi mildly, "you may well bury a fourth."

Leone shot him a quick look from under his shaggy brows. "And what's that supposed to mean?"

Rinaldi shrugged and spread his fine hands in a Roman gesture. "Just what it says. We're all too old. There are not more than half a dozen of us who can give the Church what it needs at this moment: personality, a decisive policy, time and continuity to make the policy work."

"Do you think you're one of the half dozen?"

Rinaldi smiled with thin irony. "I know I'm not. When the new man is chosen—whoever he is—I propose to offer him my resignation and ask his permission to rusticate at home. It's taken me fifteen years to build a garden in that place of mine. I'd like a little while to enjoy it."

"Do you think I have a chance of election?" asked Leone bluntly.

"I hope not," said Rinaldi.

Leone threw back his great mane and laughed. "Don't worry. I know I haven't. They need someone quite different; someone"—he hesitated, fumbling for the phrase—"someone who has compassion on the multitude, who sees them, as Christ saw them—sheep without a shepherd. I'm not that sort of man. I wish I were."

Leone heaved his bulky body out of the chair and walked to the big table, where an antique globe stood among a litter of books. He spun the globe slowly on its axis, so that now one country, now another, swam into the light. "Look at it, my friend! The world, our vineyard! Once we colonized it in the name of Christ. Not righteously always, not always justly or wisely, but the Cross was there, and the Sacraments were there, and however a man lived—in purple or in chains—there was a chance for him to die like a son of God. Now . . . ? Now we are everywhere in retreat. China is lost to us, and Asia and all the Russians. Africa will soon be gone, and the South Americas will be next. You know it. I know it. It is the measure of our failure that we have sat all these years in Rome and watched it happen." He checked the spinning globe with an unsteady hand, and then turned to face his visitor with a new question. "If you had your life over, Rinaldi, what would you do with it?"

Rinaldi looked up with that deprecating smile which lent him so much charm. "I think I should probably do the same things again. Not that I'm very proud of them, but they happened to be the only things I could do well. I get along with people because I've never been capable of very deep feelings about them. That makes me, I suppose, a natural diplomat. I don't like to quarrel. I like even less to be emotionally involved. I like privacy and I enjoy study. So I'm a good canonist, a reasonable historian, and an adequate linguist. I've never had very strong passions. You might, if you felt malicious, call me a cold fish. So I've achieved a reputation for good conduct without having to work for it. . . . All in all, I've had a very satisfactory life—satisfactory to myself, of course. How the recording angel sees it is another matter."

"Don't underrate yourself, man," said Leone sourly. "You've done a great deal better than you'll admit."

"I need time and reflection to set my soul in order," said Rinaldi quietly. "May I count on you to help me resign?"

"Of course."

"Thank you. Now, suppose the inquisitor answers his own question. What would you do if you had to begin again?"

"I've thought about it often," said Leone heavily. "If I didn't marry—and I'm not sure but that's what I needed to make me halfway human—I'd be a country priest with just enough theology to hear confession, and just enough Latin to get through Mass and the sacramental formulae. But with heart enough to know what griped in the guts of other men and made them cry into their pillows at night. I'd sit in front of my church on a summer evening and read my office and talk about the weather and the crops, and learn to be gentle with the poor and humble with the unhappy ones. . . . You know what I am now? A walking encyclopaedia of dogma and theological controversy. I can smell out an error faster than a Dominican. And what does it mean? Nothing. Who cares about theology except the theologians? We are necessary, but less important than we think. The Church is Christ—Christ and the people. And all the people want to know is whether or no there is a God, and what is His relation with them, and how they can get back to Him when they stray."

"Large questions," said Rinaldi gently, "not to be answered by small minds or gross ones."

Leone shook his lion's mane stubbornly. "For the people they come down to simplicities! Why shouldn't I covet my neighbor's wife? Who takes the revenge that is forbidden to me? And who cares when I am sick and tired, and dying in an upstairs room? I can give them a theologian's answer. But whom do they believe but the man who feels the answers in his heart and bears the scars of their consequences in his own flesh? Where are the men like that? Is there one among all of us who wear the red hat? Eh . . . I" His grim mouth twitched into a grin of embarrassment, and he flung out his arms in mock despair. "We are what we are, and God has to take half the responsibility even for theologians! . . . Now tell me— where do we go for our Pope?"

"This time," said Rinaldi crisply, "we should choose him for the people and not for ourselves."

"There will be eighty-five of us in the conclave. How many will agree on what is best for the people?"

Rinaldi looked down at the backs of his carefully manicured fingers. He said softly, "If we showed them the man first, perhaps we could get them to agree."

Leone's answer was swift and emphatic. "You would have to show him to me first."

"And if you agreed?"

"Then there would be another question," said Leone flatly. "How many of our brethren will think as we do?"

The question was subtler than it looked, and they both knew it. Here, in fact, was the whole loaded issue of a papal election, the whole paradox of the Papacy. The man who wore the Fisherman's ring was Vicar of Christ, Vicegerent of the Almighty. His dominion was spiritual and universal. He was the servant of all the servants of God, even of those who did not acknowledge him.

On the other hand, he was Bishop of Rome, Metropolitan of an Italian see. The Romans claimed by historic tradition a pre-emption on his presence and his services. They relied on him for employment, for the tourist trade

and the bolstering of their economy by Vatican invest-
ment, for the preservation of their historic monuments
and national privileges. His court was Italian in character;
the greater number of his household and his administrators were Italian. If he could not deal with them familiarly in their own tongue, he stood naked to palace intrigue and every kind of partisan interest.

Once upon a time the Roman view had had a pecul-
iarly universal aspect. The numen of the ancient empire
still hung about it, and the memory of the Pax Romana
had not yet vanished from the consciousness of Europe.
But the numen was fading. Imperial Rome had never subdued Russia or Asia, and the Latins who conquered South
America had brought no peace, but the sword. England
had revolted long since, as she had revolted earlier from
the legions of Roman occupation. So that there was sound
argument for a new, non-Italian succession to the papal
throne—just as there was sound reason for believing that
a non-Italian might become either a puppet of his ministers or a victim of their talent for intrigue.

The perpetuity of the Church was an article of faith;
but its diminutions and corruptions, and its jeopardy by
the follies of its members, were part of the canon of history. There was plenty of ground for cynicism. But over
and over again the cynics were confounded by the uncanny capacity for self-renewal in the Church and in the
Papacy. The cynics had their own explanations. The faithful put it down to the indwelling of the Holy Ghost. Either
way there was an uncomfortable mystery: how the chaos
of history could issue in so consistent a hold on dogma or
why an omniscient God chose such a messy method of
preserving his foothold in the minds of his creatures.

So every conclave began with the invocation of the

Paraclete. On the day of the walling-in Rinaldi led his
old men and their attendants into St. Peter's. Then Leone
came, dressed in a scarlet chasuble and accompanied by
his deacons and subdeacons, to begin the Mass of the
Holy Spirit. As he watched the celebrant, weighed down
by the elaborate vestments, moving painfully through the
ritual of the Sacrifice, Rinaldi felt a pang of pity for him
and a sudden rush of understanding.

They were all in the same galley, these leaders of the
Church—himself along with them. They were men without issue, who had "made themselves eunuchs for the
love of God." A long time since they had dedicated themselves with greater or less sincerity to the service of a hidden God, and to the propagation of an unprovable mystery.
Through the temporality of the Church they had attained to honor—more honor, perhaps, than any of them
might have attained in the secular state; but they all lay
under the common burden of age—failing faculties, the
loneliness of eminence, and the fear of a reckoning that
might find them bankrupt debtors.

He thought, too, of the stratagem which he had planned
with Leone, to introduce a candidate who was still a
stranger to most of the voters, and to promote his cause
without breaching the Apostolic Constitution, which they
had sworn to preserve. He wondered if this were not a
presumption and an attempt to circumvent Providence,
whom they were invoking at this very moment. Yet if God
had chosen, as the Faith taught, to use man as a free instrument for a divine plan, how else could one act? One
could not let so momentous an occasion as a papal election play itself like a game of chance. Prudence was en-
joined on all—prayful preparation and then considered
action, and afterward resignation and submission. Yet

however prudently one planned, one could not escape the uncanny feeling that one walked unwary and un-purged on sacred ground.

The heat, the flicker of the candles, the chant of the choir, and the mesmeric pace of the ritual made him drowsy, and he stole a surreptitious glance at his colleagues to see if any of them had noticed his nodding.

Like twin choirs of ancient archangels they sat on either side of the sanctuary, their breasts hung with golden crosses, the princely seals agleam on their folded hands, their faces scored by age and the experience of power.

There was Rahamani of Antioch, with his spade beard and his craggy brows and his bright, half-mystical eyes. There was Benedetti, round as a dumpling, with pink cheeks and candy-floss hair, who ran the Vatican bank. Next to him was Potocki from Poland, he of the high, bald dome and the suffering mouth and the wise, calculating eyes. Tatsue from Japan wanted only the saffron robe to make him a Buddhist image, and Hsien, the exiled Chinese, sat between Ragambwe, the black man from Kenya, and Pallenberg, the lean ascetic from Munich.

Rinaldi's shrewd eyes ranged along the choir stalls, naming each one for his virtues or his shortcomings, trying on each the classic label *papabile,* he-who-has-the-makings-of-a-Pope. In theory every member of the conclave could wear it; in practice very few were eligible.

Age was a bar to some. Talent or temperament or reputation was an impediment to others. Nationality was a vital question. One could not elect an American without seeming to divide East and West even further. A Negro Pope might seem a spectacular symbol of the new revolutionary nations, just as a Japanese might be a useful link between Asia and Europe. But the Princes of the Church

were old men and as wary of spectacular gestures as they
were of historic hangovers. A German Pope might alienate
the sympathies of those who had suffered in World War
II. A Frenchman would recall old memories of Avignon
and tramontane rebellions. While there were still dictator-
ships in Spain and Portugal, an Iberian Pope could be a
diplomatic indiscretion. Gonfalone, the Milanese, had the
reputation of being a saint, but he was becoming more
and more of a recluse, and there was question of his fit-
ness for so public an office. Leone was an autocrat who
might well mistake the fire of zealotry for the flame of
compassion.

The lector was reading from the Acts of the Apostles.
"'In those days, Peter began and said, Men, Brethren, the
Lord charged us to preach to the people and to testify
that He is the one who has been appointed by God to be
judge of the living and of the dead. . . .'" The choir sang,
"*Veni, Sancte Spiritus* . . . Come, Holy Spirit, and fill
the hearts of the faithful." Then Leone began to read in
his strong stubborn voice the Gospel for the day of the
conclave: "'He who enters not by the door into the
sheepfold, but climbs up another way is a thief and a
robber. But he who enters by the door is the shepherd of
the sheep.'" Rinaldi bent his head in his hands and
prayed that the man he was offering would be in truth a
shepherd, and that the conclave might hand him the
crook and the ring.

When the Mass was over, the celebrant retired to the
sacristy to take off his vestments and the Cardinals relaxed in the stalls. Some of them whispered to one another, a couple were still nodding drowsily, and one was
seen to take a surreptitious pinch of snuff. The next part
of the ceremony was a formality, but it promised to be a

boring one. A prelate would read them a homily in Latin, pointing out once again the importance of the election and their moral obligation to carry it out in an orderly and honest fashion. By ancient custom, the prelate was chosen for the purity of his Latin, but this time the Camerlengo had made another arrangement.

A whisper of surprise stirred round the assembly as they saw Rinaldi leave his place and walk down to the far end of the stalls on the Gospel side of the altar. He offered his hand to a tall, thin Cardinal and led him to the pulpit. When he stood elevated in the full glare of the lights, they saw that he was the youngest of them all. His hair was black, his square beard was black, too, and down his left cheek was a long, livid scar. On his breast, in addition to the cross, was a pectoral ikon representing a Byzantine Madonna and Child. When he crossed himself, he made the sign from right to left, in the Slavic manner; yet when he began to speak, it was not in Latin but in a pure and melodious Tuscan. Across the nave Leone smiled a grim approval at Rinaldi, and then like their colleagues, they surrendered themselves to the simple eloquence of the stranger:

"My name is Kiril Lakota, and I am come the latest and the least into this Sacred College. I speak to you today by the invitation of our brother the Cardinal Camerlengo. To most of you I am a stranger because my people are scattered and I have spent the last seventeen years in prison. If I have any rights among you, any credit at all, let this be the foundation of them—that I speak for the lost ones, for those who walk in darkness and in the valley of the shadow of death. It is for them and not for ourselves that we are entering into conclave. It is for them and not for ourselves that we must elect a Pontiff. The

first man who held this office was one who walked with
Christ, and was crucified like the Master. Those who have
best served the Church and the faithful are those who
have been closest to Christ and to the people, who are
the image of Christ. We have power in our hands, my
brothers. We shall put even greater power into the hands
of the man we elect, but we must use the power as servants and not as masters. We must consider that we are
what we are—priests, bishops, pastors—by virtue of an
act of dedication to the people who are the flock of Christ.
What we possess, even to the clothes on our backs, comes
to us out of their charity. The whole material fabric of the
Church was raised stone on stone, gold on golden offering,
by the sweat of the faithful, and they have given it into
our hands for stewardship. It is they who have educated
us so that we may teach them and their children. It is
they who humble themselves before our priesthood, as
before the divine Priesthood of Christ. It is for them that
we exercise the sacramental and the sacrificial powers
which are given to us in the anointing and the laying on
of hands. If in our deliberations we serve any other cause
but this, then we are traitors. It is not asked of us that we
shall agree on what is best for the Church, but only that
we shall deliberate in charity and humility, and in the
end give our obedience to the man who shall be chosen
by the majority. We are asked to act swiftly so that the
Church may not be left without a head. In all this we
must be what, in the end, our Pontiff shall proclaim himself to be—servants of the servants of God. Let us in these
final moments resign ourselves as willing instruments for
His hands. Amen."

It was so simply said that it might have been the customary formality, yet the man himself, with his scarred

face and his strong voice and his crooked, eloquent
hands, lent to the words an unexpected poignancy. There
was a long silence while he left the pulpit and returned
to his own place. Leone nodded his lion's head in approval, and Rinaldi breathed a silent prayer of gratitude.
Then the Master of Ceremonies took command and led
the Cardinals and their attendants with their confessor
and their physician and surgeon, and the Architect of the
Conclave, and the conclave workmen, out of the Basilica
and into the confines of the Vatican itself.

In the Sistine Chapel they were sworn again. Then
Leone gave the order for the bells to be rung, so that all
who did not belong to the conclave should leave the
sealed area at once. The servants led each of the Cardinals
to his apartment. Then the prefect of the Master of Ceremonies, with the Architect of the Conclave, began the
ritual search of the enclosed area. They went from room
to room pulling aside draperies, throwing light into dark
corners, opening closets, until every space was declared
free from intruders.

At the entrance of the great stairway of Pius IX they
halted and the Noble Guard marched out of the conclave
area, followed by the Marshal of the Conclave and his
aides. The great door was locked. The Marshal of the
Conclave turned his key on the outside. On the inside the
Masters of Ceremonies turned their own key. The Marshal ordered his flag hoisted over the Vatican, and from
this moment no one might leave or enter, or pass a message, until the new Pope was elected and named.

Alone in his quarters, Kiril Cardinal Lakota was beginning a private purgatory. It was a recurrent state whose
symptoms were now familiar to him: a cold sweat that

broke out on face and palms, a trembling in the limbs, a twitching of the severed nerves in his face, a panic fear that the room was closing in to crush him. Twice in his life he had been walled up in the bunkers of an underground prison. Four months in all, he had endured the terrors of darkness and cold and solitude and near starvation, so that the pillars of his reason had rocked under the strain. Nothing in his years of Siberian exile had afflicted him so much nor left so deep a scar on his memory. Nothing had brought him so close to abjuration and apostasy.

He had been beaten often, but the bruised tissue had healed itself in time. He had been interrogated till every nerve was screaming and his mind had lapsed into a merciful confusion. From this, too, he had emerged, stronger in faith and in reason, but the horror of solitary confinement would remain with him until he died. Kamenev had kept his promise. "You will never be able to forget me. Wherever you go, I shall be. Whatever you become, I shall be part of you." Even here, in the neutral confines of Vatican City, in the princely room under Raphael's frescoes, Kamenev, the insidious tormentor, was with him. There was only one escape from him, and that was the one he had learned in the bunker—the projection of the tormented spirit into the arms of the Almighty.

He threw himself on his knees, buried his face in his hands, and tried to concentrate every faculty of mind and body into the simple act of abandonment.

His lips commanded no words, but the will seized on the plaint of Christ in Gethsemane. " 'Father, if it be possible, let this Chalice pass.' "

In the end he knew it would pass, but first the agony must be endured. The walls pressed in upon him relentlessly. The ceiling weighed down on him like a leaden vestment. The darkness pressed upon his eyeballs and packed itself inside his skull case. Every muscle in his body knotted in pain, and his teeth chattered as if from the rigors of fever. Then he became deathly cold, and deathly calm, and waited passively for the light that was the beginning of peace and of communion.

The light was like a dawn seen from a high hill, flooding swiftly into every fold of the landscape, so that the whole pattern of its history was revealed at one glance. The road of his own pilgrimage was there like a scarlet ribbon that stretched four thousand miles from Lvov, in the Ukraine, to Nikolayevsk, on the Sea of Okhotsk.

When the war with the Germans was over, he had been named, in spite of his youth, Metropolitan of Lvov, successor to the great and saintly Andrew Szepticky, leader of all the Ruthenian Catholics. Shortly afterwards he had been arrested with six other bishops and deported to the eastern limits of Siberia. The six others had died, and he had been left alone, shepherd of a lost flock, to carry the Cross on his own shoulders.

For seventeen years he had been in prison, or in the labor camps. Once only in all that time he had been able to say Mass, with a thimbleful of wine and a crust of white bread. All that he could cling to of doctrine and prayer and sacramental formulae was locked in his own brain. All that he had tried to spend of strength and compassion upon his fellow prisoners he had had to dredge out of himself and out of the well of the Divine Mercy. Yet his body, weakened by torture, had grown miraculously strong again at slave labor in the mines and on the road gangs, so that even Kamenev could no longer mock him, but was struck with wonder at his survival.

For Kamenev, his tormentor in the first interrogations, would always come back; and each time he came he had risen a little higher in the Marxist order. Each time, he had seemed a little more friendly, as if he were making a slow surrender to respect for his victim.

Even from the mountaintop of contemplation he could still see Kamenev—cold, sardonic, searching him for the slightest sign of weakness, the slightest hint of surrender. In the beginning he had had to force himself to pray for the jailer. After a while they had come to a bleak kind of brotherhood, even as the one rose higher and the other seemed to sink deeper into a fellowship with the Siberian slaves. In the end it was Kamenev who had organized his escape—inflicting on him a final irony by giving him the identity of a dead man.

"You will go free," Kamenev had said, "because I need you free. But you will always owe me a debt because I have killed a man to give you a name. One day I shall come to you to ask for payment, and you will pay, whatever it may cost."

It was as though the jailer had assumed the mantle of prophecy, because Kiril Lakota had escaped and made his way to Rome, to find that a dying Pope had made him a Cardinal "in the breast"—a man of destiny, a hingeman of Mother Church.

To this point the road in retrospect was clear. He could trace in its tragedies the promise of future mercies. For every one of the bishops who had died for his belief, a man had died in his arms in the camp, blessing the Almighty for a final absolution. The scattered flock would not all lose the faith for which they had suffered. Some of them would remain to hand on the creed, and to keep a small light burning that one day might light a thousand

torches. In the degradation of the road gangs he had seen
how the strangest men upheld the human dignities. He
had baptized children with a handful of dirty water and
seen them die unmarked by the miseries of the world.

He himself had learned humility and gratitude and the
courage to believe in an Omnipotence working by a
mighty evolution toward an ultimate good. He had
learned compassion and tenderness and the meaning of
the cry in the night. He had learned to hope that for Kamenev himself he might be an instrument, if not of ultimate enlightenment, then at least of ultimate absolution.
But all this was in the past, and the pattern still had to
work itself out beyond Rome into a fathomless future.
Even the light of contemplation was not thrown beyond
Rome. There was a veil drawn, and the veil was the limit
imposed on prescience by a merciful God. . . .

The light was changing now; the landscape of the
steppes had become an undulant sea, across which a figure
in antique robes was walking toward him, his face shining,
his pierced hands outstretched, as if in greeting. Kiril
Cardinal Lakota shrank away and tried to bury himself in
the lighted sea, but there was no escape. When the hands
touched him and the luminous face bent to embrace him,
he felt himself pierced by an intolerable joy, and an intolerable pain. Then he entered into the moment of
peace.

The servant who was assigned to care for him came
into the room and saw him kneeling rigid as a cataleptic,
with his arms outstretched in the attitude of crucifixion.
Rinaldi, making the rounds of the conclavists, came upon
him and tried vainly to wake him. Then Rinaldi, too, went
away, shaken and humbled, to consult with Leone and
with his colleagues.

In his cluttered and unelegant office George Faber, the
gray-haired dean of the Roman press corps, fifteen years
Italian correspondent for the New York *Monitor,* was
writing his background story on the papal election:

". . . Outside the small medieval enclave of the Vatican, the world is in a climate of crisis. Winds of change
are blowing and storm warnings are being raised, now in
one place, now in another. The arms race between America and Russia goes on, unabated. Every month there are
new and hostile probes into the high orbits of space.
There is famine in India, and guerrilla fighting along the
southern peninsulas of Asia. There is thunder over Africa,
and the tattered flags of revolution are being hoisted
over the capitals of South America. There is blood on the
sands in North Africa, and in Europe the battle for economic survival is waged behind the closed doors of banks
and board rooms. In the high airs above the Pacific, war
planes fly to sample the pollution of the air by lethal
atomic particles. In China the new dynasts struggle to fill
the bellies of hungry millions while they hold their minds
chained to the rigid orthodoxy of Marxist philosophy. In
the misty valleys of the Himalayas, where the prayer flags
flutter and the teapickers plod along the terraces, there
are forays and incursions from Tibet and Sinkiang. On
the frontiers of Outer Mongolia the uneasy amity of Russia and China is strained to the point of rupture. Patrol
boats probe the mangrove swamps and inlets of New
Guinea while the upland tribes try to project themselves
into the twentieth century by a single leap from the Stone
Age.

"Everywhere man has become aware of himself as a
transient animal and is battling desperately to assert his

right to the best of the world for the short time that he sojourns in it. The Nepalese haunted by his mountain demons, the coolie hauling his heart muscle into exhaustion between the shafts of a rickshaw, the Israeli beleaguered at every frontier, everyone all at once is asserting his claim to an identity; everyone has an ear for any prophet who can promise him one."

He stopped typing, lit a cigarette, and leaned back in his chair, considering the thought which he had just written—"a claim to identity." Strange how everyone had to make it sooner or later. Strange for how long one accepted with apparent equanimity the kind of person one seemed to be, the state to which one had apparently been nominated in life. Then all of a sudden the identity was called in question. . . . His own, for instance. George Faber, long-time bachelor, acknowledged expert on Italian affairs and Vatican politics . . . Why so late in life was he being forced to question what he was, what he had so far been content to be? Why this restless dissatisfaction with the public image of himself? Why this doubt that he could survive any longer without a permanent supplement to himself? . . . A woman, of course. There always had been women in his life, but Chiara was something new and special. . . . The thought troubled him. He tried to put it away and bent again to his typewriter.

"Everywhere the cry is for survival, but since the supreme irony of creation is that man must inevitably die, those who strive for the mastery of his mind or his muscle have to promise him an extension of his span into some semblance of immortality. The Marxist promises him a oneness with the workers of the world. The nationalist gives him a flag and a frontier, and a local enlargement of himself. The democrat offers him liberty through

a ballot box, but warns that he may have to die to preserve it.

"But for man, and all the prophets he raises up for
himself, the last enemy is time; and time is a relative
dimension, limited directly by man's capacity to make use
of it. Modern communication, swift as light, has diminished to nothing the time between a human act and its
consequences. A shot fired in Berlin can detonate the
world within minutes. A plague in the Philippines can
infect Australia within a day. A man toppling from a high
wire in a Moscow circus can be watched in his death
agony from London and New York.

"So at every moment every man is besieged by the consequences of his own sins and those of all his fellows. So,
too, every prophet and every pundit is haunted by the
swift lapse of time and the knowledge that the accounting for false predictions and broken promises is swifter
than it has ever been in history. Here precisely is the
cause of the crisis. Here the winds and the waves are born
and the thunderbolts are forged that may, any week, any
month, go roaring round the world under a sky black with
mushroom clouds.

"The men in the Vatican are aware of time, though
many of them have ceased to be as aware as they need to
be. . . ."

Time . . . ! He had become so vividly conscious of
this diminishing dimension of existence. He was in his
mid-forties. For more than a year he had been trying to
steer Chiara's petition of nullity through the Holy Roman
Rota so that she might be free from Corrado Calitri to
marry him. But the case was moving with desperate slowness, and Faber, although a Catholic by birth, had come
to resent bitterly the impersonal system of the Roman

Congregations and the attitude of the old men who ran them.

He typed on vividly, precisely, professionally:

"Like most old men, they are accustomed to seeing time as a flash between two eternities instead of a quantum of extension given to each individual man to mature toward the vision of his God.

"They are concerned also with man's identity, which they are obliged to affirm as the identity of a son of God. Yet here they are in danger of another pitfall: that they sometimes affirm his identity without understanding his individuality, and how he has to grow in whatever garden he is planted, whether the ground is sweet or sour, whether the air is friendly or tempestuous. Men grow, like trees, in different shapes, crooked or straight, according to the climate of their nurture. But so long as the sap flows and the leaves burgeon, there should be no quarrel with the shape of the man or the tree.

"The men of the Vatican are concerned as well with immortality and eternity. They, too, understand man's need for an extension of himself beyond the limit of the fleeting years. They affirm, as of faith, the persistence of soul into an eternity of union with the Creator, or of exile from His face. They go further. They promise man a preservation of his identity and an ultimate victory even over the terror of physical death. What they fail too often to understand is that immortality must be begun in time, and that a man must be given the physical resources to survive before his spirit can grow to desire more than physical survival. . . ."

Chiara had become as necessary to him as breath. Without her youth and her passion it seemed that he must slide all too quickly into age and disillusion. She had been his mistress for nearly six months now, but he was plagued by the fear that he could lose her at any moment to a younger man, and that the promise of children and continuity might never be fulfilled in him. . . . He had friends in the Vatican. He had easy access to men with great names in the Church, but they were committed to the law and to the system, and they could not help him at all. He wrote feelingly:

"They are caught, these old and deliberate men, in the paradox of all principality: that the higher one rises, the more one sees of the world, but the less one apprehends of the small determining factors of human existence. How a man without shoes may starve because he cannot walk to a place of employment. How a liverish tax collector may start a local revolution. How high blood pressure may plunge a noble man into melancholy and despair. How a woman may sell herself for money because she cannot give herself to one man for love. The danger of all rulers is that they begin to believe that history is the result of great generalities, instead of the sum of millions of small particulars, like bad drainage and sexual obsession and the anopheles mosquito. . . ."

It was not the story he had intended to write, but it was a true record of his personal feelings about the coming event. . . . Let it stand, then! Let the editors in New York like it or lump it . . . ! The door opened and Chiara came in. He took her in his arms and kissed her. He damned the Church and her husband and his paper to a special kind of hell, and then took her out to lunch on the Via Veneto.

The first day of the conclave was left private to the electing Cardinals, so that they might meet and talk discreetly, and probe for one another's prejudices and blind spots and motives of private interest. It was for this reason that Rinaldi and Leone moved among them to prepare them carefully for the final proposal. Once the voting began, once they had taken sides with this candidate or that, it would be much more difficult to bring them to an agreement.

Not all the talk was on the level of eternal verities. Much of it was simple and blunt, like Rinaldi's conversation with the American over a cup of American coffee (brewed by His Eminence's own servant because Italian coffee gave him indigestion).

His Eminence, Charles Corbet Carlin, Cardinal Archbishop of New York, was a tall, ruddy man with an expansive manner and a shrewd, pragmatic eye. He stated his problem as baldly as a banker challenging an overdraft:

"We don't want a diplomat, and we don't want a Curia official who will look at the world through a Roman eyeglass. A man who has traveled, yes, but someone who has been a pastor and understands what our problems are at this moment."

"I should be interested to hear your Eminence define them." Rinaldi was at his most urbane.

"We're losing our grip on the people," said Carlin flatly. "They are losing their loyalty to us. I think we are more than half to blame."

Rinaldi was startled. Carlin had the reputation of being a brilliant banker for Mother Church and of entertaining a conviction that all the ills of the world could be solved by a well-endowed school system and a rousing sermon every Sunday. To hear him talk so bluntly of the shortcomings of his own province was both refreshing and disquieting. Rinaldi asked:

"Why are we losing our grip?"

"In America? Two reasons: prosperity and respectability. We're not persecuted any more. We pay our way. We can wear the Faith like a Rotary badge—and with as little social consequence. We collect our dues like a club, shout down the Communists, and make the biggest contribution in the whole world to Peter's Pence. But it isn't enough. There's no—no heart in it for many Catholics. The young ones are drifting outside our influence. They don't need us as they should. They don't trust us as they used. For that," he added gravely, "I think I'm partly to blame."

"None of us has much right to be proud of himself," said Rinaldi quietly. "Look at France—look at the bloody things that have been done in Algeria. Yet this is a country half Catholic, and with a Catholic leadership. Where is our authority in this monstrous situation? A third of the Catholic population of the world is in the South Americas, yet what is our influence there? What impression do we make among the indifferent rich, and the oppressed poor, who see no hope in God and less in those who represent Him? Where do we begin to change?"

"I've made mistakes," said Carlin moodily. "Big ones. I can't even begin to repair them all. My father was a gardener, a good one. He used to say that the best you could do for a tree was mulch it and prune it once a year, and leave the rest to God. I always prided myself that I was a practical fellow, just as he was—you know? Build the church, then the school. Get the nuns in, then the brotners. Build the seminary and train the priests, and keep the money coming in. After that it was up to the Almighty." For the first time he smiled, and Rinaldi, who had disliked him for many years, began to warm to him. He went on whimsically, "The Romans and the Irish! We're great plotters, and great builders, but we lose the inwardness of things quicker than anybody else. Stick to the book! No meat on Fridays, no sleeping with your neighbor's wife, and leave the mysteries to the theologians! It isn't enough. God help us, but it isn't!"

"You're asking for a saint. I doubt we have many on the books just now."

"Not a saint." Carlin was emphatic again. "A man for the people, and of the people, as Sarto was. A man who could bleed for them, and scold them, and have them know all the time that he loved them. A man who could break out of this gilded garden patch and make himself another Peter."

"He would be crucified, too, of course," said Rinaldi tartly.

"Perhaps that is just what we need," said His Eminence from New York.

Whereupon Rinaldi, the diplomat, judged it opportune to talk of the bearded Ukrainian, Kiril Lakota, as a-man-with-the-makings-of-a-Pope.

In a somewhat smaller suite of the conclave Leone was discussing the same candidate with Hugh Cardinal Brandon from Westminster. Brandon, being English, was a man with no illusions and few enthusiasms. He pursed his thin gray lips and toyed with his pectoral cross, and delivered his policy in precise, if stilted, Italian:

"From our point of view, an Italian is still the best choice. It leaves us room to move, if you understand what I mean. There is no question of a new attitude or a fresh political alignment. There is no disturbance of the relations between the Vatican and the Republic of Italy. The Papacy would still be an effective barrier to any growth of Italian communism." He permitted himself a dry joke. "We could still count on the sympathy of English romantics for romantic Italy."

Léone, veteran of many a subtle argument, nodded his agreement and added almost casually, "You would not then consider our newcomer, the one who spoke to us this morning?"

"I doubt it. I found him, as everyone did, most impressive in the pulpit. But then eloquence is hardly a full qualification, is it? Besides, there is the question of rites. I understand this man is a Ukrainian and belongs to the Ruthenian rite."

"If he were elected, he would automatically practice the Roman one."

His Eminence of Westminster smiled thinly. "The beard might worry some people. A too Byzantine look, don't you think? We haven't had a bearded Pope in a very long time."

"No doubt he would shave it."

"Would he still wear the ikon?"

"He might be persuaded to dispense with that, too."

"Then we should be left with a model Roman. So why not choose an Italian in the first place? I can't believe you would want anything different."

"Believe me, I do. I am prepared to tell you now that my vote will go to the Ukrainian."

"I am afraid I can't promise you mine. The English and the Russians, you know. . . . Historically we've never done very well together. . . . Never at all."

:

"Always," said Rahamani the Syrian in his pliant, courteous fashion, "always you search a man for the one necessary gift—the gift of co-operation with God. Even among good men this gift is rare. Most of us, you see, spend our lives trying to bend ourselves to the will of God, and even then we have often to be bent by a violent grace. The others, the rare ones, commit themselves, as if by an instinctive act, to be tools in the hands of the Maker. If this new man is such a one, then it is he whom we need."

"And how do we know?" asked Leone dryly.

"We submit him to God," said the Syrian. "We ask God to judge him, and we rest secure in the outcome."

"We can only vote on him. There is no other way."

"There is another way, prescribed in the Apostolic Constitution. It is the way of inspiration. Any member of the conclave may make a public proclamation of the man he believes should be chosen, trusting that if this be a candidate acceptable to God, God will inspire the other conclavists to approve him publicly. It is a valid method of election."

"It also takes courage—and a great deal of faith."

"If we elders of the Church lack faith, what hope is there for the people?"

"I am reproved," said the Cardinal Secretary of the Holy Office. "It's time I stopped canvassing and began to pray."

Early the next morning, all the Cardinals assembled in the Sistine Chapel for the first ballot. For each there was a throne and over the throne a silken canopy. The thrones were arranged along the walls of the Chapel, and before each was set a small table which bore the Cardi-

nal's coat of arms and his name inscribed in Latin. The
Chapel altar was covered with a tapestry upon which was
embroidered a figuration of the Holy Ghost descending
upon the first Apostles. Before the altar was set a large
table on which there stood a gold Chalice and a small
golden platter. Near the table was a simple potbellied
stove whose flue projected through a small window that
looked out on the Square of St. Peter.

When the voting took place, each Cardinal would write
the name of his candidate upon a ballot paper, lay it first
on the golden platter, and then put it into the Chalice, to
signify that he had completed a sacred act. After the votes
were counted, they would be burned in the stove, and
smoke would issue through the flue into the Square of St.
Peter. To elect a Pope, there must be a majority of two
thirds.

If the majority was not conclusive, the ballot papers
would be burned with wet straw, and the smoke would
issue dark and cloudy. Only when the ballot was successful would the papers be burned without straw, so that a
white smoke might inform the waiting crowds that they
had a new Pope. It was an archaic and cumbersome
ceremony for the age of radio and television, but it
served to underline the drama of the moment and the continuity of two thousand years of papal history.

When all the Cardinals were seated, the Master of
Ceremonies made the circuit of the thrones, handing to
each voter a single ballot paper. Then he left the Chapel,
and the door was locked, leaving only the Princes of the
Church to elect the successor to Peter.

It was the moment for which Leone and Rinaldi had
waited. Leone rose in his place, tossed his white mane,
and addressed the conclave:

"My brothers, I stand to claim a right under the Apostolic Constitution. I proclaim to you my belief that there is among us a man already chosen by God to sit in the Chair of Peter. Like the first of the Apostles, he has suffered prison and stripes for the Faith, and the hand of God has led him out of bondage to join us in this conclave. I announce him as my candidate, and dedicate to him my vote and my obedience. . . . Kiril Cardinal Lakota."

There was a moment of dead silence, broken by a stifled gasp from Lakota. Then Rahamani the Syrian rose in his place and pronounced firmly:

"I, too, proclaim him."

"I, too," said Carlin the American.

"And I," said Valerio Rinaldi.

Then in twos and threes, old men heaved themselves to their feet with a like proclamation until all but nine were standing under the canopies, while Kiril Cardinal Lakota sat, blank-faced and rigid, on his throne.

Then Rinaldi stepped forward and challenged the electors. "Does any here dispute that this is a valid election, and that a majority of more than two thirds has elected our brother Kiril?"

No one answered the challenge.

"Please be seated," said Valerio Rinaldi.

As each Cardinal sat down, he pulled the cord attached to his canopy so that it collapsed above his head, and the only canopy left open was that above the chair of Kiril Cardinal Lakota.

The Camerlengo rang a small hand bell and walked across to unlock the Chapel door. Immediately there entered the Secretary of the Conclave, the Master of Ceremonies, and the Sacristan of the Vatican. These three prelates, with Leone and Rinaldi, moved ceremoniously to the throne of the Ukrainian. In a loud voice Leone challenged him:

"*Acceptasne electionem* [Do you accept election]?"

All eyes were turned on the tall, lean stranger with his scarred face and his dark beard and his distant, haunted eyes. Seconds ticked away slowly, and then they heard him answer in a dead flat voice:

"*Accepto*. . . . *Miserere mei Deus*. . . . I accept. . . . God have mercy on me!"

Extract from
the Secret Memorials of
KIRIL I, Pont. Max.

No ruler can escape the verdict of history, but a ruler who keeps a diary makes himself liable to a rough handling by the judged. . . . I should hate to be like old Pius II, who had his memoirs attributed to his secretary, had them expurgated by his kinsmen, and then, five hundred years later, had all his indiscretions restored by a pair of American bluestockings. Yet I sympathize with his dilemma, which must be the dilemma of every man who sits in the Chair of Peter. A Pope can never talk freely unless he talks to God or to himself—and a Pontiff who talks to himself is apt to become eccentric, as the histories of some of my predecessors have shown.

It is my infirmity to be afraid of solitude and isolation. So I shall need some safety valves—the diary, for one, which is a compromise between lying to oneself on paper and telling posterity the facts that have to be concealed from one's own generation: There is a rub, of course. What does one do with a papal diary? Leave it to the Vatican library? Order it buried with oneself in the triple coffin? Or auction it beforehand for the Propagation of the Faith? Better, perhaps, not to begin at all; but how else guarantee a vestige of privacy, humor, perhaps even sanity in this noble prison house to which I am condemned?

Twenty-four hours ago my election would have seemed a fantasy. Even now I cannot understand why I accepted it. I could have refused. I did not. Why? . . .

Consider what I am: Kiril I, Bishop of Rome, Vicar of Jesus Christ, Successor of the Prince of the Apostles, Supreme Pontiff of the Universal Church, Patriarch of the West, Primate of Italy, Archbishop and Metropolitan of the Roman Province, Sovereign of the Vatican City State . . . gloriously reigning, of course . . . !

But this is only the beginning of it. The Pontifical Annual will print a list two pages long of what I have reserved by way of abbacies and prefectures, and what I shall "protect" by way of orders, congregations, confraternities and holy sisterhoods. The rest of its two thousand pages will be a veritable Domesday Book of my ministers and subjects, my instruments of government, education, and correction.

I must be, by the very nature of my office, multilingual, though the Holy Ghost has been less generous in the gift of tongues to me than he was to the first man who stood in my shoes. My mother tongue is Russian; my official language is the Latin of the schoolmen, a kind of Mandarin which is supposed to preserve magically the sublest definition of truth like a bee in amber. I must speak Italian to my associates and converse with all in that high-flown "we" which hints at a secret converse between

God and myself, even in such mundane matters as the coffee "we" shall drink for breakfast and the brand of gasoline "we" shall use for Vatican City automobiles.

Still, this is the traditional mode, and I must not resent it too much. Old Valerio Rinaldi gave me fair warning when an hour after this morning's election he offered me both his retirement and his loyalty. "Don't try to change the Romans, Holiness. Don't try to fight or convert them. They've been managing Popes for the last nineteen hundred years and they'll break your neck before you bend theirs. But walk softly, speak gently, keep your own counsel, and in the end you will twist them like grass round your fingers."

It is too early, Heaven knows, to see what success Rome and I shall have with one another, but Rome is no longer the world, and I am not too much concerned— just so I can borrow experience from those who have pledged me their oaths as Cardinal Princes of the Church. There are some in whom I have great confidence. There are others . . . But I must not judge too swiftly. They cannot all be like Rinaldi, who is a wise and gentle man with a sense of humor and a knowledge of his own limitations. Meantime, I must try to smile and keep a good temper while I find my way round this Vatican maze. . . . And I must commit my thoughts to a diary before I expose them to Curia or Consistory.

I have an advantage, of course, in that no one quite knows which way I shall jump—I don't even know myself. I am the first Slav ever to sit on the Chair of Peter, the first non-Italian for four and a half centuries. The Curia will be wary of me. They may have been inspired to elect me, but already they must be wondering what kind of Tartar they have caught. Already they will be asking themselves how I shall reshuffle their appointments and spheres of influence. How can they know how much I am afraid and doubtful of myself? I hope some of them will remember to pray for me.

The Papacy is the most paradoxical office in the world; the most absolute and yet the most limited; the richest in revenues but the poorest in personal return. It was founded by a Nazarene carpenter who owned no place to rest His head, yet it is surrounded by more pomp and panoply than is seemly in this hungry world. It owns no frontiers, yet is subject always to national intrigue and partisan pressure. The man who accepts it claims divine guarantee against error, yet is less assured of salvation than the meanest of his subjects. The Keys of the Kingdom dangle at his belt, yet he can find himself locked out forever from the Peace of Election and the Communion of Saints. If he says he is not tempted by autocracy and ambition, he is a liar. If he does not walk sometimes in terror, and pray often in darkness, then he is a fool.

I know—or at least I am beginning to know. I was elected this morning, and tonight I am alone on the Mountain of Desolation. He whose Vicar I am hides His face from me. Those whose shepherd I must be do not know me. The world is spread beneath me like a campaign map—and I see balefires on every frontier. There are blind eyes upturned, and a babel of voices invoking an unknown. . . .

O God, give me light to see, and strength to know, and courage to endure the servitude of the servants of God . . . !

My valet has just been in to prepare my sleeping quarters. He is a melancholy fellow who looks very like a guard in Siberia who used to curse me at night for a Ukrainian dog and each morning for an adulterous priest. This one,

however, asks humbly if my Holiness has need of anything. Then he kneels and begs my blessing on himself and
his family. Embarrassed, he ventures to suggest that if I
am not too tired, I may deign to show myself again to the
people who still wait in St. Peter's square.

They acclaimed me this morning when I was led out
to give my first blessing to the city and to the world. Yet
so long as my light burns, it seems there will always be
some waiting for God knows what sign of power or be-
nignity from the papal bedroom. How can I tell them that
they must never expect too much from a middle-aged
fellow in striped cotton pajamas? But tonight is different.
There is a whole concourse of Romans and of tourists in the
Piazza, and it would be a courtesy—excuse me, Holiness,
a great condescension!—to appear with one small blessing. . . .

I condescend, and I am exalted once again on wave
after wave of cheering and horn-blowing. I am their Pope,
their Father, and they urge me to live a long time. I bless
them and hold out my arms to them, and they clamor
again, and I am caught in a strange heart-stopping moment, when it seems that my arms encompass the world
and that it is much too heavy for me to hold. Then my
valet—or is it my jailer?—draws me back, closes the window, and draws the drapes, so that, officially at least,
His Holiness Kiril I is in bed and asleep.

The valet's name is Gelasio, which is also the name of a
Pope. He is a good fellow, and I am glad of a minute of
his company. We talk a few moments, and then he asks
me, blushing and stammering, about my name. He is the
first who has dared to raise the question except old Rinaldi, who, when I announced that I desired to keep my
baptismal name, nodded and smiled ironically and said,

"A noble style, Holiness—provocative, too. But for God's sake, don't let them turn it into Italian."

I took his advice, and I explained to the Cardinals as I now explain to my valet that I kept the name because it belonged to the Apostle of the Slavs, who was said to have invented the modern Cyrillic alphabet and who was a stubborn defender of the right of people to keep the Faith in their own idiom. I explained to them also that I should prefer to have my name used in its Slavic form, for a testimony to the universality of the Church. Not all of them approve since they are quick to see how a man's first act sets the pattern of his later ones.

No one objected, however, except Leone, he who runs the Holy Office and has the reputation of a modern St. Jerome, whether for his love of tradition, a Spartan life, or a notoriously crusty temper I have yet to find out. Leone asked pointedly whether a Slavic name might not look out of place in the pure Latin of Papal Encyclicals. Although he is the one who first proclaimed me in the conclave, I had to tell him gently that I was more interested in having my encyclicals read by the people than in coddling the Latinists, and that since Russian had become a canonical language for the Marxist world, it would not hurt us to have the tip of one shoe in the other camp.

He took the reproof well, but I do not think he will easily forget it. Men who serve God professionally are apt to regard Him as a private preserve. Some of them would like to make His Vicar a private preserve as well. I do not say that Leone is one of these, but I have to be careful. I shall have to work differently from any of my predecessors, and I cannot submit myself to the dictate of any man, however high he stands, or however good he may be.

None of this, of course, is for my valet, who will take home only a simple tale of missionary saints and make himself a great man on the strength of a Pontiff's confidence. The *Osservatore Romano* will tell exactly the same tale tomorrow, but for them it will be "a symbol of the Paternal care of His Holiness for those who cleave, albeit in good faith, to schismatic communions. . . ." I must, as soon as I can, do something about the *Osservatore*. . . . If my voice is to be heard in the world, it must be heard in its authentic tones.

Already I know there are questions about my beard. I have heard murmurs of a "too Byzantine look." The Latins are more sensitive about such customs than we are, so perhaps it might have been a courtesy to explain that my jaw was broken under questioning and that without a beard I am somewhat disfigured. . . . It is so small a matter, and yet schisms have begun over smaller ones.

I wonder what Kamenev said when he heard the news of my election. I wonder whether he has humor enough to send me a greeting.

I am tired—tired to my bones and afraid. My charge is so simple: to keep the Faith pure and bring the scattered sheep safely into the fold. Yet into what strange country it may lead me I can only guess. . . . Lead us not into temptation, O Lord, but deliver us from evil. Amen.

II

IN THE white marble lounge of the Foreign Press Club, George Faber stretched his elegant legs and delivered his verdict on the election:

"To the East a stumbling block, to the West a foolishness, to the Romans a disaster."

A respectful laugh fluttered around the room. A man who had spent so many years on the Vatican beat had a right to make phrases—even bad ones. Sure of the attention of his audience, he talked on in his calm, confident voice:

"Look at it any way you like, Kiril I means a political mess. He's been a prisoner of the Russians for seventeen years, so at one stroke we wipe out any hope of rapprochement between the Vatican and the Soviets. America is involved, too. I think we can expect progressive abandonment of neutralist policies and a gradual lining up of the Vatican with the West. We are back again to the Pacelli-Spellman alliance. For Italy—" He flung out eloquent hands that embraced the whole peninsula. "Beh! What happens now to the Italian miracle of recovery? It was created in co-operation with the Vatican—

Vatican money, Vatican prestige abroad, Vatican help in emigration, the confessional authority of the clergy holding the Left in check. What happens now? If he starts making new appointments, the links between the Vatican and the Republic can be broken very quickly. The delicate balance can be tipped." He relaxed again and turned on his colleagues a smile of charm and deprecation, the smile of kingmaker. "At least that's my story and I'm sticking to it. You may quote me with acknowledgments, and if anyone steals my lead lines I'll sue!"

Collins, of the London *Times*, shrugged fastidiously and turned back to the bar with a German from Bonn. "Faber is a mountebank, of course, but he does have a point on the Italian situation. I'm quite staggered by this election. From all I hear, most of the Italians were in favor of it—though none of them gave any hint of it before they went into conclave. It's a wonderful weapon for Right or Left. The moment the Pope talks about any Italian business they can label him a foreigner, interfering in local politics. . . . That's what happened to the Dutchman—who was it, Adrian VI? The historical evidence shows him a wise man and a sound administrator, but when he died the Church was in a bigger mess than before. I've never liked the kind of baroque Catholicism which the Italians hand out to the world, but in affairs of state they have a great political value—like the Irish, if you understand what I mean."

". . . For a picture story the beard is wonderful." This from a hungry-mouthed brunette at the other end of the bar. "And it might be fun to have a few Greek and Russian ceremonies at the Vatican. All those odd robes and those lovely dangling ikons on their chests. One could start a craze with those—pendants for the new winter fashion! Quite a line, don't you think?" She gave a high-pitched braying laugh.

"There's a mystery about it," said Boucher, the fox-faced Frenchman. "A complete outsider after the shortest conclave in history! I talked with Morand and with some of our own people. The impression was of desperation—as if they saw the end of the world and wanted someone special to lead us toward it. They could be right. The Chinese have gone to Moscow, and the word is that they want a war now or they will split the Marxist world down the middle. They may get it, too, and then there is an end of politics, and we had all better begin to say our prayers. . . ."

"I heard an odd one this morning." Feuchtwanger the Swiss sipped a coffee and talked in a whisper with Erikson the Swede. "A courier arrived in Rome yesterday from Moscow, by way of Prague and Warsaw. This morning a personage from the Russian Embassy called on Cardinal Potocki. Of course, nobody is saying anything, but I wonder if Russia expects something from this man. Kamenev is in trouble with the Chinese, and he has always seen a lot farther than the end of his nose. . . ."

"Strange," said Fedorov the Tass man softly, "strange! Wherever you turn today, you feel the finger of Kamenev, even in this—name him or not, you see his touch."

Beron the Czech nodded wisely, but said nothing. The great Kamenev was beyond the reach of his humble pen, and after twenty years of survival he had learned that it was better to say nothing for a year than to permit himself a moment's indiscretion.

The Russian talked on with the quiet zeal of the orthodox. "Months ago I heard a rumor—it was only a rumor then—that Kamenev had organized this man's escape, and that the Praesidium would have his head for it. Now although we have been told to say nothing, the secret is out. It was Kamenev. And he must be laughing in his sleeve to see a man on whom he has left his mark sitting on the apostolic throne."

"And what does the Praesidium think of it?" asked the Czech cautiously.

Fedorov shrugged and spread his stubby fingers on the table. "They approve, of course—why should they not? Kamenev's mark is on every one of them, too. Besides, the man is a genius. Who else could have done what all the Five-Year Plans could not do—bring the Siberian plains into flower? From the Baltic to Bulgaria, look what he has done! For the first time, we have peace in the Western marches. Even the Poles don't hate us too much any more. We are exporting grain. Think of it! I tell you, whatever this man does the Praesidium and the people cannot fail to approve."

The Czech nodded soberly, and then asked another question. "This, this mark of Kamenev—what is it?"

The Tass man sipped his drink thoughtfully, and then said, "He spoke about it once, I believe. I was not there, but I heard echoes of it. He said, 'Once you have taken a man to pieces under questioning, once you have laid out the bits on the table and put them together again, then a strange thing happens. Either you love him or you hate him for the rest of your life. He will either love you or hate you in return. You cannot lead a man or a people through hell without wishing to share a heaven with them, too!' That's why our own people love him. He put them on the rack for three years and then suddenly showed them a new world." He downed his drink at one gulp and slapped the glass on the table. "A great man, the greatest we have had since Peter the Emperor!"

"And this Pope—this Kiril—what sort of a man will he be?"

"I don't know," said the Russian thoughtfully. "If Kamenev loves him, strange things may happen. Strange things may happen to both of them."

He was not yet crowned, but already Kiril the Pope had felt the impact of power. The shock of it was greater than he had ever dreamed. Two thousand years of time and all of eternity were now given into his hands. Five hundred million people were his subjects, and his tribute came in every coinage of the world. He could walk, as he walked each day now in the gardens of the Vatican, and measure the confines of his kingdom in a day's stroll; yet this narrow domain was only a foothold from which his power reached out to encompass the tilted planet.

The men who had made him he could now unmake with a word. The treasures of the centuries which they delivered to him with the Keys he could dispense at will or dissipate with a fool's gesture. His bureaucracy was more complex and yet more cheaply run than any other in the world. The toy soldiers who guarded his sacred presence were backed by thousands of levies bound to him by vow to serve with their talent, their hearts, their will, and all their celibate lives. Other men held dominion by the fickle voice of voters, by the pressure of party alignment, or by the tyranny of military juntas. He alone in all the world held it by divine delegation, and no one of all his subjects dared gainsay it.

Yet the knowledge of power was one thing, the use of it

was quite another. Whatever his plans for the Church, whatever changes he might make in the future, he had for the present to use the instruments at his disposal and the organization which his predecessors had transmitted to him. He had to learn so much so quickly, and yet in the days before his coronation it seemed almost as if there were a conspiracy to rob him of the time to think or plan. There were moments when he felt like a puppet being dressed and rehearsed for the theatre.

The cobblers came to measure him for new slippers, the tailors to stitch his white cassocks. The jewelers offered their designs for his ring and his pectoral cross. The heralds presented their drawings for his coat of arms: crossed keys for Peter's charge, a bear rampant on a white field, above it the dove of the Paraclete, and beneath, the motto "*Ex oriente lux. . . .* A light out of the East."

He approved it at first glance. It appealed to his imagination and to his sense of humor. It took time to lick a bear into shape—but once he was full-grown he was a very formidable fellow. With the Holy Ghost to guide him, he might hope to do much for the Church. And perhaps the East had been dark too long because the West had given too local a shape to a universal Gospel.

The chamberlains led him through audience after audience—with the press, with the diplomatic corps, with the noble families who claimed place about the papal throne, with prefects and secretaries of congregations and tribunals and commissions. The Chancellery of Briefs and the Secretariat of Briefs to Princes kept his desk piled with replies in impeccable Latin to all the letters and telegrams of felicitation. The Secretariat of State reminded him daily of crisis and revolution and the intrigues of the embassies.

At every step he stubbed his pontifical toe on history, ritual, and protocol, and the cumbersome methodology of Vatican bureaucracy. Wherever he turned, there was an official at his elbow, directing His Holiness' attention to this or that—an office to be filled, a courtesy to be bestowed, or talent to be elevated.

The setting was grandiose, the stage management was sedulous, but it took him nearly a week to find out the title of the play. It was an old Roman comedy, once popular, but now fallen into some disrepute: its title was *The Management of Princes*. The theme was simple—how to give a man absolute power and then to limit his use of it. The technique was to make him feel so important and to keep him so busy with pompous trifles that he had no time to think out a policy or put it into execution.

When he saw the joke, Kiril the Ukrainian laughed privately and decided to make a joke of his own.

So two days before his coronation he summoned without warning a private meeting of all the Cardinals in the Borgia rooms of the Vatican. The abruptness of the call was calculated, and the risk of it was calculated, too.

The day after his coronation all but the Cardinals of the Curia would leave Rome and return to their own countries. Each could prove a willing adjutant or a discreet hindrance to papal policy. One did not become a Prince of the Church without some ambition and some taste for power. One did not grow old in office without some hardening of heart and will. They were more than subjects, these hingemen, they were counsellors, also, jealous of their own apostolic succession and of the autonomy conferred by it. Even a Pope must deal delicately with them and not strain too far their wisdom, their loyalty, or their national pride.

When Kiril saw them seated before him, old and wise and shrewdly expectant, his heart sank and he asked himself for the hundredth time what he had to offer to them and to the Church. Then once again it seemed as though power renewed itself in him, and he made the Sign of the Cross, an invocation to the Holy Ghost, and then plunged into the business of the Consistory. He did not use the "we" of authority, but spoke intimately and personally, as if anxious to establish a relation of friendship:

"My brothers, my helpers in the cause of Christ . . ." His voice was strong, yet strangely tender, as if he pleaded with them for fraternity and understanding. "What I am today you have made me. Yet if what we believe is true, it is not you but God who has set me in these shoes of the Fisherman. Day and night I have asked myself what I have to offer to Him or to His Church—I have so little, you see. I am a man who was wrenched out of life like Lazarus, and then drawn back into it by the hand of God. All of you are men of your time. You have grown with it, you have been changed by it, you have contributed to change it for better or for worse. It is natural that each of you should guard jealously that place and that knowledge, and that authority which you have earned for yourselves in time. Now, however, I must ask you to be generous with me and lend me what you have of knowledge and experience in the name of God." His voice faltered a little, and to the old men it seemed for a moment as if he were about to weep. Then he recovered himself, and seemed to grow in size, while his voice took on a stronger tone. "Unlike you, I am not a man of my time—because I have spent seventeen years in prison and time has passed me by. So much of the world is a novelty to me. The only thing that is not new is man, and him I know and love because I have lived with him for so long in the simple intimacy of survival. Even the Church is strange to me because I have had to dispense for so long with what is unnecessary in it, and I have had to cling the more desperately to that which is of its nature and its essence— the Deposit of Faith, the Sacrifice, and the sacramental acts."

For the first time, he smiled at them, sensing their uneasiness and trying to calm them. "I know the thought that is in your mind—that you may have for Pope an innovator, a man avid for change. This is not so. Though much change is necessary, we must make it together. I try simply to explain myself so that you may understand me and help me. I cannot cling as zealously as some to ritual and to traditional forms of devotion because for years I have held to nothing but the simplest forms of prayer and the bare essentials of the Sacraments. I know, believe me, I know, that there are those for whom the straightest road is the safest one. I wish them to be as free as possible inside the bond of the Faith. I do not wish to change the long tradition of a celibate clergy. I myself am celibate as you are. Yet I have seen the Faith preserved under persecution by married priests who have handed it to their children like a jewel in silk. I cannot grow hot over the legalities of the canonists or the rivalries of religious congregations because I have seen women raped by their jailers, and I have delivered their children with these consecrated hands."

Once again he smiled and threw out his crooked hands to them in a gesture of pleading. "I am perhaps the wrong man for you, my brothers—but God has given me to you and you must make the best of me."

There was a long pause, and then he went on more strongly still, not pleading, not explaining, but demanding with all the power that surged within him:

"You ask me where I want to lead you, where I want to lead the Church. I will show you. I want to lead you back to God, through men. Understand this, understand it in mind and heart and obedient will. We are what we are, for the service of God through the service of man. If we lose contact with man—suffering, sinful, lost, confused men crying in the night, women agonizing, children weeping—then we, too, are lost because we shall be negligent shepherds who have done everything but the one thing necessary." He paused and stood facing them, tall, pale, and strange, with his scarred face, and his crooked hands, and his black Byzantine beard. Then he handed them like a challenge the formal Latin question:

"*Quid vobis videtur.* . . . How does it seem to you?"

There was a ritual to cover this moment, just as there was a ritual to cover every act of Vatican life. The Cardinals would remove their red caps and bow their heads in submission, and then wait to be dismissed to do or not to do that which they had been counselled. A papal allocution was rarely a dialogue, but this time there was a sense of urgency and even of conflict in the assembly.

Cardinal Leone heaved his lion's bulk out of his chair, tossed his white mane, and addressed himself to the Pontiff. "All of us here have pledged to your Holiness and to the Church the service of our lives. Yet we should not discharge this service if we did not offer counsel when we believed counsel was necessary."

"This is what I have asked of you," said Kiril mildly. "Please speak freely."

Leone made a grave acknowledgment and then went on firmly. "It is too early yet to measure the effect of your Holiness' election upon the world at large, and especially upon the Roman and Italian Church. I mean no disrespect when I say that until we know this reaction there should be a prudence, a reserve in public utterance and public action."

"I have no quarrel with that," said Kiril in the same mild fashion. "But you must not quarrel with me when I tell you that I want the voice of Kiril to be heard by all men—not another voice, in another accent or another mode, but my voice. A father does not speak to his son through an actor's mask. He speaks simply, freely, and from the heart, and this is what I propose to do."

The old lion held his ground and went on stubbornly. "There are realities to be faced, Holiness. The voice will change, no matter what you do. It will issue from the mouth of a Mexican peasant and an English academician and a German missionary in the Pacific. It will be interpreted by a hostile press or a theatrical television correspondent. The most your Holiness can expect is that the first voice shall be yours and the first record shall be the authentic one." He permitted himself a grim smile. "We, too, are your voices, Holiness, and even we may find it hard to render the score perfectly." He sat down amid a small rustle of approval.

Then Pallenberg, the lean, cold man from Germany, took the floor and presented his own problem. "Your Holiness has spoken of changes. It is my view and the view of my brother bishops that certain changes are long overdue. We are a divided country. We have an immense prosperity and a dubious future. There is a drift of the Catholic population away from the Church because our women must marry outside it, since our males were decimated during the war. Our problems in this regard are legion. We can solve them only at the human level. Yet here in Rome they are being dealt with by Monsignori who cannot even speak our language, who work solely by the canons, and who have no sense of our history or of our present problems. They delay, they temporize, they centralize. They treat the affairs of souls as if they were entries in a ledger. Our burden is great enough, we cannot carry Rome on our backs as well—for myself and for my brethren, *Appello ad Petrum.* . . . I appeal to Peter!"

There was an audible gasp at so much bluntness. Leone flushed angrily, and Rinaldi hid a smile behind a silk handkerchief.

After a moment Kiril the Pope spoke again. His tone was as mild as ever, but this time they noticed he used the plural of royalty. "We promise our German brothers that we shall give immediate and full consideration to their special problems and we shall confer with them privately before they return to their homeland. We would urge them, however, to patience and to charity with their colleagues in Rome. They should remember, too, that often things are left undone from habit and from tradition rather than from lack of good will." He paused a moment, letting the reproof sink in; then he chuckled. "I have had my own troubles with another bureaucracy. Even the men who tormented me did not lack good will. They wanted to build a new world in one generation, but the bureaucracy beat them each time. Let us see if we can find ourselves more priests and fewer bureaucrats

—fewer clerks and more simple souls who understand the human heart."

Now it was the turn of the Frenchman, and he was no less blunt than Pallenberg. "Whatever we do in France—whatever we propose from France—comes here to Rome under the shadow of old history. Every one of our projects, from the worker priests to studies in the development of dogma and the creation of an intelligent Catholic press, is greeted as if it were a new tramontane rebellion. We cannot work freely or with continuity in this climate. We cannot feel ourselves helped by the fraternity of the Church if a cloud of censure hangs over everything we plan or propose." He swung around angrily and flung out a challenge to the Italians. "There are heresies here in Rome, too, and this is one of them: that unity and uniformity are the same thing, that the Roman way is best for everyone from Hong Kong to Peru. Your Holiness has expressed the wish to have his voice heard in its true tone. We, too, wish to have our voice heard without distortion at the throne of Peter. Appointments need to be made, men who can represent us and the climate in which we live, truthfully and with understanding."

"You touch on a problem," said Kiril carefully, "which preoccupies us as well. We ourselves carry the burden of history so that we cannot always deal with the simplicity of a matter, but must consider a complexity of colorations and historic associations." He raised a hand to his beard and smiled. "Even this I understand to be a source of scandal to some, although our Master and the first Apostles were all bearded men. I should hate to think that the rock of Peter should split for want of a razor. *Quid vobis videtur?*"

In that moment they laughed and loved him. Their

anger with one another subsided, and they listened more humbly while the men from the South Americas told of their own problems: impoverished populations, a scarcity of trained clergy, the historic association of the Church with the wealthy and the exploiters, lack of funds, the strength of the Marxist idea held up like a torch to rally the dispossessed.

Came then the men from the East, telling how the frontiers were closing one by one on the Christian idea. And how one by one the old missionary foundations were being destroyed while the idea of an earthly paradise took hold of the minds of men who needed it so desperately because they had so little time to enjoy it. It was a brutal balance sheet for men who had to make their reckoning with the Almighty. And when finally it was done, there was a silence over the whole assembly, and they waited for Kiril the Pontiff to make his final summation.

He rose then in his place and confronted them—a figure oddly young, oddly alone, like a Christ from a Byzantine triptych. "There are those," he told them solemnly, "who believe that we are come to the last age of the world because man has now the power to destroy himself from the face of the earth, and every day the danger grows greater that he will do it. Yet we, my brothers, have no more and no less to offer for the world's salvation than we had in the beginning. We preach Christ and Him crucified—to the Jews, indeed a stumbling block; and to the Gentiles, foolishness. This is the folly of the Faith, and if we are not committed to it, then we are committed to an illusion. What do we do, therefore? From this point where do we go? I believe there is only one way. We take the truth like a lamp and we walk out like the first Apostles to tell the good tidings to whoever will listen. If history stands in our way, we ignore it. If systems inhibit us, we dispense with them. If dignities weigh us down, we cast them aside. I have one commission now for all of you —for those who are going away from Rome and those who stay here in the shadow of our triumphs and our sins—find me men! Find me good men who understand what it is to love God and love His children. Find me men with fire in their hearts and wings on their feet. Send them to me, and I will send them out to bring love to the loveless and hope to those who sit in darkness. . . . Go now in the name of God!"

Immediately after the Consistory, Potocki, the Cardinal from Poland, presented a petition for an urgent and private audience with the Pope. To his surprise, it was answered within an hour by an invitation to dinner. When he arrived at the papal apartment, he found the new Pontiff alone, sitting in an armchair, reading a small volume bound in faded leather. When he knelt to make his obedience, Kiril stretched out a hand and raised him to his feet with a smile.

"Tonight we should be brothers together. The cooking is bad, and I haven't had time to reform the papal kitchens. I hope your company will give me a better dinner than usual." He pointed to the yellowed pages of the book and chuckled. "Our friend Rinaldi has a sense of humor. He gave me a present to celebrate my election. It is an account of the reign of the Dutchman, Adrian VI. Do you know what they called the Cardinals who elected him? 'Betrayers of Christ's blood, who surrendered the fair Vatican to foreign fury, and handed the Church and Italy into slavery with the barbarians.' I wonder what they are saying about you and me at this moment?" He shut the book with a snap and relaxed once again in the chair. "It is only the beginning, and yet I do so badly, and I feel myself so much alone. . . . How can I help you, my friend?"

Potocki was touched by the charm of his new Master, but the habit of caution was strong in him and he contented himself with a formality. "A letter was delivered to me this morning, Holiness. I am told that it comes from Moscow. I was asked to deliver it directly into your hands." He brought out a bulky envelope sealed with gray wax and handed it to Kiril, who held it a moment in his hands and then laid it on the table.

"I shall read it later, and if it should concern you as well, I shall call you. Now tell me . . ." He leaned forward in his chair, begging earnestly for a confidence. "You did not speak in the Consistory today, and yet you have as many problems as the others. I want to hear them."

Potocki's lined face tightened and his eyes clouded. "There is a private fear first, Holiness."

"Share it with me," said Kiril gently. "I have so many of my own, it may make me feel better."

"History sets snares for all of us," said the Pole gravely. "Your Holiness knows this. The history of the Ruthenian Church in Poland is a bitter one. We have not always acted like brothers in the Faith, but like enemies one to another. The time of dissension is past, but if your Holiness were to remember it too harshly it could be bad for us all. We Poles are Latin by temper and loyalty. Time was when the Polish Church lent itself to persecution of its brothers in the Ruthenian rite. We were both young then, but it is possible—and we both know it—that many might have lived who are now dead had we kept the unity of the Spirit in the bond of faith." He hesitated, and then stumbled awkwardly through the next question. "I mean no disrespect, Holiness, but I must ask with loyalty what others will ask with a false purpose: How does your Holiness feel about us in Poland? How do you regard what we are trying to do?"

There was a long pause. Kiril the Pontiff looked down at his gnarled hands, and then abruptly heaved himself from the chair and laid his hands on the shoulders of his brother bishop. He said softly, "We have both been in prison, you and I. We both know that when they tried to break us it was not with the love we had, but with the resentments that we had buried deep inside us. When you sat in the darkness, trembling and waiting for the next session with the lights, and the pain, and the questions, what tempted you most?"

"Rome," said Potocki bluntly, "where they knew so much and seemed to care so little."

Kiril the Pontiff smiled and nodded gravely. "For me it was the memory of the great Andrew Szepticky, Metropolitan of Galicia. I loved him like a father. I hated bitterly what had been done to him. I remembered him before he died, a hulk of a man, paralyzed, torn with pain, watching all that he had built being destroyed, the houses of education, the seminaries, the old culture he had tried so hard to preserve. I was oppressed by the futility of it all, and I wondered whether it was worth spending so many lives, so many more noble spirits, to try again. . . . Those were bad days, and worse nights."

Potocki flushed to the roots of his thin hair. "I am ashamed, Holiness. I should not have doubted."

Kiril shrugged and smiled wryly. "Why not? We are all human. You are walking a tightrope in Poland, I am walking another in Rome. Both of us may slip, and we shall need a net to catch us. I beg you to believe that if I sometimes lack understanding I do not lack love."

"What we do in Warsaw," said Potocki, "is not always understood in Rome."

"If you need an interpreter," said Kiril briskly, "send me one. I promise him always a ready hearing."

"There will be so many, Holiness, and they will speak in so many tongues. How can you attend to them all?"

"I know." Kiril's thin frame seemed suddenly to shrink, as if under a burden. "Strange. We profess and we teach that the Pontiff is preserved from fundamental error by the indwelling of the Holy Spirit. I pray, but I hear no thunder on the mountain. My eyes see no splendors on the hills. I stand between God and man, but I hear only man and the voice of my heart."

For the first time, the harsh face of the Pole relaxed, and he spread his hands in a gesture of willing defeat. "Listen to that, Holiness. *Cor ad cor loquitur.* Heart speaks to heart, and this may well be God's dialogue with men."

"Let's go to dinner," said Kiril the Pontiff, "and forgive my nuns their heavy hand with the sauce. They are worthy creatures, but I will have to find them a good cookbook."

They ate no better than he had promised, and they drank a thin young wine from the Alban Hills; but they talked more freely, and a warmth grew between them, and when they came to the fruit and the cheese Kiril the Pontiff opened his heart on another matter.

"In two days I am to be crowned. It is a small thing, perhaps, but I am troubled by so much ceremony. The Master came into Jerusalem riding on a donkey. I am to be carried on the shoulders of nobles between the plumed fans of a Roman emperor. All over the world are barefoot men with empty bellies. I am to be crowned with gold, and my triumph will be lit with a million lights. I am ashamed that the successor of the Carpenter should be treated like a king. I should like to change it."

Potocki gave a thin smile and shook his head. "They will not let you do it, Holiness."

"I know." Kiril's fingers toyed with the broken crumbs on his plate. "I belong to the Romans, too, and they must have their holiday. I cannot walk down the nave of St. Peter's because I could not be seen, and even if the visitors do not come to pray they do come to see the Pontiff. I am a prince by treaty, they remind me, and a prince must wear a crown."

"Wear it, Holiness," said Potocki with grim humor. "Wear it for the day, and do not trouble yourself. Soon enough they crown you with thorns!"

An hour away at his villa in the Alban Hills, Valerio Cardinal Rinaldi was giving his own dinner party. His guests made a curious yet powerful assemblage, and he managed them with the skill of a man who had just proved himself a kingmaker.

Leone was there, and Semmering, the Father General of the Jesuits, whom the vulgar called "the Black Pope." There were Goldoni, from the Secretariat of State, and Benedetti, the prince of Vatican finances, and Orlando Campeggio, the shrewd, swarthy fellow who was the editor of the *Osservatore Romano*. At the foot of the table, as if for a concession to the mystics, sat Rahamani the Syrian, soft, complaisant, and always unexpected.

The meal was served on a belvedere which looked down on a classic garden, once the site of an Orphic temple,

and beyond it to the farmlands and the distant glow of
Rome. The air was mild, the night was full of stars,
and Rinaldi's assiduous servants had coaxed them into
comfort with one another.

Campeggio, the layman, smoked his cigar and talked
freely, a prince among the princes. ". . . First it seems we
have to present the Pontiff in the most acceptable light.
I have thought a great deal about this, and you will all
have read what we have already done in the press. The
theme so far has been 'in prison for the Faith.' The reaction to this has been good—a wave of sympathy—an expression of lively affection and loyalty. Of course, this is
only the beginning, and it does not solve all our problems. Our next thought was to present 'a Pope of the people.' We may need some assistance with this, particularly
from an Italian point of view. Fortunately, he speaks good
Italian and therefore can communicate himself in public functions, and in contacts with the populace. . . .
Here we shall need both direction and assistance from
the members of the Curia. . . ." He was a deft man, and
he broke off at this point, leaving the proposition for the
clerics.

It was Leone who took it up, worrying it in his stubborn
fashion, while he peeled an apple and sliced it with a
silver knife. "Nothing is quite as simple as it sounds. We
have to present him, yes, but we have to edit him and
comment him as well. You heard what went on in the
Consistory today." He thrust the knife blade at Rinaldi
and Rahamani. "Print what he said baldly and without
explanation, and it would read as if he were ready to
throw two thousand years of tradition out the window. I
saw his point, we all did, but I saw, too, where we have to
protect him."

"Where is that?" Semmering, the spare blond Jesuit, leaned forward in his place.

"He showed us his own Achilles' heel," said Leone firmly. "He said he was a man who had dropped out of time. He will need, I think, to be reminded constantly what our times are and what instruments we have to work with."

"Do you think he is unaware of them?" asked the Jesuit again.

Leone frowned. "I'm not sure. I have not yet begun to read his mind. All I know is that he is asking for something new before he has had time to examine what is old and permanent in the Church."

"As I remember," said the Syrian mildly, "he asked us to find him men. This is not new. Men are the foundation of every apostolic work. How did he say it? 'Men with fire in their hearts and wings on their feet.'"

"We have forty thousand men," said the Jesuit dryly, "and they are all bound to him by solemn vows of service. We stand, all of us, at his call."

"Not all of us," said Rinaldi without rancor. "And we should be honest enough to confess it. We move familiarly where he must move for a while awkwardly and strangely, in the headquarters of the Church. We accept the inertia and the ambition, and the bureaucracy, because we have been bred to it, and in part we have helped to build it. You know what he said to me yesterday?" He paused like an actor, waiting for their attention to focus on him. "He said, 'I celebrated Mass once in seventeen years. I lived where hundreds of millions will die without having seen a priest or heard the word of God, yet here I see hundreds of priests stamping documents and punching time clocks like common clerks. . . .' I understand his point of view."

"What does he expect us to do?" asked Benedetti acidly. "Run the Vatican with IBM machines and put all the priests in the mission fields? No man can be as naïve as that."

"I don't think he is naïve," said Leone. "Far from it. But I think he may discount too readily what Rome means to the Church—for order and discipline, and a stewardship of the Faith."

For the first time, Goldoni, the gray, stocky man from the Secretariat of State, entered the argument. His harsh Roman voice crackled like twigs in a fire as he gave his own version of the new Pontiff. "He has been in to see me several times. He does not summon me, but walks in quietly and asks questions of me and of my staff. I have the impression that he understands politics very well, especially Marxist politics, but he is little interested in details and personalities. He uses one word often, *pressure*. He asks where the pressures begin in each country, and how they act on the people, and on those who rule them. When I asked him to explain, he said that the Faith was planted in men by God, but that the Church had to be built on the human and material resource of each country, and that to survive it had to withstand the pressures that were suffered by the mass of the people. He said something else, too: that we have centralized too much, and we have delayed too long to train those who can maintain the universality of the Church in the autonomy of a national culture. He spoke of vacuums created by Rome—vacuums in classes and countries—and local clergies. . . . I do not know how enlightened his own policies may be, but he is not blind to the defects of those which already exist."

"The new broom," said Benedetti tartly. "He wants to

sweep all the rooms at once. . . . He can read a balance sheet, too! He objects that we have so much in credit while there is so much poverty in Uruguay, or among the Urdus. I ask myself if he really understands that forty years ago the Vatican was almost bankrupt and Gasparri had to borrow ten thousand sterling pounds to finance the papal election. Now at least we can pay our way and move with some strength for the good of the Church."

"When he spoke to us," said Rahamani again, "I did not hear him mention money. I was reminded how the first Apostles were sent out with neither scrip nor stave nor money for the road. As I heard the story, that is how our Kiril came from Siberia to Rome."

"Possibly," said Benedetti irritably. "But have you ever looked at the travel bills for a pair of missionaries—or worked out how much it costs to train a seminary teacher?"

Abruptly Leone threw back his white mane and laughed, so that the night birds stirred in the cypresses and the echoes rolled down over the starlit valley. "That's it. We elected him in the name of God, and now suddenly we're afraid of him. He has made no threat, he has changed no appointment, he has asked nothing but what we profess to offer. Yet here we sit, weighing him like conspirators and making ready to fight him. What has he done to us?"

"Perhaps he has read us better than we like," said Semmering the Jesuit.

"Perhaps," said Valerio Rinaldi, "perhaps he trusts us more than we deserve. . . ."

Extract from
the Secret Memorials of
KIRIL I, Pont. Max.

. . . It is late and the moon is climbing high. The Square of St. Peter is empty, but the rumor of the city still reaches me on the night wind—footsteps sounding hollow on stones, a scream of motor tires, the bleat of a horn, snatches of faraway song, and the slow clip-clop of a tired horse. I am wakeful tonight, and I resent my solitude. I want to walk out through the Angelic Gate and find my people where they stroll or sit together in the alleys of Trastevere, or huddle in narrow rooms with their fears and their loves. I need them so much more than they need me.

One day soon I must do this. I must shrug off the bonds which are laid upon me by protocol and precaution and confront this city of mine so that I may see it and it may see me as we truly are. . . .

I remember the stories of my childhood, how the Caliph

Haroun disguised himself and walked out with his vizier at night to search the hearts of his people. I remember how Jesus the Master sat at meat with tax-gatherers and public women, and I wonder why His successors were so eager to assume the penalty of princes, which is to rule from a secret room and to display oneself like a demi-God only on occasions of public festivity. . . .

It has been a long day, but I have learned something of myself and of others, too. I made a mistake, I think, in the Consistory. When men are old and powerful, they need to be drawn by reason and calculation because the sap of the heart dries up with age. . . .

When one is in a position of power, one must not show oneself publicly humble because the ruler must reassure with strength and a show of decision. If one displays one's heart, it must be in private, so that the man who sees it will believe that he has received a confidence. . . .

I am writing like a cynic, and I am ashamed of it. Why? Perhaps because I was confronted with strong men who were determined to bend me to their opinions. . . .

Leone was the one who irritated me most of all. I had hoped for an ally, and instead I found a critic. I am tempted to appoint him to another office and remove him from the position of influence which he now holds. Yet this, I think, would be a mistake, and the beginning of greater ones. If I surround myself with weak and compliant men, I shall rob the Church of noble servants . . . and in the end I shall be left without counsellors. Leone is a formidable fellow, and I think we shall find ourselves opposed to each other on many issues. But I do not see him as an intriguer. I should like to have him for my friend because I am a man who needs friendship, yet I do not think he will surrender himself so far. . . .

I should like to keep Rinaldi by me, but I think I must consent to his retirement. He is not, I think, a profound man, though he is a subtle and an able one. I sense that he has come to grips with God very late in his life and that he needs a freedom to audit the accounts of his soul. This, fundamentally, is why I am here, to show men the staircase to union with God. If anyone stumbles on my account, then I shall be the one to answer for it. . . .

Kamenev's letter is open before me, and beside it is his gift for my coronation—a few grains of Russian soil and a package of sunflower seeds.

"I do not know," he writes, "whether the seeds will grow in Rome, but perhaps if you mix a little Russian earth with them they will bloom for next summer. I remember that I asked you during one interrogation what you missed most of all, and you smiled and said the sunflowers in the Ukraine. I hated you at that moment because I was missing them, too, and we were both exiles in the frozen lands. Now you are still an exile, while I am the first man in Russia.

"Do you regret us? I wonder. I should like to think so because I regret you. We could have done great things together, you and I; but you were wedded to this wild dream of the hereafter, while I believed, as I still believe, that the best a man can do is make barren earth fruitful and ignorant men wise, and see the children of puny fathers grow tall and straight among the sunflowers.

"It would, I suppose, be courteous to congratulate you on your election. For what they are worth, you have my compliments. I am curious to know what this office will do to you. I let you go because I could not change you, and yet I could not bring myself to degrade you any more. It would shame me now if you were to be corrupted by eminence.

"We may yet have need of each other, you and I. You have not seen the half of it, yet I tell you truly we have brought this country to a prosperity she has not known in all her centuries. Yet we are ringed with swords. The Americans are afraid of us; the Chinese resent us and want to drag us fifty years back in history. We have fanatics inside our own borders who are not content with bread and peace and work for all, but want to turn us all back into bearded mystics from Dostoievski.

"To you perhaps I am anti-Christ. What I believe you reject utterly. But for the present, I am Russia, and I am the guardian of this people. You have weapons in your hands, and I know, though I dare not admit it publicly, how strong they are. I can only hope you will not turn them against your homeland nor pledge them to a base alliance in East or West.

"When the seeds begin to grow, remember Mother Russia, and remember that you owe me a life. When the time comes to claim payment, I shall send you a man who will talk of sunflowers. Believe what he tells you, but deal with no others, now or later. Unlike you, I do not have the Holy Ghost to protect me, and I must still be wary of my friends. I wish I could say that you were one. Greetings. Kamenev."

. . . I have read the letter a dozen times, and I cannot decide whether it brings me to the fringe of a revelation or to the edge of a precipice. I know Kamenev as intimately as he knows me, yet I have not reached down to the core of his soul. I know the ambition that drives him, his fanatic desire to exact some goodness from life to pay for the debasement he inflicted on himself and others for so many years. . . .

I have seen peasants scoop up a handful of soil from a new plot and taste it to see whether it was sweet or sour. I can imagine Kamenev doing the same with the soil of Russia.

I know how the ghosts of history threaten him and his people because I understand how they threaten me, too. I do not see him as anti-Christ, nor even as an archheretic. He has understood and accepted the Marxist dogma as the swiftest and sharpest instrument yet devised to trigger a social revolution. I think he would throw it aside the moment he saw it fail of its purpose. I think, though I cannot be sure, that he is asking my help to preserve what he has already won of good for the people, and to give it a chance to grow peacefully into other mutations.

I believe that having thrust himself up so high, he has begun to breathe a freer air and to wish the same fortune for a people he has learned to love. If this be true, then I must help him. . . .

Yet there are events which give him the lie at every moment. There are invasions and forays on every frontier, under the banner of the sickle and the star. Men are still starved and beaten, and locked away from the free commerce of thought and the channels of grace.

The great heresy of the earthly paradise still creeps across the world like a cancer, and Kamenev still wears the robe of its high priest. This I am pledged to fight, and I have already resisted it with my blood. . . .

Yet I cannot ignore the strange working of God in the souls of the most unlikely men, and I believe I can see this working in the soul of Kamenev. . . . I see, though only dimly, how our destinies may be linked in the divine design. . . . What I cannot see is how to comport myself in the situation which exists between us. . . .

He asks for my friendship, and I would gladly give him my heart. He asks, I think, for a kind of truce, yet I cannot make truce with error, though I can ascribe the noblest motives to those who propagate it. I dare not, however, place the Church and the faithful in jeopardy for an illusion, because I know that Kamenev could still betray me, and I could still betray myself and the Church.

What do I do?

Perhaps the answer is in the sunflower—that the seed must die before the green shoots come, that the flower must grow while men pass by, heedless that a miracle is taking place under their noses.

Perhaps this is what is meant by "waiting upon the mercy of God." But we cannot only wait because the nature with which He has endowed us drives us to action. We must pray, too, in darkness and dryness, under a blind sky. . . .

Tomorrow I shall offer Mass for Kamenev, and tonight I must pray for light for Kiril the Pontiff, whose heart is restless and whose vagrant soul still hungers for its homeland. . . .

III

FOR GEORGE FABER the coronation of Kiril I was a long and elaborate boredom. The ovations deafened him, the lights gave him a headache, the sonorities of the choir depressed his spirit, and the gaudy procession of prelates, priests, monks, chamberlains, and toy soldiers was an operatic cavalcade which pricked him to resentment and gave him no entertainment at all. The exhalation of eighty thousand bodies, jammed like sardines into every corner of the Basilica, made him feel faint and nauseated.

His copy was already written and filed for transmission: three thousand glowing words on the pageantry and symbolism and religious splendor of this Roman festal day. He had seen it all before, and there was no reason for him to repeat the tedium except, perhaps, the snobbery of sitting in the place of honor in the press box, resplendent in a new frock coat, with the ribbon of his latest Italian decoration bright upon his chest.

Now he was paying for the indulgence. His buttocks were jammed tight between the broad hips of a German and the angular thighs of Campeggio, and there would be no escape for at least two hours, until the distin-

guished congregation broke out into the Square to receive
the blessing of the new-crowned Pope with the humbler
citizens and tourists of Rome.

Exasperated, he slumped forward in his seat and tried to
find a grain of consolation in what this Kiril might mean to
himself and Chiara. So far the Curia had kept him tightly
in wraps. He had made few public appearances, and no
pronouncements of any moment at all. But the word was
already about that this was an innovator, a man young
enough and strange enough to have a mind of his own and
the vigor to express it in action. There were rumors of
rough words in the Consistory, and more than one Vatican
official was talking of changes, not only in personnel, but in
the whole central organization as well.

If changes were made, some of them might affect the
Holy Roman Rota, where the petition of nullity for Chiara's marriage had lain in the pigeonholes for nearly two
years. The Italians had a wry-mouthed joke for the
workings of this august body: *"Non c'e divorzio in
Italia* . . . There is no divorce in Italy—and only Catholics can get it!" Like most Italian jokes, this one had
more than one barb to it. Neither Church nor State admitted the possibility of divorce, but both viewed with
apparent equanimity a large-scale concubinage among the
rich and a growing number of irregular unions among the
poor.

The Rota was by constitution a clerical body, but much
of its business was in the hands of lay lawyers, specialists
in canon law, who formed, for mutual profit, a union as
rigid and exclusive as any in the world, so that the business of marital causes banked up in a bottleneck, regard-
less of the human tragedies which underlay most of them.

In theory the Rota must adjudicate equally for those

who could pay and for those who could not. In practice the paying petitioner, or the petitioner with Roman influence or Roman friendship, could count on quicker decisions by far than his poorer brethren in the Faith. The law was the same for all, but its decisions were dispensed more swiftly to those who could command the best service from the advocates.

The tag of the joke made another point as well. A decree of nullity was much easier to obtain if both partners to the marriage consented to the first petition. If *error* had to be proved in the contract, or *conditio,* or *crimen,* it was much easier to do it with two voices. But if one partner only made a petition and the other presented contradictory evidence, the case was doomed to a slow progress and to very probable failure.

In such cases the Rota made a neat, if hardly satisfying, distinction: that in the private forum of conscience—and, therefore, in fact—the contract might be null and void, but until it could be proved so in the external forum, by documented evidence, the two parties must be regarded as married even though they did not live together. If the aggrieved party obtained a divorce and remarried outside the country, he or she would be excommunicated by the Church and prosecuted for bigamy by the State.

In practice, therefore, concubinage was the easier state in Italy, since it was more comfortable to be damned inside the Church than out of it and one was much happier loving in sin than serving a prison sentence in the Regina Coeli.

The which precisely was the situation for George Faber and Chiara Calitri.

As he watched the new Pontiff being vested by his assistants in front of the high altar, Faber wondered sourly how much he knew or could ever hope to know of the intimate tragedies of his subjects, of the burdens which their beliefs and loyalties laid upon their shoulders. He wondered, too, whether the time had not come to throw aside the caution of a lifetime and break a lance, or his head, for the most contentious cause in Rome, the reform of the Holy Roman Rota.

He was not a brilliant man, and certainly not a brave one. He had a capacity for close observation and urbane reportage, and a slightly theatrical knack for ingratiating himself with well-bred people. In Rome these things added up to a valuable talent for a correspondent. Now, however, with the climacteric looming, and the lonely years, the talent was not enough. George Faber was in love, and being a Nordic puritan and not a Latin, he needed at all costs to be married.

The Church, too, wanted him married, being concerned for the safety of his soul; but she would rather see him damned by default or rebellion than seem to call in question the sacramental bond which she counted, by divine revelation, indissoluble.

So whether he liked it or not, his own fate and Chiara's were held between the rigid hands of the canonists and the soft, epicene palms of Corrado Calitri, Minister of the Republic. Unless Calitri slackened his grip—which he showed no sign of doing—they could both stay suspended till doomsday in the limbo of those outside the law.

Across the nave, in the enclosure reserved for dignitaries of the Republic of Italy, Faber could see the slim patrician figure of his enemy, his breast resplendent with decorations, his face pale as a marble mask.

Five years ago he had been a spectacular young deputy

with Milanese money behind him and a cabinet career
already in promise. His only handicaps were his bachelor
estate and a fondness for gay young men and visiting
aesthetes. His marriage to a Roman heiress, fresh from
convent school, had put the ministry in his pocket and
set the Roman gossips laughing behind their hands.
Eighteen months later Chiara, his wife, was in hospital
with a nervous breakdown. By the time she had recovered, their separation was an accomplished fact. The next
step was to file a petition for a declaration of nullity with
the Holy Roman Rota, and from this point began the tedi-
ous dialogue of the tragicomedy:

"The petitioner, Chiara Calitri, alleges first a defect of
intention," so the lawyers deposed on her behalf, "in that
her husband entered into the bond of matrimony without the full intent to fulfill all the terms of the contract,
with respect to cohabitation, procreation, and normal sexual commerce."

"I had the fullest intention to fulfill all the terms of
the contract. . . ." Thus Corrado Calitri in reply. "But
my wife lacked both the will and the experience to assist
me to carry them out. The married state implies mutual
support; I did not get support or moral assistance from my
wife."

"The petitioner alleges also that it was a condition
of the marriage that her husband should be a man of normal sexual habits."

"She knew what I was," said Corrado Calitri in effect.
"I made no attempt to conceal my past. Much of it was
common knowledge. She married me in spite of it."

"Fine!" said the auditors of the Rota. "Either of the
pleas would be sufficient for a decree of nullity, but a simple statement is not proof. How does the petitioner pro-

pose to prove her case? Did her husband express his
defective intentions to her or to another? Was the condition made explicit before the contract? On what occasion? In what form of speech or writing? And by whom
can the condition be verified?"

So inevitably the wheels of canonical justice ground to
a halt, and Chiara's lawyers advised her discreetly that it
was better to suspend the case while new evidence was
being sought than to force it to an unfavorable conclusion. The men of the Rota stood firm on dogmatic principle and the provisions of the law; Corrado Calitri was
safely married and happily free while she herself was
caught like a mouse in the trap he had set for her. The
whole city guessed at the next step before she made it.
She was twenty-six years old, and within six months she
and George Faber were lovers. Rome in its cynical fashion
smiled on their union and turned to the merrier scandals
of the film colony at Cinecittà.

But George Faber was no complaisant lover. He had an
itch in his conscience, and he hated the man who forced
him to scratch it every day. . . .

He felt suddenly dizzy. A sweat broke out on his face
and palms, and he struggled to compose himself as the
Pope mounted the steps of the altar, supported by his assistants.

Campeggio cocked an astute eye at his queasy colleague, and then leaned forward and tapped him on the
shoulder. "I don't like Calitri, either; but you'll never
win the way you're going."

Faber sat bolt upright and stared at him with hostile
eyes. "What the devil do you mean?"

Campeggio shrugged and smiled. "Don't be angry, my
friend—it's an open secret. And even if it weren't, you

have it written on your face. . . . Of course you hate
him, and I don't blame you. But there are more ways
than one to skin a cat."

"I'd like to hear them," said Faber irritably.

"Call me for lunch one day, and I'll tell you."

And with that Faber had to be content, but the hope
buzzed in his head like a gadfly while Kiril the Pontiff
chanted the Coronation Mass and the voices of the choir
pealed around the dome of the Basilica.

Rudolf Semmering, Father General of the Society of
Jesus, stood rigid as a sentinel at his post in the nave and
addressed himself to a meditation on the occasion and its
meanings.

A lifetime of discipline in the Ignatian exercises had
given him the facility of projecting himself out of the
terms of time and space into a solitude of contemplation.
He did not hear the music, or the murmur of the concourse, or the sonorous Latin of the ceremony. His subdued senses were closed against all intrusion. A vast
stillness encompassed him while the faculties of his spirit
concentrated themselves upon the essence of the moment:
the relationship between the Creator and His creatures,
which was being affirmed and renewed by the installation
of His Vicar.

Here, in symbol, ceremony, and sacrificial act, the nature of the Mystical Body was being displayed—Christ
the God-man as head, with the Pontiff as His Vicar, en-
livening the whole body by His permanent presence and
through the indwelling of the Paraclete. Here was the
whole physical order which Christ had established as
the visible symbol and the visible instrument of His working with humankind—the *ecclesia*, the hierarchy of

Pope, bishops, priests, and common folk, united in a single faith with a single sacrifice and a single sacramental system. Here the whole mission of redemption was summarized—the recall of man to his Maker by the dispensation of grace and by the preaching of the New Testament.

Here, too, was the darkness of a monstrous mystery: why an omnipotent God had made human instruments capable of rebellion, who could reject the divine design or deface it or inhibit its progress: why the All-Knowing should permit those whom He had made in His own image to grope their way to union with Him on a knife-edge path, in daily danger of losing themselves forever from His face. Here finally was the mystery of the *ministerium*, the service to which certain men—himself among them— were called: to assume a greater responsibility and a greater risk, and to show forth in themselves the image of the Godhead for the salvation of their fellows.

Which brought him by a round turn to the application of his whole meditation: what he himself must do for service to the Pontiff, the Church, and the Christ, to whom he was bound by perpetual vow. He was the leader, by election, of forty thousand celibate men, dedicated to the bidding of the Pontiff in whatever mission he might choose to give them. Some of the best brains in the world were at his command, some of the noblest spirits, the best organizers, the most inspired teachers, the most daring speculators. It was his function not merely to use them as passive instruments, but to help each one to grow according to his nature and his talent, with the spirit of God working in him.

It was not enough, either, that he should present the massive network of the Society to the Pontiff and wait for a single command to set it working. The Society, like every other organization and every individual in the Church, had to seek and to propose new modes and new efforts to further the divine mission. It could not surrender itself either to the fear of novelty or to the comfort of traditional methods. The Church was not a static body. It was, according to the Gospel parable, a tree whose whole life was implicit in a tiny seed, but which must grow each year into a new shape and a new fruitfulness, while more and more birds made nests in its branches.

But even a tree did not always grow at the same rate or with the same profusion of leaf and flower. There were times when it seemed that the sap was sparse, or the ground less nourishing, so that the gardener must come and open up the soil and inject new food into the roots.

For a long time now Rudolf Semmering had been troubled by the reports that came to him from all over the world of a slackening of the influence of his Society and of the Church. More students were drifting away from religious practice in the first years after college. There were fewer candidates for the priesthood and for religious orders. The missionary drive seemed to lack impetus. Pulpit preaching had declined into formality—and this in an age when the whole world lived under the shadow of atomic destruction, and men were asking more poignantly than ever before to what end they were made, and why they should breed children into so dubious a future.

In his younger days in the Society, he had been trained as a historian, and all his later experience had confirmed him in the cyclic and climatic view of history. All his years in the Church had shown him that it grew and changed with the human pattern in spite of—or perhaps

because of—its perennial conformity with the Divine One.
There were seasons of mediocrity and times of decadence.
There were centuries of brilliance, when genius seemed
to spring from every lane and alley. There were times
when the human spirit, burdened too long by material
existence, leapt from its prison and went shouting, free
and fiery, across the rooftops of the world, so that men
heard thunders out of a forgotten Heaven and saw once
more the trailing splendors of divinity.

When he looked up at the great altar and saw the
celebrant, moving stiffly under sixty pounds of gilded vestments, he asked himself whether this might not be the
forerunner of such a time. Remembering the Pope's plea
for men with winged feet and burning hearts, he wondered whether this was not the first offering he should
make out of the resources of the Society—a man who
could speak the old truths in a fresh mode and walk as a
new apostle in the strange world that had been born out
of the mushroom cloud.

He had the man, he was sure of it. Even in the Society
he was little known because most of his life had been
spent in strange places, on projects that seemed to have
little relation to matters of the spirit. Yet now it appeared
from his writing and his correspondence that he was ready
to be used otherwise.

His meditation over, Rudolf Semmering, the spare me-
thodical man, took out his notebook and made a memo-
randum to send a cable to Djakarta. Then from the dome
of the Basilica the trumpets broke out in a long, melodious fanfare, and he lifted his eyes to see Kiril the Pontiff
raise above his head the body of the God whom he represented on earth.

On the night of his coronation Kiril Lakota dressed himself in the black cassock and the platter hat of a Roman priest and walked alone out of the Angelic Gate to survey his new bishopric. The guards at the gate hardly glanced at him, being accustomed to the daily procession of Monsignori in and out of the Vatican. He smiled to himself and hid his scarred face behind a handkerchief as he hurried down the Borgo Angelico toward the Castle of Sant' Angelo.

It was a few minutes after ten. The air was still warm and dusty, and the streets were alive with traffic and the passage of pedestrians. He strode out freely, filling his lungs with the new air of freedom, excited as a schoolboy who had just broken bounds.

On the Bridge of Sant' Angelo he stopped and leaned on the parapet, staring down at the gray waters of the Tiber, which had mirrored for five thousand years the follies of emperors, the cavalcade of Popes and princes, and the dozen births and deaths of the Eternal City.

It was his city now. It belonged to him as it could never belong to anyone else but the successor of Peter. Without the Papacy it could die again and crumble into a provincial relic, because all its resource was in its history, and the history of the Church was half the history of Rome. More than this, Kiril the Russian was now Bishop of the Romans—their shepherd, their teacher, their monitor in matters of the spirit.

A long time ago it was the Romans who elected the Pope. Even now they claimed to own him, and in a sense, they did. He was anchored to their soil, locked within their walls until the day he died. They might love him, as he hoped they would. They might hate him, as they had many of his predecessors. They would make jokes about him, as they had done for centuries, calling the hoodlums of the town *figli di papa,* sons of the Pope, and blaming him for the shortcomings of his Cardinals and his clergy. Provoke them enough, and they might even try to murder him and throw his body in the Tiber. But he was theirs and they were his, though half of them never set foot in a church and many of them carried cards which showed them to be Kamenev's men and not the Pope's. His mission was to the world, but his home was here, and like any other householder, he must get along with his neighbors as best he could.

He crossed the bridge and plunged into the network of lanes and alleys between the Street of the Holy Spirit and the Via Zanardelli, and within five minutes the city had engulfed him. The buildings rose on either hand, gray, pitted, and weather-stained. A pale lamp glimmered at the shrine of a dusty Madonna. An alley cat, scrabbling in a heap of refuse, turned and spat at him. A pregnant woman leaned in a doorway under the coat of arms of some forgotten prince. A youth on a clattering Vespa shouted as he passed. A pair of prostitutes, gossiping under a street lamp, giggled when they saw him, and one of them made the sign against the evil eye. It was a trivial incident, but it made a deep impression on him. They had told him of this old Roman custom, but this was the first time he had seen it. A priest wore skirts. He was neither man nor woman, but an odd creature who probably was *mal'occhio.* It was better to be sure than sorry and show him the horns.

A moment later he broke out into a narrow square at whose angle there was a bar with tables set on the sidewalk. One of the tables was occupied by a family group munching sweet pastries and chattering in harsh Roman dialect; the other was free, so he sat down and ordered an espresso. The service was perfunctory, and the other guests ignored him. Rome was full of clerics, and one more or less made no matter.

As he sipped the bitter coffee, a wizened fellow with broken shoes sidled up to sell him a newspaper. He fumbled in his cassock for change, then remembered with a start that he had forgotten to bring any money. He could not even pay for his drink. For a moment he felt humiliated and embarrassed, then he saw the humor of the situation and decided to make the best of it. He signaled the bartender and explained his situation, turning out his pockets as evidence of good faith. The fellow made a surly mouth and turned away, muttering an imprecation on priests who sucked the blood of the poor.

Kiril caught at his sleeve and drew him back. "No, no! You misunderstand me. I want to pay and I shall pay."

The news vendor and the family waited silently for the beginning of a Roman comedy.

"Beh!" The barman made a sweeping gesture of contempt. "So you want to pay! But when and with what? How do I know who you are or where you come from?"

"If you like," said Kiril with a smile, "I'll leave you my name and address."

"So I'm to go trotting all over Rome to pick up fifty lire?"

"I'll send it to you or bring it myself."

"Meantime, who's out of pocket? Me! You think I have so much that I can buy coffee for every priest in Rome?"

They had their laugh then, and they were satisfied. The father of the family fished in his pocket and tossed a few coins expansively on the table. "Here! Let me pay for it, Padre. And for the paper, too."

"Thank you. . . . I'm grateful. But I would like to re-pay you."

"Nothing, Padre, nothing!" Pater familias waved a tol-erant hand. "And you must forgive Giorgio, here. He's having a bad time with his wife."

Giorgio grunted unhappily and shoved the coins into his pocket. "My mother wanted me to be a priest. Maybe she was right at that."

"Priests have their problems, too," said Kiril mildly. "Even the Pope has a few, I'm told."

"The Pope! Now there's a funny one." This from the paper vendor, who, being a seller of news, claimed the right to comment upon it as well. "They've really cooked us beautifully this time. A Russian in the Vatican! Now there's a story for you!" He spread the paper on the table and pointed dramatically to the portrait of the Pontiff, which covered nearly half the front page. "Now tell me if he isn't an odd one to foist on us Romans. Look at that face and the—" He broke off and stared at the bearded visage of the newcomer. His voice dropped to a whisper. "*Dio!* You look just like him."

The others craned over his shoulder, staring at the portrait.

"It's queer," said Giorgio, "very queer. You're almost his double."

"I am the Pope," he told them, and they gaped at him as if he were a ghost.

"I don't believe it," said Giorgio. "You look like him. Sure! But you're sitting here, without a lire in your pocket, drinking coffee, and it's not very good coffee at that."

"It's better than I get in the Vatican."

Then seeing their confusion and their trouble, he asked

for a pencil and wrote their names and their addresses on the back of a bar check. "I'll tell you what I'll do. I'll send each of you a letter and ask you to come to lunch with me in the Vatican. I'll pay you back the money then, too."

"You wouldn't joke with us, Padre?" asked the news vendor anxiously.

"No. I wouldn't joke with you. You'll hear from me."

He stood up, folded the newspaper, and shoved it into the pocket of his cassock. Then he laid his hands on the old man's head and murmured a benediction. "There now. Tell the world you've had a blessing from the Pope." He made the Sign of the Cross over the little group. "And all of you, tell your friends that you have seen me and that I didn't have enough money for coffee."

They watched him, stupefied, and he strode away, a dark, gaunt figure, but oddly triumphant from his first encounter with his people.

It was a petty triumph at best, but he prayed desperately that it might be the presage of greater ones. If Creation and Redemption meant anything at all, they meant an affair of love between the Maker and His creatures. If not, then all existence was a horrible irony, unworthy of Omnipotence. Love was an affair of the heart. Its language was the language of the heart. The gestures of love were the simplicities of common intercourse, and not the baroque rituals of ecclesiastical theatre. The tragedies of love were the tragedies of a waiter with sore feet and a wife who didn't understand him. The terror of love was that the face of the Beloved was hidden always behind a veil, so that when one lifted one's eyes for hope one saw only the official face of priest or Pope or politician.

Once, for a short space in a narrow land, God had

shown His face to men in the person of His Son, and they had known Him for a loving shepherd, a healer of the sick, a nourisher of the hungry. Then He had hidden Himself again, leaving His Church for an extension of Himself across the centuries, leaving, too, His vicars and His priesthood to show themselves other Christs for the multitude. If they disdained the commerce of simple men and forgot the language of the heart, then all too soon they were talking to themselves. . . .

The alleys closed around him again, and he found himself wishing that he could peer beyond their blank doors and their blind windows into the lives of their inhabitants. He felt a strange momentary nostalgia for the camps and the prisons, where he had breathed the breath of his fellows in misfortune and wakened at night to the muttering of their dreams.

He was halfway along a reeking lane when he found himself caught between a closed door and a parked automobile. At the same moment, the door opened and a man stepped out, jostling him against the panels of the car.

The man muttered an apology, and then catching sight of the cassock, stopped in his tracks. He said curtly, "There's a man dying up there. Maybe you can do more for him than I can—"

"Who are you?"

"A doctor. They never call us until it's too late."

"Where do I find him?"

"On the second floor. . . . Be a little careful. He's very infectious. T.B.—secondary pneumonia and haemothorax."

"Isn't there anyone looking after him?"

"Oh yes. There's a young woman. She's very capable—better than two of us at a time like this. You'd better hurry. I give him an hour at most."

Without another word he turned and hurried down the alley, his footsteps clattering on the cobbles.

Kiril the Pontiff pushed open the door and went in. The building was one of those decayed palaces with a littered courtyard and a stairway that smelled of garbage and stale cooking. The treads cracked under his feet, and the banister was greasy to the touch.

On the second landing he came on a small knot of people huddled around a weeping woman. They gave him a sidelong, uneasy stare, and when he questioned them one of the men jerked a thumb in the direction of the open door.

"He's in there."

"Has he seen a priest?"

The man shrugged and turned away, and the wailing of the woman went on, unchecked.

The apartment was a large, airless room, cluttered as a junk shop and full of the morbid smell of disease. In one corner was a large matrimonial bed where a man lay, fleshless and shrunken, under a stained counterpane. His face was unshaven, his thin hair clung damp about his forehead, and his head rolled from side to side on the piled pillows. His breathing was short, painful, and full of rales, and a small bloody foam spilled out of the corners of his mouth.

Beside the bed sat a girl, incongruously well groomed for such a place, who wiped the sweat from his forehead and cleansed his lips with a linen swab.

When Kiril entered she looked up, and he saw a young face, strangely serene, and a pair of dark, questioning eyes.

He said awkwardly, "I met the doctor downstairs. He thought I might be able to do something."

The girl shook her head. "I'm afraid not. He's in deep shock. I don't think he'll last very long."

Her educated voice and her calm professional manner intrigued him. He asked again, "Are you a relative?"

"No. The people around here know me. They send for me when they're in trouble."

"Are you a nurse, then?"

"I used to be."

"Has he seen a priest?"

For the first time, she smiled. "I doubt it. His wife's Jewish, and he carries a card for the Communist Party. Priests aren't very popular in this quarter."

Once again Kiril the Pontiff was reminded how far he was from being a simple pastor. A priest normally carried in his pocket a small capsule of the Holy Oils for the administration of the Last Sacraments. He had none, and here a man was dying before his face. He moved to the bed, and the girl made place for him while she repeated the doctor's warning:

"Just watch yourself. He's very infectious."

Kiril the Pontiff took the slack, moist hand in his own, and then bent so that his lips touched the ear of the dying man. He began to repeat slowly and distinctly the words of the Act of Repentance. When it was done he urged quietly, "If you can hear me, press my hand. If you cannot do that, tell God in your heart you're sorry. He's waiting for you with love; it needs only a thought to take you to Him."

Over and over again he repeated the exhortation while the man's head lolled restlessly and the fading breath gurgled in his gullet.

Finally the girl said, "No use, Father. He's too far gone to hear you."

Kiril the Pontiff raised his hand and pronounced the absolution. "*Deinde ego te absolvo a peccatis tuis . . .* I absolve you from your sins in the name of the Father, and of the Son, and of the Holy Ghost. Amen."

Then he knelt by the bed and began to pray passionately for the soul of this shabby voyager who had begun his last lonely pilgrimage while he himself was being crowned in the Basilica of St. Peter.

In ten minutes the little tragedy was over, and he said the prayers for the departed spirit while the girl closed the staring eyes and composed the body decently in the attitude of death. Then she said firmly:

"We should go, Father. Neither of us will be welcome now."

"I would like to help the family," said Kiril the Pontiff.

"We should go." She was very definite about it. "They can cope with death. It's only living that defeats them."

When they walked out of the room, she announced the news bluntly to the little group. "He's dead. If you need help, call me."

Then she turned away and walked down the stairs, with Kiril at her heels. The high mourning cry of the woman followed them like a malediction.

A moment later they were alone in the empty street. The girl fumbled in her handbag for a cigarette and lit it with an unsteady hand. She leaned back against a car and smoked a few moments in silence. Then she said abruptly, "I try to fight against it, but it always shakes me. They're so helpless, these people."

"At the end we're all helpless," said Kiril soberly. "Why do you do this sort of thing?"

"It's a long story. I'd rather not talk about it just now. I'm driving home—can I drop you off somewhere?"

It was on the tip of his tongue to refuse; then he checked himself and asked, "Where do you live?"

"I have an apartment near the Palatine, behind the Foro Romano."

"Then let me ride with you as far as the Foro. I've never seen it at night—and you look as though you need some company."

She gave him an odd glance, then without a word opened the door of the car. "Let's go, then. I've had more than enough for one night."

She drove fast and recklessly until they broke out into the free space where the Forum lay, bleak and ghostly, under the rising moon. She stopped the car. They got out together and walked over to the railing, beyond which the pillars of the Temple of Venus heaved themselves up against the stars. In the terse fashion which seemed habitual to her, she challenged him:

"You're not Italian, are you?"

"No, I'm Russian."

"And I've seen you before, haven't I?"

"Probably. They've printed a lot of pictures of me lately."

"Then what were you doing in Old Rome?"

"I'm the bishop of the city. I thought I should know at least what it looked like."

"That makes us both foreigners," said the girl cryptically.

"Where do you come from?"

"I was born in Germany, I'm an American citizen, and I live in Rome."

"Are you a Catholic?"

"I don't know what I am. I'm trying to find out."

"This way?" asked Kiril quietly.

"It's the only one I know. I've tried all the others."
Then she laughed, and for the first time since their meeting she seemed to relax. "Forgive me, I'm behaving very badly. My name is Ruth Lewin."

"I'm Kiril Lakota."

"I know. The Pope from the steppes."

"Is that what they call me?"

"Among other things. . . ." She challenged him again. "These stories they print about you, your time in prison, your escape, are they true?"

"Yes."

"Now you're in prison again."

"In a way, but I hope to break out of it."

"We're all in prison, one way or another."

"That's true. . . . And it's the ones who understand it that suffer most of all."

For a long moment she was silent, staring down at the tumbled marbles of the Forum. Then she asked him, "Do you really believe that you stand in God's shoes?"

"I do."

"How does it feel?"

"Terrifying."

"Does He speak to you? Do you hear Him?"

He thought about it for a moment, and then answered her gravely. "In one sense, yes. The knowledge of Himself which He revealed in the Old Testament and in the New pervades the Church. It is there in the Scripture and in the tradition which has been handed down from the time of the Apostles, and which we call the Deposit of Faith. This is the lamp to my feet. . . . In another sense, no. I pray for divine light, but I must work by human reason. I cannot demand miracles. At this moment, for instance, I ask myself what I must do for the people of

this city—what I can do for you. I have no ready answer. I have no private dialogue with God. I grope in the
dark and hope that His hand will reach out to guide me."

"You're a strange man."

"We are all strange," he told her with a smile, "and
why not, since each of us is a spark struck off from the
fiery mystery of the Godhead?"

Her next words were uttered with a poignant simplicity
that touched him almost to tears:

"I need help, but I don't know how, or where, to get it."

For a moment he hesitated, torn between prudence
and the promptings of a vulnerable heart. Then once
again he felt within him the subtle stirring of power. He
was the Pastor and none other. Tonight one soul had
slipped through his fingers; he dare not risk another. "Take
me home with you," he told her. "Make me a cup of coffee, then talk it out. Afterwards you can drive me back to
the Vatican."

In a small apartment huddled under the shadow of the
Palatine Hill she told him her story. She told it calmly
and gravely, and with no trace of that hysteria which
every confessor feared in his relations with women.

"I was born in Germany thirty-five years ago. My family was Jewish, and it was the time of the pogroms. We
were chased about from one country to another, until
finally a chance came to enter Spain. Before we applied
for visas we were told it might help if we became Catholics. . . . So my parents went through the motions and
became converts—Moriscos might be a better name! We
took the new identity and we were admitted.

"I was a child then, but it seemed that the new country and the new religion opened their arms to welcome

me. I remember the music, the color, the Holy Week processions winding through the streets of Barcelona, while little girls like me, with white veils and flower wreaths in their hair, threw rose petals before the priest who carried the Monstrance. I had lived so long in fear and uncertainty that it was as if I had been transported into a land of fairy tale.

"Then, early in 1941, we were granted visas for America. The Catholic Charities Bureau took care of us, and with their help I was placed in a convent school. For the first time, I felt thoroughly safe and, strangely enough, thoroughly Catholic.

"My parents did not seem to mind. They, too, had reached safe harbor, and they had their own lives to rebuild. For a few years I was serenely happy; then—how do I say it?—my world and I myself began to crack down the middle. I was a child still, but the minds of children open more quickly than adults ever believe.

"In Europe millions of Jews were dying. I was a Jew and I was oppressed by the thought that I was a renegade who had bought my safety by forswearing my race and my religion. I was a Catholic, too, and my belief was identified with the freest and happiest time of my life. Yet I could not accept the freedom or the happiness because it seemed they had been bought with blood money.

"I began to rebel against the teaching and the discipline of the convent and yet all the time I knew that I was rebelling against myself. When I began to go out with boys, it was always with the rebels, the ones who rejected any kind of belief. It was safer that way. Perhaps in the end it would be better to believe nothing than to be torn apart by a double allegiance.

"Then, after a while, I fell in love with a Jewish boy. I

was still a Catholic, so I went to discuss the case with my parish priest. I asked for the usual dispensation to marry someone outside the Faith. To my surprise and my shame, he read me a bitter lecture. I heard him out and then walked out of the rectory, and I have never set foot inside a church since. He was a foolish man, blind and prejudiced. For a while I hated him, and then I understood that I was really hating myself.

"My marriage was happy. My husband had no fixed belief, nor, it seemed, did I; but we had a common race and a common heritage, and we were able to live in peace with one another. We made money, we made friends. It was as if I had achieved the continuity which my life had lacked from the beginning. I belonged to someone, to a settled order, and at long last, to myself.

"Suddenly, and for no apparent reason, a strange thing happened. I became morbid and depressed. I would wander around the house disconsolate, tears rolling down my cheeks, sunk in utter despair. Sometimes I would break out into violent rages at the slightest provocation. There were times when I contemplated suicide, convinced that I would be better dead than inflicting so much unhappiness on myself and on my husband.

"In the end my husband forced the issue. He demanded that I see a psychiatrist. At first I refused angrily, and then he told me bluntly that I was destroying myself and destroying our marriage. So I agreed to begin treatment, and entered on a course of analysis.

"This is a strange and frightening road, but once you begin to walk it you cannot turn back. To live life is hard enough. To relive it, to retrace every step in symbol and fantasy and simple memory, is a weird experience. The person who makes the journey with you, the analyst, assumes a multitude of identities: father, mother, lover, husband, teacher—even God.

"The longer the journey, the harder the road, because each step brings you closer to the moment of revelation where you must face once and forever the thing from which you have been fleeing. Time and again you try to step off the road or turn back. Always you are forced forward. You try to defer, to temporize. You create new lies to deceive yourself and your guide, but the lies are demolished one by one.

"In the middle of my analysis my husband was killed in an automobile accident. For me it was another guilt added to all the others. Now I could never restore to him the happiness of which I had robbed him. My whole personality seemed to disintegrate under the shock. I was taken to a nursing home, and the therapy began again. Slowly the nature of my hidden fear became clear to me. When I reached the core of myself, I knew that I should find it empty. I should not only be alone, but hollow as well, because I had built a God in my own image and then destroyed Him, and there was no one to take His place. I must live in a desert, without identity, without purpose, since even if there were a God, I could not accept Him because I had not paid for His presence.

"Does this seem strange to you? It was a terror to me. But once I stood in the desert, empty and solitary, I was calm. I was even whole. I remember the morning after the crisis when I looked out from the window of my room and saw the sun shining on the green lawn. I said to myself, 'I have seen the worst that can happen to me, and I am still here. The rest, whatever it is, I can endure.'

"A month later I was discharged. I settled my husband's estate and came to Rome. I had money, I was free,

I could plan a new life for myself. I might even fall in love again. . . . I tried it, too; but in love one must commit oneself, and I had nothing to commit.

"Then I began to understand something. If I lived for myself and with myself I should always be hollow, always in solitude. My debts to my people and my past were still unpaid; I could accept nothing from life until I had begun to pay them.

"You asked me tonight why I do this kind of service. It's simple enough. There are many Jews in Rome—the old Sephardic families who came from Spain in the time of the Inquisition, immigrants from Bologna and the Lombard cities. They are still a people apart. Many of them are poor, like the ones you saw tonight. . . . I can give them something. I know I do. But what do I give myself? Where do I go? . . . I have no God although I need one desperately. . . . You tell me you stand in His shoes—can you help me . . . ?"

Extract from
the Secret Memorials of
KIRIL I, Pont. Max.

. . . I am troubled tonight. I am solitary and perplexed. My installation in the See of Peter is complete. I have been crowned with the triple tiara. The ring of the Fisherman is on my finger. My blessing has gone out to the city and to the world. In spite of it all—because of it all, perhaps—I have never felt so empty and inadequate. I am like the scapegoat driven into the desert, with the sins of all the people on my back. . . .

I must ask Rinaldi to find me a wise priest to whom I can confess myself each day, not only for absolution and the sacramental grace, but for a purging of this pent, stopped-up spirit of mine. I wonder if the faithful understand that the Vicar of Christ has often more need of the confessional than they themselves. . . .

I have seen many men die, but the sad and solitary exit which I witnessed tonight in a Roman tenement afflicts me strangely. The words of the woman who saw it with me still ring in my ears: "They can cope with death. It's the living that defeats them." It seems to me that this defeat is the measure of our failure in the ministry of the Word.

Those who need us most are those who are bowed the lowest under the burden of existence—whose life is a daily struggle for simple sustenance, who lack talent and opportunity, who live in fear of officials and tax-gatherers and debt collectors, so that they have no time and hardly any strength to spend on the care of their souls. Their whole life becomes a creeping despair. . . . If it were not for the infinite knowledge and the infinite mercy of God, I, too, could easily despair.

The case of the woman Ruth Lewin gives me more hope. While I was in prison and under the long ordeals of interrogation, I learned much about the intricate functioning of the human mind. I am convinced that those who devote themselves to the study of its workings, and of its infirmities, can do a great service to man and the cause of his salvation. . . . We should not, as shepherds of souls, treat this infant science with suspicion or hasty censure. Like every other science, it can be wrested to ignoble ends. It is inevitable that many who explore the misty country of the soul will make mistakes and false guesses, but every honest research into the nature of man is also an exploration of the divine intent in his regard.

The human psyche is the meeting ground between God and man. It is possible, I think, that some of the meaning of the mystery of Divine Grace may be revealed when we understand better the working of the subconscious mind, where buried memories and buried guilts, and buried impulses, germinate for years and then break out into a strange flowering. . . . I must encourage competent men inside the Church to pursue this study, and to co-operate with those outside it, to make the best use possible of their discoveries. . . .

The sick mind is a defective instrument in the great symphony which is God's dialogue with man. Here perhaps we may see a fuller revelation of the meaning of human responsibility and God's compassion for His creatures. Here we may be able to illuminate the difference between formal guilt and the true status of the soul in the sight of God. . . .

It might scandalize many if I declared openly that in a woman like this Ruth I see—or think I see—a chosen spirit. The key to such spirits is their recognition that their wrestling with life is in reality a wrestling with God. . . .

The strangest story in the Old Testament is the story of Jacob, who wrestled with the angel and conquered him and forced the angel to tell his name. . . . But Jacob went away from the struggle limping.

I, too, am a limping spirit. I have felt reason and the foundations of my faith rock in the dark bunker and under the lights and the relentless inquisition of Kamenev.

I believe still. I am committed more completely than ever before to the Deposit of Faith, but I am no longer content to say, "God is thus. Man is thus," and then make an end of it. Wherever I turn on this high pinnacle, I am confronted with mystery. I believe in the Godly harmony which is the result of the eternal creative act. . . . But I do not always hear the harmony. I must wrestle with the cacophony and apparent discord of the score, knowing that I shall not hear the final grand resolution until the day I die and, hopefully, am united with God. . . .

This is what I tried to explain to Ruth, though I am not sure that I did it very well. I could not bring myself to present her with blunt theological propositions. Her troubled spirit was not ready to receive them.

I tried to show her that the crisis of near despair which afflicts many people of intelligence and noble spirit is often a providential act, designed to bring them to an acceptance of their own nature, with all its limitations and inadequacies, and of the conformity of that nature with a divine design whose pattern and whose end we cannot fully apprehend.

I understand her terrors because I have endured them myself. This I am sure she understood. I advised her to be patient with herself and with God, who, even if she could not believe in Him, still worked in His own fashion and His own secret time.

I told her to continue the good work she was doing, but not to regard it always as a payment of debts. No one of us could pay his debts were it not for the redemptive act consummated on the Cross by Christ.

I tried to show her that to reject the joy of living is to insult Him who provides it, and who gave us the gift of laughter along with the gift of tears. . . .

These things I think I should write for others because the sickness of the mind is a symptom of our times, and we must all try to heal one another. Man is not meant to live alone. The Creator Himself has affirmed it. We are members of one body. The cure of a sick member is a function of the whole organism. . . .

I have asked Ruth to write to me, and sometimes to

come and see me. I dare not let this office separate me from direct contact with my people. . . . For this reason I think I should sit in the confessional for an hour each week and administer the Sacrament to those who come into St. Peter's.

The nearest I came to losing my faith and my soul was when I lay naked and solitary in an underground bunker. . . . When I was brought back to the huts, to the sound of human talk—even to the sound of anger and ribaldry and blasphemy—it was like a new promise of salvation. . . .

I wonder whether this is not the way in which the creative act renews itself daily: the spirit of God breathing over the dark waters of the human spirit, infusing them with a life whose intensity and diversity we can only guess. . . .

"*In manus tuas, Domine* . . . Into thy hands, O God, I commend all troubled souls."

✳
IV

IT WAS nearly six weeks after the coronation before George Faber arranged his luncheon with Campeggio. He might have put it off even longer had not Chiara argued him into it with tears and tantrums. He was by nature a prompt man, but he had lived long enough in Rome to be suspicious of any gratuitous gesture. Campeggio was a distinguished colleague, to be sure, but he was in no sense a friend, and there was no clear reason why he should concern himself with the bedding and wedding of Chiara Calitri.

So somewhere in the offing was a *combinazione*—a proposition—with the price tag carefully hidden until the very last moment. When one lunched with the Romans, one needed a long spoon and a steady hand, and George Faber was still a little shaken by his quarrel with Chiara.

Spring was maturing slowly into summer. The azaleas made a riot of color on the Spanish Steps, and the flower sellers did a brisk business with the new roses from Rapallo. Footsore tourists found refuge in the English Tea-room, and the traffic swirled irritably around Bernini's marble boat in the Piazza.

To stiffen his small courage, George Faber bought a red carnation and pinned it jauntily in his buttonhole before he crossed the Square and entered the Via Condotti. The restaurant which Campeggio had named for their rendezvous was a small, discreet place, far away from the normal haunts of newsmen and politicians. . . . In a matter of such delicacy, he claimed, one should not risk an eavesdropper, though Faber saw little point in secrecy since the Calitri story was common property in Rome. However, it was part of the game that every *combinazione*, every *progetto*, must be dressed up with a little theatre. So he submitted with as much good grace as he could muster.

Campeggio entertained him for half an hour with a vivid and amusing chronicle of the Vatican, and how the clerical dovecotes were fluttering as the new Pope asserted himself. Then with a diplomat's care he steered the talk toward Faber:

". . . It may please you to know, my dear fellow, that your own dispatches have been very favorably noticed by His Holiness. I am told he is anxious to make more direct contact with the press. There is talk of a regular luncheon with senior correspondents, and your name is, of course, first on the list."

"I'm flattered," said Faber dryly. "One tries always to write honestly, but this man is an interesting subject in his own right."

"Leone, too, has a soft spot for you, and you are well regarded in the Secretariat of State. . . . These are important sources and important voices, as you know."

"I'm well aware of it."

"Good," said Campeggio briskly. "Then you understand the importance of preserving a good relation without, shall we say, embarrassing incidents."

"I've always understood that. I'm interested to know why you bring it up now."

Campeggio pursed his thin lips and looked down the backs of his long, manicured hands. He said carefully, "I make the point to explain my next question. Do you propose setting up house with Chiara Calitri?"

Faber flushed and said testily, "We've discussed it. So far we haven't made any decision."

"Then let me advise you very strongly not to do it at this moment. . . . Don't misunderstand me. Your private life is your own affair."

"I'd hardly call it private. Everyone in Rome knows the situation between Chiara and myself. I imagine the rumor has reached the Vatican long before this."

Campeggio gave him a thin smile. "So long as it remains a rumor, they are content to suspend judgment and leave you in the hands of God. There is no question of public infamy which could damage your case with the Rota."

"At this point," Faber told him bluntly, "we have no case. The whole business is suspended until Chiara can get new evidence. So far she hasn't been able to find any."

Campeggio nodded slowly, and then began to trace an intricate pattern on the white tablecloth. "I am told by those who understand the thinking of the Rota that your best hope of a verdict rests on the plea of defective intention. In other words, if you can prove that Calitri entered into the marriage contract without the full intention of fulfilling all its terms—and that intention includes fidelity—then you have a good chance of a favorable decision."

Faber shrugged unhappily. "How do you prove what's in a man's mind?"

"Two ways: by his own sworn statement or by the evidence of those who heard him express the defective intention."

"We looked for people like that. We couldn't find any, and I'm damn sure Calitri won't give evidence against himself."

"Put enough pressure on him, and I think he might."

"What kind of pressure?"

For the first time, Campeggio seemed uncertain of himself. He was silent awhile, tracing long, flowing lines with the point of his fork. Finally he said deliberately, "A man like Calitri, who holds a high position and who has, shall we say, an unusual private life, is very vulnerable. He is vulnerable to his party, and to public attack. He is vulnerable to those who have fallen out of his favor. . . . I don't have to tell you that this is an odd world he lives in—a world of strange loves and curious hates. Nothing in it is very permanent. Today's favorite is rejected tomorrow. There are always bleeding hearts ready to tell their story to a good listener. I've heard some myself. Once you have enough stories you go to Calitri."

"I go to him?"

"Who else? You report the news, don't you?"

"Not that sort of news."

"But you know plenty who do?"

"Yes."

"Then I don't have to draw pictures for you."

"It's blackmail," said George Faber flatly.

"Or justice," said Orlando Campeggio. "It depends on the point of view."

"Even if we did frighten a testimony out of him, he

could then allege undue pressure and the whole case would be thrown out of court for good."

"That's a risk you have to take. If the stakes are high enough, I think you might be wise to take it. . . . I should add that I may be able to give you a little help in your inquiry."

"Why?" asked Faber sharply. "Why should you care a row of beans what happens to Chiara and me?"

"You've become a Roman," said Campeggio with cool irony. "Still, its a fair question. I like you. I think you and your girl deserve better than you're getting. I don't like Calitri. Nothing would give me greater satisfaction than to see him destroyed. That's almost impossible, but if your Chiara wins her case it will damage him a great deal."

"Why do you dislike him so much?"

"I'd rather not answer that question."

"We have common interests. We should at least be honest with each other."

The Roman hesitated a moment, and then threw out his hands in a gesture of defeat. "What does it matter, anyway? There are no secrets in Rome. I have three sons. One of them works in Calitri's department and has, shall we say, fallen under his influence. I don't blame the boy. Calitri has great charm, and he doesn't scruple to use it."

"A dirty business!"

"It's a dirty town," said Orlando Campeggio. "I'm the last man who should say it, but I often wonder why they call it the City of Saints."

While George Faber was still chewing unhappily over his luncheon dialogue, Chiara Calitri was sunning herself on the beach, at Fregene.

She was a small dark girl, lithe as a cat; and the youths

who passed, idling along the beach, whistled and preened themselves for her attention. Safe behind her sunglasses, she watched them come and go, and stretched herself more decoratively on the colored towel.

A sense of comfort and well-being pervaded her. She was young, the admiration of the youths told her she was beautiful. She was loved. Faber in his uneasy fashion was committed to fight her battles. She was freer than she had ever been in her life.

It was the freedom which intrigued her most of all, and each day she became more conscious of it, more curious about it, and more eager for its enlargement. This morning she had wept and shouted like a market woman at poor George because he had seemed unwilling to risk a talk with Campeggio. If he wavered again, she would fight him again, because from now on she could not love without the liberty to be herself.

With Corrado Calitri she had felt herself torn apart, blown this way and that, like paper shredded on the wind. For a time—a terrifying time—it was, as if she had ceased to exist as a woman. Now at last she had put herself together again—not the same Chiara but a new one, and no one ever again must have the power to destroy her.

Deliberately she had chosen an older man because such were more tolerant and less demanding. They asked a more placid life. They offered affection as well as passion. They moved with authority in a wider world. They made a woman feel less vulnerable. . . .

She sat up and began to toy with the warm sand, filtering it between her fingers so that it spilled out and made a small mound at her feet. Inconsequently she thought of an hourglass, in which time measured itself inexorably in a spilth of golden grains. Even as a child she had been obsessed with time, reaching out for it as she now reached for freedom, spending it recklessly, as if by so doing she could bring the future into today. When she was at home she had cried to go to school. At school she had wanted always to grow up. Grown up at last, she had wanted to be married. In marriage—the bitter fiasco of her marriage to Corrado Calitri—time had suddenly and dreadfully stood still, so that it seemed she must be anchored eternally to this union with a man who despised her womanhood and debased it at every opportunity.

It was from this terror of static time that she had fled finally into hysteria and illness. The future toward which she had reached so eagerly was now intolerable to her. She no longer wanted to advance, but only to retreat into the dark womb of dependence.

Even here time was still her enemy. Life was time; an unendurable extension of loveless years. The only ways to end it were to die or to stay forever in retreat. But in the hospital the vigilant nurses held death away from her, while the physicians drew her slowly and patiently back to another meeting with life. She had fought against them, but they, too, were inexorable. They stripped her illusions away one by one like layers of skin until the naked nerves were exposed, and she screamed in protest against their cruelty.

Then they had begun to show her a strange alchemy: how pain might transmute itself into a mercy. Endure it long enough, and it began to diminish. Run from it, and it followed, always more monstrous, like a pursuer in a nightmare. Fight it, and in the end you could come to terms with it—not always the best terms, not always the wisest, but a treaty that was at least bearable.

She had made her own treaty with life now, and she was living better than she had hoped under the terms of it. Her family disapproved of the bargain, but they were generous enough to give her love and a measure of affection. She could not marry, but she had a man to care for her. The Church condemned her, but so long as she preserved a public discretion it would withhold a public censure.

Society, in its paradoxical fashion, registered a mild protest and then accepted her with good enough grace. . . . She was not wholly free, not wholly loved, nor wholly protected, but she had enough of each to make life bearable, and time endurable, because each now held a promise of betterment.

Yet it was not the whole answer, and she knew it. The treaty was not half as favorable as it looked. There was a catch in it—a dragnet clause which, once invoked, could cancel all the rest.

She looked out at the empty water of the Tyrrhenian Sea and remembered her father's tales of all the strange life that inhabited its deeps: corals like trees, whales as big as ships, fish that flapped their wings like birds, jewels that grew in oyster slime, and weeds like the hair of drowned princesses. Under the sunlit surface was a whole mysterious world, and sometimes the waters opened and swallowed down the voyager who risked them too boldly. Sometimes, but not always. . . . The most unlikely sailormen survived and came to safe harbor.

Here precisely was the risk of her own contract with life. She believed in God. She believed in the Church's teaching about Him. She knew the penalty of eternal ruin that hung over the heads of those who rashly dared the divine displeasure. Every step, every hour, was a tightrope venture of damnation. At any moment the contract might be called in. And then . . . ?

Yet even this was not the whole mystery. There were others, and deeper ones. Why she and not another had been submitted to the first injustice of a false marriage contract. Why she and not another had been forced into the suicidal confusion of a breakdown. And this precipitate grasping at any straw for survival. Why? Why?

It was not enough to say, like the parish confessor, that this was God's dispensation for her. It was Corrado's dispensation first. Did God compound injustice and then hold damnation over the heads of those who wilted under its weight? It was as if the sea rose up and swirled her back into the confusion of her illness.

There was no cure for the untimely thought that came in nighttime or daytime, prickling along the flesh like a cold wind. One could not surrender to it for fear of a new madness. One could not blot it out except by the exercise of love and passion, which in a strange way seemed to affirm what the preachers said they denied: the reality of love and mercy, and the hand that helped the most hapless sailormen out of the damnation of the deep. . . .

She shivered in the warm air and stood up, wrapping the towel about her. A brown youth with the figure of a Greek god whistled and called to her, but she ignored him and hurried up the beach toward the car. What did he know of life who vaunted it like a phallic emblem in the sun? George knew better—dear middle-aged, uneasy George, who shared her risk and was at least working to rid her of it. She longed for the comfort of his arms and the sleep that came after the act of love. . . .

:

Rudolf Semmering, Father General of the Society of Jesus, sat in the airport at Fiumicino and waited for his man from Djakarta. To those who knew him well his vigil was of singular significance. Rudolf Semmering was an efficient man, adapted by nature and ascetic exercise to the military spirit of Ignatius Loyola. Time to him was a precious commodity because only in time could one prepare for eternity. A waste of time was therefore a waste of the currency of salvation. The affairs of his order were complex and pressing, and he might easily have sent a deputy to meet this obscure member who was already thirty minutes late.

Yet the occasion seemed to demand a more than normal courtesy. The newcomer was a Frenchman, a stranger to Rome. He had spent more than twenty years in exile—in China, in Africa, in India, and the scattered islands of Indonesia. He was a simple priest, and a distinguished scholar, whom Rudolf Semmering had held in silence under his vow of obedience.

For a scholar the silence was worse than exile. He was free to work, to correspond with his colleagues all over the world, but he was prevented by a formal obedience from publishing the results of his research or teaching on any public rostrum. Many times in the last decade Rudolf Semmering had questioned his own conscience about this prohibition laid on so brilliant a mind. Yet always he had come to rest on his first conviction, that this was a chosen spirit which discipline would only refine, and whose bold speculations needed a term of silence to found themselves firmly.

A man with a sense of history, Semmering was convinced that the effectiveness of an idea depended on the temper of the time into which it was first introduced. It was too late in history to risk another Galileo affair or the burning of a new Giordano Bruno. The Church was still suffering from the sad debates over the Chinese rites. He was less afraid of heresy than of a climate of thought which could make heresy out of a new aspect of truth. He lacked neither compassion nor understanding of the sacrifices he demanded of a noble mind such as this one, but Jean Télémond, like every other member of the Society, had vowed himself to obedience, and when it had been exacted of him he had submitted himself.

For Semmering this was the final test of the metal of a religious man, the final evidence of his capacity for a Godly work in a position of trust. Now the test was over, and he wanted to explain himself to Télémond and to offer him the affection that every son had a right to expect from his father in the spirit. Soon he would be asking Télémond to walk a new road, no longer solitary, no longer inhibited, but exposed, as he had never been exposed before, to the temptations of influence and the attacks of jealous interests. This time, he would need support more than discipline, and Semmering wanted to offer them with warmth and generosity.

Diplomacy was involved as well. Since the time of Pacelli the Cardinals of the Curia and the Bishops of the Church had been afraid of any attempt to introduce a Gray Eminence into the counsels of the Pontiff. They wanted, and so far they had had, a return to the natural order of the Church, where the Curia were the counsellors of the Pontiff and the bishops were his co-workers, acknowledging his primacy as the successor of Peter, but holding equally to their own apostolic autonomy. If the Society of Jesus gave any appearance of attempting to push a favorite into the Papal Court, it would inevitably meet suspicion and hostility.

Yet the Pontiff had called for men, and the question was now how to offer this one without appearing to canvass for him. . . . The voice of the traffic-caller crackled over the amplifiers, announcing the arrival of a BOAC flight from Djakarta, Rangoon, New Delhi, Karachi, Beirut. Rudolf Semmering stood up, smoothed down his cassock, and walked toward the customs entrance to meet the exile.

Jean Télémond would have been a striking man in any company. Six feet tall, straight as a ramrod, lean of visage, with gray hair and cool, humorous blue eyes, he wore his clerical black like a military uniform, while the yellow malarial tinge of his skin and the furrows about his upturned mouth told the story of his campaigns in exotic places. He greeted his superior with respectful reserve, and then turned to the porter who was struggling with three heavy suitcases.

"Be careful with those. There's half a lifetime of work in them."

To Semmering he said with a shrug, "I presumed I was being transferred. I brought all my papers with me."

The Father General gave him one of his rare smiles. "You were right, Father. You've been away too long. Now we need you here."

A spark of mischief twinkled in Télémond's blue eyes. "I was afraid I was to be hauled before the Inquisition."

Semmering laughed. "Not yet. . . . You're very, very welcome, Father."

"I'm glad," said Télémond with curious simplicity. "These have been difficult years for me."

Rudolf Semmering was startled. He had not expected a man so brusque and aware. At the same time, he felt a small glow of satisfaction. This was no vague savant, but a man with a clear mind and a stout heart. Silence had not broken him, nor exile subdued him. An obedient spirit was one thing, but a man with a broken will was no use to himself or to the Church.

Semmering answered him gravely. "I know what you've done. I know what you've suffered. I have, perhaps, made your life more difficult than it needed to be. I ask only that you believe I acted in good faith."

"I've never doubted that," said Jean Télémond absently. "But twenty years is a long time." He was silent awhile, watching the green meadows of Ostia, dotted with old ruins and new excavations, where red poppies grew between the cracks of ancient stones. Suddenly he said, "Am I still under suspicion, Father?"

"Suspicion of what?"

Télémond shrugged. "Heresy, rebellion, a secret modernism, I don't know. You were never very clear with me."

"I tried to be," said Semmering mildly. "I tried to explain that prudence was involved, and not orthodoxy. Some of your early papers and lectures came under the notice of the Holy Office. You were neither condemned nor censured. They felt, and I agreed with them, that you needed more time, and more study. You have great authority, you see. We wanted it used to the best advantage of the Faith."

"I believe that," said Jean Télémond. "Otherwise I think I should have abandoned the work altogether." He hesitated a moment, and then asked, "Where do I stand now?"

"We have brought you home," said Semmering gently, "because we value you, and we need you. There is work for you here, urgent work."

"I have never made conditions; you know that. I have never tried to bargain with God or with the Society. I worked as best I could within the limits imposed on me. Now . . . now I should like to ask something."

"Ask it," said Rudolf Semmering.

"I think," said Télémond carefully, "I think I have gone as far as I can on this lonely road. I think what I have done needs to be tested by discussion and debate. I should like to begin to publish, to submit my thesis to open criticism. This is the only way knowledge grows, the only way the horizons of the spirit are enlarged. . . . I have never asked for anything before, but in this I beg for your support, and for the support of the Society."

"You have it," said Rudolf Semmering.

In the cramped seats of the speeding automobile they faced each other, superior and subject, the man under obedience, the man who exacted the fulfillment of the vow.

Télémond's lean face crumpled a little, and his blue eyes were misty. He said awkwardly, "I—I did not expect so much. This is quite a home-coming."

"It is better than you know," said the Father General gently. "But there are still risks."

"I've always known there would be. What do you want me to do?"

"First you have to pass a test. It will be a rough one, and you have less than a month to prepare yourself."

"What sort of test?"

"July thirty-first is the feast day of St. Ignatius Loyola."

"I was ordained on that day."

"It makes a good omen, then, because on that same day His Holiness will visit the Gregorian University, which, you know, owed its beginning to our founder and St. Francis Borgia. . . . I want you to deliver the memorial lecture in the presence of His Holiness, the teaching staff, and the students."

"God help me," said Jean Télémond. "God help my stumbling tongue."

As they turned into the clamor of the city, through the Porta San Paolo, he buried his face in his hands and wept.

Ruth Lewin sat under a striped umbrella on the Via Veneto, sipped an *aranciata*, and watched the lunch-time crowds disperse toward siesta. The soft air of summer lifted her spirits, and she felt as if all the weight of the world could be shrugged off with one long comfortable yawn. Even the city seemed to have taken on a new face. The clamor of the traffic was a friendly sound. The folk were better dressed than usual. The waiters were more courteous. The ogling of the men was a compliment.

Nothing had changed in her situation. None of her doubts or dilemmas had resolved themselves, yet their burden was lighter, and she wore it with a better humor. It was as if her long convalescence were over and she could take her place confidently in the normal commerce of the world.

It was not all an illusion. She had suffered too long the perilous alternations of exaltation and depression to deceive herself about her cure. But the swings were shorter now—the heights less dizzy, the deeps less terrifying. The pulse of life was returning to a regular beat. The fever had broken at last, and the moment of crisis had been her meeting with Kiril the Pontiff in a Roman back alley.

Even now the memory was lit by a kind of wonder. His aspect was so strange—the scar, the beard, the contrast between his office and his humble dress. Yet when she had confronted him in her own house, over the banality of coffee and biscuits, the impression was not of strangeness but of extraordinary simplicity.

Ever since her break with the Church she had had a creeping distaste for clerical talk and the forms of clerical convention. This man had none of them. He wore his belief like a skin, and his convictions were expressed with the gentleness of one who had acquired them at a price he would not ask others to pay. His words came out new-minted and ringing with sincerity:

". . . All life is a mystery, but the answer to the mystery is outside ourselves, and not inside. You can't go on peeling yourself like an onion, hoping that when you come to the last layer you will find what an onion really is. At the end you are left with nothing. The mystery of an onion is still unexplained because like man, it is the issue of an eternal creative act. . . . I stand in God's shoes, but I can't tell you any more. Don't you see? This is what I am here to teach—a mystery! People who demand to have Creation explained from beginning to end are asking the impossible. Have you ever thought that by demanding to know the explanation for everything you are committing an act of pride? We are limited creatures. How can anyone of us encompass infinity . . . ?"

In the mouth of another the words would have sounded dry and stilted, but from this Kiril they came endowed with a quality of healing, because they were not read from a book, but from the palimpsest of his own heart. He had not reproached her for the dereliction of a baptismal faith, but had talked of it with kindness, as if it were even a sort of mercy in itself.

"No two people come to God by the same road. There are very, very few who reach Him without stumbling and falling. There are seeds that grow a long time in darkness before they push up shoots into the sun. . . . There are others that come to the light at one thrust in a single day. . . . You are in darkness now, but if you want the light you will come to it in time. . . . The human soul, you see, meets barriers that it must cross, and they are not always crossed at one stride. The direction in which the soul travels is the important thing. If it travels away from itself, then it must ultimately come to God. If it turns back upon itself, this is a course of suicide, because without God we are nothing. . . . Everything, therefore, that urges you to an outward growth—service, love, the simplest interest in the world—can be a step toward Him. . . ."

Disturbed as she was on that night, she had not taken in the full import of all that he had said. But the words had remained imprinted on her memory, and each day she found in them a new meaning and a new application. If now she could sit calm in a summer sun, watching the folly and flirtation of the town, passing no judgment on it or on herself, it was because of this Kiril, who sat in the seat of judgment and yet withheld verdict. If love were possible again, it would be because of him who lived solitary in the celibate city of the Vatican.

Love . . . ! It was a chameleon word, and she had seen more of its changes and colorations than she could admit without blushing.

Every big city had its enclave of cripples and oddities and vagrants who sustained life on the best terms they could get and were grateful for the most temporary easement from lonely misery. Here in Rome the kingdom of the beggars of love was a weird and polyglot domain, and in her time she had wandered over most of it.

It was a treacherous journey for a widow of thirty-five with money in the bank and a heart empty of resources. Unhappy boys had wept at her breast for their mothers. Straying husbands and playing tourists had come knocking on her door. Men with noble names had made her the confidante of their exotic attachments. The secret sisterhood had offered her entry to the sapphic mysteries. In the end she had emerged, shaken and unsatisfied, knowing that even in the half-world of the odd ones there was no place for her.

Love . . . ! Here on the Via Veneto pretty girls with poodles on a leash sold it by the night's installment. In the clubs and bars any woman with a foreign accent could buy it for a smile and the flirting of a lace handkerchief. . . . But where and how did one find the person on whom to spend this newly discovered self—so fragile and suddenly so precious?

Miraculously, Humpty-Dumpty had been picked up and put together again. He was sitting back on the wall, smiling and clapping hands at the concourse. But if he tumbled again and the glue came unstuck . . . who then could patch the eggshell? O little white wandering spirit, please, please stay in one piece!

Out of the clamor of the traffic she heard her own name spoken. "Ruth Lewin! Where have you been hiding yourself?"

She looked up to see George Faber, gray-haired and dapper as any Roman dandy, looking down at her.

In his private study Kiril the Pontiff was closeted with two of his senior ministers: Cardinal Goldoni, his Secretary of State, and Cardinal Clemente Platino, Prefect of the Congregation for the Propagation of the Faith. The purpose of their meeting was a daylong stock-taking of the affairs of the Church, Holy, Universal, and Apostolic. The study was a large room bare of ornament save for a carved wooden crucifix behind the Pontiff's desk and, on the opposite wall, a case full of maps showing the distribution of Catholic communities throughout the world.

In another setting and another dress they might have been a trio of international businessmen: the Pontiff, dark, bearded, and exotic; the Secretary of State, gray, stocky, and harshly eloquent; Platino, tall, olive-skinned, urbane, with a great eagle beak inherited from some Spanish ancestor.

But in this place and in this time they were dedicated, each to the limit of his own talent, to a folly that promised small profit to any business: the preparation of all men for death and for union with an unseen God. Their talk ranged over a multitude of subjects: money, politics, military treaties, economic agreements, personalities in high places round the globe; yet the core of the discussion was always the same: how to spread throughout the world the knowledge of Christ, His teaching, and the society which He had set up to preserve and disseminate it.

For them every question—how a man married, how he was educated, what he was paid, his national allegiance —was at root a theological proposition. It had to do with the Creator and the creatures and the eternal relationship of one with the other. Everything that was done in the dimension of time had its roots and its continuity in eternity.

When the Secretary of State appointed an ambassador to Austria or a legate to Uruguay, his function was to maintain an official relationship with the government so that in a climate of accord between Church and State human souls might be led the more easily to the knowledge and the practice of a saving truth.

When Platino appointed this missionary congregation or that to go into the jungles of the Amazon, he did so with the fullest conviction that he was obeying a clear command of Christ to carry a Gospel of hope to those who sat in darkness and the shadow of death.

It was, however, a point of view that raised special problems of its own. Men who did a Godly work were apt to become careless about the human aspect of it. Men who dealt with the currency of eternity were apt to rest too hopefully on the future and let the present slip out of their control. Those who were sustained by the two-thousand-year-old structure of the Church were protected too softly from the consequence of their own mistakes. With so much tradition to rest on, they were often prickly and suspicious about new modes of Christian action.

Yet in spite of all, men like Platino and Goldoni had an acute awareness of the world in which they lived and of the fact that to do the work of God they had to come to terms with what man had done for himself or to himself. Platino was making this point now. His long brown finger pointed to a spot in Southeast Asia.

". . . Here, for example, Holiness, is Thailand. Constitutionally it is a monarchy. In fact it is a military dictatorship. The religion of the state is Buddhism. At one time or another in his life every male of the royal family, and every senior official, takes the saffron robe and spends some time in a monastery. We have schools here. They are run by nuns and teaching priests. They are free to give religious instruction, but not within normal school hours. Those who wish to be instructed in the Faith must come outside these times. This is our first difficulty. There is another. Government appointments—and any position of consequence is a government appointment—are only open to Buddhists. Officially, of course, this is not admitted, but in fact it is true. The country is underdeveloped. Most commerce is in the hands of Chinese, so that for all practical purposes, a man who becomes a Christian must give up all hope of economic or social advancement. . . . The temper of the people, which has also been conditioned by Buddhist belief, is resistant to change and suspicious of outside influence. . . .

"On the other hand, there is evident among the young men a growing interior conflict. They are being brought every day into closer contact with Western civilization through American military and economic aid, but there is little opportunity or work for them. I have been given what I believe is a reliable statistic, that twenty-five per cent of senior male students are addicted to heroin before they leave school. You see the problem. How do we move to make a real penetration of the minds and hearts of the people?"

"How do you summarize the work we are doing now?" asked the Pontiff gravely.

"Basically as a work of education and charity. On the human level we are helping to raise the standard of literacy. We run hospitals which are used as training centers. There is a home for the rehabilitation of girls who have been taken out of the brothels. . . . We serve the community. We display the Faith to those who pass through our hands. However, the number of conversions is small, and we have not yet entered effectively into the mind and heart of the country."

"We have a worse position in Japan," said Goldoni in his brisk fashion. "We have a concordat which gives us much more effective working conditions than we have in Thailand, but here again we have made no real break-through."

"Yet we did once make a break-through," said Kiril with a smile. "It was begun by one man. St. Francis Xavier. The descendants of his converts are still there— the Old Christians of Nagasaki and Nara. Why do we fail now? We have the same message. We dispense the same grace as the Church of the Catacombs. Why do we fail?" He heaved himself out of the chair and stood by the map, pointing to one country after another and measuring the failures and retreats of the Church. "Look at Africa. My predecessors proclaimed constantly the need for the swift training of a native clergy: men identified with their own people, speaking their language, understanding their symbols and their special needs. Too little was done too slowly. Now the continent is moving toward a federation of independent African nations, and the ground has been cut from under our feet. . . . Here in Brazil you have an immense industrial expansion, and a huge population of peasants living in the most grinding poverty. To whom are they turning to champion their cause? To the Communists. Do we not preach justice? Should we not be prepared to die for it as for any other Article of Faith? I ask you again. Where do we miss?"

Goldoni breathed a silent sigh of relief and left the answer to his colleague. After all, a Secretary of State had to deal with a situation as it was, with diplomats and politicians as they were—good or bad, pagan or Christian. Platino, on the other hand, was charged directly with the spread of Christian belief throughout the world. His authority was enormous, and inside the Church they called him "the Red Pope," as the Father General of the Jesuits was called the black one.

Platino did not answer directly, but picked up from the desk two photographs, which he held out to the Pontiff. One of them showed a fuzzy-haired Papuan in a white shirt and white lap-lap, with a small crucifix hung round his neck. The other was the picture of a native from the uplands of New Guinea with a headdress of bird-of-paradise feathers and a pig tusk thrust through his nose.

As the Pontiff examined the photographs, Platino explained them carefully:

"Perhaps these two men will answer your Holiness' question. They both come from the same island, New Guinea. It is a small place, economically unimportant, but politically it may become so as the pivot of a federation of South Pacific islands. In two years, five at most, New Guinea will be an independent country. This man . . ." He pointed to the photograph of the man who wore the crucifix. "This is a mission boy. A teacher in one of our Catholic schools on the coast. He has lived all his life in a mission colony. He speaks English and pidgin and Motu. He teaches the catechism, and has been proposed as a candidate for the priesthood. . . . This one is a tribal chief from the mountains: a leader of twenty thousand men. He speaks no English, he understands pidgin, but speaks only his own upland dialect. He is wearing now a ceremonial dress. He still holds to the old pagan beliefs. . . . Yet when independence is granted to this country, he is the most likely leader, while our mission boy will have no influence at all."

"Tell me why," said Kiril the Pontiff.

"I have thought about it a long time, Holiness," said Platino deliberately. "I have prayed much. I am still not sure that I am right, but this is what I believe. With our mission boy we have in one sense succeeded admirably. We have educated a good human being. We have set him in the way of salvation. He lives chastely, deals justly, and displays in himself the example of a Godly life. If he becomes a priest, he will teach the Word and dispense the grace of the Sacraments to those with whom he comes in contact. In him and those like him the Church fulfills her prime mission—the sanctification of individual human souls. . . . In another sense, however, we have failed because in this boy—how shall I say it?—we have limited the relevance of the Faith. . . . In the mission we have created a small, safe world for him. A Christian world, yes, but one that has cut itself off from the larger world which is still God's vineyard. We have made him an apolitical individual, and man by his nature is a political and social animal who has an immortal soul. . . . We have left him, in large part, unprepared for the dialogue which he must sustain throughout his life with the rest of his fellows in the flesh. . . . Look at our friend here, the one with the tusk through his nose. He is a man of power because he practices polygamy and each wife brings him a plot of land and then cultivates it for him. He holds to the old beliefs because these are his ground of communication with his tribe. He is their mediator with the spirits as he is their mediator with men of other tongues. He understands tribal law and tribal justice. In the difficulty and confusion which will follow the granting of independence, he will speak with more authority and more relevance than our mission boy because he has not been divorced from the realities of social existence. . . . Your Holiness spoke of Brazil and the South Americas. There is an analogy between the two situations. The Church has to deal with man in the circumstances in which he lives. If he is hungry, we have to feed him; if he is oppressed, we must defend him so that he may have, at least, a minimum freedom to set his soul in order. We cannot preach from the pulpit, 'Thou shalt not steal,' and then stand by, inactive, while political or social injustice is done to those who sit and listen to our preaching. . . . We see a strange example in Poland, where the Church has had for very survival to enter actively into a conversation with elements hostile to it. It has had to prove itself relevant, and it has done so. It lives the more strongly for that very reason, even though it lives more painfully. . . ."

He paused and mopped his forehead with a handkerchief.

"Forgive me, Holiness, if I speak more strongly still. We have all seen the progress that was made under your predecessor toward a growth of unity between the separated Christian communities. Our work in this field has only begun, but it seems to me that where we have been defensive, where we have retreated, holding the Faith to ourselves as though it could be tarnished by contact with the world, there we have failed. Where we have held it up for a witness, where we have affirmed most boldly that the Gospel is relevant to every human act and every situation, there we have done well."

"You affirm it," said Kiril the Pontiff bluntly. "I affirm it, as do our brother bishops scattered across the world, but the affirmation does not reach the people with the same clearness and the same fruitfulness—it does not even reach my Romans here. Why?"

"I think," said the Secretary of State brusquely, "the world is educating itself more quickly than the Church. Put it another way. The knowledge that is necessary to make an Act of Faith, and an Act of Repentance, is not enough to found a Christian society or create a religious climate. In the last twenty years men have been projected into a new and terrifying dimension of existence. . . . The graph of human science from the invention of the wheel to the internal-combustion engine is a long, gradual slope. It covers—what?—five, ten, fifteen thousand years. From the internal-combustion engine to this moment the line leaps almost vertically, pointing to the moon. . . . 'Tempora mutantur . . .'" he quoted wryly. "'Times change, and man changes with them.' If our mission means anything, it means that each new enlargement of the human mind should be an enlargement of man's capacity to know, love, and serve God."

"I think," said Kiril the Pontiff with a smile, "I should send you both out on a missionary journey." He crossed to his desk and sat down, facing them. He seemed to gather himself for a moment, and then very quietly, almost humbly, he explained himself. "I am, as you know, an eager man. It has been my fear, since I have sat in the Chair of Peter, that I should act too hastily and damage the Church, which is given into my hands. . . . I have tried to be prudent and restrained; I have understood also that one man in his lifetime cannot change the world. The symbol of the Cross is a symbol of the apparent failure and folly of God himself. . . . But it is my office to teach and to direct, and I have decided now where I want to begin. . . . What you have told me confirms me in the decision. I am grateful to you both. I want you both to pray for me."

The two Cardinals sat silent, waiting for him to go on. To their surprise, he shook his head. "Be patient with me. I need time and prayer before I declare myself. Go in the name of God."

"I suppose," said George Faber in his uncomfortable fashion, "I suppose you're wondering why I'm telling you all this about Chiara and me."

Ruth Lewin laughed and shrugged. "That's the way it goes in Rome—everybody's got a story. And a stranger's usually the best listener."

"We're not really strangers, though. How many times have we met? Half a dozen, at least. At the Antonellis' and at Herman Seidler's and—"

"So I'm convinced we're not strangers. Take it from there."

"I was feeling low—and I was delighted to see you."

"Thank you, kind sir."

"And I don't tell my life story to every girl I meet on a street corner."

"I don't think it matters in Rome whether you tell it or not. People know it just the same—in different versions, of course!"

Faber grinned, and looked for a moment like a self-conscious boy. "I've never heard your story, Ruth."

She parried the probe with a smile. "I've never told it. And I don't belong to the cocktail set."

"Where do you belong?"

"I've often wondered that myself."

"Do you have many friends here?"

"A few. They call me for dinner sometimes. I visit them when I feel inclined. I do a little work amongst some lame ducks in Old Rome. For the rest . . . *Mi arrangio*. I get along one way and another."

"Are you happy?"

Once again she hedged the answer. "Is anyone? Are you?"

"I'm in a mess," said George Faber bluntly.

"That's not your reputation."

Faber looked up sharply, wondering if she was mocking him. He had a small humor, and banter always made him suspicious. "What's my reputation?"

"You have the tidiest life in Rome . . . and a beautiful mistress to round it out."

"That's not the way I see it. I want to get married. It seems the only way I can do it is to mix myself up with blackmail and backstairs politics, and a bunch of gay boys and Lesbians."

"Don't you think the risk is worth it?"

His heavy, handsome face clouded and he ran a nervous hand through his gray hair. "I suppose it is. I haven't really had time to think it out."

"That means you're not sure."

"No, I'm not sure."

As if to divert her attention he signaled the waiter to bring him another cup of coffee. Then he lit a cigarette and stared moodily at the shop front on the other side of the pavement. For all her detachment, Ruth Lewin felt herself touched by a pang of pity for him. He was no longer young, though most women would find him attractive. He had built himself a comfortable career and a respectable name in his trade. Now he was being asked to risk them both for a girl who, once free, might grow tired of him and look for younger loving. She dropped her teasing tone and questioned him more gently.

"What does Chiara want?"

"Freedom at any price."

"Even at the price of your career?"

"I'm not sure of that, either."

"Don't you think you should ask her?"

"That's what bothers me. . . . I'm not even clear myself what the risks are. All I know is that on the one hand, there's an element of blackmail and I'm to be the blackmailer . . . Don't misunderstand me. I've been in this game a long time. I know that every newsman is tempted at some time or another to use his position for his own profit. My experience is that those who do it always lose in the end. I've never been a muckraker, and I'm rather proud of it. . . . On the other hand, I'm fighting for something and someone very precious to me."

"If you start a fight with Corrado Calitri," said Ruth Lewin soberly, "I can promise you it will be a very rough one."

He stared at her, surprised. "Do you know Calitri, then?"

"I know some of the people he knows. They play very dirty when their feelings are hurt."

He hesitated a moment, and then faced her with the question. "Could you help me to meet some of them?"

"No." She was very definite about it.

"Why not?"

"I lived in that little Arcady for a while. I didn't like it. I don't want to go back. Besides, you're a newsman. You have your own contacts."

"Not too many I can trust. Would you be willing to give me names . . . information?"

To his surprise, she burst out laughing, and then seeing his discomfiture, she laid an apologetic hand on his wrist.

"Poor George! I shouldn't laugh at you. But I wonder
. . . I really wonder . . ."

"What?"

"About you and Chiara. Are you both so sure you can
go through with this fight—win or lose? If you lose, you
know, they'll tear you into little pieces and feed you to
the lions like early Christians. The Church won't have
either of you. You'll never be welcome again at the Vatican or on the Quirinale. Are you both ready for that? Do
you have enough love for Chiara? Does she have enough
for you?"

He shrugged and spread his hands in a Roman gesture
of puzzlement. "Beh! Everybody in Rome talks about love.
Everybody plays at it in his own fashion. I've played, too,
but now it's late in the day for me. I don't want to make a
mistake."

"I'd like to help you," she told him quietly, "but it's
your life and your girl. . . . I should go now; it's getting
late."

"Would you let me take you home?"

"Better not. I'll get a taxi."

"Could I see you again?"

"Why, George?"

He flushed unhappily. "I've enjoyed talking to you. I
hope you'll decide to help me. And if I go ahead with this
Calitri business, I'll need to talk to someone I can trust."

"What makes you think you can trust me?"

"You said yourself you don't belong to the gossip circuit. I'd like to add that you're a very grown-up girl."

"Is that the best recommendation you can give me?"

Once again his rare humor asserted itself. "Give me
time, and I may think of others."

"If and when you do, you can call me. I'm in the telephone book."

On which indecisive note they parted. As she rode home through the clamor of the afternoon traffic, she remembered that it was late in the day for her, too, and she felt again the pang of treacherous pity for George Faber and his puzzled middle-aged heart.

Extract from
the Secret Memorials of
K I R I L I, Pont. Max.

. . . It is an hour after midnight—the beginning of a new day. An important day for me because for the first time I shall begin to address myself to the whole Church. Late last evening I asked my confessor to come to me so that I might purge myself from the sins of the day and purify myself for the task I am about to undertake.

Afterwards I begged him to stay with me a little while and serve the Mass which I wanted to celebrate immediately after midnight. . . . It is strange how much variety there can be for a priest in the offering of the Sacrifice. Sometimes one is dry and unmoved, one has to make an effort of will to concentrate on the familiar ritual and on the staggering significance of the Act of Consecration. At other times it is as if one is caught out of oneself and "into the spirit," as St. John puts it. One is aware of God. One is at the same moment humbled and exalted, afraid and rapturously glad. . . .

Tonight it was different again. I began to understand in a new fashion the nature of my office. When, at the moment of elevation, I lifted the Host above my head, I saw the real meaning of the "we" with which the Pontiffs have addressed themselves customarily to the world. It is not "I" who am to speak or to write, it is the Church through me and Christ through me and the Church. . . .

I am myself, yes. But if I speak only of myself, and for myself, I am nothing. I am like the wind bells, whose sound changes with every breeze. . . . But the Word cannot change. The Word is immutable. . . . "In the beginning was the Word, and the Word was with God, and the Word was God." Yet in another sense the Word must renew itself in me as the redemptive act of the Crucifixion renews itself at the hands of every priest when he says Mass. I am the reed through which the voice of the spirit must be blown so that men may hear it in the mode of their own times. . . .

The paper is blank before me, the pens are ready. Is Kiril ready? I pray that he may be. What must he write? And how and to whom?

My subject is education, the preparation of a man to take his place in this world and in the next. My letter will be a discussion of the educative office of the Church—its mission to "lead out" the soul of man from the darkness of ignorance, from the bondage of the flesh, into the light and the freedom of the sons of God. . . .

How shall I write? As simply as I can because the deepest truth is the most simply stated. I must write from the heart—*cor ad cor loquitur*. And I must write in my own tongue because this is the best fashion for every man to talk of God, and to Him. Later the Latinists will take my words and harden them into the antique form which will preserve them for a permanent record in the Church. After them will come the translators, who will turn them into a hundred other tongues in which the Word of God must be preached. . . . The world is a Babel Tower of conflicting voices, but inside the Church there is and must always be "the unity of the spirit in the bond of faith."

Outside the Church, too, there is a unity which we neglect too often. It is the unity of men who suffer together a common existence, delight in common joys, and share the same confusions, regrets, and temptations. . . .

I am reminded of something forgotten too often by us the shepherds, Tertullian's *Testimony of the Soul*. . . . "Man is one name belonging to every nation upon earth. In them all is one soul though many tongues. Every country has its own language, yet the subjects of which the untutored soul speaks, are the same everywhere."

There is another reason why I want to write in Russian. I want Kamenev to see my letter as it came from my own hand. I want him to hear through it the tones of my voice so that he may know that I love him and the people among whom I was born. If it were possible I should like him to have my manuscript, but it may be difficult to get it into his hands, and I could not risk compromising him.

To whom shall I write? . . . To the whole Church—to my brother bishops, to all priests and monks and nuns, to all the faithful, without whom our office is meaningless. I must show them how their mission is not merely to teach but to educate one another with love and forbearance, each lending of his own strength to the weak, of his own knowledge to the ignorant, of his charity to all. . . .

And when I have written, what then? I must begin to act through the administration of the Church to see that reforms are made where they are needed and that the inertia of a large and scattered organization does not stand in the way of God's intention. I must have patience, too, and tolerance, understanding that I have no right to demand of God a visible success in all I attempt. I am the gardener. I plant the seed and water it, knowing that death may take me before I see the bud or the flower. It is late and I must begin. . . .

"Kiril, the servant of the servants of God, to the bishops and brethren of all the Churches, peace and apostolic benediction. . . ."

V

THE HOME-COMING of Jean Télémond, S.J., was a drab little affair that belied the warmth of his superior's welcome.

The headquarters of the Society, at No. 5 Borgo Santo Spirito, was a large gray building, bleak as a barracks, that nestled under the shadow of St. Peter's dome. Its furnishings were sparse, functional, and without discernible beauty. The only man to greet him was the brother porter, a gray and crusty veteran who had seen so many members come and go that one more made no matter.

The whole aspect of the place was cheerless and temporary, a shelter for men whose training was to divest themselves of comfort and human attachment and make themselves soldiers of Christ. Even the religious emblems were ugly and mass-produced, reminders only of the interior life which no symbol could properly convey.

After they had prayed together, the Father General led him to his room, a small, whitewashed box, furnished with a bed, a *prie-dieu,* a crucifix, a desk, and a set of bookshelves. Its dusty windows looked out on a courtyard, chill and deserted even under the summer sun. Jean

Télémond had lived more harshly than most and in less
friendly places, but this first look at the Mother House
plunged him into a deep depression of spirit. He felt
solitary and naked and strangely afraid. The Father
General gave him the timetable of the House, promised to
introduce him to his colleagues at suppertime, and then
left him to his own devices.

It took him only a few moments to unpack his meager
personal belongings, and then he set about the task of
laying out the mass of notes, manuscripts, and bulky
folders which represented his life-work. Now, when the
time had come to make the tally of it and present it to
the world, it seemed small and insignificant.

For twenty years he had worked as a paleontologist, in
China, in Africa, in America, and the far Indies, plotting
the geography of change, the history of life recorded in
the crust of the earth. The best scientific minds had been
his colleagues and co-workers. He had survived war and
revolution and disease and loneliness. He had endured the
perilous dichotomy between his function as a scientist
and his life as a religious priest. To what end?

For years the conviction had been growing in him that
the only intelligible purpose of so much effort and sacrifice
was to display the vast concordance of Creation, the ultimate convergence of the spiritual and physical which
would mark the eternal completion of an eternal creative
Impulse. Many times he had pondered the significance of
the old proverb "God writes straight with crooked lines,"
and he was convinced to the marrow of his bone that
the final vector of all the diverse forces of Creation was an
arrow pointing straight to a personal divinity.

Many another before him had attempted this justification of God to men. Their achievements and their fail-

ures were the milestones of human thought—Plato, St.
Augustine, Albertus Magnus, Thomas of Aquin . . . Each
had used the knowledge of his own time to build a theology or a philosophy or a cosmology. . . . Each had
added another stage to the journey of unaided reason;
each had elevated man thus much above the jungle that
spawned him.

For Télémond the project presented itself in another
form: to trace, from the text of the living earth, the journey from unlife to life, from life to consciousness, from
consciousness to the final unity of Creation with its Creator.

The study of the past, he believed, was the key to the
pattern of the future. The justification of the past and of
the present lay in the tomorrow that would thrust out of
them. He could not believe in a wasteful Creator or in a
diffuse, accidental, purposeless Creation. At the root of all
his thought and, he believed, at the root of every human
aspiration was an instinctive desire for a unity and a
harmony in the cosmos. Once men abandoned their hope
for it, they condemned themselves to suicide or madness.

That the harmony did exist, he was convinced beyond
doubt. That it could be demonstrated, he believed also—
though in another mode of credence. The pattern was
laid, but it was not yet complete. He believed he had
grasped the main lines of it, but his problem was to explain them in terms intelligible and acceptable. So vast
an exposure needed new words, new levels of thought,
new analogies, and a new boldness in speculation.

For too long Western thought had been disinclined
toward a unified knowledge of the world. Even in the
Church the spiral thinking of the Eastern fathers, the traditional Christian *gnosis*, had been overshadowed by the

nominalist and rationalist tradition of Western theologians. Now, if ever, the hope of the world's survival seemed to rest on a leap out of mere logic into a recognition of new and bolder modes of communication.

Yet the terror of this first moment in Rome was that under the first impact of this noisy, brawling city, where past and present rubbed elbows with each other at every step, his conviction seemed to be weakening. Rome was so sure of itself, so sophisticated, so skeptical, so certain that everything that had happened or could happen had been weighed and judged beyond dispute—that his own voice must sound small and meaningless.

A long time ago, from a hut on the fringe of the Gobi Desert, he had written, "I understand now how little mere travel gives to a man. Unless the spirit expands with the explosion of space about him, he returns the same man as he went out." Here in the Mother House of the Society, where all the rooms looked the same, where everyone was dressed in the same black cassock and attended the same exercises of devotion and ate at the same table, he wondered whether in truth he had changed at all, and whether the enlargement which he thought to have attained was not a bitter illusion.

With a gesture of impatience he stacked the last manuscripts on the desk, closed the door on them, and walked out to view the city which threatened him so vividly.

A few moments' walking brought him out onto the broad reach of the Street of Conciliation and in full view of the Piazza of St. Peter. The slim finger of the obelisk pointed to the sky, and on either hand Bernini's colonnades swept backward to the sunlit dome of the Basilica. The sudden majesty of it all—the towering cupola, the gigantic figures of windy stone, the rearing masses of columns and pilasters—oppressed him, and he felt drunk with the suddenness of sun and space.

Instinctively he lowered his eyes to the human aspect: the straggle of afternoon tourists, the coachmen gossiping at their horses' heads, the peddlers with their little boxes of rosaries, the buses and automobiles, and the slim jets of the fountains. Once again the cogs of memory slipped into gear, and he remembered what he had written after his first look at the Grand Canyon of the Colorado. . . . "I am either unmoved or tremendously troubled by the sight of natural grandeur, or even by a spectacular artifact deserted by its makers. As soon as man appears, I am comforted again because man is the only significant link between the physical order and the spiritual one. Without man the universe is a howling wasteland contemplated by an unseen Deity. . . ." If man deserted even this ageless splendor of St. Peter's, it would decay and rot into a goat-cropping, where tree roots grew out of the stones and animals drank from the muddy basins of the fountains.

Encouraged, he strolled across the Piazza toward the entrance of the Basilica, pausing to look up at the papal apartments and ask himself what manner of man now dwelt in them. Soon they would meet face to face, and Jean Télémond would have to justify his own life's work to a man charged to perpetuate the life of the whole Church. Already rumors were rife about the new Pontiff and his challenge to the reactionaries and the extreme traditionalists in the Vatican. There were those who saw him as the prime mover of a second renaissance within the Church, a new and unexpected link between the logical West and the illuminated East.

If the rumors were true, then there was hope that Jean Télémond might be freed at last from his exile. If not . . .

On the opposite side of the Piazza lay the Palace of the Holy Office, where the Hounds of God kept watch over the Deposit of Faith. To them Jean Télémond was known already. Once a priest came under their scrutiny he was never forgotten, and everything he wrote must pass through their hands before it could be printed. Cardinal Leone was still there, too, he of the white mane and the cold eye and the uncertain temper. It was an open secret that Leone had small liking for the Father General of the Jesuits and that he favored more the opinions and the manners of the older orders in the Church. Télémond wondered what had prompted Semmering to risk the displeasure of the old lion by bringing back to Rome a man of suspect opinions.

There were politics inside the Church as well as out of it. There were questing minds and reluctant ones. There were blind traditionalists and too eager innovators. There were men who sacrificed order to growth, and others who reached so boldly for change that they held it back for centuries. There were rank pietists and fierce ascetics. There were administrators and apostles—and God help any luckless fellow who was caught between the millstones.

There was only one refuge; one committal, which he had made a long time ago. A man could walk only the path he saw at his own feet or that which was pointed out to him by a lawful superior. After that he was in the hands of God. . . . And their compass was more generous, their hold more reassuring, than the hands of any man.

In spite of the warmth he shivered and quickened his

steps toward the interior of the Basilica. Looking neither
to right nor left, he walked down the echoing nave toward the sanctuary, and then knelt for a long time, praying at the tomb of Peter.

In the small, cold hours between midnight and dawn
George Faber lay wakeful and grappled with his new
situation. Beside him Chiara lay sleeping like a child,
satiated and tranquil. Never in the months of their loving had he experienced a passion so tumultuous, a mat-
ing so abandoned as on this night. Every sense had
quickened, every emotion had surged up and spent itself
in a climax of union so intense that death itself had
seemed only a whisper away. Never had he felt so much
a man. Never had Chiara shown herself so generously a
woman. Never had speech been stifled so swiftly by the
outpourings of tenderness and the transports of desire.
. . . Never in all his life had he been so suddenly over-
whelmed by the sadness of the afterward.

When their loving was done, Chiara had given a small
contented sigh, buried her face in the pillow, and lapsed
immediately into sleep. It was as if she had left him without warning and without farewell to embark on a private journey—as if having touched the limit of love, he
were left solitary to face the darkness and the terrors of
an endless night.

The terrors were more real than they had ever been
before. For so rich a pleasuring, sometime, somehow,
a price must be paid. And he knew beyond the shadow of
a doubt that he would be the one to pay it. What he had
felt this night was a springtime flowering which might
never repeat itself, because for him it was late summer,

late harvest, with the taxman waiting at the gate to claim his due.

For Chiara life was still her debtor. Payment had been deferred too long and her body was greedy for the tribute. For himself, a man on the wrong side of forty, the case was far other. He knew where the price tags were hidden. He knew the needs that followed the brisk satisfaction of the act of union: the need of continuity, the need of children to be born of the seed so richly spent in lust or love, the need of quiet harbor and a morning sunlight after the storms of the night.

Even as he thought about it, Chiara stirred and turned toward him for warmth. It was a gesture made in a dream, but it was more eloquent than words. Until her marriage to Calitri she had been protected at every step—by rich and doting parents, by cosseting nuns, by the traditions of her class. When her marriage had failed, she had found another refuge, and now she had come to rest in his arms to forgetfulness in his practiced embrace. So long as he held her strongly and securely, she would stay. But the moment his grip slackened or his courage faltered, she would slip away.

The strange thing was that she saw nothing one-sided in the bargain. She had given him her body, she had given him her reputation; what else was there to demand? Had he told her, she would never have understood. Married and the mother of children, she would grow in the end to maturity, but in this halfway state she would always be the girl-woman, half delighted by the adventure, half afraid of its consequences, but never wholly understanding that the debt of love was not all paid in the coinage of the flesh.

For her even tonight's encounter, rich, ruinous and wonderful, was a kind of flight—and he was too old, too wise, or too calculating to make it with her. Instinctively he turned, threw his arms about her, and drew her to him, wondering even as he did so why the miraculous oneness of the flesh should last so short a time, and why in the end two lovers must lie so often and so long like islands in a dark sea. Her slack hand lay across his body, her hair brushed his lips, her perfume surrounded him. But sleep would not come, and he rehearsed over and over again their dinner-table talk, when he had told her of Campeggio's advice, and where it might lead the pair of them. . . .

She had listened attentively, chin cupped in her hands, her dark eyes bright with eagerness, intrigued by the prospect of a plot.

"Of course, darling! It's so simple. Why didn't we think of it before? There must be twenty people in Rome who'd be happy to give evidence against Corrado. All we've got to do is find them."

"Do you know any of them, Chiara?"

"Not really. Corrado was always fairly discreet with me. Still, I'm sure if we talked around we'd get a whole list of names."

"The one thing we mustn't do," he told her firmly, "is talk around. If word gets out about what we're doing, we're finished. Don't you understand? This is a conspiracy."

"George, darling, don't be so melodramatic. All we're trying to do is get justice for me. You couldn't call that conspiracy, surely."

"It wears the color of it. And in the eyes of the Church, and civil law, it comes to the same thing. There are only two things we can do—employ a professional investigator or I'll have to do the investigation myself. If we use an investigator, it will cost me more money than I can afford, and in the end he could sell me out to your husband. If I do the job myself . . . I'm immediately embroiled up to the neck."

She stared at him, wide-eyed and innocent. "Are you afraid, George?"

"Yes, I am."

"Of my husband?"

"Of his influence, yes."

"Don't you want to marry me, darling?"

"You know I do. But once we're married we have to live. If I lose my reputation in Rome I can't work here any longer. We'd have to go back to America."

"I wouldn't mind that. . . . Besides, what about my reputation? I didn't throw that in your face, did I?"

"Please, Chiara! Please try to understand this isn't a matter of morals, it's a matter of authority, professional status . . . the credit I live by. If I'm held up as a common blackmailer . . . where do I start again? This is the double standard, sweetheart. You can sleep around as much as you like. You can make a million by exploiting the poor. But if you pass a bad check for ten dollars or breach the code of professional ethics, you're dead and buried and there's no coming back. That's the way the world is, rough as guts. Do what you want. Take what you want. But if you trip—God help you! That's what we have to face—together."

"If I'm not afraid, George, why should you be?"

"I've got to be sure that you know what's involved."

"I wonder if you really know what's involved for me. A woman needs to be married, George. She needs to have a home and children, and a man who belongs to her. What we have is wonderful, but it isn't enough. If you won't fight for it, George, what can I do?"

. . . And there it was, the challenge that had taken him at one stride to her arms—a challenge to his virility, a challenge to the one folly he had never indulged—to count the world well lost for love. But George Faber was a man of his own world. He knew himself too well to believe that he could live without it. He had made the gesture, to be sure. He had flung his cap at the whirling windmills, but when the time came to assault them with sword and lance, how would he be then? A knight in shining armor with his lady's favor on his helm . . . ? Or an aging Quixote on a spavined nag, an object of laughter for men and angels?

Valerio Cardinal Rinaldi sat on the terrace of his villa and watched the day decline toward the sea. The folds of the land were full of purple shadows, the hills were touched with gold and bronze, and the rooftops of village and farmhouse shone russet in the glow. A small breeze stirred across the land, carrying the scent of lilac and roses, and mown grass. The sound of childish laughter rose from the garden below, where his niece's daughter played among the Orphic marbles.

This was the good time—the hour between day and dusk, when the eye was rested from the harshness of the sun and the spirit was not yet touched by the melancholy of twilight. The cicadas were still, and the crickets had not begun their mournful chirping. He picked up the book that lay on his lap and began to read the crabbed Greek characters which hid the magical words of Euripides:

And O for that quiet garden by the Western sea
   Where the daughters of Evening sing
Under the golden apple-tree;
   Where the bold sailor wandering
   Finds the Ocean-god has barred
His Westward path over the purple waste!
   Where huge Atlas lives to guard
   The solemn frontiers of the sky!
Where Zeus' palace fountains of ambrosial wine
   Flow by the festal couch divine,
   While holy Earth heaps high
   Her fruits of rarest taste
To bless the immortal feast with bountiful supply!

He was a lucky man and he knew it. It was given to few to arrive at eminence and then survive it with a strong heart and a good digestion to enjoy the quiet garden where the Daughters of Evening sang. It was given to few in his profession to hear the voices of children in his own orchard close, to have them cluster about his knee for a story, to give them a kiss and an old priest's blessing at bedtime.

Others he knew had died before their time. Others, again, survived painfully, with blear eyes or palsied limbs or slow cankers, on the charity of the Church. Some lapsed into senility or a poverty of possession and spirit. But he sat here in the splendor of a fading day—prosperous, independent, the last of the princely Cardinals of the Church. He had few regrets, because regret had always seemed a vanity and alien to his nature. He was ready for retirement—prepared for it, too, by a curious and scholarly mind and a diversity of friendships and interests. He did not fear death because in the normal course it was still a long way off, and he had lived an orderly life, investing his talents as best he knew for the service of the Church.

Yet sometimes—in the twilight hour, in the wakeful nights of an old man, or when he watched the peasants bending over the tillage of his estate—the poignant question presented itself: Why have I so much? Why am I endowed so richly and others in so niggardly a fashion? Or is this all a divine irony whose point will be revealed only in eternity?

Old Euripides had raised the same question and yet answered it no better:

> They wander over the waves, visit strange cities,
>   Seeking a world of wealth,
> All alike sure of achievement; yet
> One man's aim misses the lucky moment,
>   Another finds fortune in his lap.

And there was another question still. What did one do with all this fruitage of life? Toss it away, like little Brother Francis, and walk the world singing the praise of Lady Poverty? It was too late in the day for that. The grace of abandonment had passed him by—if, indeed, it had ever been offered. For better or for worse, he was saddled with the career he had built.

He was neither gluttonous nor spendthrift. He was educating his sister's children, and a pair of needy students for the priesthood. When he died half his wealth would go to his family, the other half to the Church. The Pontiff himself had approved the disposition. For what, then, should he reproach himself? For nothing, it seemed, except, perhaps, a certain mediocrity of spirit, a need of his nature to have the best of both worlds. And yet God

Almighty had made them both, the seen and the unseen, for man's habitation and benefit. He had made man, too, and it was the nature of His mercy to exact no more than a just return on the talent He had given to each one.

Valerio Rinaldi was wise enough not to rejoice too freely in his good fortune. Yet he could not weep because there was nothing to weep for. So he sighed a little as the shadows drew closer over the land and went on reading the story of Hippolytus, the son of Theseus:

To go into the dark! Now let me die, and pass
To the world under the earth, into the joyless dark!
Since you, dearer than all, are at my side no longer,
And the death you have dealt is more than the death
    that has swallowed you.

When twilight came at last, he closed his book and went in to say evening prayers with his household, and then prepare himself for dinner with Cardinal Leone.

The white-haired inquisitor was growling and crusty as ever, but he softened instantly at the entry of the children. When they bobbed before him, three dark-haired little maids, to receive his blessing, his eyes clouded and his hands trembled as he laid them on their foreheads. When the children backed away respectfully, he drew them to him and talked gravely as any grandfather about their lessons and their dolls and the momentous event of a day at the zoo. Rinaldi smiled secretly to see the old lion tamed so swiftly. He was even more surprised when the man who was the guardian of so many mysteries fumbled his way through a jigsaw puzzle and begged for time for the children to finish it with him.

When at last the children were dismissed and dinner

was announced, Leone was strangely subdued. He said soberly, "You're a lucky man, Rinaldi. For this you should be grateful to God all the days of your life."

"I am grateful," said Rinaldi. "It troubles me that I have done so little to deserve my happiness."

"Enjoy it, my friend. It's the purest one you will ever know." Then he added a poignant afterthought. "When I was in the seminary, one of my old masters said that every priest should be given a child to rear for five years. I didn't understand what he meant then. I do now."

"Do you have any relatives?" asked Rinaldi.

"None. I used to think that as priests we didn't need them. That's an illusion, of course. . . . One gets lonely in the cloth as well as out of it." He grunted and gave a wintry smile. "Eh! We all get sentimental when we're old."

They dined alone as befitted a pair of princes, men who were charged with the weightiest secrets of the Church. An elderly manservant waited on them and withdrew after each course was served, so that they might talk freely. Leone seemed oddly moved by his meeting with the children, and as he picked absently at his fish he reverted once more to the problems of a celibate life.

". . . Every year, as you know, we get a small crop of cases at the Holy Office: priests who get into trouble with women, unsavory affairs between teachers and pupils, and allegations of soliciting by priests in the confessional. It's inevitable, of course. There are bad apples in every barrel, but the older I get the less sure I am of how to deal with them."

Rinaldi nodded agreement. He himself had served as a commissioner of the Holy Office and was privy to its most diverse deliberations.

Leone went on: "We have a very bad case in front of us now, affecting a Roman priest and a young woman of his congregation. The evidence is pretty conclusive. The girl has fallen pregnant, and there is possibility of open scandal. I felt bound to bring the affair to the personal notice of the Holy Father."

"How did he take it?"

"More calmly than I expected. The priest in question has, of course, been suspended from his duties; but His Holiness ordered that he be required to submit to a medical and psychiatric examination before the case is finally decided. . . . It's an unusual step."

"Do you disagree with it?" asked Rinaldi quizzically.

"The way it was put to me," said Leone thoughtfully, "I was in no position to disagree. His Holiness pointed out that no matter what a priest does he is still an erring soul in need of help; that punishment was not enough; that we had to help the man to mend his error and his life. He went on to say that modern research had shown that many sexual aberrations had their roots in a real sickness of the mind, and that the celibate life raised special problems for those of a psychotic disposition. . . . The ruling of the canons is guarded on this point, but not, of course, prohibitive. A priest may seek or be given psychiatric treatment only in grave cases and with the permission of the bishop. The authority of the Holy Father is supreme in the matter."

"You still haven't said whether you agreed with his decision," said Rinaldi in his mild, ironic fashion.

Leone chuckled. "I know, I know. I have a bad reputation. To the Church at large I am still the Grand Inquisitor, ready to purge out error by rack and fire. . . . But it isn't true. I am always in dilemma in these matters.

I have to be so careful of discipline. I am torn always between compassion and my duty to enforce the law. . . . I've met this man. He's a sad, troubled creature. We can break him with a word, and set him with the same word in the way of damnation. On the other hand, what about the woman, and the child which is to be born?"

"What did His Holiness have to say about that?"

"He wants the child made a ward of the Church. He wants the girl provided with employment and a dowry. Once again, you see, there is a question of precedent. But I admire his attitude even though I am not sure I can agree with all of it. He has a soft heart. . . . The danger is that it may be too soft for the good of the Church."

"He has suffered more than we. Perhaps he has more right to trust his heart than we have."

"I know that. I could wish he trusted me a little more."

"I know he trusts you." Rinaldi made the point firmly. "I know he has a great respect for you. Has he moved against you in any way?"

"Not yet. I think the real test is still to come."

"What do you mean?"

Leone cocked a shrewd eye at his host. "Don't tell me you haven't heard. The Father General of the Jesuits has brought this Télémond fellow back to Rome. He's arranged for him to speak in the presence of the Pope on the feast of St. Ignatius Loyola."

"I heard about it. I'm invited to be present. I don't think it means too much. Télémond is a distinguished scholar. I think it's only natural that Semmering should want to reinstate him and give him a wider field of action in the Church."

"I think it's a calculated step," said Leone bluntly.

"Semmering and I rub each other the wrong way. He knows that Télémond's opinions are still suspect."

"Come, come, old friend! He's had twenty years to revise them, and you certainly can't call him a rebellious spirit. He submitted, didn't he, when silence was imposed on him? Even the Holy Office can't refuse him the opportunity to restate his position."

"The occasion is too public. Too symbolic, if you want. I think Semmering has committed an indiscretion."

"What are you really afraid of, my friend? A victory for the Jesuits?"

Leone growled and tossed his white mane. "You know that isn't true. They do God's work, as we try to do it, in our own fashion."

"What, then?"

"Have you met this Jean Télémond?"

"No."

"I have. He's a man of great charm and, I think, of singular spirituality. I think he may make a very favorable impression on the Holy Father. I believe that's what Semmering's expecting, too."

"Is that a bad thing?"

"It could be. If he has the patronage of the Pontiff, then he is much freer to promulgate his opinions."

"But the Holy Office is still there to monitor them."

"It would be much more difficult to move against a man under papal patronage."

"I think you're making two unfounded assumptions —that he will get papal patronage, and that you will have to move against him."

"We have to be ready for anything that happens."

"Isn't there a simpler way? Why not raise the matter with the Holy Father now?"

"And what do I tell him? That I mistrust his discretion, or that he doesn't trust me enough?"

"I can see that might be difficult." Rinaldi laughed and rang the bell for the next course. "I'll give you my advice. Relax. Enjoy your dinner, and let the affair take its own way. Even the Holy Office can't do as well for the Church as the Holy Ghost. . . ."

Leone smiled grimly and addressed himself to the roast. "I'm getting old, my friend—old and stubborn. I can't get used to the idea that a youngster of fifty is wearing the triple crown."

Rinaldi shrugged like a true Roman. "I think the tiara fits him very well. And there is nothing in the Faith which prescribes that the Church must be a gerontocracy —a government of old men. I have time to think now, and I am sure age doesn't always make us wiser."

"Don't mistake me. I see the good that this man brings to us. He goes out like a true shepherd among the flock. He visits the hospitals and the prisons. Last Sunday, believe it or not, he sat through three sermons, in three different Roman churches . . . just to hear what kind of preaching we had in our pulpits."

"I hope he was impressed."

"He was not," said Leone with tart humor. "He made no secret of it. He talked of 'turgid rhetoric' and 'vague devotion.' I think we may hear something of this in the encyclical which he is preparing now."

"Is it ready yet?"

"Not yet. I hear he is still working on the first Russian version. . . . We may be in for some surprises. . . ." He laughed ruefully. "I've already had a few myself. His Holiness disapproves of the tone of certain Holy Office proclamations. He feels they are too stringent, too harsh.

He wants us to refrain from outright condemnation, especially of persons, and to adopt a tone rather of admonition and warning."

"Did he say why?"

"He put it very clearly. He said we must leave room to move for men of good will even when they are in error. We must point out the error, but we must not do injustice to the intentions of those who commit it."

Rinaldi permitted himself a thin smile. "I begin to see why you are worried about Jean Télémond."

Leone ignored the joke and growled, "I'm inclined to agree with Benedetti. This man *is* a reformer. He wants to sweep all the rooms at once. He is talking, I believe, of a reform of the Rota, of changes in seminary training, and even of separate commissions to represent the various national Churches in Rome."

"That could be a good move," said Rinaldi thoughtfully. "I think that everyone but us Romans agrees that we have centralized too much. We live in troubled times, and if there is another war, then the Churches of the world will be much more isolated than they have ever been. The sooner they can develop a vigorous local life, the better for the Faith."

"If there is another war, my friend . . . it may well be the end of the world."

"Thank God things seem to be a little calmer at present."

Leone shook his head. "The calm is deceptive, I think. The pressure is building up, and before another year is out I think we may see a renewal of crisis. Goldoni was talking to me about it only yesterday. He is making a special report to the Pontiff."

"I wonder," asked Rinaldi softly. "I wonder how the

crisis looks to a man who has sat for seventeen years in the shadow of death."

To Kiril the Pontiff the crisis presented itself in a variety of aspects.

He saw it first in microcosm, on the battleground of his own soul. At the lowest level—the level at which he had lived in the prison bunker—there was the simple impulse to survival: the desperate effort to cling to that single spark of life which, once extingushed, could never be lit again. There was only one infusion of life into the frail vessel of the body. Once the vessel was broken, it would never be put together again until the day of the last restoration. So with the infusion of life was infused also the instinct to preserve it at all costs against whatever threatened, or seemed to threaten it, from within or without.

Every animal contained within itself a mechanism of survival. Only man, the last and noblest of the animal kingdom, understood, however dimly, that the mechanism must run down and that sooner or later he must make a conscious act of abandonment of the gift into the hand of the Creator, Who had first given it. This was the act for which all his living was a preparation; to refuse it was to commit the final rebellion, from which there was no recanting.

Yet every day of every man's life was a series of small rebellions against the fear of death or of sporadic victories for hope in the unseen. Even for Kiril, the Vicar of God on earth, there was no retreat from the daily war. The impulse to survival took many forms: the delight in power which gave a man the illusion of immortality; the fear of opposition which might limit the illusion; the de-

sire for friendship to buttress the weak body and falter-
ing spirit; the urge to action which affirmed a man's
potency against threatening circumstance; the desire to
possess what must in the end be foregone; the cowardice
which thrust him into isolation as if he could close every
crack against the ultimate invasion of death. Even for a
Pontiff, who stood by presumption nearest to God, there
was no guarantee of victory over himself. Each day
brought its own tally of defeats which must be repented
and purged in the penitential tribunal.

But what of other men, so much less enlightened, so
much more vulnerable, so much more oppressed by the
terror of bodily extinction? On them the pressures of existence built up to the breaking point every day. For
them he must find in himself a strength to lend, and a
charity to spend, lest they collapse utterly under the burden, or turn and rend each other in a feral war, which
would blot them out quicker than the merciful death
from which they fled.

This was the other aspect of the crisis which he read in
every report which was laid on his desk, in every newspaper and bulletin which came under his notice.

When a man in a capsule was shot into a new dimension of space and time, the world exulted as if he were
coming back with a promise of eternity in his pocket.

When a new program of armament was announced, it
seemed that those who promoted it wrote with the one
hand a new profit into the stock market while with the
other they inscribed their own epitaph.

Each economic treaty brought advantage to those who
signed it and a degree of injustice to those whom it excluded.

The populations of the East and the Africas were ex-

ploding into a new magnitude, and yet men put their
trust in islands of color or race, as though they were
endowed with a divine right of election to an earthly
paradise.

Every new victory over disease made a corresponding
drain on the diminishing resources of the planet. Every
advance in science was another patch on the shabby
cloak which man wrapped about himself against the cold
wind of dissolution.

And yet . . . and yet this was the nature of man. This
was the historic method of his progress—a tightrope
walk toward a destiny dimly perceived, but profoundly
felt. The Church was in the world, though not of it—
and it was her function to hold up the truth like a lamp
to light the farther shore of man's ultimate arrival.

So Kiril the Pontiff, caught like all his fellows in the
human dilemma, sat at his desk and traced in the formal
words of his Secretary of State the shadows of the gathering storm.

"The pivot of the present situation is China. The most
reliable reports indicate that the agricultural program
has again broken down and that there will be a very
light harvest this summer. This will mean, almost inevitably, a military push toward the rice-bowl areas of
Southeast Asia immediately after the next monsoons. Military training is already being stepped up, and there are
reports reaching us every day of repressive measures
against disaffected elements. Our own people are being
subjected to new campaigns of surveillance and open
persecution.

"In America the economic recession has eased, but this
is largely due to an increase in the program of military

armament. Our sources in the United States inform us
that any new Chinese expansion toward Burma or Indo-
China or Siam would create an immediate danger of
war. . . .

"In Bonn and Paris there is new talk of France and
Germany participating in a joint program for the development of atomic weapons. This is a logical outcome of
their status as senior partners in the European bloc, but
it is clear that it must present itself as an open threat to
East Germany and Moscow. . . .

"It has been our hope for some time that Russia's fear
of the Chinese might bring about a betterment of her
relations with the West, but this situation introduces a
dangerous and contrary element.

"It would seem timely for your Holiness to make some
clear and public comment on the dangers of this new
armament race, which is being justified as a strengthening
of the Western alliance against communism.

"It is difficult to see how it could be done, but if it were
possible for us to make any contact with the Praesidium
in the Kremlin and to introduce ourselves as a mediating
element in East-West relations, there would be no time
better than the present. Unfortunately, our opposition to
the doctrines of communism is all too easily interpreted as
a political alliance with the West. We have instructed our
legates and nuncios everywhere to emphasize, both in
public and in their conversations with political personalities, the dangers of the present situation.

"As your Holiness knows, we are now maintaining
friendly relations with representatives of the Orthodox
Church, and with senior members of other Christian
bodies. We may look with confidence to their co-

operation in this matter. However, the creation of a moral climate always lags far behind the creation of a political one, and we do have to face the fact that the next six or twelve months may well bring the world to the threshold of another war. . . .

"In Africa . . ."

Kiril the Pontiff put down the typescript and covered his tired eyes with the palms of his hands. Here again in macrocosm was the struggle for human survival. The Chinese wanted a bowl of rice. The Russian wanted to hold the civilized comfort which had just become familiar to him. A hundred and eighty million Americans had to be kept working, lest the precarious consumer economy should collapse. France and Germany, stripped of their colonies, had to maintain their bargaining power in the European community of nations.

"What we have we hold, because it is ours, because we have earned it. All that increases us is a good. All that diminishes us is a threat. . . . Jungle law . . . Survival of the fittest . . . There are no morals in politics. . . ."

Yet, boil it down, survival even for the individual was never a simple equation. The definition of rights and duties had occupied theologians and legalists for two thousand years of the Christian dispensation, and for thousands of years before that. It was one thing to state the law, but to apply it, to bring all the diverse millions of mankind to see it with the same eye, to recognize it as a divine decree . . . this was, on the face of it, a rank impossibility. Yet there was the promise. "I, if I be lifted up, will draw all things to myself." And without the promise there was no foothold of reason left in the universe.

If one did not believe that the spinning orb of the earth was held safe by the continuance of a creative act, then one might well despair and wish it dissolved in fire, to make place for a better one.

Once again memory struck off at a tangent, to a conversation he had had with Kamenev nearly ten years before!

"The difference between you and me, Kiril, is that I am dedicated to the possible while you are dedicated to a nonsense. . . . 'God wishes that all men should be saved and come to the knowledge of truth.' That's what you preach, isn't it? Yet you know it's folly. A sublime folly, I agree. But still—a folly. . . . It doesn't happen. It won't happen. It can't happen. What is your heaven but a carrot to make the donkey trot? What is your hell but a rubbish heap for all your failures—God's failures, my friend! And you say He's omnipotent. Where do you go from here? Do you come with me to achieve the small possible or go chasing after the great impossible? . . . I know what you want to say: God makes all possible. Don't you see? I am God to you at this moment because you can't even move from that chair until I give the order. . . . Here! God gives you a little gift. A cigarette. . . ."

He had taken the cigarette, he remembered, and smoked it gratefully while his tired mind grappled with the paradox which Kamenev had presented to him. . . . The little gain or the great loss? Which? The limited wisdom or the monstrous folly? He had chosen the folly, and been consigned again to stripes and starvation and solitude to purge it out of him.

And now the paradox had reversed itself. Kamenev

was faced with a situation impossible to resolve, while Kiril, the abject prisoner, stood in the shoes of God, to whom all things were possible.

For a long time he sat pondering the gigantic humor of the situation. Then he lifted the receiver and called Goldoni in the Secretariat of State.

"I'm reading your report. I'm impressed. I'm grateful. I'm also very worried. Now tell me something. . . . If I wanted to get a message to the Premier of Russia—a private message—how would I do it?"

Extract from
the Secret Memorials of
KIRIL I, Pont. Max.

. . . It is well that I have kept a sense of humor; otherwise I should be harassed to madness by the consequences of my most trivial actions. When a man in my position asks a simple question, the whole Vatican begins to flutter like a nest of birds. If I make the smallest motion, it is as if I were trying to shake the foundations of the world. I can only do what I believe to be right, but there are always twenty people with as many reasons why I should not move at all. . . . And I am a fool if I do not at least listen to their opinions.

When I proposed to Goldoni that I should make a pastoral visitation of the whole of Italy, and see on the spot the problems of my local clergy, he was aghast. Such a thing had not been done for centuries. It would create problems with the Italian government. It would raise God knows what questions of protocol and logistics and local ceremony. He pointed out that I was a prince and that the paying of princely honors would impose hardship on poor and depressed areas. I had to be very firm with him on this point and tell him that I am first and foremost a pastor, successor to a fisherman who was executed like a common criminal in the City of the Emperors. Even so, we have not yet agreed how and when I shall make this journey; but I am determined to do it before very long.

I want to make other journeys, too. I want to cross the frontiers of Europe and the oceans of the world to see my people—where and how they live, and the burdens they carry on their journey to eternity. . . . This, I know, is a project not easily accomplished. It will involve opposition from governments, a risk to myself and to the administration of the Holy See. . . . But it would, I believe, restate as nothing else could the apostolic mission of the Pontiff. . . . For the present, however, I have a more pressing concern: to establish and maintain a personal contact with Kamenev.

Immediately after my telephone call Goldoni came rushing across from the Secretariat of State to talk with me. He is a shrewd man, much practiced in diplomacy, and I have great respect for his opinion. His first counsel was a negative one. He could see no possible ground of communication with those who preach an atheistic heresy and who are engaged in an active persecution of the faithful. . . . He made the point, too, that all those who are members of the Communist Party are automatically excommunicated from the Church. I could not help remarking that in the twentieth century excommunication was a blunt weapon and very possibly an outmoded one. . . . He offered then the very valid caution that even a private dialogue with the Kremlin might constitute a diplomatic affront to Western governments.

I could not disagree with him, but I am obsessed by the belief that the prime mission of the Church is a pastoral and not a diplomatic one. I showed Goldoni the letter which Kamenev had written to me, and he understood my anxiety to begin some kind of conversation. Goldoni gave me, however, another warning: any step that I take may be misinterpreted as a sign of weakness and may be used as a propaganda weapon by the Communists. . . .

Goldoni is right, of course; but I do not believe he is wholly right. The truth has a virtue of its own; the good act has a virtue of its own, and we must never discount the fructifying power of the Almighty. . . .

I have never believed that everyone who comes to Rome must come here by way of Canossa. This, I think, has been one of our historic errors. The good shepherd seeks out the lost sheep and carries them home on his shoulder. He does not demand that they come crawling back, draggle-tailed and remorseful, with a penance cord around their necks. . . . It was St. Augustine who said, "It takes a big mind to make a heresy." And there are noble minds and noble spirits from whom the gift of faith is withheld and for whom salvation comes by way of the uncovenanted mercy of God. With all such we must deal in patience, tolerance, and brotherly charity, humbled always by the gratuitous mercy of God in our own regard. For them we must exercise in a special fashion the *ministerium* of the Faith and not insist too harshly upon its magistracy.

So, finally, Goldoni and I agreed on a compromise. We

would try to get a message to Kamenev, to tell him that I have received his letter and that I have nothing but the most friendly disposition toward him and toward my own people. The problem was, of course, how to deliver the message, but Goldoni in his subtle fashion proposed an amusing solution. A South American diplomat who has social contacts in the Kremlin will seek an opportunity to speak with the Premier at a cocktail party and tell him that a friend of his would like to talk more about the growing of sunflowers. . . . In this way neither one of us will be compromised and the next effective move will be for Kamenev to make. God knows where the move may point, but I must pray and rest in hope. . . .

It is curious, but I am more deeply perturbed by the case which Leone has transmitted to me from the Holy Office: a priest accused of soliciting in the confessional, who is now in danger of being cited in a civil paternity suit. . . . This sort of scandal is, of course, sporadic in the Church, but I am troubled by the spectacle of a soul in a mortal sickness.

There are men who should never be priests at all. The system of seminary training is designed to filter out unsuitable candidates, but there are always the odd ones who slip through the net. There are those whose sole hope of a normal and fruitful life is in the married state, yet the discipline of the Western Church imposes on all priests a perpetual celibacy.

It is within my power as the Pontiff to dispense this unfortunate man from his vows and permit him to marry. My heart urges me to do it, and yet I dare not. To do so would be to create a precedent which might do irreparable damage to clerical discipline and to a tradition which has its roots in Christ's teaching on the state of dedicated virginity.

I have the power, yes, but I must use it to build and not to demolish what has been given into my keeping. I am aware that I may be increasing the danger of damnation of this unhappy soul. I want to deal with him as mercifully as I can, but I dare not, for one soul, put ten thousand others in jeopardy. . . .

The Keys of the Kingdom are given into my hands, but I do not hold them absolutely. They are mine in trust under law. . . . There are times—and this is one of them —when I wish I could take upon myself the sins of all the world and offer my life in expiation for them. I know, however, that I am only a man, and that the expiation was made once for all on Calvary. Through the Church I administer the fruits of redemption. I cannot change the covenant of God with man which governs their distribution. . . .

It is late, and my letter to the Church is still unfinished. Tonight I am working on the text "A chosen generation, a kingly priesthood." A priest is only a man, and we have only a few short years to train him for the burden of kingship. . . . To those who stumble under its weight, we must extend the maternal love of the Church. For them we must invoke the patronage of the Virgin Mother of all men. . . .

It is warm tonight. Summer is coming in, but there are those who walk in a lifetime winter, lost and alone. Let me not fail them who have felt the winter in my own bones, who have cried at night for love in a loveless prison. . . .

VI

THE PRINCESS Maria Caterina Daria Poliziano was a small gray woman who admitted to seventy-five years and was prepared to sue anyone bold enough to dispute her accounting.

Her hair was thin, her skin was shrunken. Her sharp beak and her black agate eyes gave her the look of a mummified eagle dug from some ancient tomb. But the Princess Maria-Rina was very far from dead and was, on the contrary, a very formidable old lady.

She kept an apartment in Rome—which she rarely used "because all Romans are beginning to look like commercial travelers"—a villa in Fiesole, where she held habitual court, estates in Sicily, farms in the Abruzzi, and holdings in beets and rice in the Romagna and along the valley of the Po. Her portfolio, begun by her father and augmented by the fortunate deaths of two husbands, was full of the fattest stocks in Italy, and she traded them as shrewdly as a gypsy tinker.

Her bony finger stirred every political pudding north of Lazio, and those whispers of power which did not begin in her drawing room circulated there, inevitably, before they blew into a wind. A summons to her table was either a warrant for execution or a promise of promotion. And more than one too bold politico had braved her anger only to find himself running out of funds, favor, and votes at the next election.

Her dress was antique, her manner more tyrannical than regal. She drank Scotch whisky and smoked Egyptian cigarettes in a long gold holder. She had a scandalous tongue, a dangerous memory—and an unexpected discretion. She despised the old, and courted the young like a crotchety but humorous vampire who could pay richly for youthful blood. In her villa garden, among the fountains and the cypresses and the avenues of weathered marbles, it seemed, in very truth, as if time stood still at her aged but imperious bidding.

Her favorite resort was an arbor hung with maturing grapes and fronting a small fountain where an antique Leda was courted by languid swans to the sound of water music. In a younger time the Princess Maria-Rina had been courted there as well—now, instead, she bargained with the legacies of her youth: power, money, and prestige. Once a month the Archbishop of Florence came to drink coffee with her. Once a week someone from the Quirinale came to lunch and make a private report from the Premier. Where the dandies of another age had bent over her small hand, now the bankers and the stockbrokers came to pay her a reluctant homage, and a tribute of secret confidence.

She was sitting there now, this summer morning, reading a blunt lecture to a Minister of the Republic, her nephew, Corrado Calitri:

"You're a fool boy! You come a certain way and you think it is the end of the journey. You want to sit down and play with the flowers. It's delightful, I'm sure, but it isn't politics."

Calitri's pale classic face flushed, and he put down his coffee cup with a clatter. "Now listen, Aunt, you know that isn't true. I do my work. I do it very well. Only yesterday the Premier was good enough to say—"

"Was good enough to say!" Her old voice crackled with contempt. "Why should you care what he says? What is praise, anyway, but breakfast for the prisoner before they cut his throat? You disappoint me, Corrado. You're a baby. You can't see past your nose."

"What do you expect me to see, Aunt?"

"The future!" said the Princess crisply. "Twelve months from now, when the election comes. Are you prepared for it?"

"Of course I am. The funds are there. My committees are working day and night, even now. I don't think there is any doubt I shall be re-elected. . . . I think the party will have a reduced majority. We'll have to open out a little further in coalition with the Left, but even so I'm assured of a seat in the Cabinet."

"And that's the end of the story?" Her dark agate eyes bored into him; her withered lips twitched into a smile of pity.

Calitri shifted uneasily in his chair. "Do you see another ending, Aunt?"

"Yes!" Her old hands reached across the table and fastened like talons on his wrist. "You have twelve months left to plan it, but if you plan aright you can lead the country." He stared at her, gape-mouthed, and she gave a high, cackling laugh. "Never underrate your old aunt, my boy. When you're as old as I am, you've learned to

see round corners, and I tell you without a doubt you can
lead the Republic . . ."

"You really believe that?" Calitri's voice was almost a
whisper.

"I never tell fairy tales, my boy—and I gave up listening to them a long while ago. At lunch today you will
meet some people who will show you how you can do it.
There will be a certain amount of"—she rubbed her fingertips together in the gesture that signified money—"but
that part we can handle. I want to talk to you about something else. There's another price to be paid, and you're
the only one who can pay it."

Corrado Calitri cocked a shrewd eye at his relative.
"And what is the price, Aunt?"

She fixed him with a beady and predatory eye and
told him. "You'll have to clean up your life, and do it
quickly. Get rid of this bunch of pimps and playboys
that you hang around with. Push this marriage business
through the courts. Get rid of Chiara. She's no good to
you. And get yourself married again, quickly and quietly.
I'll find you a woman who can manage you. You need a
strong one—not a dewy-eyed schoolgirl."

"I won't do it!" Corrado Calitri exploded into sudden
anger. "I won't be bought and sold like a piece of mer-
chandise!"

He heaved himself out of his chair and began to pace
restlessly up and down the flagged pathway between the
arbor and the fountain while the old Princess watched
him with a calm and calculating eye.

When his anger had spent itself a little, she went to
him and linked her arm in his and led him slowly round
the circuit of the villa plantations. She was a different

woman now. She made no effort to tease or provoke him,
but talked soberly and quietly, as if he were her son:

". . . I told you I don't listen to fairy stories any more
—even about myself. I know what I am, Corrado—a
dried-up old woman with paint on her face, and her past
a million years away. . . . But I've lived, my boy. I've
lived every minute of every hour. I've sucked the orange
dry and spat out the pips. So listen to me, please. . . . I
know you're not like other men. You were always different, even as a little boy. . . . Watching you, I used to
think of someone trying to rub out the world and paint it
new and clean again. I could have made it different for
you, I think; but your father would never have me near
the house. . . ." She gave a short, bitter chuckle. "He
thought I was a corrupting influence. He was a strait-
laced fellow, with no sense of humor. I never could see
what your mother found in him."

"Misery," said Corrado Calitri harshly. "Misery and
loneliness, and no love at all. I hated that man from the
bottom of my heart."

"But you can't run away from him any longer," said
the old woman softly. "He's dead, and the daisies are
growing out of his ears. I know what you look for—the
love you didn't get from him. I know you find it sometimes, but it doesn't last. I know the dangers when you
go on looking desperately and without caution." Her thin
hands clutched at his arm. "You do have enemies, don't
you?"

"Who hasn't in a job like mine?"

"Have you ever been blackmailed?"

"It's been tried a couple of times."

"Then you know what I'm talking about. The enemies

get more numerous and they grow bigger—bigger than you realize. Take Campeggio, for instance—"

"Campeggio!" He swung round to face her, genuinely startled. "Campeggio! I've never done him any harm."

"You have his boy," said Maria-Rina gravely.

"So that's the story." Calitri threw back his patrician head and laughed, startling the birds in the olive trees. "The boy works for me. I like him. He has talent, and charm and—"

"Beauty?"

"That, too, if you want. But not for me. You think I want to fall foul of Campeggio and the Vatican?"

"You've already done it," said the Princess Maria-Rina. "And without the Vatican you can't lead the country at the next election. Now—now do you see what I'm talking about?"

For a long moment he did not answer her, but seemed to shrink back into himself. His youthful face furrowed. His eyes misted with sudden emotion. Finally he said softly, "Life is very long, Aunt. Sad, too, sometimes, and solitary."

"You think I don't know that, boy? You think when Louis died I wasn't sad and solitary? You think I didn't know what it was like to be middle-aged and rich, and able to buy what I couldn't get for love? I tried it, too, for a little while. Does that shock you?"

"No. I understand it."

"Then I woke up, as you have to wake up. You can't get out of bed every morning fearing to lose what you don't own, anyway. You can't wait and weigh the risks of the blackmailer. You can't govern your life by the snap of a pretty boy's fingers. No! One day you have to say to yourself: 'What have I got that is really mine? How best can I enjoy it?' When you come to add it up, you find there's a great deal. And there may even be a little loving as well."

"In marriage?" he asked with heavy irony.

"In it or outside. It makes small matter. For you . . ." Her skeleton finger stabbed at him like a dagger. "For you marriage is necessary. Very necessary."

"I tried it, remember."

"With a baby who was still playing with dolls."

"And this time?"

"First," said the old woman briskly, "we must get you out of the mess you're in now, and this is where you make your first payment."

"How much?" asked Corrado Calitri.

"In money, nothing. In pride . . . a great deal, perhaps. You will have to approach the Rota and reverse all your previous testimony."

"How do I make them believe me?"

The Princess Maria-Rina laughed again. "You repent. There will be joy in Heaven and in the Vatican when you come to repair the grave injustice that you have done to an innocent girl. You will be mending your ways, too, and they will be happy to have you back in the fold."

"I can't do it," said Corrado Calitri heavily. "It's a monstrous hypocrisy."

"It needn't be," said the Princess. "And even if it is, the Quirinale is worth a Mass, isn't it?"

In spite of himself Calitri smiled and laid an affectionate hand on the old woman's cheek. "Sometimes, Aunt, I think you're descended directly from the Borgias."

"I am," said the old Princess, "but on the wrong side of the blanket! Now . . . Will you do what I ask?"

"I'll have to think about it."

"You have thirty minutes, boy. At lunch they will want your answer and mine."

In a third-floor tenement, a stone's throw from the Pantheon, Ruth Lewin was caught up in another of the daily dramas of Old Rome. From the evening Angelus until nearly midnight she had been working with a twenty-year-old wife to help her give birth to her first child. For the last two hours the doctor had been with her, a haggard young man who seemed far too embroiled in the drama for his own good, or for that of his patient.

When finally they had dragged the child into the light with forceps, it was a monster—a tiny, whimpering deformity with a human head and a penguin body, whose feet and hands were attached directly to the trunk.

Ruth Lewin stared at it in horror, and the young doctor swore savagely.

"Sweet Jesus! Sweet suffering Jesus, look at it!"

Ruth Lewin found herself stammering helplessly, "But why? What caused it? What—"

"Shut up!" said the doctor harshly. "Shut up and give me water and a towel."

Mechanically she did as he asked and watched in fascinated horror while he swaddled the deformed body and then poured a few drops of water on the head and muttered the ritual words: "I baptize thee in the name of the Father, and of the Son, and of the Holy Ghost. Amen."

Ruth Lewin found voice again. "What's going to happen now?"

"That's my business. You get the mother cleaned up."

Angry and near to tears, she set about the menial task, bathing the torn young body, comforting the girl as she struggled back, moaning, into consciousness. When finally it was done and the young mother lay composed and decent on the pillows, Ruth Lewin looked up. "What now, Doctor?"

He was standing by the table, his back towards her, fumbling with the wrapping that covered the child. He turned a stony face to her and said:

"It's dead. Get the father in."

She opened her mouth to ask a question, but no sound issued. She searched his face for an answer, but his young eyes were blank as pebbles. He repeated the order. "Please call the father."

Ruth Lewin went to the door and beckoned to a tall, muscular boy who was drinking a glass of wine and talking with a group of neighbors on the landing. "Will you come in, please."

Puzzled, the youth approached her with the neighbors at his heels. She drew him inside and closed the door against the other curious faces.

The doctor confronted him, holding the swaddled body in his arms. "I have bad news for you, my friend. The baby was born dead."

The boy stared at him stupidly. "Dead?"

"It happens sometimes. We don't really know why. Your wife is well. She will be able to have other children."

Dumbly the boy moved toward the bed and bent, crooning, over the pale, half-conscious girl.

"Let's go," said the doctor abruptly. "I want to deliver this to the general hospital."

To the boy he said, "I have to take the body away. It's the law. I'll be back in the morning to see your wife and give you a death certificate."

Neither the boy nor the wife seemed to hear him, and

he went out, carrying the small pathetic bundle, with Ruth Lewin following like a professional mourner. The crowd on the landing stared silently at their passing, and then crowded into the door of the room, whispering excitedly among themselves.

When they reached the street, the doctor laid the body of the child on the back seat of his car and slammed the door. Then he faced Ruth Lewin and said abruptly, "Don't ask any questions. I'll deliver the cadaver to the general hospital and make a report."

"Won't there be an autopsy?"

"No. Even if there were, it would show nothing. The child died of asphyxiation. . . ."

In a single moment all his control seemed to drain away. His body was shaken with rigors, and his young face twisted as if with an intolerable pain. Suddenly in a fury of desperation he was pleading with her. "Don't leave me now. For God's sake, don't leave me. Come to the hospital, and then . . . then let's go somewhere. Somewhere sane. If I'm alone tonight I think I'll go mad."

"Of course I'll come with you. But you can't blame yourself for this. You're a doctor; you know these things happen every day."

"I know! Oh yes, I know." He tried to smile, but it was more like a rictus of agony. "I'll tell you something you don't know. I've got twenty more babies to be born in the next eight weeks, and at least half of them are going to be like that."

"Oh God," said Ruth Lewin softly. "Oh God Almighty, why . . . ?"

In her quiet house under the haunted shadow of the Palatine he told her the why. He told her savagely and brusquely, as if the whole paradox of the healing art—its half promise of perpetuity, its ultimate surrender to mortality—had proved too much for him.

". . . It's a crazy thought . . . but medical pharmacy always seems to come with the elixir of life in one hand and a phial of poison in the other. . . . There are antibiotics that cure some people and kill others. There was the French drug that boiled men's brains. There was thalidomide, which gave sleep and then grew monsters in the womb. Now there's another one. It came on the market about twelve months ago—a combination formula to prevent nausea in pregnancy and reduce the danger of toxaemia. . . . Three months ago we started to get the first warnings from Germany about deformities induced by the drug. . . . It looks like thalidomide all over again, only this time everyone's trying to hush it up. . . ." He lay back in his chair, an image of dejection, fatigue, and pure misery. "I used to think I was a kind of medical apostle. I paid for drugs for poorer patients out of my own pocket. I bought the bloody stuff for that girl tonight, and for all the others in the quarter."

"There's no hope that the other births will be different?"

"Some of them will be normal. But the rest . . ." He flung out his hands in passionate appeal. "What do I do? I can't murder them all."

"First, you must never use that word again. I saw nothing tonight. I heard nothing."

"But you know, don't you?"

"I don't know anything—except this. You mustn't blame yourself, and you mustn't ever again play God. There's a kind of madness in that."

"Madness is right." He ran a shaking hand through his hair. "It was a madness tonight, and yet . . . What equipment do those people have to cope with such a situation? You know what they would have said if they'd seen that birth tonight? '*Mal'occhio!*' The evil eye. Someone looked on the mother and laid a curse on her while the child was still in her womb. You have no idea of the power of superstition over the minds of these poor folk. What would they do with the child? Some few might care for it. Others might stifle it or try to throw it in the river. Some few might sell it to professional beggars who would make profit from its deformity. . . . What about all the others still to come? What do I do about them? Sweet Jesus, what do I do?"

Without warning he was racked by deep weary sobs, so that Ruth Lewin ran to him and threw her arms about him for comfort and soothed him with soft and helpless words. When he was calm at last, she made him lie down on her bed, and covered him with a blanket, and then sat beside him, holding his hand until he lapsed into the mercy of sleep. Then she was alone—alone in the mournful hours, confronted by the ultimate mystery of life and death and pain, and the bloody stinking mess of the world.

She had seen a monster come to birth as the result of an act of healing and kindness. She had seen murder done in the name of mercy and found her heart more than half approving the act. Here in little was the whole mighty tragedy of man, the whole bleak mystery of his existence and his destiny.

Confronted by that pitiful embryo, how could one say that the cogs of Creation did not slip out of kilter and grind into a monstrous confusion? How could one talk of Omnipotence and Omniscience and an ever present Goodness? How could one find a soul or spirit in the weak, puling, fishlike creature, swimming blindly out of the fluid of the womb to affront the light of day?

Where now were the foundations of faith, and hope, and love? Where was one vestige of sanity in this madhouse of sick, maimed, helpless victims of civilization? If there was none, then it was time to quit and be gone. The exit was easy enough, and once she had almost passed through it. One could not go on blundering wildly through a hall of mirrors, confused, disordered, purposeless, and afraid. If there was no resolution to the discord, then pack up the band and send it home. But if there was, then it must be soon, before the tattered nerves frayed themselves into a screaming horror.

The weariness of the vigil crept into her bones, and she stretched out on the bed beside the sleeping man. But the contact of his body troubled her, and when he muttered and turned to her in sleep, she withdrew and went into the kitchen to make herself a cup of coffee.

She remembered another night with another man in this same house, and how for a while she had glimpsed a beginning of light. She asked herself what he would have made of tonight's affair, and what would have been his answer for the horrors that were still to come. Then the thought struck her, cold and reviving. This was his city. He had claimed it for his own. He had named himself as the shepherd and servant of its people. . . .

Ruth Lewin was still awake when the gray of the false dawn crept across the Palatine Hill. And before the city had rubbed the sleep out of its eyes, she had written her letter, begging a private audience with Kiril the Pontiff.

:

His own letter to the Church was already finished, and the Russian draft was in the hands of the translators. Now that it was done, he felt strangely empty, oppressed by a sense of futility and frustration.

While he was writing he had felt seized as never before by the power of the Word, by the conviction of its inevitable fruitfulness in the hearts of good men. Yet now he was faced with the cold fact that without the grace of God—and men co-operating with the grace of God—the seed might lie fertile but fruitless for a hundred years. Among the millions of believers who professed an obedience to the Word, and to his authority as its Supreme Preacher, how many were there from whom he could exact a full performance?

He saw all too clearly what would happen to his letter. It would be read within a few months in every Catholic pulpit in the world. He would receive acknowledgments from bishops pledging their loyalty to his counsels and promising to carry them out as best they could. But between the promise and the fulfillment stood a hundred obstacles: shortage of men, shortage of money, shortness of sight and courage sometimes, and the natural resentment of the man at the point of action, who wondered why he was being asked to make so many bricks with so little straw.

The best one could hope was that here and there the Word would take fire in the soul of a man, would brighten his eyes with vision, and set him striding out to achieve a divine impossible. For himself he knew there was no other choice but to go on preaching, teaching, urging to action, and to wait, empty of all but hope, on the promise of the Paraclete.

There was a knock on his door, and the Maestro di Camera entered to inquire whether His Holiness was ready to begin the morning's audiences. Kiril glanced briefly at the list and saw that the first name was that of Ruth Lewin.

Her letter had troubled him deeply because it had reached him in a moment of temptation—the temptation to immerse himself in the political aspects of the Church and to challenge, by a display of power, those men, like Leone, who made no secret of their disagreements with him. There were those, he knew, who found his encyclical something of a novelty. It was too personal, they felt, too specific. It was too openly critical of past policy. It called for new modes of action in the training of the clergy and in the direction of missionary education. For himself, the man at the top, it was all too easy to thrust his authority down the throats of his subordinates and stifle their criticism by a summons to religious obedience.

Ruth Lewin's letter reminded him that the real battleground was elsewhere—in lonely rooms and solitary hearts, among folk who had no theology, but only an intimate and frightening familiarity with the problems of living and dying. Ruth Lewin represented a contact with such people. If he could make the Faith efficacious for her, then whatever the outcome of his pontificate, he would not have failed utterly.

When she was ushered into his presence, he greeted her warmly and then, without preamble, addressed himself to the subject:

"I had you called as quickly as I could because I know that you must be suffering a good deal."

"I'm grateful to your Holiness," she told him in her

blunt fashion. "I have no right to bother you, but this is a terrible affair."

"For you?" asked Kiril quizzically.

"For me it calls everything into question. But I want to talk about the others first."

"What others?"

"The women who are going to give birth to these children. Most of them, I believe, are quite unprepared for what is going to happen."

Kiril's lean face clouded, and a nerve began throbbing under the scar on his cheek. "What do you want me to do?"

"We . . . That is, the mothers need help. They need a place where they can leave these children if they're not capable of looking after them themselves. The children have to be cared for. I'm told the expectation of life is short, but they will need a special kind of care—a special kind of loving."

"You think the Church can provide it?"

"It has to," said Ruth Lewin flatly. "If it means what it teaches." She flushed, understanding that she had committed an indiscretion; then she hurried into an explanation. "I'm a woman, your Holiness. I asked myself the other night what I would do, how I would feel, if I were the mother of such a child. I don't know. I don't think I should behave very well."

Kiril the Pope gave a small wintry smile of approval. "I think you underrate yourself. You have more courage than you realize. . . . Tell me. How many of these births are there likely to be in Rome?"

"We expect about twenty in the next two months. There may be many more."

He sat for a moment, silent and thoughtful. Then he gave a crooked, boyish grin and said:

"Well! Let's see what sort of authority I have in the Church." He picked up the telephone and dialed the number of the Secretary of the Sacred Congregation of the Religious.

Crisply he explained the situation, and then asked, "Which of our nursing nuns in Rome are best equipped to look after these children?"

There was an indistinguishable clatter of talk from the other end of the line, and Ruth Lewin saw the Pontiff's mouth tighten in anger. He said sharply, "I know it is difficult. Everything is difficult. But this is an urgent work of charity, and it must be done. If money is needed, we will provide it. It will be your business to find the accommodation and the nursing aid. I want it arranged within the next twenty-four hours."

He put down the phone with a bang and said testily, "These people live in a little world of their own. One has to bounce them out of it into reality. . . . Anyway, you can take it for granted that we shall provide care and hospital accommodation for those who need it. You will be informed by letter and telephone of the details. Then I shall have an announcement published in the *Osservatore* and circulated to the Roman press."

"I'm very grateful to your Holiness."

"I'm grateful to you, young woman. Now, what can I do for you?"

"I don't know," said Ruth Lewin unhappily. "I've been asking myself the same question all the way to the Vatican. Why do these things happen? Why does a good God let them happen?"

"If I could tell you that," said Kiril the Pontiff soberly,

"I'd be God myself. I don't know, though I sometimes wish I did. You mustn't imagine that the mystery of faith is any simpler for me than it is for you. The Act of Faith is an act of acceptance—not an explanation. I'll tell you a story about myself. . . . When I was first taken to prison, it was in the bad time in Russia. There was much torture, much cruelty. One night a man was brought back to my hut who had been handled more brutally than any other I had ever seen. He was in agony, and he kept crying over and over again for someone to kill him and put him out of his misery. I tell you truly I was tempted. It's a terrible thing to see so much suffering. It degrades and terrifies those who see it but cannot alleviate it. That's why I can understand, though I cannot condone, what your doctor friend did. It seems almost as though one would be bestowing a divine mercy with the gift of death. But one is not divine, one cannot dispense either life or death."

He seemed for a moment to sink back into a private contemplation.

Ruth Lewin prompted him gently. "What was the end of the story, Holiness?"

"The man died in my arms. I should like to tell you that he died in a Godly fashion, but I have no way of knowing. I could not penetrate through his pain to touch the springs of his will. He just died, and I had to commit him to God. . . . That's the only answer I can give you."

"It's a leap into the dark," said Ruth Lewin gravely. "I'm not sure I can make it."

"Is it any less hard to stay where you are?"

"It's harder, I think."

"But you have already made one step into the dark."

"I don't understand."

"You could not condone this murder, even of a monstrous birth."

"Not wholly, no."

"And you have turned to me for help, not for yourself, but for the children."

"I just felt so inadequate. I needed someone who could act . . ."

"Perhaps," said Kiril the Pontiff softly, "perhaps that is part of the meaning of pain—that it challenges our arrogant possession of life; that it confronts us with our own frailty and makes us aware, however dimly, of the sustaining power of the Creator."

"I wish I could believe that. But how do you see God in a human child that looks like a fish?"

"It's not a new mystery, Ruth. It's a very old one. How do you see God in a dying criminal nailed on a gallows tree?"

"It isn't enough to say that," said Ruth Lewin harshly. "There has to be some loving somewhere. There has to be."

"True. . . . There has to be some loving. If the mystery of pain is not a mystery of love, then all this . . ." His crooked hands embraced the ornate room and all the Sacred City beyond it. "Then all this is a historic nonsense. And my office is a role for a mountebank."

His bluntness took her by surprise. For a moment she stared at him, caught by the contrast between his crooked, quizzical face and the religious formality of his dress. Then she said:

"Your Holiness really believes that?"

"I do."

"Then why can't I?"

"I think you do believe it," said Kiril the Pontiff gently. "That's why you are here to see me. That's why you act within a context of belief, although you are still wrestling with God."

"If I could only know that I was loved—that I was worth loving."

"You don't ask that of someone you love—why should you ask it of yourself?"

"Your Holiness is too clever for me."

"No! I am not a clever man. I understand you, Ruth Lewin, better than you know, because I have walked on the same road that you are walking now. I'm going to tell you another story, and then I'm going to send you away because there are lots of people waiting to see me. . . . My escape from Russia was arranged, as you know. I was released from prison and sent to a hospital because I had been very ill for some time. The doctors treated me well, and I was nursed solicitously. After seventeen years of endurance it was a strange experience. I did not have to fight any more. It was as if I became another human being overnight. I was clean, and well fed. I had books to read, and leisure, and a kind of freedom. I enjoyed it. I was proud to be decent. . . . It took a little time to understand that I was being submitted to a new temptation. I felt loved again. I wanted to be loved. I used to look forward to the coming of the nurse, to her smile and her service of me. Then came a moment when I understood that what Kamenev my tormentor had not been able to do to me I was doing to myself. I was demanding an experience of love. In spite of my priesthood and my bishopric I was being tempted by this attraction of a simple human communion. . . . Do you understand what I'm trying to say?"

"Yes, I understand it. It's what I feel every day."

"Then you will understand something else. That the

taking and the demanding is only one side of the medal
of love. The giving is the side that proves the true minting.
If I took, I should have nothing to give. If I gave, the
giving renewed the resource, and it was this that had kept
me whole for seventeen years of imprisonment. . . ."

"And the return of love?"

"You are part of it," said Kiril the Pontiff gently. "You
and these children whom we shall love together, and those
whom I shall reach here and there in the Church, because my voice echoes in their hearts. . . . I am still
lonely often, as you are. But to be lonely is not to be un-
loved, but only to learn the value of love—and that it
takes many forms, and is sometimes hard to recognize."
He rose and held out his hand. "Now I must send you
away, but we shall see each other again."

She had long since rejected the authority which he
represented; yet she bowed her knee and laid her lips to
the Fisherman's ring on his finger, and listened with gratitude to the words of the blessing:

*"Benedictio Dei omnipotentis descendat, Patris et Fili et
Spiritus Sancti, super te et maneat semper. . . ."*

For Kiril the Pontiff it was a startling irony that his
encyclical on Christian education made far less stir than
his statement in the *Osservatore Romano* on the victims
of the new drug. Every correspondent in Rome cabled the
full text of the *Osservatore* release, which was interpreted
in Europe and America as a clear papal command to
place the medical and social resources of the Church at
the disposal of mothers and offspring who were affected
by the deadly medicine.

For a week afterwards his desk was piled with letters

and telegrams from bishops and lay leaders, commending his action as a timely demonstration of the charity of the Church. Cardinal Platino wrote expansively:

". . . It seems to me that your Holiness has shown in a very special fashion the relevance of the Church's mission to every act and circumstance of human life. It may well be that your Holiness' pronouncement points the way to a missionary method of great importance—the reintroduction of the Church into private and public life through works of practical charity. Historically speaking, this method has been the beginning of the most permanent evangelical activity, and it is, in fact, a true copy of the work of the Master, who in the words of the Gospel, 'went about healing the sick and doing good. . . .'"

Another man might have been flattered by so spontaneous a response to an executive action, but Kiril Lakota was preoccupied by those aspects of the problem which the press either ignored or built into a factitious drama.

Day and night he was haunted by the picture of a woman waiting through nine months of fear and uncertainty to give birth to a deformity, of a doctor urged to intervene before the tragic moment, of the child itself, and what might happen to it when it grew to maturity. For all these the charity of the Church was at best a postscript, at worst an unwelcome prolongation of grief and despair.

The mission of the Church to all these people was far other than a dispensation of kindness. It was to confront with them the naked fact of their existence, with all its risks and all its terror, and another fact, that their existence set them in a precise relationship with the Creator, who had called them into being. The Church could not change the relationship. It could not eliminate one sin-

gle consequence of it. Its sole functions were to interpret
it in the light of reason and revelation and to dispense the
grace by which alone the relationship was made workable.

In theory every one of the thousands of priests who
trotted about the streets of Rome in platter hats and
black skirts was an official interpreter of doctrine, an official dispenser of grace, and a shepherd with a sackful of
compassion for his flock. In fact there were all too few
with the talent or the understanding to participate truly
in these intimate tragedies of humankind.

It was as if the symbiosis of the Church failed at a certain point and the lives of its people diverged thencefor-
ward from the lives of its clergy. It was as if the interpretation of God to man became a didactic exercise and
the realities of God's grace were blotted out by the realities of pain and loss.

In the methodology of the Church the priest was always available to the people of his parish. If they did not
turn to him, it was because of their own negligence and
want of faith. This at least was the text of many a Sunday
sermon, but in truth the breakdown came because the
cleric no longer shared the tragedy of his people, was
even protected from it by his cloth and by his education. . . .

Education! He came back to it again by a round turn,
seeing more clearly than he ever had before that the fruit
of his mission to the world must never be judged by spectacle or acclamation, but only by its flowering in the secret
heart of the individual.

Buried under the pile of congratulations there were
other and more disquieting letters. Like the one from
Cardinal Pallenberg, in Germany:

". . . With the greatest respect, therefore, I would beg

your Holiness to undertake an examination of the present constitution and method of working of the Holy Roman Rota. Your Holiness is well aware that because of our special circumstances in Germany, a large number of marital cases are being referred each year to Rome. Many of these have been delayed for three and four years, with consequent hardship and grave spiritual danger to the parties concerned. It seems to me and my brother bishops that there is need of swift reform in this matter, either by way of fuller reference of powers to provincial courts or by an increase in the number of Rota officials and the institution of a speedier method of examination. It is suggested that instead of all documents being translated into Latin—a slow and expensive progress—they might be presented and examined in their original vernacular. . . ."

On the face of it the Holy Roman Rota was a far shout away from an act of infanticide in a third-floor slum. Yet the causes which found their way into the slow files of this august body were no less dramas of love and passion. The Holy Roman Rota was the last court of appeal for marital cases within the Church, and every marital case was a history of love or the lack of it, and of a human relationship—defective or not—which had to be measured beside the divine one.

To the theologian and the canonist the function of the Rota was very simple. It had to render a decision as to whether or no a marriage was valid according to the moral law and the prescriptions of the canons. To many inside the Church, it seemed that this view was altogether too simple. The Rota was meticulously careful that justice should be done. It cared not one whit that it should seem to be done. Its methods were antique and often dilatory. Every document and every deposition had to be translated into Latin. The number of personnel, both clerical and lay, was hopelessly inadequate to handle the volume of business with any degree of speed. The least sympathetic of men could not fail to guess at the hardship which such slowness inflicted on those who had appealed to the tribunal.

Kiril the Pontiff understood the problem more clearly than others, but he had already learned that to accomplish a reform in Rome one had to prepare slowly and act strongly at the right moment; otherwise one ended fighting the bureaucracy, which was tantamount to fighting oneself.

He penciled a note on his calendar to discuss the question with Valerio Rinaldi, who, having retired from the politics of the Church, might give him good advice about how to beat them.

From Ragambwe, the black Cardinal in Kenya, came a note of even greater urgency:

". . . Events in Africa are moving much more swiftly than would have seemed possible two years ago. Within the next twelve months I believe we may see a bloody uprising of black against white in South Africa. This is an almost inevitable consequence of the brutal repressive measures exercised by the South African government under the banner of Apartheid, and by the archaic feudal and often brutal methods of the Portuguese. If this revolution is successful—and with the support of other African nations there is reason to believe it will be—then it may well be the end of Christianity for a hundred years in the southern continent of Africa. We are training catechists as fast as we can, but we cannot hope to train even a minimal number of native priests in the time at our disposal. I know that this may well seem a revolutionary suggestion, but I ask myself whether we should not consider very seriously a new program of training in which the local language, and not Latin, will be the basis of instruction, and in which the whole liturgy will be celebrated in the vernacular. If this course were approved, it might be possible to train a native clergy in about half the time it takes now to train them under the system laid down by the Council of Trent.

"I understand very well that this would mean a clergy less well educated than that in other lands, but the question is whether we shall have such a clergy, preaching the Word and dispensing the Sacraments validly and religiously, or whether we shall have no clergy at all. Your Holiness will understand that I speak of desperate measures for a desperate time, and that . . ."

Once again he was brought back to the subject of his letter, the education of the ministers of the Word. Once again he was faced with the intangible X that dominated the whole thinking of the Church—the infusion of the Holy Spirit supplying what was defective in man so that the Mystical Body was kept always alive. How far, therefore, could one go in entrusting the Church to this dominating influence of the Spirit? How far was it lawful to risk the Word and the Sacraments to men partly instructed, trusting to the Paraclete to supply the rest? And yet who but himself was to say what was a partial and what was a sufficient instruction? Did the Holy Ghost work less strongly now, in the twentieth century, than in the primitive Church, when twelve fishermen were entrusted with the Deposit of Faith and the mission to preach it to all nations . . . ?

Outside, the summer day was dying. The bells of the

city were tolling their vain cry for recollection and withdrawal. But the city was full of other sounds, and it was left to Kiril the Pontiff to gather his household about him for vespers and a remembrance of the hidden God.

"You've done a very thorough job, my friend." Campeggio laid down the typescript and looked at George Faber with a new respect. "That's the most complete dossier I've ever seen on Corrado Calitri and his friends."

Faber shrugged unhappily. "I was trained as a crime reporter. I have a talent for this sort of thing. . . . But I can't say that I'm very proud of it."

"Love's an expensive business, isn't it?" Campeggio smiled as he said it, but there was no humor in his shrewd dark eyes.

"I was going to talk to you about that. The information in that document cost me a thousand dollars. I may have to spend a lot more."

"On what?"

"To get a signed statement out of one or more of the people mentioned in the dossier."

"Have you any idea how much it will cost?"

"No. But from what I've gathered so far, several of them are short of money. The most I can afford is another thousand dollars. I want to know if you're prepared to put up any more."

Campeggio sat silent awhile, staring down at Faber's littered desk. Finally he said deliberately, "I'm not sure that I should discuss the proposition in those terms."

"What do you mean?"

"From the point of view of the Rota, and of civil law, it could amount to a subornation of witnesses."

"I've thought of that myself."

"I know you have. You're an honest man—too honest for your own comfort, or mine. Let's look at it from another angle. How do you propose to approach your prospective witnesses?"

"I've marked three names in the document. Each one of them has open animosity to Calitri. One is an actor who hasn't had a good part for twelve months. One is a painter. Calitri financed one exhibition for him, and then dropped him. The third is a woman. I'm told she's a writer, though I've never seen anything she's published. The two men always spend the summer at Positano. The woman has a house on Ischia. I propose to go south during the summer holidays and try to make contact with each one."

"Are you taking Chiara with you?"

"No. She wants to come, but I don't think it's good diplomacy. Besides I . . . I need to test myself away from her."

"You may be wise, at that." Campeggio's shrewd eyes searched his face. "I wonder if any of us knows himself before his middle years? . . . Now tell me something else. Why do you think your witnesses will ask for money?"

"It's the way of the world," said George Faber wryly. "Nobody really wants to be persecuted for justice's sake. Everybody wants to make a profit on the process."

"You're a Catholic, Faber. How do you feel in conscience about this transaction?"

Faber flushed. "My conscience is compromised already. I'm committed to Chiara; I can't afford the luxury of scruples."

Campeggio agreed sourly. "It's a very Nordic point of view. It's probably more honest than mine."

"And what is your point of view?"

"About the money? I'm prepared to give you another thousand dollars. But I don't want to know what you do with it."

Faber's rare wintry humor asserted itself for a moment. "And that leaves your conscience clear?"

"I'm a casuist," said Campeggio with a thin smile. "I can split hairs as well as the Jesuits. It suits me to be in doubt. But if you want the truth . . ." He stood up and began to pace up and down Faber's office. "If you want the truth, I'm in deep confusion. I think Chiara has justice on her side. I think you have a right to try to get it for her. I think there is justice on my side, too, when I want to remove my son from Calitri's influence. I'm doubtful about the means, so I don't want to question them too closely. That's why I'm co-operating with you while leaving you to carry the burden of moral and legal decision. . . . It's a very Latin trick. . . ."

"At least you're open with me," said Faber with odd simplicity. "I'm grateful for that."

Campeggio stopped his pacing and looked down at Faber, who sat slumped and vaguely shrunken behind his desk. "You're a soft man, my friend. You deserve a simpler loving."

"It's my fault more than Chiara's. . . . I have to work double time to be free for the vacation. I'm worried about money. I'm scared that I may not be able to control the consequences of what we are doing."

"And Chiara?"

"She's young. She's been hurt. She's in an uncomfortable position for a woman . . . So she wants to be diverted. . . . I don't blame her. But I don't have the stamina for five nights a week at the Cabala or the Papagallo."

"How does she occupy herself while you're working?"

Faber gave a small, rueful grin. "What does any young matron of fashion do in Rome? . . . Luncheon parties, mannequin shows, cocktails. . . ."

Campeggio laughed. "I know, I know. Our women make good lovers and good mothers. As wives, even as unofficial ones, they lack something. They resent their husbands and spoil their sons."

For a moment Faber seemed to lose himself in a private contemplation. He said absently, "The loving is still good. . . . But I have the feeling that we're both starting to calculate. When Chiara came to me first she was almost broken. I seemed to be able to supply everything she needed. Now she's back to normal and I am the one with the needs."

"Doesn't she understand that?"

"That's the sixty-four-dollar question. . . . By nature she's impulsive and generous, but living with Calitri has changed her. It's as if . . ." He fumbled uneasily for the words. "As if she thinks men owe her a special kind of debt."

"And you're not sure you can pay it all?"

"No, I'm not sure."

"Then if I were you," said Campeggio emphatically, "I should cut loose now. Say good-by, cry into your pillow, and forget the whole business."

"I'm in love with her," said Faber simply. "I'm ready to pay any price to hold her."

"Then we're both in the same galley, aren't we?"

"What do you mean?"

Campeggio balked a moment, and then explained himself deliberately. "In the beginning possession always seems the ultimate triumph of love. You have your Chiara now, but you cannot be wholly happy until you possess her by legal contract. Then, you feel, you will be safe. You pluck the rose and put it in a vase in the drawing room, but after a while the bloom fades, and it is no longer so important that you own a wilting flower. When children come, they are another kind of possession. They depend on you utterly. You hold them to you by their need of sustenance and security. As they grow, you find that the bond weakens, and that you no longer possess them as you once did. . . . I want my son. I want him to be the image and the continuum of myself. I tell myself that what I do is for his good, but I know, deep in my heart, that it is also for my own satisfaction. I cannot bear that he should withdraw himself from me and give himself to another—man or woman—whom I consider less worthy. . . . But in the end he will go, for better or for worse. . . . Look at me now. I am a man of confidence at the Vatican. As editor of the *Osservatore* I am the mouthpiece of the Church. I have a reputation for integrity and I believe I have earned it. Yet today I am beginning to compromise myself. Not for you! Don't think I'm blaming you! It is for my son, whom I shall lose anyway, and for myself, because I have not yet begun to come to terms with age and loneliness. . . ."

George Faber heaved himself out of his chair and stood facing his colleague. For the first time, he seemed to take on an unfamiliar strength and dignity. He said evenly, "I have no right to hold you to any bargains. You're in a more delicate position than I am. You're free to withdraw your offer."

"Thank you," said Orlando Campeggio simply. "But I can't withdraw. I'm committed . . . because of what I want and what I am."

"And what are you? What am I?"

"We should have been friends," said Orlando Campeggio with dry irony. "We've known each other a long time. But we missed the chance. So I'm afraid we're just conspirators—and not very good ones at that!"

Ten days before the feast of St. Ignatius Loyola, Jean Télémond received a letter from His Eminence Cardinal Rinaldi:

Dear Reverend Father,

This is not an official communication, but a personal one. Just before your arrival in Rome the Holy Father granted me permission to retire from office, and I am now living privately in the country. I am, however, invited to be present next week when you address the students and faculty at the Gregorian University. Before that day I should very much like to have the opportunity of meeting and talking with you.

Already I know a great deal—more, perhaps, than you realize—about you and your work. I judge you to be a man favored by God with what I can only call the grace of commitment.

This grace is a rare gift. I myself have missed it, but for this reason, perhaps, I am the more aware of it in others. I am aware, too, that it comes to the recipient more often as a cross than as a consolation.

I believe that your recall to Rome may be an event of great importance to the Church. I know that it is a decisive one for you. I should like, therefore, to offer you my friendship, my support, and perhaps my advice in your future activities.

If it is convenient, perhaps you would be good enough to visit me next Monday and spend the afternoon with me. You will be doing me a favor, and I hope sincerely I may be of some service to you.

Yours fraternally in Christ Jesus,
Valerio Rinaldi
Cardinal Priest

For a man in crisis it was a princely encouragement, and it touched Télémond deeply. It reminded him—when he needed the reminder most—that for all its monolithic faith, the Church was a habitation of diverse spirits amongst whom still dwelt a virtue of fraternity and compassion.

In the clattering, gregarious, clerical society of Rome he felt like an alien. Its conventions irked him. Its brusque orthodoxy troubled him as if he were being reproached for his twenty-year solitude among the mysteries of Creation. The melancholy of the climacteric weighed upon his soul. On the one hand, he found himself dreading the moment when he must present the speculation of a lifetime to the public view. On the other, he found himself approaching the moment with a kind of calculation which made the risks he had sustained, in flesh and spirit, seem futile and even guilty.

Now suddenly there was a hand stretched out to welcome him, and a voice that spoke with an accent of rare understanding and gentleness. He had not lacked friendship in his life. His work had not wanted patronage and encouragement. Yet no one had ever seen it so clearly for what it was. A gamble, a commitment to living and knowing and believing, with a complete conviction that every moment of existence, every extension of

knowledge, every act of faith, was a step in the same
direction, toward God-made-man and man made in the
image of God.

What had troubled him most in Rome was the feeling
that certain people in the Church regarded his work as
an arrogance. Yet an arrogant man could not have embarked upon such a journey, nor risked so much in a
single-minded search for truth.

He had never been afraid of error since all his experience had shown him that knowledge was self-corrective
and that a search honestly pursued must bring a man
closer to the shores of revelation, even though their out-
line remained forever hidden from his view.

There was an attitude of orthodoxy which was itself
a heresy: that to state the truth, as it had been stated
and restated in every century of the Church, was to display it forever in all its fullness. Yet the history of the
Church was the history of an immutable revelation un-
folding itself into greater and greater complexity as
men's minds opened to receive it more fully. The history
of spiritual progress for an individual was the history of
his preparation of himself to co-operate more willingly,
more consciously, and more gratefully with the grace of
God.

For Jean Télémond the letter of Valerio Rinaldi wore
the aspect of such a grace. He accepted it thankfully, and
made an appointment to visit the Cardinal in his country retreat.

They were instantly at ease with each other. Rinaldi
walked his guest round the pleasances of the villa and
rehearsed its history from the first Etruscan tomb, in the
orchard, to the Orphic temple, whose pavement lay un-
covered in the sunken garden. Télémond was charmed by

the urbanity and kindness of his host, and he opened himself more freely than he had done for a long time, so that the old man looked out through his visitor's eyes on exotic landscapes and a cavalcade of histories new and strange to him.

When they had finished the circuit, they sat beside a marble pond and drank English tea, and watched the fat carp browse languidly among the lily pads. Then, amiably but shrewdly, Rinaldi began to probe the mind of Jean Télémond.

"Rome is a chameleon city. It wears a different color for each visitor. How does it look to you, Father?"

Jean Télémond toyed with the question for a moment, and then answered it frankly. "I am uneasy. The idiom is strange to me. I am a Gaul among the Romans, a provincial among the metropolitans. I came back sure that I had learned so much in twenty years. Now I feel that I have forgotten something—some essential mode of speech, perhaps. I don't know what it is, but the lack of it troubles me."

Rinaldi put down his teacup and wiped his fastidious hands with a linen napkin. His lined patrician face softened. "I think you rate yourself too humbly, Father. It's a long time since Gaul was a province of Rome, and I think it is we who have lost the art of communication. . . . I don't deny that you have a problem, but I am inclined to read it differently."

Télémond's lean, disciplined features relaxed into a smile. "I should be grateful to hear your Eminence's interpretation."

The old Cardinal waved an eloquent hand, so that the sunlight gleamed on the emerald ring of his office.

"There are some, my friend, who wear the Church like

a glove. Myself, for instance. I am a man who was made
to grow comfortably within an established order. I understand the organization. I know where it is rigid and
where it can be made flexible. . . . There is no merit in
this, no special virtue. It is at bottom a matter of temperament and aptitude. It has nothing to do with faith, hope,
or charity. There are those who are born to be good servants of the State. There are those who have an aptitude
for the government of the Church. . . . It is a talent, if
you want, but a talent which has its own temptations, and
I have succumbed to some of them during my life. . . ."

He stared down at the lily pond, where the fish swam
gold and crimson and the flowers spread their creamy
petals under the afternoon sun. Télémond waited while
the old prince gathered the rest of his thoughts.

"There are others, my friend, who wear the Church like
a hair shirt. They believe no less. They love perhaps more
richly and more daringly; but they move, as you do, uneasily inside the discipline. For them obedience is a daily
sacrifice, whereas for me and those like me it is an accommodation—often a rewarding accommodation—to circumstance. Do you understand what I mean?"

"I understand it, but I think that your Eminence un-
derrates himself to be kind to me."

"No! No!" Rinaldi's answer was swift and emphatic.
"I am too old to pay idle compliments. I have entered
into judgment with myself and I know how much I am
found wanting. . . . At this moment you are a troubled
man. . . ."

"So very troubled, Eminence," said Télémond softly.
"I came to Rome under obedience, but there is no peace
for me here. I know that."

"You are not born to peace, my friend. This is the first

thing you must accept. You will not come to it, perhaps, till the day you die. Each of us has his own cross, you know, made and fitted to his reluctant shoulders. Do you know what mine is?"

"No."

"To be rich and content and fulfilled, and to know in this twilight of living that I have deserved none of it and that when I am called to judgment I must depend utterly upon the mercy of God and upon the merits of others more worthy."

Télémond was silent a long time, touched and humbled by this glimpse of an intimate and private agony. Finally he asked quietly, "And my cross, Eminence?"

"Your cross, my son . . ." The old man's voice took on a new warmth and compassion. "Your cross is to be always divided between the faith which you possess, the obedience which you have vowed, and your personal search for a deeper knowledge of God through the universe which He has made. You believe that there is no conflict between the two, and yet you are involved in conflict every day. You cannot recant the Act of Faith without a personal catastrophe. You cannot abandon the search without a ruinous disloyalty to yourself and to your own integrity. Am I right, Father?"

"Yes, Eminence, you're right; but it isn't enough. You show me the cross, but you do not show me how to carry it."

"You have carried it for twenty years without me."

"And now I am staggering under its weight. Believe me, I am staggering. . . . And now there is a new burden—Rome!"

"Do you want to go away?"

"Yes. And yet I should be ashamed to go."

"Why?"

"Because I hope that this may be the time of resolution for me. I feel I have been silent long enough for my thought to take shape. I feel that I have a duty to expose it to debate and dialectic. This exposure seems as much a duty as all my years of study and exploration."

"Then you must do your duty," said Rinaldi mildly.

"That makes another problem, Eminence," said Télémond with a flash of humor. "I am not a publicist. I do not present myself very well. I do not know how to accommodate myself to the climate of this place."

"Then ignore it," said Rinaldi bluntly. "You come armed with a right heart and a private vision of the truth. That is armor enough for any man."

Télémond frowned and shook his head. "I mistrust my courage, Eminence."

"I could tell you to trust in God."

"I do, and yet—" He broke off and stared unseeing across the reaches of the classic garden.

Rinaldi prompted him gently. "Go on, my son."

"I'm afraid—desperately afraid!"

"Of what?"

"That there may come a moment when this conflict in myself splits me in two and destroys me utterly. I can't put it any other way. I lack the words. I can only hope that your Eminence understands."

Valerio Cardinal Rinaldi stood up and laid his hands on the bowed shoulders of the Jesuit. "I do, my son, believe me! I feel for you as I have felt for few men in my lifetime. Whatever happens after your address next week, I want you to count me your friend. I told you you would be doing me a favor if you allowed me to help you. I put it more strongly. You may give me the opportunity of winning some small merit for myself. . . ." His habitual humor asserted itself again, and he laughed. "It's a tradition in Rome, Father. Painters, poets, and philosophers all need a patron to protect them from the Inquisition. And I may be the last real one left!"

Extract from
the Secret Memorials of
K I R I L I, Pont. Max.

. . . All this week I have been besieged by what I can only call a temptation of darkness. Never since my time in the bunker have I been so oppressed by the wild absurdity of the world, by the wastefulness of man's struggle for survival, by the apparent idiocy of any attempt to change human nature or bring about a corporate betterment in the human condition.

To reason with the temptation was simply to create another absurdity. To reason with myself was to invite a new confusion. A spirit of mockery seemed to inhabit me. Whenever I looked at myself I saw a jester in cap and bells, perched on a mountaintop, waving his silly wand at the hurricanes. When I prayed, my spirit was arid. The words were like an incantation from some ancient witchcraft—without virtue and without reward. It was a kind of agony which I thought would never come my way again, yet this time I was more deeply wounded by it than ever before.

In my confusion I addressed myself to a meditation on the passion and death of the Master. I began to understand dimly the meaning of the agony in Gethsemane garden, when the trouble of His human spirit communicated itself so poignantly to His body that its mechanism began to break down and He suffered, as a leukemia patient does, the bloody sweat which is a foretaste of dying.

For a moment also I glimpsed the meaning of His final desolate cry from the Cross. . . . "My God, my God, why hast Thou forsaken me?" In that moment I think He must have seen—as I see now—the wild folly of a world gone mad, bursting itself asunder in a tangential flight from its center.

At that moment His own life and death must have seemed a vast futility, just as my life and all my effort as His Vicar seem to me. Yet He endured it, and so must I. If He, God-man, could suffer, uncomforted by the Godhead, shall I refuse the cup which He hands on to me? . . .

I held to the thought with a kind of terror, lest it should slip away from me and leave me forever a prey to blackness and despair. Then, slowly, the darkness dissipated itself and I found myself shaken, almost physically ill, but confirmed once again in the essential sanity of belief. I did, however, see something very clearly: the plight of those who have no God to infuse a meaning into the monstrous nonsense of the whole human effort.

For a believer life is at best a painful mystery, made acceptable by a partial revelation of a divine design. To an unbeliever—and there are hundreds of millions from whom the grace of belief has been withheld—it must present itself at times as a kind of madness, always threatening, at times almost unendurable. Perhaps this is the meaning of what I am and what has happened to me: that being poor in all else, I can offer to the world the love of an understanding heart. . . .

Today a second letter arrived from Kamenev. It was delivered in Paris to the Cardinal Archbishop and forwarded to me by special messenger. It is more cryptic than the first, but I sense a greater urgency in it:

I have your message and I am grateful for it. The sunflowers are blooming now in Mother Russia, but before they come to flower again, we may have need of each other.

Your message tells me that you trust me, but I have to be honest and say that you must not trust what I do or what I am reported to say. We live in different climates, as you know. You command an obedience and a loyalty impossible in my sphere of action. I can survive only by understanding what is possible, by yielding to one pressure in order to avoid a greater one.

Within twelve months, even sooner, we may come to the brink of war. I want peace. I know that we cannot have it with a one-sided bargain. On the other hand, I cannot dictate its terms even to my own people. I am caught in the current of history. I can tack across it, but I cannot change the direction of the flow.

I believe you understand what I am trying to say. I ask you, if you can, to interpret it as clearly as possible to the President of the United States. I have met him. I respect him. In a private dealing I could trust him, but in the domain of politics he is as subject to pressure as I am—more so, perhaps, because his tenure is shorter and the influence of public opinion is stronger. If you can communicate with him, I beg you to do so, but secretly and with the greatest discretion. You know that I should have to repudiate violently any suggestion that there is a private channel of talk between us.

I cannot yet suggest a secure method by which you can write to me. From time to time, however, you will receive application for a private audience from a man named Georg Wilhelm Forster. To him you may speak freely, but commit nothing to writing. If you succeed in a conversation with the President of the United States, you should refer to him as Robert. Foolish, is it not, that to discuss the survival of the race we must resort to such childish tricks.

You are fortunate that you can pray. I am limited to action, and if I am half right for half the time I am lucky.

Again I repeat my caution. You believe you stand in God's shoes. I must wear my own, and the ground is very slippery. Trust me no further than I can trust myself. Martyrdom is out of fashion in my world. Greetings. Kamenev.

No man remains unchanged by the experience of power. Some are perverted to tyranny. Some are corrupted by flattery and self-indulgence. Some very few are tempered to wisdom by their understanding of the consequences of executive action. I believe this is what has happened to Kamenev.

He was never a gross man. When I knew him he had surrendered himself to cynicism, but this surrender was never quite complete. This was proved by his action in my regard. I would say that there is in his thinking no truly spiritual or religious domain. He has accepted too fully a materialist conception of man and of the universe. However, I do believe that within the limits of his own logic, he has arrived at an understanding of the dignity of man and a sense of obligation to preserve it as far as he can. I do not think he is governed by moral sanctions as we understand them in the spiritual sense. But he does realize that a certain practical morality is essential to social order, and even to the survival of civilization as we know it.

I think this is what he is trying to tell me: that I can trust him to proceed logically in his own system of thought, but that I must never expect him to work inside mine. For my part, I must not forget that while man is limited to the covenanted channels of grace, made available to him by the redemptive act of Christ, God is not so limited, and that in the outcome Kamenev's logic may be turned into a divine one. Even in the human order Kamenev's letter has a historic importance. The man who embodies in his office the Marxist heresy, who has tried violently to extirpate the Faith from the land of Russia, now turns to the Papacy to provide a free and secret mode of communication with the rest of the world.

I see very clearly that Kamenev offers me nothing—no entry for the Faith into Russia, no slackening of oppression or persecution. Cardinal Goldoni points out that at this very moment our schools and seminaries in Poland, and Hungary, and East Germany, are in danger of being closed altogether by the imposition of new and savage taxation. He asks me what Kamenev proposes to offer either to the Church or to the United States by way of a down payment toward peace. . . .

On the face of it he offers nothing. One might even make a good case for the opinion that he is trying to use me to his own advantage. I have to weigh this opinion very carefully. Yet I cling to the deep conviction that there is a divine design in this relationship between us and that it must not be allowed to degenerate into a political gambit. . . .

It is a historic fact that when the temporal power of the Church was greatest her spiritual life was at its lowest ebb. It is dangerous to read divine revelation into every paragraph of history, but I cannot help feeling that when we are like the Master, poorest in temporality, then we may be richest in the divine life.

From me the occasion demands prayer and prudence. . . . Normally we should communicate with the Government of the United States through our own Secretariat of State. In this instance we dare not do so. I have, therefore, sent a cable to the Cardinal Archbishop of New York, asking him to come to Rome as quickly as possible so that I may brief him on the situation and have him communicate directly with the President of the United States. Once I have spoken with Cardinal Carlin, we shall all be walking on eggs. If any hint of the matter is revealed to the American press, this small hope of peace may be lost to us forever. . . . In the morning I must offer Mass as a petition for a favorable outcome. . . .

Today I held the first of a series of conferences with the Congregation of the Religious and with the heads of the major religious orders. The purpose of the conferences is to determine how they may best adapt themselves to the changing conditions of the world and participate more actively and more flexibly in the mission of the Church to the souls of men.

There are many problems involved, and we shall not solve them all at one stroke. Each order holds jealously to its tradition and its sphere of influence in the Church. All too often the tradition is a handicap to apostolic effort. Systems of training differ. The "spirit of the order" —that mode of thought and action which gives it a special character—tends too often to harden itself into "the method of the order," so that it reacts too slowly and too stubbornly to the demands of the times.

There is another problem, too. The rate of recruitment of new members has become dangerously slow because many willing spirits find themselves too limited and constrained by an archaic constitution and even by a mode of dress and life which separates them too sharply from the times in which they live. . . .

Once again I am faced with the fundamental problem of my office—how to translate the Word into Christian action; how to scrape off the overburden of history so that the lode of the primitive faith may be revealed in all its richness. When men are truly united with God, it matters little what dress they wear, what exercises of piety they perform, what constitution they live under. Religious obedience should set a man free in the liberty of the sons of God. Tradition should be a lamp to his feet, lighting his pathway into the future. To renounce the world is not to abandon it, but to restore it in Christ to the beauty of its primal design. . . . We inherit the past, but we are committed to the present and to the future.

It is time, I think, for a deeper exploration and a clearer definition of the function of the laity in the life of the Church. Anti-clericalism is a symptom of dissatisfaction among the faithful. For the fact is that rebellion against the doctrine of the Church is less common than the gradual desertion of a religious climate which seems to be at irreconcilable odds with the world men have to live in. Those whose aspirations exceed the dimensions of the local pastor's mentality gradually fade from the pews in search of substitutes and partial truths, which as a rule, bring them neither peace nor joy, but certainly a sense of dedicated integrity. The number of these cases has become large enough to achieve some sort of recognizable status in the Church, which, though ambiguous, is radically different from the category of those whose militant darkness attempts to eradicate from human consciousness the very notion of man's existence dependent on God. . . .

In this world of ours, when men are reaching swiftly for the moon, the dimension of time seems to narrow daily, and I am perturbed that we cannot adjust ourselves more quickly to the change. . . .

In a couple of weeks the holiday season will begin in Europe. It is customary for the Pontiff to leave the Vatican and spend a vacation at Castel Gandolfo. In spite of my impatience I find myself looking forward to the change. It will give me time to think, to sum up for myself the thousand diverse impressions of these first months in office.

I have not dared to mention it to the Secretary of State, but I think I shall take the opportunity to travel a little in private, round the countryside. . . . I shall need a good driver. It would be embarrassing to me, and to the Italian government, if we had any accidents on the road—it would make a wonderful picture if the Pontiff were discovered in the middle of a highway, arguing with an Italian truck driver. . . . I find myself wishing for an agreeable companion to spend the vacation with me, but I have not yet found time to cultivate any real friendship. My isolation is all the greater because I am so much younger than the members of the Curia, and—God help me—I do not want to become an old man before my time.

I understand now how some of my predecessors have lapsed into nepotism and surrounded themselves with relatives, and how others have cultivated favorites in the Vatican. It is not good for any man to be wholly alone. . . .

Kamenev is married and has a son and a daughter. I should like to think he has made a happy match. . . . If not, he must be much more isolated than I. I have never regretted my own celibacy, but I envy those whose work in the Church is with children. . . .

A sudden dark thought. If there is another war, what of the little ones? They are the inheritors of our misdeeds, and how will they fare in the broadcast horror of an atomic Armageddon? . . .

It must not be . . . it must not!

VII

IN HIS bachelor apartment on Parioli, Corrado Calitri, Minister of the Republic, was conferring with his lawyers. The senior advocate, Perosi, was a tall, spare man with a dry, academic manner. His junior had a round dumpling face and a deprecating smile. In the far corner of the room the Princess Marina-Rina sat withdrawn and wary, watching them with hooded predatory eyes.

Perosi laid the tips of his fingers together like a bishop about to intone a Psalm, and summed up the situation:

". . . As I understand it, you have been troubled in conscience for some time. You have taken counsel with a confessor, and he has advised you that it is your duty to change your testimony with respect to your marriage."

Calitri's pale face was blank, his voice devoid of expression. "That's the position, yes."

"Let us be very clear, then, where we stand. Your wife's petition for a decree of nullity is made under the terms of Canon 1086, which states two things: first, the internal consent of the mind is always presumed to be in agreement with the words or signs which are used in the celebration of the marriage; second, if either party or both

parties, by a positive act of the will, exclude marriage itself, or all right to the conjugal act or any essential property of the marriage, the marriage contract is invalid." He
rustled his papers and went on in his professorial fashion.
"The first part of the canon does not really concern us. It
simply expresses a presumption of the law, which may be
overcome by contrary proof. Your wife's plea leans on the
second part. She claims that you deliberately excluded
from your consent her right to the conjugal act, and that
you did not accept the contract as unbreakable, but as a
form of therapy to be laid aside if the therapy failed. If
her plea could be sustained, the marriage would, of
course, be declared invalid. You understand that?"

"I've always understood it."

"But you denied in a written and sworn statement that
your intention was defective."

"I did."

"Now, however, you are prepared to admit that the
statement was false and that, in fact, you perjured yourself."

"Yes. I understand that I have done a grave injustice,
and I want to repair it. I want Chiara to be free."

"You are prepared to make another sworn statement,
admitting the perjury and the defective intention?"

"I am."

"So far, so good. This will give us a ground to reopen
the case with the Rota." Perosi pursed his pale lips and
frowned. "Unfortunately, it will not be sufficient for a
decree of nullity."

"Why not?"

"It's a question of procedure covered by Canon 1971,
and by commentaries on the code dated March 1929,
July 1933, and July 1942. A party to a marriage who is the

guilty cause of the nullity is deprived of the right to impugn the contract. He has no standing in court."

"Where does that leave us?"

"We need one or more witnesses to testify that you expressed to them, clearly and explicitly, your defective intentions before the marriage took place."

The brisk old voice of the Princess intruded itself into the conversation. "I think you can take it for granted that such testimony would be available."

"In that case," said Advocate Perosi, "I think we have a sound case, and we may look with some confidence to a favorable outcome."

He sat back in his chair and began rearranging his papers. As if on a prearranged signal, the dumpling man added a footnote to the discussion:

"With respect to my senior colleague, I should like to make two suggestions. It would be an advantage if we had a letter from your confessor, indicating that you are acting under his advice in trying to repair the injustice done. It might help, too, if you wrote a friendly letter to your wife, admitting your fault and asking her to forgive you. . . . Neither of these two documents would have any value in evidence, but they might, shall we say, help the atmosphere."

"I'll do as you suggest," said Calitri in the same colorless fashion. "Now I'd like to ask a couple of questions. I admit default, I admit perjury. On the other hand, I do have a public position and a reputation to protect."

"All the deliberations of the Rota, and all the depositions made before it, are protected by rigid secrecy. You need have no fear on that score."

"Good. How long do you think the business will take?"

Perosi considered the question a moment. "Not too

long. Nothing can be done, of course, during the holiday period, but if all the depositions were in our hands by the end of August, we could have the translation done in two weeks. Then, in view of your position and the long suspension of the case, I think we would get a speedy hearing. . . . I should say two months at the outside. It might even be sooner."

"I am grateful," said Corrado Calitri. "I'll have the papers ready by the end of August."

Perosi and his colleague bowed themselves out. "We are always at the disposal of the minister."

"Good day, gentlemen, and thank you."

When the door closed behind them, the Princess threw back her bird's head and laughed. "There, now. I told you, didn't I? It's as simple as shelling peas. Of course we have to find you a confessor. There's a nice understanding Monsignore who attends me from Florence. Yes, I think he'd be the one. He's intelligent, cultivated, and quite zealous in his own way. I'll have a talk with him and arrange an appointment. . . . Come on now, smile. In two months you'll be free. In a year you'll be leading the country."

"I know, Aunt, I know."

"Oh, there's one more thing. Your letter to Chiara. There's no need to be too humble about it. Dignity, restraint, a desire to make amends, yes. But nothing compromising. I don't trust that girl. I never have."

Calitri shrugged indifferently. "She's a child, Aunt. There's no malice in her."

"Children grow up—and there's malice in every woman when she can't get what she wants."

"From what I hear, she's getting it."

"With the dean of the foreign press. What's his name?"

"George Faber. He represents one of the New York dailies."

"The biggest one," said the old Princess firmly. "And you can't shrug him off like a cold in the head. You're too vulnerable now, my boy. You have the *Osservatore* against you and Chiara in bed with the American press. You can't afford a situation like that."

"I can't change it."

"Why not?"

"Campeggio's son works for me. He likes me and dislikes his father. Chiara will probably marry this Faber as soon as she gets the decree of nullity. There's nothing I can do about either situation."

"I think there is." She fixed him with a shrewd and rheumy eye. "Take young Campeggio first. You know what I should do?"

"I'd like to hear it."

"Promote him. Push him forward as fast as you can. Promise him something even bigger after the election. Bind him to you with trust and friendship. His father will hate you, but the boy will love you, and I don't think Campeggio will fight his own son. . . . As for Chiara and her American boy friend, leave them to me."

"What do you propose to do?"

The old Princess gave her high birdlike chuckle and shook her head. "You have no talent with women, Corrado. Just sit quietly and leave Chiara to me."

Calitri spread his eloquent hands in a gesture of resignation. "Just as you say, Aunt. I'll leave her to you."

"You won't regret it."

"I'll take your advice, Aunt."

"I know you will. Give me a kiss now, and cheer up.

You'll have dinner with me tomorrow night. There are some people from the Vatican I want you to meet. Now that you're back in the bosom of the Church, they can begin to be useful to you."

He kissed her withered cheek and watched her leave, wondering the while that so much vitality should reside in so frail a body, and whether he had enough to sustain the bargain he had made with his backers.

All his life he had been making deals like this one. Always the price had to be paid in the same coin—another fragment of himself. Each depletion made him less assured of his identity, and he knew that in the end he would be altogether empty and the spiders would spin webs in the hollow of his heart.

Depression came down on him like a cloud. He poured himself a drink and carried it over to the window seat from which he could look down on the city and the flight of pigeons over its ancient roofs. The Prime Ministry might be worth a Mass, but nothing—nothing—was worth the lifetime damnation to emptiness which was demanded of him.

To be sure, he had made a contract. He would be the White Knight without fear and without reproach, and the Christian Democrats would let him lead them into power. But there was room still for a footnote, and the Princess Maria-Rina had spelled it out for him. . . . Trust and friendship. . . . Perhaps even more! In the sour bargain he had made, there was suddenly a hint of sweetness.

He picked up the telephone, dialed the number of his office, and asked young Campeggio to bring the afternoon's correspondence to his apartment.

:

At ten-thirty of a cloudless morning Charles Corbet Carlin, Cardinal Archbishop of New York, landed at Fiumicino Airport. An official of the Secretariat of State met him at the steps of the aircraft and hurried him past the customs and immigration officials into a Vatican limousine. An hour and a half later he was closeted with Kiril the Pontiff and Goldoni the Secretary of State.

Carlin was by nature a peremptory man, and he understood the usages of power. He was quick to see the change that a few months of office had wrought in the Pope. He had lost none of his charm, none of his swift, intuitive warmth. Yet he seemed to have reached a new dimension of authority. His scarred face was leaner, his speech more brisk, his whole manner more urgent and concerned. Yet, characteristically, he opened the discussion with a smile and an apology:

"I'm grateful that your Eminence came so promptly. I know how busy you are. I wanted to explain myself more fully, but I could not trust the information even to a coded cable."

Then in crisp, emphatic sentences he explained the reason for the summons and showed Carlin the text of Kamenev's two letters.

The American scanned them with a shrewd and calculating eye, and then handed them back to the Pontiff. "I understand your Holiness' concern. I confess I am less clear on what Kamenev hopes to gain by this maneuver."

Goldoni permitted himself a faint smile. "Your Eminence's reaction is the same as mine . . . A maneuver! His Holiness, however, takes a different view."

Kiril spread his crooked hands on the desk top and explained himself simply. "I want you to understand first that I know this man. I know him more intimately than I know either of you. For a long time he was my interrogator in prison. Each of us has had a great influence on the other. It was he who arranged my escape from Russia. I am profoundly convinced that this is not a political maneuver, but a genuine appeal for help in the crisis which will soon be upon us."

Carlin nodded thoughtfully. "Your Holiness may be right. It would be folly to discount your experience with this man and your intimate knowledge of the Russian situation. On the other hand—and I say it with all respect— we have had another kind of experience with Kamenev and with the Soviets."

"When you say 'we,' do you refer to the Church or to the United States of America?"

"To both," said Carlin flatly. "So far as the Church is concerned, the Secretariat of State will bear me out. There is still active persecution in the satellite countries. In Russia the Faith has been totally extinguished. Our brother bishops who went to prison with your Holiness are all dead. The Soviet frontiers are sealed against the Faith. I see no prospect of their being opened in our time."

Goldoni added agreement. "I have already put this view very clearly to His Holiness."

"And I," said Kiril the Pontiff, "do not disagree with it. . . . Now tell me about the American view."

"At first blush," said Carlin, "this looks to me like another version of the old summit meetings. We all remember the arguments . . . 'Let's bypass the lower echelons and let the leaders talk freely and familiarly about our problems. Let's skip the details and get down to the fundamental issues that divide us. . . .' Well, we had the meetings. They were always abortive. In the end every discussion was wrecked by the details. Whatever good will existed before the meetings was diminished, if not wholly destroyed. In the end, you see, the lower echelons of government are more decisive than the upper ones because under our system, and under the Russian one, the leader is always subject to the pressures of political and administrative advice from below. No single man can sustain the burden of decision on major issues." He smiled expansively at the Pontiff. "Even in the Church we have the same situation. Your Holiness is the Vicar of Christ. Yet the effectiveness of your decisions is limited by the co-operation and obedience of the local ordinaries."

Kiril the Pontiff picked up the letters from his desk and held them out to his two counsellors. "So what would you have me do about these? Ignore them?"

Carlin side-stepped the question. "What does Kamenev ask your Holiness to do?"

"He is very clear, I think. He asks me to communicate the letters to the President of the United States, and communicate also my own interpretation of his mind and his intentions."

"What is his mind, Holiness? What are his intentions?"

"Let me quote again what he says. 'Within twelve months, even sooner, we may come to the brink of war. I want peace. I know that we cannot have it with a one-sided bargain. On the other hand, I cannot dictate its terms even to my own people. I am caught in the current of history. I can tack across it, but I cannot change the direction of the flow. . . . I believe you understand what I am trying to say. I ask you, if you can, to interpret it as clearly as possible to the President of the

United States. . . .' To me, in my knowledge of the man, the message is quite evident. Before the crisis becomes irreversible, he wants to establish a ground of negotiation so that peace may be preserved."

"But what ground?" asked Goldoni. "Your Holiness must admit that he is somewhat less than precise."

"Put it another way," said Carlin in his pragmatic fashion. "I go back home. I call Washington and ask for a private interview with the President of the United States. I show him these letters. I say, 'It is the view of the Holy See that Kamenev wants to begin secret talks to fend off the crisis we all know is coming. The Pope will be the intermediary of the talks. . . .' What, do you think, the President will say or do then? What would your Holiness do in his place?"

Kiril's scarred face twitched into a smile of genuine amusement. "I should say, 'Talk costs nothing. So long as men can communicate, however haltingly, then there is a hope of peace. But close all the doors, cut all the wires, build the walls even higher—then each nation is an island, preparing in secret a common destruction.'"

Abruptly Carlin challenged the argument. "There is a flaw in the logic, Holiness. Forgive me, but I have to show it to you. Talk always costs something—this kind of talk especially. Secret parleys are dangerous because once they are brought into the open—and inevitably they must be—then they can be denied by those who took part in them. They can be used as weapons in political dealings."

"Remember!" Goldoni added the potent afterthought. "There are no longer two grand powers in the world. There is Russia, and the United States. There is the European bloc. There is China, and there are the un-

committed nations of Asia and Africa and the South
Americas. There is not only the arms race. There is the
race to feed the hungry and the race to align vast numbers of mankind with one ideology or another. We dare
not take too simple a view of this very complex world."

"I hesitate to say it, Holiness," said Carlin gravely,
"but I should not like to see the Holy See compromised
by offering itself as an intermediary in bilateral and
probably abortive discussions. . . . Personally I mistrust
a truce with the Russian bear, no matter how prettily
he dances."

"You have him in the papal coat of arms," said Kiril
tartly. "Do you mistrust him there, too?"

"Let me answer the question with another. Can your
Holiness trust himself completely in this matter? This
is not doctrine or dogma, but an affair of State. Your
Holiness is as open to error as the rest of us."

He had been dangerously frank and he knew it. To be
Cardinal Archbishop of New York was to sit high in the
Church, to dispose great influence, to command money
and resources vital to the economy of the Vatican. Yet
in the constitution of the Faith the Successor of Peter
was paramount, and in its history many a Cardinal Prince
had been stripped of his preferment by a single word
from an outraged Pontiff. Charles Corbet Carlin sat back
in his chair and waited, not without uneasiness, for the
papal answer.

To his surprise, it was delivered in a tone of restraint
and real humility. "Everything you tell me is true. It is,
in fact, a reflection of my own thought on the matter. I
am grateful that you have chosen to be open with me,
that you have not tried to bend me by diplomatic words.
I do not want to bend you, either. I do not want to force

you to act against your own prudence. This is not a matter of faith or morals, it is a matter of private conviction,
and I should like to share mine with you. . . . Let us
have lunch first, and then I want to show you both something. You have seen it before, but I hope today it may
take on another meaning for you."

Then seeing the doubt and surprise on their faces, he
laughed almost boyishly. "No, there are no plots, no
Borgia subtleties. I've learned something in Italy. One
should never discuss weighty matters on an empty stomach. I think Goldoni will agree that I've reformed the
Vatican kitchens, if nothing else. Come now, let's relax
for a while."

They ate simply but well in Kiril's private apartment.
They talked discursively of men and affairs and the hundred intimacies of the hierarchic society to which they
belonged. They were like members of an exclusive international club, whose fellows were scattered to every
point of the compass, but whose affairs were common knowledge in all tongues.

When the meal was over and the Vatican had lapsed
into the somnolence of siesta time, Kiril put on a black
cassock and led his two guests into the Basilica of
St. Peter.

The tourists were sparse now, and no one paid any
attention to three middle-aged clerics halted by the confessional boxes near the sacristy. Kiril pointed to one of
them, which carried on its door the laconic legend "Polish and Russian."

"Once a week I come and sit here for two hours, to
hear the confession of anyone who chances to come. I
should like to hear them in Italian as well, but the dia-
lects escape me. . . . You both know what this minis-

try of the tribunal is like. The good ones come. The bad
ones stay away; but every so often there arrives the soul
in distress, the one who needs a special co-operation from
the confessor to lead him back to God. . . . It's a lot-
tery always—a gamble on the moment and the man, and
the fruitfulness of the Word one plucks from one's own
heart. And yet there, in that stuffy little box, is the
whole meaning of the Faith—the private speech of man
with his Creator, myself between as man's servant and
God's. There, encompassed by the smell of blood sau-
sage and cabbage water, and the sweat of a frightened
man, I am what I was ordained to be: a sublime opportunist, a fisher of men, not knowing what I shall
catch in my net or whether I shall catch anything at
all. . . . Now come over here."

He beckoned to an attendant to accompany them.
Then he took the arms of the two Cardinals and walked
them across to the steps that led down to the confession
of St. Peter, in front of the great altar of Bernini. They
descended the steps. The attendant unlocked the bronze
grille in front of the kneeling statue of Pope Pius VI.
When they entered the recess, he closed the door on them
and retired to a respectful distance. Kiril led his two
counsellors to the space where a dark hole plunged down
toward the grottoes of the Vatican. Then he turned to
face them. His voice dropped to a murmur that echoed
softly round the enclosure.

"Down there, they say, is the tomb of Peter the Fisherman. Whenever I am afraid or in darkness, I come here
to pray, and ask him what I, his inheritor, should do. He
was an opportunist, too, you know. The Master gave him
the Keys of the Kingdom. The Holy Ghost gave him the
gift of wisdom and the gift of tongues. Then he was left,

still a fisherman, an alien in the empire of Rome, to plant
the seed of the Gospel wherever there was earth to receive it. . . . He had no method. He had no temple. He
had no book but the living Gospel. He was conditioned
by the time in which he lived, but he could not be bound
by the condition. . . . Neither can I. Do you remember
the story of Paul coming into the city of Athens, among
the philosophers and the rhetors, and seeing the altar of
the Unknown God? Do you remember what he did? He
cried out with a loud voice, 'Men, brethren! What you
worship without knowing, I preach!' Is not this an opportunist, also? He does not reason with the moment. He
does not appeal to a system or a history. He gambles
himself and his mission on a word tossed into a milling
crowd. Don't you see? This is the meaning of faith. This
is the risk of belief."

He turned a luminous face on Carlin, not commanding
but pleading with him. "Before your Eminence came to
see me, I was in darkness. I saw myself as a fool shouting
a folly to a heedless world. So be it! That is what we
preach: transcendent nonsense, which we trust in the
end will make a divine logic. . . ."

Abruptly he relaxed and grinned at them mischiev-
ously. "In prison I learned to gamble, and I found that
in the end the man who always won was he who never
hedged his bets. I know what you're thinking. I want to
navigate the barque of Peter by the seat of my papal
breeches. . . . But if the wind is blown by the breath
of God and the water is rocked by His hands . . .
how better can I do it? Answer me! How better can I
do it?"

In the narrow enclosure Goldoni shifted uneasily on
his feet.

Carlin stood as obstinate and unshakable as Plymouth Rock. He said evenly, "This is perhaps the faith that moves mountains, Holiness. I regret that it has not been given to me in the same measure. I am compelled to work by normal prudence. I cannot agree that the affairs of the Church can be administered by private inspiration."

Kiril the Pontiff was still smiling when he answered. "You elected me by inspiration, Eminence. Do you think the Holy Ghost has deserted me?"

Carlin was not to be put off. He pressed his argument stubbornly. "I did not say that, Holiness. But I will say this: No one is large enough to make himself the universal man. You want to be all things to all men, but you can never truly succeed. You're a Russian, I am an American. You ask me to risk more on this Kamenev than I would risk on my own brother if he were President of the United States. I cannot do it."

"Then," said Kiril with unexpected mildness, "I will not ask you to do it. I will not ask you to risk anything. I will give you a simple command. You will present yourself to the President of the United States. You will offer him these letters, and one which I shall write myself. If your opinion is asked, you will be free to say whatever you wish, as a private cleric and as an American, but you will not attempt to interpret my mind or Kamenev's. This way I hope you will feel free to discharge your duty to the Church and to your country."

Carlin flushed. He said awkwardly, "Your Holiness is generous with me."

"Not generous, only logical. If I believe the Holy Ghost can work through me and through Kamenev, why should he not work through the President of the United States? It is never wise to discount Omnipotence. Besides," he added gently, "you may do better for me in opposition. At least you will guarantee the good faith of the Holy See toward the United States of America. . . . I think now, perhaps, we should pray together. It is not expected that we should agree on what is prudent, only that our wills should be set toward the service of the same God."

As the month of July drew to a close and the summer exodus from Rome began, Ruth Lewin found herself caught up once more in the cyclic drama of mental distress.

The onset of the action was always the same: a deep melancholy, a sensation of solitude, a feeling of rootlessness, as though she had been set down suddenly on an unfamiliar planet, where her past was meaningless, her future was a question mark, and communication lapsed into gibberish.

The melancholy was the worst sensation of all. As a symptom it was familiar to her, yet she could neither reason with it nor dispel it. It drove her into fits of weeping. When the tears stopped, she felt empty and incapable of the simplest pleasure. When she looked in a mirror, she saw herself old and ravaged. When she walked out into the city, she was a stranger, an object of derision to the passers-by.

The flaw in her personality must be evident to everybody. She was a German by birth, a Jew by race, an American by adoption, an exile in the country of the sun. She demanded belief and refused it with the same gesture. She needed love and knew herself impotent to express it. She wanted desperately to live, yet was haunted by the insidious attraction of death. She was everything and nothing. There were times when she huddled helpless in her apartment like a sick animal, afraid of the clamorous health of her kind.

All her relationships seemed to fail her at once. She moved like a stranger among her protégés in Old Rome. She made expensive telephone calls to friends in America. When they failed to answer, she was desolate. When they responded with casual thanks, she was convinced she had made a fool of herself. She was oppressed by the prospect of summer, when Rome was deserted and the heat lay like a leaden pall over the alleys and the sluggish life of the piazzas.

At night she lay wakeful, with aching breasts, tormented by a fire in the flesh. When she drugged herself into sleep, she dreamed of her dead husband and woke sobbing in an empty bed. The young doctor with whom she worked came to visit her, but he was too immersed in his own problems, and she was too proud to reveal her own to him. He was in love with her, he said, but his demands were too blunt, and when she drew away he was quickly bored, so that in the end he stopped coming, and she blamed herself for his neglect.

A couple of times she tried the old prescription for unhappy widows in Rome. She sat herself in a bar and tried to drink herself into recklessness. But three drinks made her ill, and when she was accosted she was brusquely and unreasonably angry.

The experience was salutary. It made her cling with a kind of desperation to the last vestige of reason. It gave her a little more patience to support the illness which she knew must pass, even though she dare not wait too long upon the cure. Each petty crisis depleted her reserves and brought her one step nearer the medicine cabinet, where the bottle of barbiturates mocked her with the illusion of forgetfulness.

Then, one heavy and threatening day, hope stepped into her life again. She had wakened late and was dressing listlessly when the telephone rang. It was George Faber. He told her Chiara was out of town. He was feeling lonely and depressed. He would like to take her to dinner. She hesitated a moment, and then accepted.

The incident was over in two minutes, but it wrenched her out of depression and into an almost normal world. She made a hasty appointment with her hairdresser. She bought herself a new cocktail frock for twice the money she could afford. She bought flowers for her apartment and a bottle of Scotch whisky for Faber, and when he came to call for her at eight o'clock she was as nervous as a debutante on her first date.

He was looking older, she thought, a trifle stooped, a little grayer than at their last meeting. But he was still the dandy, with a carnation in his buttonhole, an engaging smile, and a bunch of Nemi violets for her dressing table. He kissed her hand in the Roman fashion, and while she mixed his drink he explained himself ruefully:

"I have to go south on this Calitri business. Chiara hates Rome in the summer, and the Antonellis have asked her to go to Venice with them for a month. They've taken a house on the Lido. . . . I hope to join them later. Meantime . . ." He gave a little uneasy laugh. "I've lost the habit of living alone. . . . And you did say I could call you."

"I'm glad you called, George. I don't like living alone, either."

"You're not offended?"

"Why should I be? A night on the town with the dean of the foreign press, that's an event for most women. Here's your drink."

They toasted each other, and then fenced their way through the opening gambits of talk.

"Where would you like to dine, Ruth? Do you have any preferences?"

"I'm in your hands, good sir."

"Would you like to be quiet or gay?"

"Gay, please. Life's been all too quiet lately."

"That suits me. Now, would you like to be a Roman or a tourist?"

"A Roman, I think."

"Good. There's a little place over in Trastevere. It's crowded and noisy, but the food's good. There's a guitar player, an odd poet or two, and a fellow who draws pictures on the tablecloth."

"It sounds wonderful."

"I used to like it, but I haven't been there in a long time. Chiara doesn't like that sort of thing." He blushed and fiddled nervously with his liquor. "I'm sorry. That's the wrong beginning."

"Let's make a bargain, George."

He gave her a quick, shamefaced glance. "What sort of bargain?"

"Tonight nothing is wrong. We say what we feel, do what we like, and then forget it. No strings, no promises, no apologies. . . . I need it like that."

"I need it, too, Ruth. Does that sound like disloyalty?"

She leaned across and placed a warning finger on his lips. "No second thoughts, remember!"

"I'll try. . . . Tell me about yourself. What have you been doing?"

"Working. Working with my *Juden* and wondering why I do it."

"Don't you know why?"

"Sometimes. At others it's pretty meaningless."

She got up and switched on the record player, and the room was filled with the saccharine tones of a Neapolitan singer. Ruth Lewin laughed. "Pretty schmaltzy, isn't it?"

Faber grinned and lay back in his chair, relaxed for the first time. "Now who's having second thoughts? I like schmaltz—and I haven't heard the word three times since I left New York."

"It's the Yiddish in me. It slips out when I'm off my guard."

"Does that worry you?"

"Occasionally."

"Why should it?"

"That's a long story, and it's not for now. Finish your drink, George. Then take me out and make a Roman of me, just for tonight."

At the doorway of the apartment he kissed her lightly on the lips, and then they walked, arm in arm, past the ghostly marbles of the Forum. Then for a final surrender to whimsy, they hailed a *carrozza* and sat holding hands while the tired horse carried them clippity-clop over the Palatine Bridge and into the populous lanes of Trastevere.

The restaurant was called 'o Cavalluccio. Its entrance was an old oaken door, studded with rusty nails. Its sign was a prancing stallion, roughly carved into the weathered stone of the lintel and picked out with whitewash. The interior was a large, vaulted cellar, hung with dusty lanterns and set with heavy wooden refectory tables. The clientele was mostly families from the quarter, and the spirit of the place was one of amiable tyranny.

The proprietor, a dumpy fellow in a white apron, set them down in a dark corner, planked a flask of red and a flask of white wine in front of them, and announced his policy with a flashing smile:

"As much wine as you can drink! Good wine, too, but no fancy labels. Two kinds of pasta only. Two main dishes —a roast of chicken and a stew of veal in Marsala. After that you're in the hands of God!"

As Faber had promised, there was a guitar player, a swarthy youth with a red bandana round his neck and a tin cup tied to his belt for an alms box. There was a bearded poet, dressed in blue denims, homemade sandals, and a sackcloth shirt, who turned an honest penny by mocking the guests with verses improvised in the Roman dialect. For the rest, the entertainment was provided by the clowning of the guests themselves and an occasional raucous chorus called by the guitar player. The pasta was served in great wooden bowls, and an impudent waiter tied a huge napkin round their necks to protect their noble bosoms from the sauce.

Ruth Lewin was delighted with the novelty, and Faber, plucked out of his normal ambience, seemed ten years younger and endowed with an unsuspected wit.

He charmed her with his talk of Roman intrigues and Vatican gossips, and she found herself talking freely of the long and tortuous journey which had brought her at last to the Imperial City. Encouraged by Faber's sympathy, she exposed her problems more freely than she had ever done, except to an analyst, and found to her surprise that she was no longer ashamed of them. On the contrary, they seemed to define themselves more clearly, and the terror they had once held for her was magically diminished.

". . . For me everything boiled itself down to a question of security and the need to put down some kind of roots in a world that had shifted too quickly for my childish understanding. I never seemed to be able to do it. Everything in my life, people, the Church, the happiness I enjoyed—and I did have moments of great happiness—everything seemed to have the look of 'here one day and gone the next.' I found that I could not believe in the permanence of the simplest relationship. The worst moments were when I found myself doubting that anything that had happened to me was real at all. It was as if I had been living a dream—as if I, the dreamer, were a dream, too. Does that sound strange to you, George?"

"No, not strange. Sad, yes, but rather refreshing, too."

"Why do you say that?"

He sipped his wine thoughtfully, and then gave her a long, searching look over the rim of his glass. "I suppose because Chiara is just the opposite. In spite of everything that has happened to her, she seems completely certain of what she wants in life and how she's going to get it. There's only one way to be happy—her way. There's only one way to be amused or content—the way to which she has been bred. Her marriage to Calitri shocked her dreadfully, but basically it didn't change her view of life. . . . I think in the end you may be more fortunate than she is."

"I wish I could believe that."

"I think you must. You may not be happy yet. You may never be truly secure. But you're more flexible, more ready to understand the thousand ways people live, and think, and suffer."

"I often wonder if that is a good thing—or whether it's just another illusion on my part. You know, I have the same dream over and over again. I talk to someone. He does not hear me. I reach out for someone. He does not even see me. I am waiting to meet someone. He walks right past me. I'm convinced that I don't exist at all."

"Take my word for it," said George Faber with a rueful smile. "You do exist, and I find you very disturbing."

"Why disturbing?"

Before he had time to answer, the bearded poet came and took his stand by their table, and declaimed a long rigmarole that sent the diners into roars of laughter. George Faber laughed, too, and handed him a bank note for reward. The poet added another couplet that raised another roar of laughter, then backed away, bowing like a courtier.

"What did he say, George? I missed most of the dialect."

"He said we weren't young enough to be single, but we weren't too old to look like lovers. He wondered if your husband knew what you were doing, and whether the baby would look like him or me. When I gave him the money, he said I was rich enough not to care, but if I wanted to keep you I'd better marry you in Mexico."

Ruth Lewin blushed. "A very uncomfortable poet, but I like him, George."

"I like him, too. I wish I could afford to be his patron."

They were silent awhile, listening to the clatter and the muted, melancholy music of the guitar. Then casually enough, Faber asked:

"What will you do with yourself during the summer?"

"I don't know. Just now I'm dreading it. In the end I'll probably take one of those CIT tours. They can be pretty dull, I know, but at least one isn't alone."

"You wouldn't think of joining me for a few days? Positano first, then Ischia."

She did not shrink away from the question, but faced it in her forthright fashion. "On what terms, George?"

"The same as tonight. No strings, no promises, no apologies."

"What about Chiara?"

He gave her a shrugging, uneasy answer. "I won't question what she does in Venice. I don't think she'll question me. Besides, what harm is there? I'll be working for Chiara. You and I are both grown-up. I'd like you to think about it."

She smiled and refused him gently. "I mustn't think about it, George. You're finding it hard enough to cope with the woman you have. I doubt you could handle me as well." She reached out and took his hand between her palms. "You have a rough fight ahead of you, but you can't win it if you split down the middle. I can't divide myself, either. . . . Please don't be angry with me. I know myself too well."

He was instantly penitent. "I'm sorry. I guess it sounded pretty crude, but I didn't mean it like that."

"I know you didn't, and if I try to tell you how grateful I am I'll cry. Now will you please take me home?"

Their driver was still waiting for them, patient and knowing, in the darkened alley. He roused his dozing horse and set him on the long way home: the Margherita Bridge, the Villa Borghese, the Quirinale piazza, and down past the Colosseum to the Street of St. Gregory. Ruth Lewin laid her head on Faber's shoulder and dozed fitfully while he listened to the clip-clop of the ancient nag and searched his troubled heart.

When they reached Ruth Lewin's apartment, he helped her alight and held her for a moment in the shadow of the doorway.

"May I come up for a little while?"

"If you want to."

She was too sleepy to protest, and too jealous of the little that was left of the evening. She made him coffee, and they sat together listening to music, each waiting for the other to break the dangerous spell. Impulsively George Faber took her in his arms and kissed her, and she clung to him in a long and passionate embrace. Then he held her away from him and pleaded without reserve:

"I want to stay with you, Ruth. Please, please let me stay."

"I want you to stay too, George. I want it more than anything in the world . . . But I'm going to send you home."

"Don't tease me, Ruth. You're not a girl like that. For God's sake, don't tease me."

All the needs of the years welled up in her and forced her toward surrender, but she drew away from him and pleaded in her turn. "Go home, George. I can't have you like this. I'm not strong enough for it. You'll wake in the morning and feel guilty about Chiara. You'll thank me and slip away. And because you feel disloyal I won't see you again. I do want to see you. I could be in love with you if I let myself, but I don't want half a heart and half a man. . . . Please, please go!"

He shook himself like a man waking out of a dream. "I will come back; you know that."

"I know it."

"You don't hate me?"

"How can I hate you? But I don't want you to hate yourself because of me."

"If it doesn't work out with Chiara—"

She closed his lips with a last light kiss. "Don't say it, George! You'll know soon enough. . . . Perhaps too soon for both of us."

She walked with him to the portico, watched him climb into the *carrozza*, and waited until the fading hoofbeats had died into the murmur of the city. Then she went to bed, and for the first time in months she slept dreamlessly.

In the Great Hall of the Gregorian University, Jean Télémond stood facing his audience.

His address lay before him on the rostrum, translated into impeccable Latin by a colleague of the Society. His back was straight. His hands were steady. His mind was clear. Now that the moment of crisis had come, he felt strangely calm, even elated by this final and resolute commitment of a lifetime's work to the risk of open judgment.

The whole authority of the Church was here, summed up in the person of the Pontiff, who sat, lean, dark, and oddly youthful, with the Father General on one side of him and Cardinal Leone on the other. The best minds of the Church were here: six Cardinals of the Curia; the theologians and philosophers, dressed in their diverse habits—Jesuits, Dominicans, Franciscans, and men of the ancient order of St. Benedict. The future of the Church was there—in the students with scrubbed and eager faces, who had been chosen from every country in the world to study at the seat of Christendom. The diversity of the Church was here, too, expressed in himself, the exile, the solitary seeker, the exotic who yet wore the black tunic of brotherhood and shared the ministry of the servants of the Word.

He waited a moment, gathering himself. Then he made the Sign of the Cross, delivered the opening allocution to the Pontiff and the Curia, and began his address:

"It has taken a journey of twenty years to bring me to this place. I must therefore beg your patience while I explain myself and the motives which prompted this long and often painful pilgrimage. I am a man and a priest. I became a priest because I believed that the primary and the only perfectly sustaining relationship was that between the Creator and the creature, and because I wished to affirm this relationship in a special fashion by a life of service. But I have never ceased to be a man, and as a man I have found myself committed, without recourse, to the world in which I live.

"My deepest conviction as a man—confirmed by all my experience—is that I am one person. I who think, I who feel, I who fear, I who know and believe, am a unity. But this unity of my self is part of a greater unity. I am separate from the world, but I belong to it because I have grown out of its growth just as the world has grown out of the unity of God as the issue of a single creative act.

"I, therefore, the one, am destined to participate in the oneness of the world, as I am destined to participate in the oneness of God. I cannot set myself in isolation from Creation any more than I can, without destroying myself, set myself in isolation from the Creator.

"From the moment that this conviction became clear to me, another followed it by inevitable consequence. If God is one, and the world is one issue of His eternal act, and I am a single person spawned out of this complex unity, then all knowledge—of my self, of Creation, of the Creator—is one knowledge. That I do not have all knowledge, that it presents itself to me by fragments and in diversity, means nothing except that I am finite, limited by time and space and the capacity of my brain.

"Every discovery I make points in the same direction. No matter how contradictory the fragments of knowledge may appear, they can never truly contradict one another. I have spent a lifetime in one small branch of science, paleontology. But I am committed to all sciences, to biology, to physics, to the chemistry of inorganic matter, to philosophy, and to theology, because all are branches of the same tree and the tree grows upwards toward the same sun. Never, therefore, can we risk too much or dare too boldly in the search for knowledge, since every step forward is a step toward unity—of man with man, of men with the universe, of the universe with God. . . ."

He glanced up, trying to read in the faces of his audience a reaction to his words. But there was nothing to read. They wanted to hear his whole case before they committed themselves to a verdict. He turned back to the typescript and read on.

"Today I want to share with you a part of the journey which I have made for the past twenty years. Before we begin it, however, there are two things I want to say. The first is this: An exploration is a very special kind of journey. You do not make it like a trip from Rome to Paris. You must never demand to arrive on time and with all your baggage intact. You walk slowly, with open eyes and open minds. When the mountains are too high to climb, you march around them and try to measure them from the lowlands. When the jungle is thick, you have to cut your way through it, and not resent too much the labor or the frustration.

"The second thing is this: When you come to record the journey, the new contours, the new plants, the strangeness and the mystery, you find often that your vocabulary is inadequate. Inevitably your narrative will fall far short of the reality. If you find this defect in my record, then I beg you to tolerate it and let it not discourage you from contemplation of strange landscapes which, nevertheless, bear the imprint of the creative finger of God.

"Now to begin . . ."

He paused, twitched his cassock over his thin shoulders, and lifted his lined face to them in a kind of challenge.

"I want you to come with me, not as theologians or philosophers, but as scientists—men whose knowing begins with seeing. What I want you to see is man: a special kind of being who exists in a visible ambience at a determinable point in time and space.

"Let us look at him in space first. The universe which he inhabits is immense, galactic. It stretches beyond moon and sun into an enormity of dimension which our mathematics can express only by an indefinite extension of zeros.

"Look at man in time. He exists now at this moment, but his past goes back to a point where we lose him in a mist. His future prolongs itself beyond our conception of any possible circumstance.

"Look at man by numbers, and you find yourself trying to count the grains of sand on a shore line without limit.

"Look at him by scale and proportion, and you find him on the one hand a minuscule dwarf, in a universe without apparent limits. Measure him by another scale, and you find him in partial control of the enormity in which he lives. . . ."

The most skeptical of his hearers—and there were many in the audience who were disposed to be dubious of him —found themselves being caught up and carried along by the strong current of his eloquence. The passion of his conviction expressed itself in every line of his weathered face, in every gesture of his thin, expressive hands.

Rudolf Semmering, the grim, soldierly man, found himself nodding approval of the noble temper of his subject. Cardinal Rinaldi smiled his thin, ironic smile and wondered what the pedants would make of this valiant intruder into their private domain. Even Leone, the harsh old watchdog of the Faith, leaned his craggy chin on his hand and registered a reluctant tribute to the unflinching courage of this suspect spirit.

In Kiril the Pontiff the conviction grew, swift as a conjuror's mango plant, that this was the man he wanted: a man totally committed to the risk of living and knowing, yet anchored firm as a sea-battered rock to belief in a divinely planned unity. The waves might tear at him, the winds might score his spirit, but he would stand unshaken and unshakable under the assault. He found himself murmuring a message to sustain him. "Go on! Don't be afraid. Your heart is right, and it beats in time with mine. No matter that the words stumble and the record falters. The vision is clear, the will points straight and true toward the Center. Go on! . . ."

Télémond was in full course now, expounding to them his view of matter—the material of the universe, which expressed itself in so many different appearances, and finally in the appearance of man.

". . . 'God made man of the dust of the earth'! The

Biblical image expresses aptly the most primitive conviction of man—a conviction confirmed by the most advanced scientific experiment—that the stuff of which he is formed is capable of indefinite scaling down to particles infinitely small. . . . At a certain point of this scaling down man's vision of himself becomes blurred. He needs spectacles, then a microscope, then a whole array of instrumentation to supplement his failing sight. For a moment he is lost in diversity—molecules, atoms, electrons, neutrons, protons . . . so many and so different! Then suddenly they all come together again. The universe, from the farthest nebulae to the simplest atomic structure, is a whole, a system, a quantum of energy—in other words, a unity. But—and I must ask you to lean and linger and think upon this most important 'but'—this universe is not a static whole, it is in a constant state of change and transformation. It is in a state of genesis . . . a state of becoming, a state of evolving. And this is the question which I ask you to face with me now. The universe is evolving and man is evolving with it—into what? . . ."

They were with him now. Critics or captives of the idea, they were with him. He could see them leaning forward in their benches, intent on every phrase and every inflection. He could feel their interest projected toward him like a wave. He gathered himself once again and began to sketch, with swift, decisive strokes, the picture of a cosmos in motion, rearranging itself, diversifying itself, preparing itself for the coming of life, for the coming of consciousness, for the arrival of the first subhuman species, and the ultimate arrival of man.

He was on his own ground now, and he marched them forward with him, out of the misty backward of a crystallizing world to the moment when the change from life to non-life took place, when the megamolecule became the micro-organism and the first biotic forms appeared on the planet.

He showed them how the primitive life forms spread themselves in a vast network around the surface of the spinning globe; how they joined and disjoined into a multitude of combinations; how some conjunctions were swiftly suppressed because they were too specially adapted to a time and a condition of the evolutionary march; how others survived by changing themselves, by becoming more complex in order to guarantee their own endurance.

He showed them the first outlines of a fundamental law of nature—the too specialized life form was the first to perish. Change was the price of survival.

He did not shrink from the consequences of his thought. He took his audience by the scruff of their necks and forced them to face the consequences with him.

". . . Even so early in the evolutionary chain we are faced with the brutal fact of biological competition. The struggle for life is endless. It is always accompanied by death and destruction, and violence of one kind or another. . . . You will ask yourselves, as I have asked myself a thousand times, whether this struggle necessarily transfers itself, at a later stage of history, into the domain of man. At first blush the answer is yes. But I object to so crude and total an application of the biological pattern. Man does not live now on the same level upon which he lived when he first made his appearance on the planet. He has passed through successive levels of existence; and it is my belief, supported by considerable evidence, that man's evolution is marked by an effort to find other, less brutal, and less destructive modes of competition for life. . . ."

He leaned forward over the rostrum and challenged them with the thought that he knew was already in their minds.

"You ask me why I do not invoke at this moment a divine intervention in the pattern of human evolvement. It is because we must continue to walk along the exploratory path which we have set ourselves. We are limiting ourselves only to what we see. And all we are seeing at this moment is man emerging as a phenomenon in a changing universe. If we are troubled by what we see, we must bear the trouble and not seek too easy an answer for it. I make this point although man has not yet appeared to our exploring eyes. We have leapt forward to meet him. Now we must go back."

He could almost feel their tension relax. He stole a swift glance at the front row of the audience. Leone was shaking his white head and making a whispered comment to a Cardinal on his left. Rinaldi was smiling, and he lifted one hand in an almost imperceptible gesture of encouragement. Kiril the Pontiff sat erect in his chair, his scarred face immobile, his dark eyes bright with interest.

Gently now Télémond led them back to the main stream of his story. He showed them the primitive life forms reproducing themselves, multiplying, joining and rejoining, groping ingeniously but indifferently toward stability and permanence. He drew for them the tree of life and showed how it branched and yet grew upwards; how certain twigs died and fell off; how certain branches ceased to grow; but how, always, the main thrust of growth was upwards in the direction of the large brain and the complex organism, and the most flexible mechan-

ism of survival. He showed them the first subhuman species—the hominoid, which was the prelude to the human
—and finally he showed them man.

Then, brusquely, he presented them with a puzzle.

". . . From where we stand now, we see a continuity
and a unity in the evolutionary process. But if we look
closely, we see that the line of advance is not always a
firm and a definite stroke. It is dotted in places, or broken.
We cannot say where, in point of time, life began. Yet
we know that it did begin. We know that the pterodactyl
existed. We have dug his bones out of the earth. But
where and by what mutations he came to be is not wholly
clear to us. We see him first as plural . . . many ptero-
dactyls. But was there a first couple or were they always
many? We do not know. . . . So, with man, when we
first find him on the earth, he is many. Speaking as scientists, we have no record of the emergence of man as a single couple. In the historic record written in primal clay,
men are suddenly present. I do not say that they came
suddenly, any more than that the pterodactyl came suddenly. All the evidence points to a slow emergence of the
species, but at a certain point in history man is there, and
with man something else is there as well. . . . Consciousness. . . . Man is a very special phenomenon. He is a being who knows, he is also a being who knows that he
knows. We have come, you see, to a very particular
point of history. A creature exists who knows that he
knows. . . .

"Now, my friends, I want you to address yourself to my
next question only as scientists, only as witnesses of the
visible evidence. How did this special phenomenon
emerge?

"Let us step back from him a moment. Let us consider

all those phenomena which preceded him, many of which still co-exist with him, from the micro-organism to the hominoid ape. All of them have something in common—a drive, a groping, an urge to fit themselves for survival. To use an overworked and imprecise term, it is an instinct to do those things, to enter into those combinations and those associations which will enable them to proceed along their proper line of continuity. I prefer to choose another word than *instinct*. I prefer to say that this drive, or this capacity, is a primitive but evolving form of what culminates in man. . . . Consciousness. . . ."

Once again he had brought them to a crisis, and he knew it. For the first time, he felt really inadequate to display to them the whole range and subtlety of the thought. Time was against him, and the simple semantic limitation and the rhetorical power to persuade them into a new but still harmonious view of the nature and origin of humankind. Still, he went on resolutely, developing for them his own view of the cosmic pattern—primal energy, primitive life, primitive consciousness, all evolving and converging to the first focal point of history, thinking man. He took them further yet, by a bold leap into their own territory, showing all the lines of human development coverging to a final unity, a unity of man with his Creator.

More vividly than ever before he could feel the mood of his audience shifting. Some were in awe, some were dubious, some had settled themselves into complete hostility to his thought.

Yet when he came to his peroration, he knew that he had done the best he could and that for all its sometime vagueness, and sometime risky speculation, his address had been the true reflection of his own intellectual position. There was nothing more he could do but commit himself to judgment and rest courageous in the outcome. Humbly, but with deep emotion, he summed it up for them.

"I do not ask you to agree with me. I do not put any of my present conclusions beyond reconsideration or new development, but of this I am totally convinced: the first creative act of God was directed toward fulfillment, and not destruction. If the universe is not centered on man, if man as the center of the universe is not centered on the Creator, then the cosmos is a meaningless blasphemy. The day is not far distant when men will understand that even in biological terms they have only one choice: suicide or an act of worship."

His hands trembled and his voice shook as he read them the words of Paul to the Colossians:

" 'In Him all created things took their being, heavenly and earthly, visible and invisible. . . . They were all created through Him and in Him; He takes precedence of all, and in Him all subsist. . . . It was God's good pleasure to let all completeness dwell in Him, and through Him to win back all things, whether on earth or in Heaven, unto union with Himself, making peace with them through His blood, shed on the Cross.' "

He did not hear the thunder of applause as he stepped down from the pulpit. As he knelt to pay his respects to the Pontiff and lay the text of his address in his hands, he heard only the words of the blessing and the invitation— or was it a command?—that followed:

"You're a bold man, Jean Télémond. Time will tell whether you are right or wrong, but at this moment I need you. We all need you."

Extract from
the Secret Memorials of
K I R I L I, Pont. Max.

. . . Yesterday I met a whole man. It is a rare experience, but always an illuminating and ennobling one. It costs so much to be a full human being that there are very few who have the enlightenment, or the courage, to pay the price. . . . One has to abandon altogether the search for security, and reach out to the risk of living with both arms. One has to embrace the world like a lover, and yet demand no easy return of love. One has to accept pain as a condition of existence. One has to court doubt and darkness as the cost of knowing. One needs a will stubborn in conflict, but apt always to the total acceptance of every consequence of living and dying.

This is how I read Jean Télémond. This is why I have decided to draw him to me, to ask for his friendship, to use him as best I know in the work of the Church. . . . Leone is uneasy about him. He has said so very bluntly.

He points, quite rightly, to ambiguities and obscurities in his system of thought, to what he calls a dangerous rashness in certain of his speculations. He demands another full examination of all his writings by the Holy Office before he is permitted to teach publicly or to publish his research.

I do not disagree with Leone. I am not so bold that I am prepared to gamble with the Deposit of Faith, which is, after all, the testament of Christ's new covenant with man. To preserve it intact is the whole meaning of my office. This is the task which has been delegated to Leone in the Church. . . .

On the other hand, I am not afraid of Jean Télémond. A man so centered upon God, who has accepted twenty years of silence, has already accepted every risk, even the risk that he can be mistaken. Today he said so in as many words, and I believe him. . . . I am not afraid of his work, either; I do not have the equipment or the time to judge truly of its ultimate value. This is why I have counsellors and experts learned in science, theology, and philosophy to assist me. . . .

I am convinced, moreover, that honest error is a step toward a greater illumination of the truth, since it exposes to debate and to clearer definition those matters which might otherwise remain obscure and undefined in the teaching of the Church. In a very special sense the Church, too, is evolving toward a greater fullness of understanding, a deeper consciousness of the divine life within itself.

The Church is a family. Like every family, it has its homebodies and its adventurers. It has its critics and its conformists; those who are jealous of its least important traditions; those who wish to thrust it forward, a bright lamp into a glorious future. Of all them I am the common Father. . . . When the adventurers come back scarred and travel-worn from a new frontier, from another foray, successful or unsuccessful, against the walls of ignorance, I must receive them with the charity of Christ and protect them with gentleness against those who have fared better only because they have dared much less. I have asked the Father General of the Jesuits to send Jean Télémond to keep me company at Castel Gandolfo during summer. I hope and pray that we may learn to be friends. He could enrich me, I think. I, for my part, may be able to offer him courage and a respite from his long and lonely pilgrimage. . . .

In an odd fashion he has given me courage as well. For some time now I have been engaged in a running debate with the Cardinal Secretary of the Congregation of Rites on the question of introducing the vernacular liturgy and a vernacular system of teaching into the seminaries and churches of missionary countries. This would mean inevitably a decline of the Latin liturgical language in many areas of the world. It would mean also an immense task of translation and annotation, so that the works of the Fathers of the Church would be made available to clerical students in their own language.

The Congregation of Rites takes the view that the merits of the change are far outweighed by its disadvantages. They point out that it would run counter to the decisions of the Council of Trent, and to the pronouncements of later Councils and later Pontiffs. They claim that the stability and uniformity of our organization depends much on the use of a common official tongue in the definition of doctrine, the training of teachers, and the celebration of the liturgy.

I myself take the view that our first duty is to preach the Word of God and to dispense the grace of the Sacraments, and that anything which stands in the way of this mission should be swept aside.

I know, however, that the situation is not quite so simple. There is, for example, a curious division of opinion in the small Christian community in Japan. The Japanese bishops want the Latin system preserved. Because of their unique and isolated position they are inclined to be timorous about any change at all. On the other hand, missionary priests working in the country report that work is handicapped when the vernacular is not used.

In Africa the native Cardinal Ragambwe is very clear that he wants to try the vernacular system. He is very aware of the risks and the problems, but he still feels that a trial should be made. He is a holy and enlightened man, and I have great respect for his opinion.

Ultimately the decision rests with me, but I have deferred it because I have been so vividly aware of the complexity of the problem and of the historic danger that small and isolated groups of Christians may, for lack of a common communication, be separated from the daily developing life of the Church. We are not building only for today, but for tomorrow and for eternity.

However, listening to Jean Télémond, I felt myself encouraged to make a decisive step. I have decided to write to those bishops who want to introduce the vernacular system and ask them to propose to me a definite plan for its use. If their plans seem workable, and if at the same time a certain select number of the clergy can be trained in the traditional mode, I am disposed to let the new system be tried. . . . I expect strong opposition from the Congregation of Rites, and from many bishops in the

Church, but a move must be made to break the deadlock which inhibits our apostolic work, so that the Faith may begin to grow with more freedom in emerging nations.

They are all jealous of their new identity, and they must be led to see that they can grow in, and with, the Faith toward a legitimate social and economic betterment. We are not yet one world, and we shall not be for a long time, but God is one, and the Gospel is one, and it should be spoken in every tongue under Heaven. . . . This was the mode of the primitive Church. This was the vision which Télémond renewed for me: the unity of the spirit in the bond of faith in the diversity of all knowledge and all tongues. . . .

Today I held the last series of audiences before the summer holidays. Among those whom I received privately was a certain Corrado Calitri, Minister of the Republic. I had already received most of the Italian Cabinet, but I had never met this man. The circumstance was sufficiently unusual for me to comment on it to the Maestro di Camera.

He told me that Calitri was a man of unusual talent, who had had a meteoric rise in the Christian Democratic Party. There was even talk that he might lead the country after the next elections.

He told me also that Calitri's private life had been somewhat notorious for a long time, and that he was involved in a marital case presently under consideration by the Holy Roman Rota. Now, however, it seemed that Calitri was making serious efforts to reform himself and that he had put himself and his spiritual affairs into the hands of a confessor.

There was, of course, no discussion of these matters between myself and Calitri. An audience is an affair of State and has nothing to do with the spiritual relationship of Pastor and people.

Nonetheless, I was curious about the man, and I was tempted for a moment to call for the file on his case. In the end I decided against it. If he comes to power, we shall have diplomatic connections, and it is better that it should not be complicated by a private knowledge on my part. It is better, too, that I do not interfere too minutely in the varied functions of the tribunals and the congregations. My time is very limited. My energies are limited, too, and presently they are so depleted that I shall be glad to pack and go from this place, into the comparative serenity of the countryside.

I see very clearly the shape of a great personal problem for every man who holds this office: how the press of business and the demands of so many people can so impoverish him that he has neither time nor will left to regulate the affairs of his own soul. I long for solitude and the leisure for contemplation. . . . "Consider the lilies of the field . . . they labor not, neither do they spin"! Lucky the ones who have time to smell the flowers and doze at noonday under the orange trees . . . !

VIII

GEORGE FABER left Rome early on a Saturday morning. He headed out through the Lateran Gate and down the new Appian Way toward the southern autostrada. He had a five-hour drive ahead of him, Terracina, Formia, Naples, and then out along the winding peninsular road to Castellammare, Sorrento, Amalfi, and Positano. He was in no hurry. The morning air was still fresh, and the traffic was heavy, and he had no intention of risking his neck as well as his reputation.

At Terracina he was hailed by a pair of English girls who were hitchhiking down the coast. For an hour he was glad of their company, but by the time they reached Naples he was happy to be rid of them. Their cheerful certainty about the world and all its ways made him feel like a grandfather.

The heat of the day was upon him now—a dry, dusty oppression which made the air dance and filled the nostrils with the ammoniac stink of a crowded and ancient city. He turned onto the Via Caracciolo and sat for a while in a waterfront café, sipping iced coffee and pondering the moves he should make when he reached Positano. He had two people to see: Sylvio Pellico, artist; and Theo Respighi, sometime actor—both of them, according to the record, unhappy associates of Corrado Calitri.

For weeks now he had been puzzling over the best method to approach them. He had lived long enough in Italy to know the Italian love of drama and intrigue. But his Nordic temper revolted against the spectacle of an American correspondent playing a Latin detective in raincoat and black fedora. Finally he had decided on a simple, blunt approach:

"I understand you knew Corrado Calitri. . . . I'm in love with his wife. I want to marry her. I think you can give me some evidence against him. I'm prepared to pay well for it. . . ."

For a long time he had refused to reason beyond this point. Yet now, three hours from Rome, and a long way further from Chiara, he was prepared to come to grips with the *if*. If all failed, he would have proved himself to himself. He would have proved to Chiara that he was prepared to risk his career for her sake. He would be able to demand a two-way traffic in love. If that failed, too . . . ? At long last he was beginning to believe that he would survive it. The best cure for love was to cool it down a little and leave a man free to measure woman against woman, the torment of a one-sided loving against the bleak peace of no loving at all.

One could not bounce a middle-aged heart, like a rubber ball, from one affair to another; but there was a crumb of comfort in the thought of Ruth Lewin and her refusal to commit his heart or her own to a new affliction without any promise of security.

She was wiser than Chiara. He knew that. She had been tested further and survived better. But *love* was a rainbow word that might or might not point to a crock of gold. He paid for his drink, stepped out into the raw sunshine, and began the last leg of his journey into uncertainty.

The Bay of Naples was a flat and oily mirror, broken only by the wake of the pleasure steamers and the spume of the *aliscafi*, which bounced their loads of tourists at fifty miles an hour toward the siren islands of Capri and Ischia. The summit of Vesuvius was vague in a mist of heat and dust. The painted stucco of the village houses was peeling in the sun. The gray tufa soil of the farm plots was parched, and the peasants plodded up and down the rows of tomato plants like figures in a medieval landscape. There was a smell of dust and dung, and rotting tomatoes and fresh oranges. Horns bleated at every curve, wooden carts rolled noisily over cobblestones. Snatches of music swept by, mixed with the shouts of children and the occasional curse of a farmer caught in the press of summer traffic.

George Faber found himself driving fast and free, and chanting a tuneless song. On the steep spiral of the Amalfi drive he was nearly forced off the road by a careering sports car, and he cursed loud and cheerfully in Roman dialect. By the time he reached Positano, the shabby, spectacular little town that ran in a steep escalade from the water to the hilltop, he was his own man, and the experience was as heady as the raw wine of the Sorrentine mountains.

He lodged his car in a garage, hefted his bag, and strolled down a steep, narrow alley to the city square. Half an hour later, bathed and changed into cotton slacks and a striped sailor shirt, he was sitting under an awning, drinking a Carpano, and preparing for his encounter with Sylvio Pellico.

The artist's gallery was a long, cool tunnel that ran from the street into a courtyard littered with junk and fragments of old marbles. His pictures were hung along the walls of the tunnel—gaudy abstracts, a few portraits in the manner of Modigliani, and a scattering of catch-penny landscapes to inveigle the sentimental tourist. It was easy to see why Corrado Calitri had dropped him so quickly. It was less easy to see why he had taken him up in the first place.

He was a tall, narrow-faced youth with a straggly beard, dressed in cotton sweatshirt, faded blue denims, and shoes of scuffed canvas. He was propped between two chairs at the entrance to the tunnel, dozing in the sun, with a straw hat tipped over his eyes.

When George Faber stopped to examine the pictures, he came to life immediately and presented himself and his work with a flourish. "Sylvio Pellico, sir, at your service. My pictures please you? Some of them have already been exhibited in Rome."

"I know," said George Faber. "I was at the show."

"Ah! Then you're a connoisseur. I will not try to tempt you with this rubbish!" He dismissed the landscapes with a wave of his skinny hand. "Those aren't important. They're just eating money."

"I know, I know. We all have to eat. Are you having a good season?"

"Eh! . . . You know how it goes. Everyone looks, nobody wants to buy. Yesterday I sold two little pieces to an American woman. The day before, nothing. The day before that—" He broke off and cocked a huckster's eye at George Faber. "You are not an Italian, signore?"

"No. I'm an American."

"But you speak beautiful Italian."

"Thank you. . . . Tell me, who sponsored your exhibition in Rome?"

"A very eminent man. A Minister of the Republic. A very good critic, too. Perhaps you've heard of him. His name is Calitri."

"I've heard of him," said George Faber. "I'd like to talk to you about him."

"Why?" He leaned his shaggy head on one side like an amiable parrot. "Did he send you to see me?"

"No. It's a private matter. I thought you might be able to help me. I'd be happy to pay for your help. Does that interest you?"

"Who isn't interested in money? Sit down, let me get you a cup of coffee."

"No coffee. This won't take long."

Pellico dusted off one of the chairs, and they sat facing each other under the narrow archway.

Crisply Faber explained himself and his mission, and then laid down his offer. ". . . Five hundred dollars, American money, for a sworn statement about Calitri's marriage, written in the terms I shall dictate to you."

He sat back in his chair, lit a cigarette, and waited while the artist cupped his brown face in his hands and thought for a long time. Then he lifted his head and said, "I'd appreciate an American cigarette."

Faber handed him the pack, and then leaned forward with a light.

Pellico smoked for a few moments, and then began to talk. "I am a poor man, sir. Also, I am not a very good painter, so I am likely to remain poor for a long time. For one like me five hundred dollars is a fortune, but I am afraid I cannot do what you ask."

"Why not?"

"Several reasons."

"Are you afraid of Calitri?"

"A little. You've lived in this country, you know the way things run. When one is poor, one is always a little outside the law and it never pays to tangle with important people. But that's not the only reason."

"Name me another."

His thin face wrinkled, and his head seemed to shrink lower between his shoulders. He explained himself with an odd simplicity. "I know what this means to you, sir. When a man is in love, eh! . . . It is ice in the heart and fire in the gut. . . . One loses for a while all pride. When one is out of love, the pride comes back. Often it is the only thing left. . . . I am not like you. . . . I am, if you want, more like Calitri. He was kind to me once. . . . I was very fond of him. I do not think I could betray him for money."

"He betrayed you, didn't he? He gave you one exhibition and then dropped you."

"No!" The thin hands became suddenly eloquent. "No. You must not read it like that. On the contrary, he was very honest with me. He said every man has the right to one trial of his talent. If the talent was not there, he had best forget it. . . . Well, he gave me the trial. I failed. I do not blame him for that."

"How much would you charge to blame him? A thousand dollars?"

Pellico stood up and dusted off his hands. For all his shabbiness, he seemed clothed in a curious kind of dignity. He pointed at the gray walls of the tunnel. "For twenty dollars, sir, you can buy my visions. They are not great visions, I know. They are the best I have. Myself I do not sell. Not for a thousand dollars, not for ten thousand. I am sorry."

As he walked away down the cobbled street, George Faber, the Nordic puritan, had the grace to be ashamed of himself. His face was burning, his palms were sweating. He felt a swift, unreasonable resentment toward Chiara, sunning herself in Venice, five hundred miles away. He turned in to a bar, ordered a double whisky, and began to read through the dossier of his next contact, Theo Respighi.

He was an Italo-American, born in Naples and transported to New York in his childhood. He was a middling-bad actor who had played small parts in television, small parts in Hollywood, and then returned to Italy to play small parts in Biblical epics and pseudo-classic nonsense. In Hollywood there had been minor scandals—drunken driving, a couple of divorces, a brief and turbulent romance with a rising star. In Rome he had joined the roistering bunch who kept themselves alive on hope and runaway productions and the patronage of Roman playboys. All in all, Faber summed him up as a seedy character who should be very amenable to the rustle of a dollar bill.

He ran Respighi to earth that same evening in a cliff-side bar, where he was drinking with three very gay boys and a faded Frenchwoman who spoke Italian with a Genoese accent. It took an hour to prise him away from the company, and another to sober him up with dinner and black coffee. Even when he had done it, he was left with a hollow, muscular hulk who, when he was not combing his long blond hair, was reaching nervously for the brandy

bottle. Faber stifled the wavering voice of his own conscience and once again displayed his proposition:

". . . A thousand dollars for a signed statement. No
strings, no problems. Everything that goes before the Roman Rota is kept secret. No one, least of all Calitri, will
ever know who gave the testimony."

"Balls!" said the blond one flatly. "Don't try to con me,
Faber. There's no such thing as a secret in Rome. I don't
care whether it's in the Church or Cinecittà. Sooner or
later Calitri has to know. What happens to me then?"

"You're a thousand dollars richer, and he can't touch
you."

"You think so? Look, lover boy, you know how films are
made in this country. The money comes from everywhere.
The list of angels stretches from Napoli to Milano, and
back again. There's a black list here, too, just like in Hollywood. You get on it, you're dead. For a thousand crummy
bucks, I don't want to be dead."

"You haven't earned that much in six months," Faber
told him. "I know, I checked up."

"So what? That's the way the cookie crumbles in this
business. You starve for a while, and then you eat, and eat
good. I want to go on eating. Now if you were to make it
ten thousand, I might begin to think about it. With that
much I could get myself back Stateside and wait long
enough to get a decent start again. . . . Come on, lover!
What are you playing for? The big romance or a bag of
popcorn?"

"Two thousand," said George Faber.

"No deal."

"It's the best I can do."

"Peanuts! I can get that much by lifting a phone and

telling Calitri that you're gunning for him. . . . Tell you
what. Give me a thousand, and I won't make the call."

"Go to hell." He pushed back his chair and walked out.
The laughter of the blond one followed him like a
mockery into the darkened street.

"The longer I live," said Jean Télémond musingly, "the
more clearly I understand the deep vein of pessimism that
runs through so much of modern thought, even the thought
of many in the Church. . . . Birth, growth, and decay.
The cyclic pattern of life is so vividly apparent that it
obscures the pattern that underlies it, the pattern of constant growth, and—let me say it bluntly—the pattern of
human progress. For many people the wheel of life simply
turns on its own axis; it does not seem to be going anywhere."

"And you, Jean, believe it is going somewhere?"

"More than that, Holiness. I believe it must go somewhere."

They had taken off their cassocks, and they were sitting,
relaxed, in the shade of a small copse, with a bank of
wild strawberries at their backs, and in front the flat,
bright water of Lake Nemi. Jean Télémond was sucking
contentedly on his pipe, and Kiril was tossing pebbles into
the water. The air vibrated with the strident cry of cicadas, and little brown lizards sunned themselves on rock
and tree trunk.

They had long since surrendered themselves to bucolic
ease and the comfort of each other's company. In the
mornings they worked privately—Kiril at his desk, keeping
track of the daily dispatches from Rome; Télémond in the
garden, setting his papers in order for the scrutiny of
the Holy Office. In the afternoons they drove out into the

country, Télémond at the wheel, exploring the valleys and the uplands and the tiny towns that had clung to the ridges for five hundred years and more. In the evenings they dined together, then read or talked or played cards until it was time for Compline and the last prayer of the day.

It was a good time for both: for Kiril, a respite from the burden of office; for Télémond, a true return from exile into the companionship of an understanding and truly loving spirit. He did not have to measure his words. He felt no risk in exposing his deepest thoughts. Kiril, for his part, confided himself fully to the Jesuit, and found a peculiar solace in this sharing of his private burden.

He tossed another pebble into the water and watched the ripples fan out toward the farther shore until they were lost in the shimmer of sunlight. Then he asked another question:

"Have you never been a pessimist yourself, Jean? Have you never felt caught up in this endless turning of the wheel of life?"

"Sometimes, Holiness. When I was in China, for instance, far to the northwest, in the barren valley of the great rivers. There were monasteries up there. Enormous places that could have been built only by great men—men with a great vision—to challenge the emptiness in which they lived. . . . In one fashion or another, I thought, God must have been with them. Yet when I went in and saw the men who live there now—dull, uninspired, almost dolt-ish at times—I was afflicted by melancholy. . . . When I came back to the West and read the newspapers and talked with my brother scientists, I was staggered by the blindness with which we seem to be courting our own de-struction. Sometimes it seemed impossible to believe that man was really growing out of the slime toward a divine destiny. . . ."

Kiril nodded thoughtfully. He picked up a stick and teased a sleeping lizard, so that it skitted away into the leaves. "I know the feeling, Jean. I have it sometimes even in the Church. I wait and pray for the great movement, the great man, who will startle us into life again. . . ."

Jean Télémond said nothing. He drew placidly on his pipe, waiting for the Pontiff to finish the thought.

". . . A man like St. Francis of Assisi, for instance. What does he really mean? . . . A complete break with the pattern of history. . . . A man born out of due time. A sudden, unexplained revival of the primitive spirit of Christianity. The work he began still continues. . . . But it is not the same. The revolution is over. The revolutionaries have become conformists. The little brothers of the Little Poor Man are rattling alms boxes in the railway square or dealing in real estate to the profit of the order." He laughed quietly. "Of course, that isn't the whole story. They teach, they preach, they do the work of God as best they know, but it is no longer a revolution, and I think we need one now."

"Perhaps," said Jean Télémond with a twinkle in his shrewd eyes, "perhaps your Holiness will be the revolutionary."

"I have thought about it, Jean. Believe me, I have thought about it. But I do not think even you can understand how limited I am by the very machinery which I inherit, by the historic attitudes by which I am enclosed. It is hard for me to work directly. I have to find instruments apt to my hand. I am young enough, yes, to see big changes made in my lifetime. But there will have to be others to make them for me. . . . You, for instance."

"I, Holiness?" Télémond turned a startled face to the Pontiff. "My field of action is more limited than yours."

"I wonder if it is?" asked Kiril quizzically. "Have you ever thought that the Russian Revolution, the present might of Soviet Russia, was built on the work of Karl Marx, who spent a large part of his life in the British Museum and is now buried in England? The most explosive thing in the world is an idea."

Jean Télémond laughed and tapped out his pipe on a tree bole. "Doesn't that rather depend on the Holy Office? I have still to pass their scrutiny."

Kiril gave him a long, sober look, then quizzed him again. "If you fail to pass, Jean, what will you do then?"

Télémond shrugged. "Re-examine, I suppose. I hope I shall have the energy to do it."

"Why do you say that?"

"Partly because I am afraid, partly because . . . because I am not a well man. I have lived roughly for a long time. I am told my heart is not as good as it should be."

"I'm sorry to hear that, Jean. You must take care of yourself. I shall make it my business to see that you do."

"May I ask you a question, Holiness?"

"Of course."

"You have honored me with your friendship. In the eyes of many—though not in mine—it will seem that you have given your patronage to my work. What will you do if it is found wanting by the Holy Office?"

To his surprise, Kiril threw back his head and laughed heartily. "Jean, Jean. There speaks the true Jesuit. What will I do? I shall always be your friend, and I shall pray that you have health and courage to continue your studies."

"But if I should die before they are done?"

"Does that worry you?"

"Sometimes. . . . Believe me, Holiness, whatever the outcome, I have tried to prepare myself for it. But I am convinced that there is a truth in my researches. . . . I do not want to see it lost or suppressed."

"It will not be suppressed, Jean. I promise you that."

"Forgive me, Holiness. I have said more than I should."

"Why should you apologize, Jean? You have shown me your heart. For a lonely man like me that's a privilege. . . . Courage now. Who knows? We may see you a Doctor of the Church yet. Now if it will not offend your Jesuit's eyes, the Pope of Rome is going for a swim."

When Kiril stripped off his shirt and made ready for the plunge, Jean Télémond saw the marks of the whip on his back, and he was ashamed of his own cowardice.

Two days later a courier from Washington delivered to the Pontiff a private letter from the President of the United States:

. . . I read with lively interest your Holiness' letter and the copies of the two letters from the Premier of the U.S.S.R. which were handed to me by His Eminence Cardinal Carlin. I agree that we shall need to preserve the most rigid secrecy about this whole situation.

Let me say first that I am deeply grateful for the information which you give me about your private association with Kamenev, and your views on his character and his intention. I was also deeply impressed by the frank disagreement of Cardinal Carlin. I know that he would not have spoken so freely without the permission of your Holiness, and I am encouraged to be equally frank with you.

I have to say that I am very dubious about the value of private conversations at this level. On the other hand, I am happy to pursue them so long as there seems the slightest hope of avoiding the explosive crisis which now seems inevitable in the next six or twelve months.

The problem as I see it is both simple and complex. Kamenev has expressed it very well. We are caught in the current of history. We can tack across it, but we cannot change the direction of the flow. The only thing that can do that is an action of such magnitude and such risk that none of us would be allowed to attempt it.

I could not, for example, commit my country to one-sided disarmament. I could not abandon our claims for a re-unification of Germany. I should very much like to be quit of Quemoy and Matsu, but we cannot relinquish them without a serious loss of face and influence in Southeast Asia. I can understand that Kamenev is afraid of the Chinese, yet he cannot abandon an alliance—even a troublesome and dangerous one—which guarantees a solid Communist bloc from East Germany to the Kuriles.

The most we can hope for is to keep the situation elastic, to give ourselves a breathing space for negotiation and historic evolution. We must avoid at all costs a head-on clash, which will inevitably cause a cataclysmic atomic war.

If a secret correspondence with Kamenev will help at all, I am prepared to risk it, and I am very happy to accept your Holiness as the intermediary. You may communicate my thoughts to Kamenev and make known to him the contents of this letter. He knows that I cannot move alone, just as he cannot. We both live under the shadow of the same risk.

I do not belong to your Holiness' faith, but I commend myself to your prayers and the prayers of all Christendom. We carry the fate of the world on our shoulders, and if God does not support us, then we must inevitably break under the burden. . . .

When he had read the letter, Kiril breathed a sigh of relief. It was no more than he had hoped for, but no less, either. The storm clouds were still piled, massive and threatening, over the world, but there was a tiny break in them and one could begin to guess at the sunlight. The problem was now to enlarge the break, and he asked himself how best he might co-operate in doing it.

Of one thing he was certain: it would be a mistake for the Vatican to assume the attitude of a negotiator, to propose grounds for a bargain. The Church, too, carried the burden of history on her back. Politically she was suspect; but the very suspicion was a pointer to her task—to affirm not the method, but the principles of a human society capable of survival, capable of ordering itself to the terms of a God-given plan. She was appointed to be a teacher, not a treaty maker. Her task was not to govern men in the material order, but to train them to govern themselves in accordance with the principles of the natural law. She had to accept the fact that the end product—if, indeed, one could talk without cynicism about an end—must always be an approximation, a stage in an evolutionary growth.

It was this thought that led him once more into the garden of Castel Gondolfo, where Jean Télémond, studious and absorbed, was annotating his papers under the shade of an old oak tree.

"Here you sit, my Jean, writing your visions of a world perfecting itself, while I sit like a telephone operator between two men, each of whom can blast us into smithereens by pressing a button. . . . There's a dilemma for you. Does your science tell you how to resolve it? What would you do if you were in my shoes?"

"Pray," said Jean Télémond with a puckish grin.

"I do, Jean. Every day—all day, for that matter. But prayer isn't enough; I have to act, too. You had to be an explorer before you came to rest in this place. Tell me now, where do I move?"

"In this situation I don't think you move at all. You sit and wait for the appropriate moment."

"You think that's enough?"

"In the larger sense, no. I think the Church has lost the initiative it should have in the world today."

"I do, too. I should like to think that in my Pontificate we may be able to get some of it back. I'm not sure how. Do you have any ideas?"

"Some," said Jean Télémond crisply. "All my life I've been a traveler. One of the first things a traveler has to do is learn to accommodate himself to the place and time in which he lives. He has to eat strange food, use an unfamiliar coinage, learn not to blush among people who have no privies, search for the good that subsists in the grossest and most primitive societies. Every individual, every organization, has to sustain a conversation with the rest of the world. He cannot talk always in negatives and contradictions."

"You think we have done that?"

"Not always, Holiness. But of late, all too often. We have lived to ourselves and for ourselves. When I say *we*, I mean the whole Church—pastors and faithful alike. We have hidden the lamp of belief under a cover instead of holding it up to illuminate the world."

"Go on, Jean. Show me how you would display it."

"This is a plural world, Holiness. We may wish it to be one in faith, hope, and charity. But it is not so. There are many hopes and strange varieties of love. But this is the world we live in. If we want to participate in the drama of God's action with it, then we must begin with the words we all understand. Justice, for instance. We understand

that. . . . But when the Negroes in America seek justice
and full citizenship, is it we who lead them? Or we who
support most strongly their legitimate demands? You know
it is not. In Australia there is an embargo on colored mi-
grants. Many Australians feel that this is an affront to
human dignity. Do we support their protests? The record
shows that we do not. In principle, yes; but in action, no.
We proclaim that the Chinese coolie has a right to work
and subsistence, but it was not we who led him toward
it. It was the men who made the Long March. If we object to the price they put on the rice bowl, we must blame
ourselves as much as we blame them. . . . If we want to
enter once more into the human dialogue, then we must
seek out whatever common ground is available to us—as I
take it your Holiness is trying to do with Kamenev—the
ground of human brotherhood and the legitimate hopes of
all mankind. . . . I have thought often about the Gospel
scene when Christ held up the coin of the tribute and proclaimed, 'Render to Caesar the things that are Caesar's, and
to God the things that are God's.' To what Caesar? Has
your Holiness ever thought about it? . . . To a murderer,
an adulterer, a paederast. . . . But Christ did not abrogate the conversation of the Church with such a one. On
the contrary, he affirmed it as a duty. . . ."

"But what you show me, Jean, is not one man's commitment. It is the commitment of the whole Church—Pope,
pastors, and five hundred million faithful."

"True, Holiness—but what has happened? The faithful
are uncommitted only because they lack enlightenment
and courageous leadership. They understand risk better
than we do. We are protected by the organization. They
have only God's cloak to shelter them. They grapple each
day with every human dilemma—birth, passion, death,

and the act of love. . . . But if they hear no trumpets, see no crusader's cross lifted up—" He shrugged and broke off. "Excuse me, Holiness. I am too garrulous, I think."

"On the contrary, Jean. I find you a very serviceable man. I am glad to have you here."

At that moment a servant approached, bringing coffee and iced water, and a letter which had been received that moment at the gate. Kiril opened it and read the brief, unceremonious message:

"I am a man who grows sunflowers. I should like to call upon you at ten-thirty tomorrow morning."

It was signed: "Georg Wilhelm Forster."

He proved a surprise in more ways than one. He looked like a Bavarian incongruously dressed by an Italian tailor. He wore thick German shoes and thick spectacles, but his suit and shirt and his tie came from Brioni, and on his small, pudgy hand he wore a bezel ring, half as large as a walnut. His manner was deferent, but vaguely ironic, as though he were laughing at himself and all he stood for. In spite of his German name he spoke Russian with a strong Georgian accent.

When Kiril received him in his study, he went down on one knee and kissed the papal ring; then he sat bolt upright in the chair, balancing his Panama hat on his knees, for all the world like a junior clerk being interviewed for a job. His opening words were a surprise, too. "I understand your Holiness has received a letter from Robert."

Kiril looked up sharply, to catch a hint of a smile on the pudgy lips.

"There is no mystery about it, Holiness. It is all a matter of timing. Timing is very important in my work. I knew when Kamenev's letter would reach the Vatican. I knew

when Cardinal Carlin returned to New York. I was told
the date and time of his interview with Robert. From that
point it was a simple deduction that Robert's letter would
reach you at Castel Gondolfo."

Now it was Kiril's turn to smile. He nodded approval and
asked, "Do you live in Rome?"

"I have lodgings here. But as you can guess, I travel a
good deal. . . . There is an extensive business in sunflower seeds."

"I imagine there is."

"May I see Robert's letter?"

"Of course."

Kiril handed the paper across his desk. Forster read it
carefully for a few moments, and then passed it back.

"You may have a copy if you like," Kiril said. "As you
see, the President is perfectly willing that Kamenev
should see the letter."

"No copy will be necessary. I have a photographic memory. It's worth a lot of money to me. I shall see Kamenev
within a week. He will have an accurate transcript of the
letter and of my conversation with you."

"Are you empowered to talk for Kamenev?"

"Up to a certain point, yes."

To Kiril's amazement, he quoted verbatim the passage
from Kamenev's second letter:

" 'From time to time . . . you will receive application
for a private audience from a man named Georg Wilhelm
Forster. To him you may speak freely, but commit nothing
to writing. If you succeed in a conversation with the
President of the United States, you should refer to him as
Robert. Foolish, is it not, that to discuss the survival of
the human race we must resort to such childish tricks.' "

Kiril laughed. "That's an impressive performance. But

tell me, if you know of whom we are speaking why do I have to refer to the President as Robert?"

Georg Wilhelm Forster was delighted to explain himself. "You might call it a mnemonic trick. No man can guard altogether against talking in his sleep, or against verbal slips when he is under questioning. . . . So one practices this kind of dodge. It works, too. I've never been caught out yet."

"I hope you won't be caught out this time."

"I hope so, too, Holiness. This exchange of letters may have long consequences."

"I should like to be able to guess what they may be."

"Robert has already pointed to them in his letter." He quoted again. " 'An action of such magnitude and such risk that none of us would be allowed to attempt it.' "

"The proposition contradicts itself," said Kiril mildly. "Both Kamenev and the President—excuse me, Robert— point to the need for such action, but each in the same breath says that he is not the man to begin it."

"Perhaps they are looking to a third man, Holiness?"

"Who?"

"Yourself."

"If I could promise that, my friend, believe me, I should be the happiest man in the world. But as our countryman Stalin once remarked, 'How many divisions has the Pope?' "

"It is not a question of divisions, Holiness, and you know it. It is at bottom a question of influence and moral authority. Kamenev believes that you have, or may come to have, such an authority. . . ." He smiled and added an afterthought of his own. "From the little I have learned, I should say that your Holiness has a greater stature in the world than you may realize."

Kiril considered the thought for a few moments, and then delivered himself of a firm pronouncement. "Understand something, my friend. Report it clearly to Kamenev, as I have already reported it directly on the other side of the Atlantic. I know how small are our hopes of peace. I am prepared to do anything that is morally right and humanly possible to preserve it, but I will not allow myself or the Church to be used as a tool to advantage one side or the other. Do you understand that?"

"Perfectly. I have only been waiting for your Holiness to say it. Now may I ask a question?"

"Please do."

"If it were possible, and if it seemed desirable, would your Holiness be prepared to go to another place than Rome? Would you be prepared to use another channel of communication than the Vatican radio and the Vatican press, and the pulpits of Catholic churches?"

"What place?"

"It is not mine to suggest it. I put the proposition as a generality."

"Then I will answer it as a generality. If I can speak freely, and be reported honestly, I will go anywhere and do anything to help the world breathe freely, for however short a time."

"I shall report that, Holiness. I shall report it very happily. Now there is a practical matter. I understand the Maestro di Camera has a list of those who may be admitted readily to private audience with your Holiness. I should like my name added to the list."

"It is already there. You will be welcome at whatever time . . . Now I, too, have a message for Kamenev. You will tell him first that I am not bargaining, I am not pleading, I am not making any conditions at all for the free passage of talk through me. I am a realist. I know how much he is limited by what he believes and by the system to which he is subject, as I am subject to mine. Having said this, tell him from me that my people suffer in Hungary and Poland and East Germany and in the Baltic. Whatever he can do to ease their burden—be it ever so small—I shall count as done to myself, and I shall remember it with gratitude and in my prayers."

"I shall tell him," said Georg Wilhelm Forster. "Now may I have your Holiness' leave to go?"

"Go with God," said Kiril the Pontiff.

He walked with the strange little man to the gate of the garden and watched him drive away into the bright and hostile world beyond.

The Princess Maria-Rina was a doughty old general, and she had planned her nephew's campaign with more than usual care. First she had set him to rights with the Church, without which he could neither arrive at power nor begin to rule comfortably. Then she had isolated Chiara for a whole month from her American lover. She had set her down in a gay playground, surrounded by young men, one at least of whom might be ardent enough to seduce her into a new attachment. Now she was ready for her next move.

Accompanied by Perosi, and with Calitri's letter tucked into her handbag, she drove to Venice, plucked Chiara off the beach, and hurried her off to lunch to a quiet restaurant on Murano. Then she added her own brusque commentary to Calitri's letter:

". . . You see, child, all of a sudden it is very simple.

Corrado has come to his senses. He has set his conscience in order, and in a couple of months you will be free."

Chiara was still shocked and delighted by the news. She was prepared to trust the whole world. "I don't understand it. Why? What made him do it?"

The old Princess dismissed the question with a wave of her hand. "He's growing up. For a long time he was hurt and bitter. Now he has better thoughts. . . . For the rest, you need not concern yourself."

"But what if he changes his mind?"

"He won't, I promise you. Already his new depositions are in the hands of Perosi, here. The final papers will be ready for presentation to the Rota immediately after the holidays. After that it's just a formality. . . . As you will see from his letter, Corrado is disposed to be generous. He wants to pay you quite a large sum by way of settlement. On the understanding, of course, that you will make no further claims on him."

"I don't want to make any claims. All I want is to be free."

"I know, I know. And you're a sensible girl. There are, however, a couple of other matters. Perosi, here, will explain."

It was all so neatly done that she was totally disarmed. She simply sat there, looking from one to the other, while Perosi explained himself with smooth formality:

"You understand, signora, that your husband is a public figure. I think you will agree that it would be most unfair, after this generous gesture, to expose him to comment and notoriety."

"Of course. I wouldn't want that, either."

"Good. Then we understand each other. Once the affair is over, then we should let it die quietly. No publicity. No word to the newspapers, no hasty action on your part."

"What sort of action? I don't understand."

"He means marriage, child," said the Princess Maria-Rina gently. "It would be most undesirable for you and for Corrado if you were to rush into a hasty union as soon as the decree of nullity is granted."

"Yes, I see that."

"Which brings us to the next question," said Perosi with elaborate care. "Your present association with an American correspondent. His name, I believe, is George Faber."

Chiara flushed, and was suddenly angry. "That's my business. It doesn't concern anyone else."

"On the contrary, my dear young lady. I hope to persuade you that it is the business of everyone. The settlement, for example, would not be payable if you were to marry Faber—or, indeed, if you were to marry anyone within six months."

"Then I don't want the settlement."

"I shouldn't be too hasty about that, child. It's a lot of money. Besides . . ." She reached out a skinny claw and imprisoned Chiara's hand. "Besides, you don't want to make another mistake. You've been hurt enough already. I should hate to see you wounded again. Take time, child. Enjoy yourself. You're still young. The world's full of attractive men. Kick up your heels awhile. Don't tie yourself down before you've had three looks at what's offering in the marriage market. There's another thing, too. . . . Even if you did want to marry Faber, there might well be certain difficulties."

"What sort of difficulties?"

She was frightened now, and they read the fear in her

eyes. Perosi pressed the advantage shrewdly. "You are both Catholics, so naturally, I presume you will want to be married in the Church."

"Of course, but—"

"In that case you both come immediately into conflict with canon law. You have, if I may put it bluntly, been living in sin. It is a delicate question whether in the terms of canon law this would constitute 'public and notorious concubinage.' My own view is that it might. In this case a principle applies: that a guilty person shall not be permitted to enjoy the fruits of guilt. In canon law this is called *crimen*, and it is an invalidating impediment to marriage. It would be necessary to approach the Church for a dispensation. I have to tell you that there is no certainty that it would be granted."

The old Princess added a final rejoinder. "You don't want this kind of complication, do you? You deserve better. One mess is enough for any lifetime. . . . You do see that, don't you?"

She saw it very clearly. She saw that they had her trapped and beleaguered and that they would not let her go without a struggle. She saw something else, too. Something that shamed and excited her at once. She wanted it this way. She wanted to be rid of an attachment which had already grown stale for her. She wanted to be free to hold hands and play love games with young Pietro Antonelli while the moon shone and the mandolins played soft music in a gondola on the Grand Canal.

The day after his encounter with Theo Respighi George Faber drove back to Naples. His self-esteem had been badly damaged—by a man with too much honor

and by another with too little. He felt shaken and sordid.
He could hardly bear the sight of himself in a shaving
mirror. The image of the great correspondent was still
there, but behind it was an empty man who lacked the
courage even to sin boldly.

He was desperate for reassurance and the forgetfulness of loving. He tried to telephone Chiara in Venice,
but each time she was out, and when she did not return
his call he was filled with sour anger. His imagination ran
riot as he pictured her carefree and flirtatious while he,
for her sake, was making this drab and uncomfortable
journey to the hollow center of himself.

He had one more person to see—Alicia de Nogara,
authoress of Ischia. But he had to restore himself before
he could confront her. He spent a day in Naples, hunting
for copies of her books, and finally came up with a
slim, expensive volume, *The Secret Island.* He sat in the
gardens, trying to read it, and then gave up, discouraged
by its florid prose and its coy hints of perverted love
among the maidens. In the end he skimmed through it to
get enough information for a conversation piece and
then gave it to a ragged urchin who would pawn it for
the price of a biscuit.

He went back to the hotel and put in a call to Ruth
Lewin. Her maid told him she was on vacation and was
not expected back for several days. He gave up in disgust,
and then, in sullen reaction, he determined to divert
himself. If Chiara could play, so could he. He set off for
a three-day bachelor jaunt to Capri. He swam in the
daytime, flirted sporadically in the evening, drank twice
as much as he needed, and ended with an abortive night
in bed with a German widow. More disgusted with him

self than ever, he packed his bag the next morning and set out for Ischia.

The villa of Alicia de Nogara was a rambling pseudo-Moorish structure set on the eastern slope of Epomeo, with a spectacular view of terraced vineyards and blue water. The door was opened to him by a pale, flat-chested girl, dressed in a gypsy shirt and silk slacks. She led him into the garden, where the great authoress was at work in a vine arbor. The first sight of her was a shock. She was dressed like a sibyl, in filmy and flowing draperies, but her face was that of a faded girl and her blue eyes were bright with humor. She was writing with a quill pen on thick, expensive paper. When he approached, she stood up and held out a slim, cool hand to be kissed.

It was all so stylized, so theatrical in character, that he almost laughed aloud. But when he looked again into her bright, intelligent eyes, he thought better of it. He introduced himself formally, sat down in the chair she offered him, and tried to marshal his thoughts. The pale girl hovered protectively beside her patron.

Faber said awkwardly, "I've come to see you about a rather delicate matter."

Alicia de Nogara waved an imperious dismissal. "Go away, Paula. You can bring us some coffee in half an hour."

The pale one wandered away disconsolately, and the sibyl began to question her visitor:

"You're rather upset, aren't you? I can feel it. I am very sensitive to emanations. Calm yourself first. Look at the land and the sea. Look at me if you want to. I am very calm because I have learned to float with the air as it moves. This is how one should live, this is how one should love, too. Floating on the air, whichever way it blows. You have been in love, haven't you . . . ? Many times, I should say. Not always happily."

"I'm in love now," said George Faber. "That's why I've come to see you."

"Now there's a strange thing! Only yesterday I was saying to Paula that although my books are not widely read they still reach the understanding heart. I think you have an understanding heart. Haven't you?"

"I hope so. Yes. I understand you know a man called Corrado Calitri."

"Corrado? Oh yes, I know him very well. A brilliant boy. A little perverted, I'm afraid, but very brilliant. People say I'm perverted, too. You've read my books, I presume. Do you think so?"

"I'm sure you're not," said George Faber.

"There, you see. You do have an understanding heart. Perversion is something different. Perversion is the urge to destroy the thing one loves. I want to preserve, to nurture. That's why Corrado is doomed. He can never be happy. I told him that many times. . . . Before he was married, after his marriage broke up."

"That's what I wanted to talk to you about. Calitri's marriage."

"Of course. I knew it. That's what the emanations were telling me. You're in love with his wife."

"How did you know?"

"I'm a woman. Not an ordinary woman. Oh no! A sapphic woman, they call me, but I prefer to say a full woman, a guardian of the deep mysteries of our sex. . . . So you're in love with Corrado's wife."

"I want to marry her."

The sibyl leaned forward, cupping her small face in her hands and fixing him with her bright blue eyes. "Marriage.

That's usually a terrible mistake. The air, remember! One must be free—to float, to rise, to fall, to be held or to be let go. Strange that men never understand these things. I was married once, a long time ago. It was a great mistake. Sometimes I think men were born defective. They lack intuition. They were born to be slaves of their own appetite!"

"I'm afraid we were," said George Faber with a grin. "May I tell you what I want?"

"Please, please do."

"I want evidence for the Holy Roman Rota. For Chiara to be free, we have to prove that Corrado Calitri entered into marriage with a defective intention. We have to prove that he expressed this defective intention to a third person before the marriage took place." He fished in his pocket and drew out a typewritten statement which he had prepared that morning. "That, more or less, is the thing we want. Would you be prepared to sign it?"

Alicia de Nogara picked up the paper with fastidious fingers, read it, and laid it down on the table. "How crude! How terribly crude of the Church to demand this sort of indignity. Freedom again, you see! If people fail in love, let them be free to begin again. The Church tries to close up the soul in a bottle as if it were a foetus preserved in formaldehyde. . . . So very vulgar and medieval. . . . Tell me, does Corrado know that you've come to me?"

"No, he doesn't. For a reason I can't understand, he wants to hold on to Chiara. . . . Not to live with her, of course, but to hold her like a piece of land or an apartment."

"I know, I know. I told you he was perverse, didn't

I? This is how it shows. He likes to torment people. He tried to torment me even though I wanted nothing from him. All I wanted to do was teach him how to give and return love. I thought I had succeeded, too. He seemed very happy with me. Then he went away, back to his boys, back to his little game of promises and refusals. I wonder if he's as happy now as he was with me."

"I doubt it."

"Do you want to hurt him?"

"No. I just want Chiara to be free and to have the chance of making her happy."

"But if I sign this, it will hurt him, won't it?"

"It will hurt his pride, probably."

"Good! That's where he needs to be hurt. When one loves, one must be humble. When you commit yourself to the air, you have to be humble. Are you humble, Faber?"

"I guess I have to be," said Faber ruefully. "I haven't very much pride left. Are you prepared to sign that document? I shouldn't say this, but I was prepared to pay for the evidence."

"Pay?" She was dramatically insulted. "My dear man, you are desperate, aren't you? In love one must never pay. One must give, give, give! Freely, and from the full heart. Tell me something. Do you think you could love me?"

He had to swallow hard to get the thought down, but he did it. He twisted his mouth into what he hoped was a smile and answered elaborately, "It would be my good fortune if I could. I'm afraid I shouldn't deserve it."

She reached out and patted his cheek with a cool, dry hand. "There, there, I'm not going to seduce you, though I think you would seduce very easily. I'm not sure I should let you throw away your life in marriage, but you have to learn in your own way, I suppose. . . . Very well, I'll sign it."

She picked up the quill and subscribed the document with a flourish. "There, now. Is that all?"

"I think we should have a witness."

"Paula!"

The pale girl came hurrying to her cry. She set her signature at the foot of the paper, and George Faber folded it and put it into his pocket. The thing was done. He had soiled himself to do it, but it was done. He let them lead him through the rituals of coffee and endless, endless talk. He exerted himself to be gentle with them. He laughed at their pathetic jokes and bent like a courtier over the hand of the sibyl to say good-by.

As the taxi drove him down to the crowded port, as he leaned against the rail of the lake steamer that took him back to Naples, he felt the document crackling and burning against his breast. *Finita la commèdia!* The shabby farce was over, and he could begin to be a man again.

When he got back to Rome, he found Chiara's letter telling him that her husband had agreed to co-operate in her petition and that she had fallen in love with another man. *Finita la commèdia!* He tore the paper into a hundred shreds, and then proceeded, savagely and systematically, to get himself drunk.

Extract from
the Secret Memorials of
K I R I L I, Pont. Max.

I have had a wonderful holiday, the first in more than
twenty years. I feel rested and renewed. I am comforted
by a friendship which grows in depth and warmth each
day. I never had a brother, and my only sister died in
childhood. So my brotherhood with Jean Télémond has become very precious to me. Our lives are full of contrasts.
I sit at the summit of the Church; he lies under the rigid
obedience of his order. I spent seventeen years in
prison; he has had twenty years of wandering in the far
corners of the earth. Yet we understand each other perfectly. We communicate swiftly and intuitively. We are
both caught up in this shining hope of unity and common
growth toward God, the Beginning, the Center, and the
End. . . .

We have talked much these last few days of the grains
of truth that underlie even the most divergent errors. For

Islam, God is one, and this is already a leap from paganism to the idea of a single spiritual Creator. It is the beginning of a God-centered universe. Buddhism has degenerated into a series of sterile formulae, but the Buddhist code, although it makes few moral demands, conduces to co-operation, to non-violence, and to a polite converse among many people. Communism has abrogated a personal God, but there is implicit in its thesis an idea of the brotherhood of man. . . .

My immediate predecessor encouraged the growth of the Ecumenical spirit in Christendom—the exploration and the confirmation of common grounds of belief and action. Jean Télémond and I have talked much about the possibility of the Christian idea beginning to infuse the great non-Christian religions. Can we, for example, make any penetration of Islam, which is spreading so quickly through the new nations of Africa and through Indonesia. A dream, perhaps, but perhaps, also, an opportunity for another bold experiment like that of the White Fathers.

The grand gesture! The action that changes the course of history! I wonder if I shall ever have the opportunity to make it. . . . The gesture of a Gregory the Great, or a Pius V. Who knows? It is a question of historic circumstance and the readiness of a man to co-operate with God and in the moment. . . .

Ever since the visit of Georg Wilhelm Forster, I have been trying to think myself into the minds of Kamenev and the President of the United States. It is true, I think, that all men who arrive at authority have certain attitudes in common. They are not always the right attitudes, but at least they provide a ground of understanding. The man in power begins to see more largely. If he has not been corrupted, his private passions tend to diminish with age and responsibility. He looks, if not for permanence, at least for a peaceful development of the system he has helped to create. On the one hand, he is vulnerable to the temptations of pride. On the other, he cannot fail to be humbled by the magnitude and complexity of the human problem. . . . He understands the meaning of contingency and mutual dependence. . . .

It is well, I think, that the Papacy has been slowly stripped of its temporal power. It gives the Church the opportunity to speak more freely, and with less suspicion of material interest, than in other ages. I must continue to build this moral authority, which has its analogies in the political influence of small nations like Sweden and Switzerland, and even Israel.

I have given instructions to the Secretariat of State to encourage the visit of representatives of all nations and all faiths to the Vatican. At the lowest they constitute a useful diplomatic courtesy; at their best they may be the beginning of a fruitful friendship and understanding. . . .

This week I had Cardinal Rinaldi to lunch. I like this man. I talked with him about the possible reform of the Roman Rota, and he gave me valuable information about its methods and its personalities. In his quiet fashion he administered a reproof as well. He told me that Cardinal Leone felt that I did not repose enough trust in him. He pointed out that for all his vigor, he was an old man who had deserved well of the Church, and that I should perhaps bestow on him a mark of favor and acknowledgment. I find it hard to like Leone; he is so very much a Roman. But I agree with Rinaldi. I have written a gentle letter to Leone, thanking him for his work and asking him to wait on me as soon as I return to Rome. I have also asked for his private advice on the appointment of a new Cardinal to take the place of the Englishman, Brandon, who died two days ago. Brandon was one of those who voted against me in the conclave, and our relations were always rather formal and distant. Yet he was an apostolic man, and one always regrets deeply the passing of a laborer from the vineyard. I said a special Mass yesterday morning for the repose of his soul. . . .

News from Hungary and Poland is bad. The new taxation laws have already put several more schools and seminaries out of existence. Potocki is ill in Warsaw. My information is that he will recover. But the illness is serious, and we shall have to think of appointing a new man to help him and later to take over his office as Primate of Poland. Potocki is a man of political genius and deep spiritual life. We shall not easily find another to match him. . . .

Jean Télémond's first volume, *The Progress of Man*, is now ready for publication. This is the crucial part of his work, upon which all the rest depends. He is anxious to have it assessed by the Holy Office as soon as possible. For his sake I am anxious, too. I have asked Cardinal Leone to appoint commissioners to scrutinize it and report to me as quickly as may be. I have suggested that these commissioners be different men from those who made the first examination. We shall then have two sets of opinions and there will be no question of a carry-over from earlier, and far less complete, works. I am glad to say that Jean is very calm about it. He seems to be well, although I notice that he tires easily and is sometimes out of breath after a small exertion. I have ordered him to submit to an examination by the Vatican physician as soon as we go back to Rome. . . .

I want to keep him by me, but he is afraid of doing me

a disservice. The hierarchy and the Curia are suspicious and uncomfortable about a Gray Eminence in the Vatican. Cardinal Rinaldi repeated his invitation to have Jean work at his villa. Jean likes the idea, so I suppose I shall have to let him go. At least we shall not be far from each other, and I shall have the pleasure of his company at dinner on Sundays. Now that I have found him, I am loath to let him go. . . .

I learned so much with him during our journeys through the Italian countryside. The thing that impressed me most vividly was the contrast between entrenched wealth and the grinding poverty in which so many of the people still live. This is the reason for the strength and attraction of communism in Italy. It will take a long time—longer than I have at my disposal—to redress the balance. However, I have thought of a gesture which may become a symbol of what is needed.

The Congregation of Rites has informed me that they are ready to proceed to the beatification of two new servants of God. Beatification is a long and expensive process, and the ceremonies which conclude it are also very expensive. I am informed that the total cost may well be as much as fifty thousand American dollars. It could be that I shall be accused of diminishing the splendor of the liturgical life of the Church, but I have decided to reduce the ceremony to a simple formality and to devote whatever funds are available to the establishment of local works of charity. I shall take steps to see that my reasons are published as widely as possible so that people will understand that the service of the servants of God is much more important than their glorification.

Oddly enough, I am reminded at this moment of the woman Ruth Lewin and the work which she and others like her are doing, without encouragement and without apparent spiritual help in various places in the world. I am reminded, too, of the saying of the Master that even a cup of water given in His name is a gift made to Him. A thousand candles in St. Peter's mean nothing beside a poor man grateful to God because he is grateful to one of his fellows. . . .

Wherever I turn, I find myself being drawn irresistibly to the primitive thought of the Church, and I cannot believe that I am being drawn into error. I have no private inspiration. I am in the Church and of the Church, and if my heart beats in tune with its pulse I cannot be too far wrong. . . . "Judge me, O God, and distinguish my cause from that of the unholy."

✠
IX

SUMMER was in decline. The first colors of autumn were showing across the land. There was a pinch in the air, and soon the cold winds would begin to blow from the steppes down along the Alpine ridges. But the Sunday crowds in the Villa Borghese were still jealous of the warmth, and they paraded themselves cheerfully among the sellers of sweetmeats and the peddlers of novelties while their children stood gaping at the antics of Pulcinella.

Ruth Lewin was among them, playing nursemaid to a child—a tiny spastic creature with bobbing head and slobbering mouth—whom she had brought out from the slums for an airing. They were sitting on a bench, watching a fiddler with a dancing monkey while the child crammed himself with candy and bobbed a grotesque balloon in happy ignorance of his misfortune.

For all the pathos of her mission, Ruth Lewin felt calm and content. Her illness was over. She had come back from her holiday refreshed. She had made, at long last, a landfall. After the years of confusion her mind was clear. She knew what she was and what she had a right to be. It was not a conversion but an arrival. If she was not

fulfilled, at least she was no longer in flight. If she was
not satisfied, at least she could rest in hope of a betterment.

She was a Jew. She had inherited a race and a history.
She was prepared to accept them both, not as a burden,
but as an enrichment. She understood now that she had
never really rejected them, but had been forced into flight
from them by the circumstance of childhood. The flight
was not a guilt, but an affliction, and she had survived it,
as her ancestors had survived the captivities and the dis-
persions and the obloquy of the European ghettos. By
the simple fact of this survival, by the half-conscious
act of accepting, she had earned the right to be what she
wanted to be, to believe what she needed to believe to
grow to whatever shape her nature dictated.

She understood something else: that joy was a gift
which one accepted gratefully and should not try to pay
for, any more than one tried to pay for sunlight and bird
song. One held out grateful hands to take the gift, and
then held up the gift for a sharing. Payment was too
gross a word to describe a disbursal like this. Flowers
grew out of the eyes of the dead, but because one picked
the flowers one should not carry a corpse on one's back
for all the days of living. Children were born maimed and
misshapen, but to deny them beauty and love by way of
personal penance was a monstrous paradox. Doubt was a
burden on all questing spirits, but when the doubt was
resolved one should not cling to it in the luxury of self-
torment.

She had no doubts now. She had entered into the Christian faith in childhood. She had made it a refuge, and
then launched herself out of it into terror and confusion.
Now it was no longer a refuge but an ambience in which

she wanted to live and to grow. Like the sunlight, the bird song and the flower, it was free. She had no right to it, but she had no reason to refuse it, either. Everyone had a claim to sleep on his own pillow, hard or soft, because without sleep one died; and dying paid no debts, but only canceled them.

So, quite simply, on this Sunday morning she found herself at home.

To the traveler tossing on a windy ocean, home-coming always presented itself as a drama, a moment of revelation or of conquest. But the moment, when it came, was usually very trite. There were no banners and no trumpets. One was there, walking down a familiar street, seeing familiar faces in the doorways, wondering if the passage of time, the cavalcade of events, were not an illusion after all.

The child tugged at her arm with sticky fingers, begging to be taken to a toilet. She laughed aloud at the irony. This was the true shape of life at last—a succession of simplicities: snotty noses and soiled linen, bacon and eggs for breakfast, some laughter, some tears, and hanging over it all the majesty of mere existence. She took the child's hand and led him, stumbling and crowing, across the grass to unbutton his breeches. . . .

When she reached home, it was already dusk and the chill autumn was settling down on the city. She bathed and changed, and then because her maid was out she made her own supper, put a stack of disks on the record player, and settled down to a comfortable evening.

Time was, not so long ago, when the prospect of a solitary night would have driven her to desperation. Now, at peace with herself, she was glad of it. She was not sufficient to herself, but life, with its small services and its occasional piquant encounters, might now be sufficient to her. She was no longer an alien. She had her domain of giving, and sooner or later there might be a time of receiving, too. She could commune with herself because she had discovered herself. She was one, she was real. She was Ruth Lewin, widow, Jew by birth, Christian by adoption. She was old enough to understand, and still young enough to love if love was offered. For one day and one new woman it was more than enough.

Then the bell rang, and when she opened the door she found George Faber, drunk and mumbling, at the top of the stairs. His shirt was limp. His clothes were stained, his hair was in disorder, and he had not shaved for days.

It took her nearly an hour to sober him with black coffee and make sense out of his story. Ever since Chiara had left him, he had been drinking steadily. He had done no work at all. His bureau was being kept open by a stringer and by the kindness of his colleagues, who filed stories for him, answered his cables, and kept him out of trouble with New York.

For a man so urbane and precise it was a sorry downfall. For one so prominent in Rome the tragedy could quickly develop beyond remedy. Yet George Faber seemed to have no heart left to help himself. He despised himself utterly. He poured out the story of his affronted manhood. He abandoned himself to maudlin tears. Ambition had deserted him, and he seemed to have no foothold left from which to grope his way back to dignity.

He submitted like a child when she ordered him to take a bath and then tucked him into her bed to sleep off the rest of the drink. While he slept, muttering and restless, she emptied his pockets, bundled up his soiled clothes, and then set off to his apartment to find a new suit, clean linen, and a razor. He was still sleeping when she returned, and she settled down to another vigil and a critical examination of her own role in the drama of George Faber.

It would be all too easy now to present herself as Our Lady of Succor, ready with salve and sticking plaster to patch up his wounded pride. It would be dangerously simple to wrap up her love in a candy box and offer it as a solace for the lost one. For her own sake and for his, she must not do it. Love was less than half the answer when the pillars of a man's self-respect were shaken and the rooftrees came tumbling round his ears. Sooner or later he had to walk out of the wreckage on his own two feet, and the truest recipe of love was to let him do it.

When he came down to breakfast, haggard but tidy, she told him so, bluntly:

"This has got to stop, George—here and now! You've made a fool of yourself over a woman. You're not the first. You won't be the last. But you can't destroy yourself for Chiara or for anyone else."

"Destroy myself!" He made a gesture of defeat. "Don't you understand? That's what I found out! There's nothing to destroy. There's no me at all. There's just a bundle of good manners and journalist's habits. . . . Chiara was shrewd enough to see it. That's why she got out."

"For my money, Chiara is a selfish little bitch. You're lucky to be rid of her."

He was still stubborn in self-pity. He shook his head. "Campeggio was right. I'm too soft. One push, and I fell apart."

"Comes a time when we all fall apart, George. The real test is when we have to put ourselves together again."

"And what do you expect me to do? Dust myself off, stick a flower in my buttonhole, and walk back into business as if nothing happened?"

"Just that, George!"

"Schmaltz!" He threw the word at her in angry derision. "Yiddisher schmaltz! Straight out of Brooklyn and *Marjorie Morningstar!* Rome is laughing its head off about Chiara and me. You think I can sit up and let them throw coconuts at me just for laughs!"

"I think you must."

"I won't do it."

"Fine! So what's the alternative? Drink yourself silly every day? On money that other men are earning for you?"

"Why the hell should you care what I do?"

It was on the tip of her tongue to say, "I love you," but she bit back the words and gave him a more brutal answer. "I don't care, George! You came to me! I didn't go to you! I've cleaned you up and made you look like a man again! But if you don't want to be a man, then it's your own affair!"

"But I'm not a man, sweetheart! Chiara proved it to me. Two weeks away, and she's playing kiss-me-quick on the Lido with someone else. I risked everything for her, and then she put the horns on me. So I'm a man already?"

"Are you more of a man because you drink like a pig?"

She had silenced him at last, and now she began to plead with him. "Look, George, a man's life is his own business. I'd like to make you my business, but I'm not going to unless you tell me clearly and soberly that you want it like that. I'm not going to pity you because I can't afford it. You've made a fool of yourself. Admit it! At least you'll wear it with more dignity than the horns. You think I haven't felt the way you do? I have, and for much longer. In the end I grew up. I'm grown-up now, George. It's late in the day, but I'm grown-up. You've got to grow up, too."

"I'm so damn lonely," said George Faber pathetically.

"So am I. I've made the round of the bars, too, George. If I didn't have a weak stomach, I'd be a lush three times over. It's no answer, believe me."

"What is the answer?"

"A clean shirt and a flower in the buttonhole."

"Nothing else?"

"Oh yes! But that's for afterward. Please give it a try."

"Will you help me?"

"How?"

"I don't quite know. Maybe"—for the first time he smiled ruefully—"maybe, let me wear you in my buttonhole."

"If it's for pride, George. Yes."

"What do you mean?"

"I'm half a Roman, too, you know. You lose one woman, you have to find another. It's the only way to get rid of the horns."

"I didn't mean that."

"I know you didn't, darling; but I do. The moment you can tell yourself that I'm trying to mother you, or make myself another Chiara, then I'm no good to you. You're up and away, and on the bottle again. So let's make me a buttonhole. Wear me to show the town that George Faber is back on the job. Is it a bargain?"

"It's a bargain. . . . Thanks, Ruth."

"*Prego, signore.*" She poured him a fresh cup of coffee, and then asked him quietly, "What else is on your mind, George?"

He hesitated a moment, and then told her. "I'm afraid of Calitri."

"You think he knows what you did?"

"I think he could know. There was a man at Positano who threatened to tell him. If there were money in it, he would have told him by now."

"But you haven't heard from Calitri."

"No. But he could be biding his time."

"For what?"

"Revenge."

"What sort of revenge?"

"I don't know. But I'm in a ticklish position. I've committed a criminal act. If Calitri wanted to, he could bring me to law."

She answered him resolutely. "You'll wear that too, George, if it happens."

"I'll have to. . . . Meantime, I think I should tell Campeggio."

"Is he involved in this?"

"Not openly, but he lent me money. He makes no secret of his enmity for Calitri. . . . And Calitri could easily guess at a connection between us. As a servant of the Vatican, Campeggio is even more vulnerable than I am."

"Then you must tell him. . . . But, George . . ."

"Yes?"

"Whatever happens, remember the clean shirt and the flower in the buttonhole!"

He gave her a long, searching look, and then said softly, "You do care, don't you?"

"Very much."

"Why?"

"Ask me in a month, and I'll tell you. . . . Now you get yourself down to the bureau and start work. . . . Leave me your key, and I'll clean up your apartment. The place is like a barnyard."

When they parted, he kissed her on the cheek, and she

watched him striding down the street to his first encounter with reality. It was too early to tell whether he would be able to restore his own dignity, but she had kept hers, and the knowledge was a strength. She went upstairs, dressed herself in a new frock, and half an hour later was kneeling in the confessional in the apse of St. Peter's basilica.

"He has beaten us," said Orlando Campeggio. "At our own game—and with nothing but profit to himself."

"I still don't understand what made him do it," said George Faber.

They were sitting together in the same restaurant where they had made their first conspiracy. Campeggio was drawing the same pattern on the tablecloth, and George Faber, grim and perplexed, was trying to fit the jigsaw together.

Campeggio stopped his tracing and looked up. He said evenly, "I hear you've been out of circulation for a while."

"I went on a bender."

"Then you've missed the beginning of a good story. Calitri is being groomed to lead the country after the next election. The Princess Maria Poliziano is handling the campaign belowstairs."

"My God!" said George Faber. "As simple as that."

"As simple and as complicated. Calitri needs the favor of the Church. His return to the confessional has been discreetly publicized. The next and most obvious step is to regularize his marriage."

"And you think he'll bring it off?"

"I'm sure he will. The Rota, like any other court, can deal only with the evidence presented to it. It can make no judgments in the internal forum of conscience."

"The clever bastard," said George Faber with feeling.

"As you say, a clever bastard. He's been clever with me, too. My son has been promoted. He thinks the sun, moon, and stars shine out of Calitri's backside."

"I'm sorry."

Campeggio shrugged. "You have your own problem."

"I'll survive it—I hope! I'm expecting Calitri to move against me at any moment. I'm trying to figure out what he may do."

"At worst," said Campeggio thoughtfully, "he could have you tried on a criminal charge and then expelled from the country. Personally I don't think he'll do it. He has too much to lose if there is a public scandal over his marriage case. At best—and it's not a very good best, I admit—he could make things so uncomfortable for you that you would have to go, anyway. You can't function as a correspondent if you are not on reasonable terms with the men who make the news. Also, he could embarrass you with a whole lot of minor legalities."

"Those are my thoughts, too. But there is a chance that Calitri hasn't heard of my activities. Our drunken friend in Positano may have been bluffing."

"That's true. You won't know, of course, until the verdict has been handed down from the Holy Roman Rota. Whether Calitri knows or not, he won't make any move until after the case is over."

"So I sit pat."

"May I ask you a question, Faber?"

"Sure."

"Have you ever mentioned my connection with you to anybody else?"

"Well, yes. To Chiara and to another friend. Why do you ask?"

"Because in that case I'm afraid I can't sit pat. I have to make a move."

"For God's sake! What sort of move?"

"I have to resign from the *Osservatore*. I told you I was a man of confidence at the Vatican. I could not compromise myself or my employers by continuing to work under a constant threat of exposure."

"But there may be no exposure."

Campeggio smiled and shook his head. "Even so, I find that I cannot come to terms with an uneasy conscience. I am no longer a man of confidence because I can no longer trust myself. I must resign. The only question is how I shall do it. . . . On the basis of full disclosure to the Pontiff, or on a plea of age and infirmity."

"If you make a disclosure," said George Faber, "you ruin me more quickly than Calitri can do it. The Vatican is my beat as much as the Quirinale."

"I know that. You have problems enough without me. So this is what I propose to do. I shall wait until after a decision on the Calitri case is handed down from the Rota. If Calitri does not move against you, then I shall go to the Holy Father and offer him my resignation, telling him simply that I am acting under doctor's orders. If on the other hand, Calitri moves against you, then I shall make a full disclosure. That way we may both salvage a little from the wreckage." He was silent a moment, and then in a more friendly tone he added, "I'm sorry, Faber, sorrier than I can say. You've lost your Chiara, I've lost my son. We have both lost something more important."

"I know," said Faber moodily. "I should do what you're doing. Pack up quietly and head back home. But I've been here fifteen years. I hate the thought of being uprooted by a son of a bitch like Calitri."

Campeggio waved an expressive hand and quoted gently, "'*Che l'uomo il suo destin fugge di raro.* . . . It's a rare man who dodges his destiny!' And you and I were born for a troubled one. Don't fight it too long. One should always save a little dignity for the exit."

In his office at No. 5 Borgo Santo Spirito, Rudolf Semmering, Father General of the Jesuits, talked with his subject, Jean Télémond. There were letters under his hand which contained the reports of the Vatican physicians. He held them out to Télémond. "You know what these say, Father?"

"I do."

"Your cardiographs show that you have already suffered one and possibly two heart attacks."

"That's right. I had a mild seizure in India the year before last, and another while I was in the Celebes last January. I understand I may expect another at any time."

"Why didn't you write and tell me you had been so ill?"

"It seemed of small consequence. There was nothing anyone could do about it."

"We should have given you an easier way of life."

"I was happy in my work. I wanted to go on doing it."

The Father General frowned and said firmly, "It was a matter of rule and obedience, Father. You should have told me."

"I'm sorry. I did not look at it like that. I should have known better."

The stern features of the Father General relaxed, and he went on more mildly. "You know what this means, Father? You're a man in the shadow of death. You may be called without warning at any time."

"I've known that for months."

"Are you ready for it?"

Jean Télémond said nothing, and the Father General went on quietly. "You understand, Father, that this is the essential meaning of my office—a care of the souls entrusted to me by the Society and by the Church. Rightly or wrongly, I have laid heavy burdens on you. Now I want to be as much help to you as I can."

"I am very grateful, Father," said Jean Télémond. "I'm not sure how I should answer your question. Is any man ever truly ready for death? I doubt it. The best I can say is this: I have tried to live a logical life as a man and a priest. I have tried to develop my talents to make them serviceable to the world and to God. I have tried to be a good minister of the Word, and of the grace of the Sacraments. I have not always succeeded, but I think my failures have been honest ones. I am not afraid to go. . . . I do not think God wants any of us to fall out of His hands."

Semmering's lined face puckered into a smile of genuine affection. "Good. I am very happy for you, Father. . . . I hope we shall have you with us a long time yet. I want to tell you that I was deeply impressed by your address at the Gregoriana. I am not sure that I can agree with all of it. There were certain propositions which troubled me and still do. But of you I am sure. Tell me something else. How firmly do you hold to what you propounded then, and in your other works?"

Télémond considered the question carefully, and then answered. "From a scientific point of view, Father, I should explain it this way. Experiment and discovery bring one by a certain line to a certain point of arrival. . . . Up to that point one is scientifically certain because the discoveries have been documented and the logic has been proved by experiment. . . . Beyond the arrival point, the line projects itself infinitely further. One follows it by hypothesis and by strides of speculation. . . . One believes that the logic will continue to prove itself as it has done before. . . . One cannot be certain, of course, until the logic of speculation has proved itself against the logic of discovery. . . . So—again as a scientist—one has to preserve an open mind. I think I have done that. . . . As a philosopher I am perhaps less well equipped, but I believe that knowledge does not contradict itself. It develops onto successive planes, so that what we see first as a symbol may enlarge itself on another plane into a reality which to our unfamiliar eyes is different. Again, one tries to keep the mind open to new modes of thought and knowledge. . . . One understands that language is at best a limited instrument to express our expanding concepts. As a theologian I am committed to the validity of reason as an instrument for attaining to a limited knowledge of the Creator. I am committed also by an Act of Faith to the validity of divine revelation, expressed in the Deposit of Faith. . . . Of one thing I am sure—as I am sure of my own existence—that there is no possible conflict of knowledge at any plane, once the knowledge is wholly apprehended. . . . I remember the old Spanish proverb 'God writes straight with crooked lines,' but the final vector is an arrow which leads straight to the Almighty. This is the reason why I have tried to live fully in and with the world, and not in separation from it. The redemptive act is barren without the co-operation of man . . . but man as he is, in the world in which he lives—" He broke off and gave a little shrug of deprecation. "Forgive me, Father, I didn't mean to read lectures."

"It's a very good lecture, Father," said Rudolf Semmer-

ing. "But I want you to add something else to it. By your
vow you are a child of obedience, an obedience of formal
act, of submissive will, and humble intellect. Have you
conformed the terms of your vow with the terms of your
personal search?"

"I don't know," said Jean Télémond softly. "I am not
sure that I can know until I am put to a final test. Cardinal Rinaldi expressed it very clearly when he said that
this was the cross I was born to bear. I admit that often
its weight oppresses me. Of this, however, I am sure, that
there cannot be in the ultimate any conflict between what
I seek and what I believe. I wish I could put it more
clearly."

"Is there any way in which I can help you now, Father?"

Télémond shook his head. "I don't think so. If there
were, believe me I should ask it. I think at this moment I
am more afraid of this dilemma than I am of dying."

"You do not think you have been reckless?"

"No, I do not. I have had to dare much because all exploration is a risk. But reckless? No. Confronted with the
mystery of an orderly universe, one cannot be anything
but humble. Confronted by death, as I am, one cannot
be anything but truthful. . . ." A new thought seemed to
strike him. He paused a moment to weigh it, and then
said bluntly, "There is a problem, though, in one's relations with the Church—not with the Faith, you understand, but with the human body of the Church. The
problem is this. There are some believers who are as ignorant of the real world as certain unbelievers are ignorant of the world of faith. 'God is great and terrible,' they
say. But the world also is great and terrible and wonderful, and we are heretics if we ignore or deny it. We are

like the old Manichees who affirm that matter is evil and
the flesh is corrupt. This is not true. It is not the world
which is corrupt, or the flesh. It is the will of man, which
is torn between God and the self. This is the whole meaning of the Fall."

"One of the things which bothered me in your address
is that you did not mention the Fall. I know it will bother
the Holy Office as well."

"I did not mention it," said Jean Télémond stoutly, "because I do not believe that it has any place in the phe-
nomenal order, but only in the moral and spiritual one."

"They will say," persisted Rudolf Semmering, "that you
have confused the two."

"There has never been any confusion in my mind.
There may be some in my expression."

"It is on your expression that they will judge you."

"On that ground I am amenable to judgment."

"You will be judged, and soon. I hope you will find
patience to support the verdict."

"I hope so, too," said Jean Télémond fervently. "I get
so very tired sometimes."

"I am not afraid of you," said Rudolf Semmering with
a smile. "And His Holiness speaks very warmly of you.
You know he wants to keep you at the Vatican."

"I know that. I should like to be with him. He is a great
man and a loving one, but until I am tested I should not
want to compromise him. Cardinal Rinaldi has invited
me to work at his villa while the Holy Office is examining
my work. Have I your permission to do that?"

"Of course. I want you to be as free and comfortable as
possible. I think you deserve that."

Jean Télémond's eyes were misty. He clasped his hands

together to stop their trembling. "I am very grateful, Father—to you and to the Society."

"And we are grateful to you." Semmering stood up, walked round his desk, and laid a friendly hand on the shoulder of his subject. "It's a strange brotherhood, this of the Faith and of the Society. We are many minds and many tempers. But we walk a common road, and we have much need of a common charity."

Jean Télémond seemed suddenly withdrawn into a private world of his own. He said absently, "We are living in a new world. But we do not know it. Deep ideas are fermenting in the human mass. Man, for all his frailness, is being subjected to monstrous tensions, political, economic, mechanical. Knowledge is reaching like a rocket toward the galaxies. I have seen machines that make calculations beyond the mind of Einstein. . . . There are those who fear that we are exploding ourselves into a new chaos. I dare not contemplate it. I do not believe it. I think, I know, that this is only a time of preparation of something infinitely wonderful in God's design for His creatures. I wish—I wish so much—I could stay to see it."

"Why wait?" said Rudolf Semmering with rare gentleness. "When you go, you will go to God. In Him and through Him you will see the fulfillment. Wait in peace, Father."

"On the judgment?" asked Jean Télémond wryly.

"On God," said Rudolf Semmering. "You will not fall out of His hands."

Immediately after his return from Castel Gandolfo, Kiril the Pontiff was caught in a press of new and varied business.

The Institute for Works of Religion had prepared its annual survey of the financial resources of the Papacy. It was a long and complex document, and Kiril had to study it with care and concentration. His reactions were mixed. On the one hand, he had to command the industry and acumen of those who had built the Papal State and the Vatican bank into stable and solvent institutions, with operations stretching all over the world. This was the nature of their stewardship. Five Cardinals and a staff of highly competent financiers administered the temporal goods of the Church. They bought and sold in the stock markets of the world. They invested in real estate and hotels and public utilities, and on their efforts depended the stability of the Holy See as a temporal institution, whose members had to be fed, clothed, housed and hospitalized so that they might be free to work with reference to eternity.

But Kiril was too much an ironist not to see the disparity between the efficiency of a financial operation and the doubt that hung over so many works for the salvation of human souls. It cost money to train a priest and maintain a nursing sister. It cost money to build schools and orphanages and homes for the aged. But all the money in the world could not buy a willing spirit or fill a slothful one with the love of God.

By the time he had finished the document and the financial conferences, he had come to a resolution. His stewards had done well. He would leave them be, but he himself must concentrate all his time and all his energy on the prime function of the Church: the leading of men to a knowledge of their relationship with their Creator. A God-centered man could sit barefoot under a tree and set the world afire. A huckster with a million in gold, and scrip stacked up to the roof, would leave the planet un-mourned and unremembered.

There was trouble in Spain. The younger clergy were in revolt against what they considered the archaic and obscurantist attitudes of certain senior prelates. There were two sides to the question. Pastoral authority had to be maintained, and at the same time the vivid and apostolic spirit of the younger Spaniards had to be pre-served. Some of the older men had become too closely identified with the dictatorial system. The new ones, iden-tified with the people and their hopes of reform, found themselves repressed and inhibited in their work. A vio-lent reaction was beginning to make itself felt against the semi-secret work of Opus Dei, which was on the face of it an institute for lay action within the Spanish Church, but which many claimed was being controlled by reac-tionary elements in Church and State. This was the cli-mate in which schism and rebellion were born, yet the climate could not be reversed overnight.

After a week of discussions with his advisors he de-cided on a double step: a secret letter to the Primate and the Bishops of Spain, urging them to accommodate them-selves with more liberality and more charity to the changing times, and an open letter to the clergy and the laity, approving the good work done, but urging upon them the duty of obedience to local ordinaries. It was at best a compromise, and he knew it. But the Church was a human society as well as a divine one, and its develop-ment was the result of checks and balances, of conflicts and retreats, of disagreements and slow enlightenment.

In England there was the question of naming a new Cardinal to succeed Brandon. The appointment posed a neat alternative! A politician or a missionary? A man of stature and reputation who would uphold the dignity of the Church—and the place it had regained in the established order? Or a rugged evangelist who understood the ferment of a crowded industrial country, and the disillusion of a once imperial society, and its fading confidence in a social and humanitarian religion?

At first blush the choice was simple. Yet given the temper of the English, their historic mistrust of Rome, their odd reaction toward revivalism, it was not half as simple as it looked.

Cardinal Leone summed it up for him neatly. "Parker, in Liverpool, is the true missionary bishop. His work among the laboring classes and the Irish immigrants has been quite spectacular. On the other hand, he is often very outspoken, and he has been accused of being a political firebrand. I do not believe that. He is an urgent man. Perhaps too urgent for the phlegmatic English. Ellison, in Wales, is in a very good standing with the establishment. He's urbane, intelligent, and understands the art of the possible. His advantage to us is that he can prepare a situation in which more apostolic men can work with some freedom."

"How long do we have?" asked Kiril. "Before a new appointment is necessary?"

"Two months, I should say, three at the outside. England needs a red hat."

"If it were left to your Eminence, whom would you choose? Parker or Ellison?"

"I should choose Ellison."

"I'm inclined to agree with you. Let's do this. We shall defer a decision for one month. During that time I should like you to make another canvass of opinion among the

Curia, and among the English hierarchy. After that we shall decide."

Then there were the reports from Poland. Cardinal Potocki had pneumonia and was critically ill. If he died, there would be two immediate problems. He was deeply loved by his people, and deeply feared by the government, against whom he had held out stubbornly for sixteen years. His funeral might well be the occasion for spontaneous demonstrations, which the government could use for provocative action against the Catholic population. Equally important was the question of his successor. He had to be named and in readiness to take office, immediately the old fighter died. He had to know of his appointment, yet it had to be kept secret lest the authorities move against him before Potocki's death. A secret emissary had to get from the Vatican to Warsaw and present the papal rescript of succession. . . .

So one by one the countries of the world came under review, and the memory of a summer holiday faded further and further into the background. Finally, toward the end of September, came a letter from Cardinal Morand, in Paris.

. . . A suggestion was made to your Holiness' Illustrious Predecessor that a papal visit to the shrine of Our Lady of Lourdes might have a spectacular effect upon the life of the Church in France. There were at that time several obstacles to the project—the health of the Holy Father, the war in Algeria, and the political climate in metropolitan France.

Now these obstacles do not exist. I am informed that the French government would look with great favor on a papal visit, and would be delighted to welcome your Holiness to Paris after the visit to Lourdes.

I need not say how delighted the clergy and faithful would be to have the Vicar of Christ on the soil of France after so long a time.

If your Holiness were prepared to entertain the idea, I should like to suggest that the most appropriate time would be the feast of Our Lady of Lourdes, on February 11, next year. The French government concurs heartily with this timing.

May I beg your Holiness most humbly to consider our request, and the good which might come from it, not only for Catholic France, but for the whole world. It would make a historic occasion—the first journey of a Pope into this land for more than a century. The eyes of all the world would be focused on the person of your Holiness, and there would be for a while a public and universal pulpit available. . . .

The letter excited him. Here was the historic gesture ready to be made. After his first exit from Rome others would follow almost inevitably. In the convergent world of the twentieth century the apostolic mission of the Pontiff might be reaffirmed in a startling style.

Immediately, and without consultation, he wrote a reply to Morand in his own hand:

. . . We are delighted by your Eminence's suggestion of a visit to France in February of next year. We have no doubt that there will be certain voices in the Church raised against it, but we ourselves are most favorably disposed. We shall discuss the matter at the earliest opportunity with Cardinal Goldoni and later with members of the Curia.

Meantime, your Eminence may accept this letter as our personal authority to initiate preliminary discussions with the French authorities concerned. We suggest that no public announcement be made until all the formalities are concluded.

To your Eminence and our brother bishops, to the clergy and all the people of France, we send from a full heart our apostolic benediction. . . .

He smiled as he sealed the letter, and sent it out for posting. Goldoni and the Curia would be full of doubts and consequential fears. They would invoke history and protocol, and logistics and political side effects. But Kiril the Pontiff was a man elected to rule in God's name, and in the name of God he would rule. If doors were open to him he would walk through them, and not wait to be led through them by the hand, like a petty princeling. . . .

The idea of a peripatetic Pope had, with the passage of time, become strange in the Church. There were those who saw in it a succession of dangers—to dignity, since a man who packed his bags and went flying round the world might look too human; to authority, since he would be required to speak extempore on many subjects, without study and without advice; to order and discipline, since the Vatican Court needed at all times a firm hand to hold it together; to stability, since modern air travel entailed a constant risk, and to lose one Pontiff and elect another was an expensive, not to say perilous, business. . . . Besides, the world was full of fanatics who might affront the august personage of Christ's Vicar, and even threaten his life.

But history was not made by those who shied away from risks. Always the Gospel had been preached by men who took death for a daily companion. . . . Above all, Kiril Lakota was an opportunist with a restless heart. If a journey were possible, he would make it, discounting all but the profit in souls. . . .

From Kamenev, holidaying by the Black Sea, came a letter delivered by the ubiquitous Georg Wilhelm Forster. It was longer and more relaxed than the others, and it carried the first clear expression of his thoughts on the approaching crisis:

. . . At last I am in private conversation with the other side of the Atlantic. I am more grateful than I can say for your good offices.

I have been resting for a while, thinking out the program for the coming year and asking myself, at the same time, where I stand at this moment of my public and private life. My career is in apogee. I can go no higher. I have perhaps five more years of full authority and activity; after that the inevitable decline will begin, and I must be prepared to accept it.

I know I have done well for this country. I should like to do better. For this betterment peace is necessary. I am prepared to go far to maintain it, yet you must understand that I want to go farther than I shall be permitted by the Party and the Praesidium.

First, therefore, let me show you the position as I see it. You can trace my thesis on a child's map of the world. China is in a bad way. That means six hundred million people are in a bad way. This year's harvests have been dangerously light. There is real starvation in many areas. There have been reports, hard to confirm because of rigid censorship, that bubonic plague has broken out in some coastal towns. We have taken a serious view of this, and we have imposed a sanitary cordon at all frontier posts along our borders with China.

Her industrial development is slow. We have deliberately made it somewhat slower by withdrawing many of our construction teams and experts, because we do not want China to grow too quickly under the present regime.

The present leaders are old men. They are subject to increasing pressures from their juniors. If the economic crisis gets any worse, they will be forced into action, and they will inevitably mount military moves in the direction of South Korea, and Burma, and the northeast frontier of India. At the same time, they will ask us to provide a diversionary front by renewing our pressure on Berlin and by pressing for a solution to the East German question, even to the point of armed intervention.

Once these moves are made, America must set herself in battle order against us.

Is there any remedy for this hair-trigger situation? I believe there is. But we must not be naïve about its efficacy. Let us get a breathing space first, so that we may proceed with a little more confidence to a long-term solution.

The first and most obvious remedy is nuclear disarmament. We have been debating this for years now, and we are no nearer to agreement. I think it is still out of the question, because public and Party opinion can be so swiftly excited by the issue. I know I cannot risk a decisive move, and neither can my opposite number. So we must discount it for a while.

The second remedy might appear to be the admission of China to the United Nations. This, again, is complicated by the fiction of the two Chinas and the existence of a rump government-in-arms on Formosa. Again we are involved in a highly political situation, too easily complicated by catchwords and prepared attitudes.

It is my view that with some preparation and a minimum of good will, a remedy may be found elsewhere. If the miseries of China were fully exposed to the world, not as a political, but as a human spectacle, and if an offer were made by America and the nations of the West to resume normal trade relations with the Chinese, by exporting food to her, by allowing the free passage of vital commodities, then we might at least defer the crisis. Of course, China would have to be prepared to accept the gesture—and to get her to do it is a delicate problem. We, on our part, would have to put our weight behind the Western offer, and we should have to make some kind of proposal of our own.

How far can we go? More properly, how far can I go with

any hope of support from the Party and the country? I must be honest with you. I must not promise more than I can hope to fulfill.

Here, I think, is my limit. We would put no further pressure on Berlin, and leave the East German question in abeyance, while we reach for a less rigid form of settlement. We would discontinue nuclear tests in return for an assurance that the United States would also discontinue. We would reopen immediately—with a more practical compromise formula—the question of nuclear disarmament, and I would add my own personal authority to any effort to achieve a settlement within a reasonable time limit.

I do not know whether the Americans will find this enough, but it is the best I could assure in any negotiations. Even so, both we and the United States will need a very favorable climate to bring off a settlement. There is not too much time to prepare it.

I can almost hear you ask yourself how far you can trust me now. I cannot swear an oath, because I have nothing to swear by, but what I have written here is the truth. How I comport myself in the public view, how I behave during the negotiation, is another matter. Politics is more than half theatre, as you know. But this is the bargain I propose, and even if the Americans hedge it a little we can do business and give the world what it desperately needs at this moment, a breathing space to measure the current value of peace against what may happen if we lose it.

I hope your health is good. Mine is fairly robust, but sometimes I am reminded sharply of the passing of the years. My son has finished his training and has now been admitted as a bomber pilot in our Air Force. If war comes, he will be one of the first victims. This is a cold thought that haunts me while I sleep. This, I think, is what saves me from the ultimate corruption of power. What do I want for him? In olden times kings murdered their sons lest they prove rivals—and when they got lonely they could always breed other ones. It is different now. There are those who say we have simply grown softer— I like to think we are growing at least a little wiser.

I am reminded of your request to ease some of the burdens of your flock in Hungary, Poland, and the Baltic areas. Here, again, I must be honest, and not promise more than I can perform. I cannot issue a direct command, nor can I reverse abruptly a traditional Party policy, to which, moreover, I am personally committed. However, there will be a meeting of premiers of the fringe countries in Moscow next week. I shall put it to them as a proposal to prepare the atmosphere for what I hope will be a discussion of the Chinese question between ourselves and America.

I am hoping your Cardinal Potocki will recover. He is a danger to us, but as things are I would rather have him alive than dead. I admire him almost as much as I admire you.

One more point, perhaps the most important of them all. If we are to negotiate along the lines I have suggested, we shall need to reach a settlement before the middle of March, next year. If the Chinese begin a military build-up, it will be early in April. Once they start, we are in real trouble.

I read a copy of your letter to the Church on education. I thought it excellent and at times moving, but we have been doing so much better than the Church for forty years. One would think that you had less to lose than we have. Forgive the irony. It is hard to lose bad habits. Help us if you can. Greetings. Kamenev.

Kiril the Pontiff sat a long time, pondering over the letter. Then he went into his private chapel and knelt in prayer for nearly an hour. That same evening after supper, he summoned Goldoni from the Secretariat of State and was closeted with him until after midnight.

:

"You are an embarrassment to me, Mr. Faber," said Corrado Calitri gently. "I imagine you are an embarrassment to Chiara as well. She is very young. Now that the Holy Roman Rota has pronounced her free to marry, I imagine she will quickly find a new husband. The presence of an elderly lover could make things very difficult for her."

He was sitting in a high carved chair behind a buhl desk, slim, pale, and dangerous as a medieval prince. His lips were smiling, but his eyes were cold. He waited for George Faber to say something, and when Faber did not answer he went on in the same silken tone. "You understand, Mr. Faber, that under the terms of the Concordat the decision of the Holy Roman Rota takes effect in civil law as well?"

"Yes, I understand that."

"Legally, therefore, your attempt to suborn a witness is a criminal offense under the laws of the Republic."

"It would be very difficult to prove subornation. No money was passed. There were no witnesses. Theo Respighi is a somewhat disreputable character."

"Don't you think his testimony would make you look disreputable, too, Mr. Faber?"

"It might. But you wouldn't come out of the affair very well, either."

"I know that, Mr. Faber."

"So it's a stalemate. I can't touch you. You can't touch me."

Calitri selected a cigarette from an alabaster box, lit it, and leaned back in his chair, watching the smoke rings curl upward toward the coffered ceiling of his office. His dark eyes were lit with malicious amusement. "A stalemate? I rather think it is a checkmate. I have to win, you see. No government, and certainly no political party, can support a situation where a correspondent for the foreign press can determine the career of one of its ministers."

In spite of himself Faber laughed dryly. "Do you think that's likely to happen?"

"After what you have done, Mr. Faber, anything is likely to happen. I certainly do not trust you. I doubt whether you will ever be able to trust yourself again. Hardly an edifying sight, was it? The dean of the press corps offering a bribe to a broken-down actor to pervert the law—and all because he wanted to go to bed legally with a girl! You're discredited, my friend! I have only to say a word, and you will never again be received in any government office, or any of the Vatican congregations. Your name will be dropped from every guest list in Italy. You see, I've never made any pretense of what I am. People have accepted me on my own terms, just as the country will accept me again at the next election. . . . So it is checkmate. The game is over. You should pack up and go home."

"You mean I'm expelled from the country?"

"Not quite. Expulsion is an official act of the administration. So far we are speaking . . . unofficially. I am simply advising you to leave."

"How long do I have?"

"How long would you need to make other arrangements with your paper?"

"I don't know. A month, two months."

Calitri smiled. "Two months, then. Sixty days from this date." He laughed lightly. "You will note, Mr. Faber, that I am much more generous with you than you would have been with me."

"May I go now?"

"In a moment. You interest me very much. Tell me, were you in love with Chiara?"

"Yes."

"Were you unhappy when she left you?"

"Yes."

"Strange," said Calitri with sardonic humor. "I have always thought that Chiara would make a better mistress than a wife. You were too old for her, of course. Not potent enough, perhaps. Or were you too much the puritan? That's the answer, I think. One has to be bold in love, Faber. In whatever kind of loving one elects. . . . By the way, is Campeggio a friend of yours?"

"He's a colleague," said Faber evenly. "Nothing more."

"Have you ever lent him money?"

"No."

"Borrowed from him?"

"No."

"That's curious. A check in the amount of six hundred thousand lire—one thousand American dollars—was drawn by Campeggio and paid into your bank account."

"That was a business transaction. How the hell did you know about it?"

"I'm a director of the bank, Mr. Faber. I like to do my work thoroughly. . . . You have two months. Why don't you take a real holiday and enjoy our lovely country? . . . You may go now."

Sick with anger and humiliation, George Faber walked out into the thin autumn sunshine. He went into a telephone booth and called Orlando Campeggio. Then he hailed a taxi and had himself driven to Ruth Lewin's apartment.

She fed him brandy and black coffee, and listened

without comment while he rehearsed his short and ig-
nominious interview with Corrado Calitri. When he had
finished, she sat silent for a moment and then asked
quietly, "What now, George? Where do you go from
here?"

"Back home, I suppose. Although after fifteen years in
Rome it's hard to think of New York as home."

"Will you have any trouble with the paper?"

"I don't think so. They'll accept any explanation I
care to give them. They'll give me a senior job in the
home office."

"So your career isn't really finished, is it?"

"Not my career. Just a way of life that I liked and
wanted."

"But it's not really the end of the world."

He gave her an odd, searching look. "No. But it is the
end of George Faber."

"Why?"

"Because he doesn't exist any more. He's just a name
and a suit of clothes."

"Is that the way you feel, George?"

"It's what I am, sweetheart. I knew it as soon as I sat
down in Calitri's office this morning. I was nothing—a
straw man. I didn't believe anything, I didn't want anything, I had nothing to fight with, I had nothing to fight
for. The wonder is that I feel quite calm about it."

"I know that calm, George," she told him gravely. "It's
the danger signal. The quiet time before the big storm.
Next, you start hating yourself and despising yourself,
and feeling empty and alone and inadequate. Then you
start to run, and you keep running until you hit a brick
wall, or fall over a cliff, or end up in the gutter with your
head in your hands. I know. I've been there."

"Then you mustn't be around when it happens to me."

"It mustn't happen, George. I'm not going to let it happen."

"Buy out, girl!" he told her with sudden harshness. "Buy out and stay out! You've had your storms. You deserve better now. I've made a damn fool of myself, I'm the one who has to pay."

"No, George!" She reached out urgent hands and forced him to turn to her. "That's the other thing I've learned. You can never pay for anything you've done, because you can't change the consequences. They go on and on. The bill keeps mounting up by compound interest until, in the end, you're crushed and bankrupt. It isn't payment we need, George. It's forgiving. . . . And we have to forgive ourselves, too. . . . You're a straw man, you say. So be it! You can either burn the straw man and destroy him. Or you can live with him and—who knows?—in the end you may get to like him. I've always liked him, George. In fact I've learned to love him."

"I wish the hell I could," said George Faber somberly. "I think he's a pompous, windy, gutless snob!"

"I still love him."

"But you can't live with him for the next twenty years and then come to despise him as he despises himself."

"He hasn't asked me to live with him yet."

"And he's not going to ask."

"Then I'll ask him: he's a straw man, I'm a straw woman. I don't have any pride, George. I don't have any pity, either. I'm just so damn glad to be alive. . . . It's not leap year, but I'm still asking you to marry me. I'm not a bad catch, as widows go. I don't have any children.

I still have some looks. I do have money. . . . What do you say, George?"

"I'd like to say yes, but I daren't."

"So what does that mean, George? A fight or a surrender?"

For a moment he was the old uneasy George, running his hands through his gray hair, half mocking, half pitying, himself. Then he said soberly, "It's the wrong thing for a man to say, but could you wait awhile? Could you give me time to get into training for the fight?"

"How, George?"

He did not answer her directly, but explained himself haltingly. "It's a thing hard to explain. . . . I—I don't want to lose you. . . . I don't want to lean on you too much, either. With Chiara I was trying to hold on to youth, and I didn't have enough of it left. I don't want to come to you as empty as I am now. I want to have something to give as well. . . . If we could be friends for a while . . . Hold hands. Walk in the Villa Borghese. Drink and dance a little, and come back here when we're tired. With you I don't want to be what I'm not, but I'm still not sure what I am. These next two months are going to be strange. All the town will be laughing up its sleeve. I'm going to have to rake up some dignity."

"And then, George?"

"Then maybe we can go home together. Can you give me that long?"

"It may take longer, George," she warned him gently. "Don't be too anxious."

"What do you mean?"

But even when she had explained, she was not sure that he had understood.

Extract from
the Secret Memorials of
KIRIL I, Pont. Max.

. . . Today has been long and troublesome. Early this morning Orlando Campeggio, editor of the *Osservatore*, waited upon me to offer his resignation. He told me an involved and sordid story of a conspiracy to introduce suborned evidence into the marital case of Corrado Calitri, which has just been decided by the Holy Roman Rota. Campeggio told me that he himself had been a party to the conspiracy.

The attempt was unsuccessful, but I was deeply shocked by this revelation of the tangled lives of people who are old enough and educated enough to do better. I had no alternative but to accept Campeggio's resignation. I had, however, to commend his honesty, and I told him that his pension arrangements would not be disturbed. I understand very well the motives which led him to this breach of trust, but I cannot for that reason condone the act.

When Campeggio left me, I called immediately for the file on the Calitri case, and went over it carefully with an official of the Rota. There is no doubt in my mind that on the evidence presented, the Rota acted rightly in issuing a decree of nullity. There was another side to the picture, however: Corrado Calitri, a man of power and influence in Italy, has been living for a long time in mortal danger of his soul. I have little doubt that his sincerity in this case is suspect, but the Holy Roman Rota can give judgment only in the external forum. A man's soul can be judged only in the tribunal of the confessional.

So I am brought to a curious position. As a Minister of the Republic, Corrado Calitri is not amenable to my authority. Our relationship in the temporal order is defined by treaty and limited by diplomacy. If we quarrel, I may do much harm to the Church and to Italy, especially as I am not an Italian. In the spiritual order, however, Calitri is subject to me. As Bishop of Rome, I am his pastor. And I am not only authorized, but obliged if I can to intervene in the affairs of his soul. I have, therefore, asked him to wait upon me at a suitable time, and I hope that I may be able to offer him a pastoral service in the regulation of his conscience.

I have had a short but cheerful letter from Ruth Lewin. She tells me that she has finally resolved her position, and has decided to return to the practice of the Catholic faith. She was kind enough to say that she was indebted to me for the enlightenment and the courage to make the step. I know that this is only half the truth, and that I am at best an instrument for the working of Divine Grace. I am consoled, however, that having stepped outside the rigid confines of my office, I was permitted to make contact with her and to co-operate in re-establishing her peace of soul. . . .

Once more I have been brought to see vividly that the real battleground of the Church is not in politics or in diplomacy or finance or material extension. It is the secret landscape of the individual spirit. To enter into this hidden place the pastor needs tact and understanding, and the very particular grace bestowed by the Sacrament of Holy Orders. If I am not to fail Corrado Calitri—and it is very easy to fail those who are framed differently from other men—then I must pray and consider carefully before I meet him. If I do fail, if he leaves me in enmity, then I shall have created a new problem since I shall have to deal with him in public matters for a long time.

The President of the United States has received Kamenev's letter and my commentary on it. His reply is before me as I write:

. . . On the face of it Kamenev does seem to offer a feasible basis for a short-term solution to our problem. I think we must get a better bargain than the one he offers. He is too good a horse trader to offer everything at once. I am not prepared to say how much more we need without submitting the project to study and taking the advice of my counsellors.

However, you may tell Kamenev that I am prepared to open negotiations at this point, but that in my view they should now be initiated at diplomatic level. And he must be the one to begin them. If he is prepared to co-operate in this fashion, then like your Holiness, I believe we may make progress.

I, too, am very concerned about the political climate in which these negotiations are begun. One always expects a certain amount of skirmishing and propaganda. We have to use it as much as the Russians. However, it must not be allowed to go beyond a safe limit. We shall need an atmosphere of moderation and good will, not only in our own negotiations but in our talks with members of the European bloc and with the representatives of uncommitted nations. In a deal like this there are so many limiting factors that it is difficult enough to maintain patience and restraint without calculated provocation.

I agree in the main with Kamenev's estimate of the political and military situation. It is broadly confirmed by my own advisors. They agree also that if the situation still remains unsettled at the end of next March, the crisis will already be upon us.

I note with lively interest the fact that your Holiness is considering a journey to France early next February. This would be a very notable event, and I ask myself—as I ask your Holiness—whether it might not be possible to use it to good purpose for the whole world.

I understand very clearly that the Holy See cannot, and does not wish to, enter directly or indirectly into a political negotiation between the great powers. But if on this occasion your Holiness could sum up the hopes of all men for peace and a negotiated settlement of our differences, then at one stroke we might have the climate we need.

I know that it will not be so easy to do. The Holy See may well have to speak for those countries where she has suffered the greatest injustice, but a historic occasion calls for a historic magnanimity. I wonder whether something like this was not in Kamenev's mind when he wrote to you first. I know that it is now in mine.

With all respect I should like to make a suggestion. The churches of Christendom are still, unhappily, divided. However, there have been signs for a long time of a growing desire for reunion. If it were possible to associate other Christian bodies with your Holiness' plea for peace, then it would be an even greater advantage.

I understand that a decision has not yet been made. I understand the weighty and prudent reasons for the delay. I can only say that I wish and hope that your Holiness will finally decide to go to Lourdes. . . .

Goldoni has seen the letter, and I know that he is torn between the excitement of the project and a prudent wish to consider all the possible consequences before a decision is made.

He suggested, diffidently, that I might care to discuss the matter with members of the Curia. I am inclined to agree with him. My authority is absolute, but common sense dictates that in so large and consequential a matter I should get the best advice available to me. I think also that I should call Cardinal Pallenberg from Germany and Morand from Paris to take part in the discussion. We have decided finally to name Archbishop Ellison, Cardinal Archbishop of Westminster. This might be a suitable occasion to call him also to Rome and offer him the red hat. . . .

Jean Télémond came yesterday to have dinner with me. He looks thinner and rather tired. He tells me, however, that he is feeling well and working steadily. He is very happy with Cardinal Rinaldi, and the two of them have become good friends. I am a little jealous of Rinaldi's good fortune because I miss my Jean, and in all this press of business I could use a little of his wondering vision of the world. Rinaldi sent me a short note by his hand, thanking me for my kindness to Leone. I have to admit that it was not so much a kindness as a calculated gesture. However, it did not go unnoticed and I am glad.

I know that Jean is still worried about the verdict of the Holy Office on his first volume. However, it is impossible to hurry an examination like this, and I have urged him to be patient. Cardinal Leone has promised to let me have an interim opinion by the end of October. I notice that he is treating the matter with extreme moderation, and is displaying personally a careful good will toward Jean Télémond. However, he is most emphatic that we should not appoint him to any office of preaching or teaching until the conclusions of the Holy Office are known.

I cannot disagree with him, but I still wish I could learn to like him. I have a free and easy commerce with other members of the Curia, but between Leone and myself there is always a kind of inhibition and uneasiness. It is my defect as much as his. I am still resentful of his Roman rigidity. . . .

Georg Wilhelm Forster has been to see me, and I have passed on to him the reply of the President of the United States. Forster is a strange little man who lives a dangerous life in apparently untroubled good humor. When I asked him about himself, he told me that his mother was a Lett and his father a Georgian. He studied in Leipzig and Moscow, and borrowed his German name for professional purposes. He is still a practicing member of the Russian Orthodox Church. When I asked him how he squared his conscience with the services of a Godless state, he turned the question very neatly:

"Is not this what you are trying to do, Holiness? Serve Mother Russia in the best fashion available to you? Systems pass, but the land is always there, and we are bound to it as if by a navel cord. . . . Kamenev understands me. I understand him. Neither demands too much of the other. . . . And God understands us all, better than we do ourselves."

The thought has remained with me all day, mixed up

with thoughts of the coming crisis, and Jean Télémond, and the pilgrimage to Lourdes, and the strange bargain of Corrado Calitri. My own understanding stumbles often. But if God understands, then we are still in hopeful case. . . . When the poet writes, the pen needs not to understand the verse. Whether the pot be whole or broken, it still stands witness to the skill of the potter. . . .

X

IN THE LAST week of October, Cardinal Leone, in private audience with the Pontiff, presented the judgment of the Holy Office on Jean Télémond's book. Leone seemed embarrassed by the occasion. He took pains to explain the nature and form of the document:

"There has been a question of time, Holiness, and a question of the special circumstances of the life of Father Jean Télémond, and the private relationship which he enjoys with your Holiness. With reference to the time factor, the Fathers of the Sacred Congregation of the Holy Office have preferred to issue an interim opinion on the work in question rather than a formal judgment. Their opinion is brief, but it is accompanied by a commentary setting down certain propositions which are basic to the whole thesis. With respect to the person of Jean Télémond, the commissioners make a special note of the evident spirituality of the man and his submissive spirit as a son of the Church and as a regular cleric. They attach no censure to him and advise no canonical process."

Kiril nodded and said quietly, "I should be grateful if your Eminence would read me this interim opinion."

Leone looked up sharply, but the Pontiff's eyes were hooded and his scarred face was as impassive as a mask. Leone read carefully from the Latin text:

" 'The most Eminent and most Reverend Fathers of the Supreme Sacred Congregation of the Holy Office, acting under instructions from His Holiness, Kiril I, Supreme Pontiff, transmitted through the Secretary of the said Sacred Congregation, have made a diligent examination of a manuscript work written by the Reverend Father Jean Télémond, of the Society of Jesus, and entitled *The Progress of Man.* They take note of the fact that this work was submitted voluntarily and in a spirit of religious obedience by its author, and they recommend that so long as he continues in this spirit no censure should attach to him, nor any process be instituted against him under the canons. They recognize the honest intention of the author and the contribution he has made to scientific research, particularly in the field of paleontology. It is their opinion, however, that the above-named work presents ambiguities and even grave errors in philosophical and theological matters which offend Catholic doctrine. A full schedule of objectionable propositions is annexed to this opinion in the form of extracts from the author's work, and commentaries by the most Eminent and Reverend Fathers of the Sacred Congregation of the Holy Office. The major grounds of objection are as follows:

" 'One: The author's attempt to apply the terms and concepts of evolutionary theory to the fields of metaphysics and theology is improper.

" 'Two: The concept of creative union expressed in the said work would seem to make the divine creation a completion of absolute being rather than an effect of efficient causality. Some of the expressions used by the author lead the reader to think he believed creation to be in some manner a necessary action in contrast with the classical theological concept of creation as an act of God's perfect and absolute freedom.

" 'Three: The concept of unity, of unifying action, strictly tied to Télémond's evolutionary theory, is more than once extended and applied even to the supernatural order. As a consequence there seems to be attributed to Christ a third nature, neither human nor divine, but cosmic.

" 'Four: In the author's thesis the distinction and difference between the natural and the supernatural order is not clear, and it is difficult to see how he can logically save the gratuitous nature of the supernatural order, and thus of grace.

" 'The most Reverend Fathers have not desired to take, letter for letter, what the author has written on these points; for otherwise they would be forced to consider some of the author's conclusions as a true and real heresy. They are very well aware of the semantic difficulties involved in expressing a new and original thought, and they wish to concede that the thought of the author may still remain in a problematic phase.

" 'It is, however, their considered opinion that the Reverend Father Jean Télémond be required to re-examine this work, and those later ones which may depend on it, to bring them into conformity with the traditional doctrine of the Church. In the meantime he should be pro-

hibited from preaching, teaching, publishing, or dissem-
inating in any other fashion the dubious opinions noted
by the Fathers of the Sacred Congregation.

" 'Given at Rome this twentieth day of October, in the
first year of the Pontificate of His Holiness, Kiril I, Gloriously Reigning.' "

Leone finished his reading, laid the document on Kiril's desk, and waited in silence.

"Twenty years," said Kiril softly. "Twenty years demolished in one stroke. I wonder how he will take it."

"I'm sorry, Holiness. There was nothing else we could
do. I myself had no part in this. The commissioners were
appointed at your Holiness' direction."

"We know that." Kiril's address was studiously formal.
"You have our thanks, Eminence. You may carry our
thanks and our appreciation also to the Reverend Fathers
of the Sacred Congregation."

"I shall do that, Holiness. Meantime, how is this news
to be conveyed to Father Télémond?"

"We shall tell him ourselves. Your Eminence has our
leave to go."

The old lion stood his ground, stubborn and unafraid.
"This is a grief to your Holiness. I know it, I wish I could
share it. But neither my colleagues nor I could have returned a different verdict. Your Holiness must know that."

"We do know it. Our grief is private to ourselves. Now
we should like to be alone."

He knew it was brutal, but he could not help himself.
He watched the old Cardinal walk, proud and erect, out
of the chamber, and then sat down heavily at the desk,
staring at the document.

They were caught now, Jean Télémond and himself. At

one stride they had come together to the point of decision. For himself the issue was clear. As custodian of the Deposit of Faith he could not accept error or even risk its dissemination. If Jean Télémond broke under the weight of judgment, he had to stand by and see him destroyed rather than permit one single deviation from the truth transmitted from Christ to His Apostles, and from the Apostles to the living Church.

For Jean Télémond, he knew, the problem was far greater. He would submit to judgment, yes. He would bend his will obediently to the Faith. But what of his intellect, that fine-tempered, far-ranging instrument that had grappled so long with a cosmic mystery? How would it bear the immense strain laid upon it? And its tenement, the weakened body with its fluttering, uncertain heart. How would it tolerate the battle soon to be waged within it?

Kiril the Pontiff bent his head on his hands and prayed an instant, desperately, for himself and the man who had become a brother to him. Then he lifted the telephone and asked to be connected with Cardinal Rinaldi, at his villa.

The old man came on almost immediately.

Kiril asked him, "Where is Father Télémond?"

"In the garden, Holiness. Do you want to talk with him?"

"No. With yourself, Eminence. . . . How is he to-day?"

"Not too well, I think. He had a bad night. He looks tired. Is something wrong?"

"I have just had the verdict from the Holy Office."

"Oh! . . . Good or bad?"

"Not good. They have gone as far as they can to minimize their objections, but their objections are still there."

"Are they valid, Holiness?"

"Most of them, I think."

"Does your Holiness want me to tell Jean?"

"No. I should like to tell him myself. Can you put him
in a car and send him to the Vatican?"

"Of course. . . . I think perhaps I should prepare him
a little."

"If you can, I shall be grateful."

"How do you feel, Holiness?"

"Worried for Jean."

"Try not to worry too much. He is better prepared than
he knows."

"I hope so. When he returns, take care of him."

"I shall, Holiness. I have a great affection for him."

"I know. And I am grateful to your Eminence."

"Who delivered the verdict, Holiness?"

"Leone."

"Was he distressed?"

"A little, I think. I have never been able to read him
very well."

"Would you like me to telephone him?"

"If you wish. . . . How long will it take Jean to get
here?"

"An hour, I should say."

"Have him come to the Angelic Gate. I shall leave orders that he is to be brought straight to my room."

"I shall do that, Holiness. . . . Believe me, I am
deeply sorry."

When Jean Télémond came in, pale of visage but
straight and soldierly, Kiril went forward to greet him
with outstretched hands. When he went to kiss the ring

of the Fisherman, Kiril drew him erect and led him to the chair by his desk. He said affectionately:

"I'm afraid I have bad news for you, Jean."

"The verdict?"

"Yes."

"I thought so. May I see it, please?"

Kiril handed the paper across the desk and watched him intently as he read it. His fine face seemed to crumple under the shock, and small beads of sweat broke out on his forehead and on his lips. When he had finished, he laid the document on the desk and looked at the Pontiff with eyes full of pain and perplexity. He said unsteadily, "It's worse than I thought. . . . They've tried to be kind, but it's very bad."

"It's not final, Jean; you know that. Some of it seems to be a matter of semantics. For the rest there is no censure. They simply ask for a re-examination."

Télémond seemed to shrink back into himself. His hands trembled. He shook his head. "There isn't time. . . . Twenty years' work depends on that volume. It's the keystone of the structure. Without it the rest falls apart."

Kiril went to him swiftly, laying his hands on Télémond's trembling shoulders. "It isn't all wrong, Jean. They don't say that. They simply challenge certain propositions. These are the only things you have to clarify. . . ."

"There isn't time. . . . At night I hear the knocking on the gate. I am being summoned, Holiness, and suddenly the work is undone. What am I to do?"

"You know what you have to do, Jean. This is the moment you were afraid of. I am here with you. I am your friend—your brother. But the moment is yours."

"You want me to submit?"

"You must, Jean; you know that."

Through his own fingertips Kiril could feel the struggle that racked Télémond in body and spirit. He felt the tremor of nerve and muscle, the dampness of sweat. He smelt the odor of a man in mortal torment. Then the tremor subsided.

Slowly Jean Télémond lifted a pain-racked face. In a voice that seemed to be wrenched out of him, he said at last, "Very well. I submit. . . . What now? I submit, but I see no light. I am deaf to all the harmony I used to hear. Where has it gone? I'm lost, left . . . I submit, but where do I go?"

"Stay here with me, Jean. Let me share the darkness with you. We're friends—brothers. This is the time of gall and vinegar. Let me drink it with you."

For a moment it seemed that he would consent. Then with a great effort he took possession of himself again. He heaved himself out of his chair and stood facing the Pontiff, ravaged, shaken, but still a whole man. "No, Holiness! I'm grateful, but no! Everyone has to drink the gall and vinegar by himself. I should like to go now."

"I shall come and see you tomorrow, Jean."

"I may need more time, Holiness."

"Will you telephone me?"

"Only when I am ready, Holiness. . . . Only when I see light. Everything is dark to me now. I feel abandoned in a desert. Twenty years down the drain!"

"Not all of it, Jean. Hold to that, I beg of you. Not all of it."

"Perhaps it doesn't matter."

"Everything matters, Jean. The right and the wrong as well. Everything matters. Take courage."

"Courage? You know all I have at this moment? A small pulse inside me that flickers and beats and tells me tomorrow I may be dead. . . . I have said it, Holiness. I submit. Please let me go now."

"I love you, Jean," said Kiril the Pontiff. "I love you as I have never loved another person in my whole life. If I could take this pain from you, I would do it gladly."

"I know it," said Jean Télémond simply. "I am more grateful than I can say. But even with loving, a man must die alone. And this, I have always known, would be ten times worse than dying."

When the door closed behind him, Kiril the Pontiff slammed his fists down on the desk and cried aloud in anger at his own impotence.

The next day and the next, and the day after, he had no word of Jean Télémond. He could only guess at what he must be suffering. For all his authority as Supreme Pastor, this was one drama, one very intimate dialogue, in which he dared not intervene.

Besides, he himself was besieged with business, from the Secretariat of State, from the Congregation for the Affairs of the Eastern Church, from the Congregation of Rites. . . . Every tribunal and commission in Rome seemed to demand his attention at once. He had to drive himself through the days with a relentless discipline, and at night his desk was still piled high with papers, and his soul cried out for the refreshment of prayer and solitude.

Still he could not put Télémond out of his mind, and on the morning of the fourth day—a day taken up with private and semi-private audiences—he called Cardinal Rinaldi at the villa.

Rinaldi's report was less than comforting:

"He is suffering greatly, Holiness. There is no doubt

about his submission, but I cannot begin to count what it is costing him."

"How is his health?"

"Indifferent. I have had the doctor to him twice. His blood pressure is dangerously high, but this, of course, is the result of tension and fatigue. There is little to be done for it."

"Is he still happy with you?"

"Happier here than anywhere else, I think. We understand each other. He is as private as he needs to be, and strangely enough, I think the children are good for him."

"What does he do with himself?"

"In the morning he says Mass, and then walks for a while in the country. At midday he goes to our parish church and reads his office alone. He rests after lunch, although I do not think he sleeps. In the afternoon he walks in the garden. He talks with the children when they come home. At night we play a game of chess together."

"He's not working?"

"No. He is in deep perplexity. . . . Yesterday Semmering came to see him. They talked together for a long time. Afterwards Jean seemed a little calmer."

"Would he like me to visit him?"

Rinaldi hesitated a moment. "I don't think so, Holiness. He has a deep affection for you. He talks of you very often with gentleness and gratitude. But he feels, I think, that he must not ask you to bend yourself, or your office, to his personal problem. He is very brave, you know, very noble."

"Does he know that I love him?"

"He knows. He has told me. But the only way he can return the love is by maintaining his own dignity. Your Holiness must understand that."

"I do. And, Valerio . . . " It was the first time he had used the Cardinal's first name. "I am very grateful to you."

"And I to you, Holiness. You have given me peace and the opportunity to share my life with a great man."

"If he gets really ill, you will call me immediately?"

"Immediately, I promise."

"God bless you, Valerio."

He put down the receiver and sat for a while, collecting his energies for the formalities of the morning. He did not belong to himself any more. He could spend no more than a part of himself even on Jean Télémond. He belonged to God, then through God to the Church. No man's purse was deep enough to stand such a constant expense of body and spirit. Yet he had to go on spending, trusting in the Almighty for a renewal of the funds.

The audience list was on his desk. When he picked it up, he saw that the first name was that of Corrado Calitri. He pressed the bell. The door of the audience chamber opened, and the Maestro di Camera led the Minister of the Republic into his presence.

When the first formalities were over, Kiril dismissed the Maestro di Camera and asked Calitri to sit down. He noted the containment of the man, the intelligent eyes, the ease with which he moved in an ambience of authority. This was one born to eminence. He had to be dealt with honestly. His pride had to be respected, his intelligence, also. Kiril sat down and addressed himself quietly to his visitor:

"I am anchored to this place, my friend. I am not so free to move as others, so I have to ask you to come to see me."

"I am honored, Holiness," said Calitri formally.

"I shall have to ask you to be patient with me, and not resent me too much. Later I believe you will sit on the Quirinal Hill; I shall sit here in the Vatican; and between us we shall rule Rome."

"There is a long way to go before then, Holiness," said Calitri with a thin smile. "Politics is a risky business."

"So this morning," said Kiril gently, "let us ignore politics. I am a priest and your bishop. I want to talk to you about yourself."

He saw Calitri stiffen under the shock, and the swift flush that mounted to his pale cheeks. He hurried on. "The editor of the *Osservatore Romano* resigned a few days ago. I think you know why."

"I do."

"I was sufficiently concerned to call for the file on your case from the Holy Roman Rota. I examined it very carefully. I have to tell you that the record of the proceedings is completely in order, and that the decree of nullity handed down was fully justified by the evidence."

Calitri's relief was evident. "I'm glad to hear that, Holiness. I did a great wrong in attempting marriage. I'm not very proud of myself, but I'm glad to see justice done at last."

Kiril the Pontiff said evenly, "There was something else in the record which interested me more than the legal process. It was the evidence of a deep spiritual dilemma in your own soul." Calitri opened his mouth to speak, but the Pontiff stayed him with an uplifted hand. "No, please! Let me finish. I did not ask you here to accuse you. You are my son in Christ; I want to help you. You have a special and very difficult problem. I should like to help you to solve it."

Calitri flushed again, and then gave an ironic shrug. "We are what we are, Holiness. . . . We have to make the best terms we can with life. The record shows, I think, that I have tried to improve the terms."

"But the problem is still there, is it not?"

"Yes. One tries to make substitutions, sublimations. Some of them work, some of them don't. Not all of us are ready for a lifelong crucifixion, Holiness. Perhaps we should be, but we are not." He gave a small, dry chuckle. "Just as well, perhaps; otherwise you might find half the world in monasteries and the other half jumping off a cliff."

To his surprise, Kiril acknowledged the irony with a smile of good humor. "Strange as it may sound, I don't disagree with you. Somehow or other, we all have to come to terms with ourselves as we are, and with the world as it is. I have never believed that we have to do it by destroying ourselves. . . . Or even more importantly, by destroying others. May I ask you a question, my son?"

"I may not be able to answer it, Holiness."

"This problem of yours. This thing that drives you. How do you define it for yourself?"

To his surprise, Calitri did not balk the question. He answered it bluntly. "I defined it a long time ago, Holiness. It is a question of love. There are many varieties of love, and—I am not ashamed to say it—I am susceptible to, and capable of, one special variety." He hurried on urgently. "Some people love children, others find them little monsters. We don't blame them, we accept them for what they are! Most men can love women—but even then, not all women. I am drawn to men. Why should I be ashamed of that?"

"You should not be ashamed," said Kiril the Pontiff. "Only when your love becomes destructive—as it has done in the past, as it may do with Campeggio's son. A man who is promiscuous is not a true lover. He is too centered upon himself. He has a long way yet to grow to maturity. Do you understand what I am trying to say?"

"I understand it. I understand also that one does not arrive at maturity in one leap. I think I am beginning to arrive there."

"Sincerely?"

"Which of us is wholly sincere with himself, Holiness? That, too, takes a lifetime of practice. Let us say that perhaps I am beginning to be sincere. But politics is not the best training ground, nor is the world."

"Are you angry with me, my friend?" asked Kiril the Pontiff with a smile.

"No, Holiness. I am not angry. But you must not expect me to surrender to you like a schoolgirl at first confession."

"I don't expect that, but sooner or later you will have to surrender. Not to me, but to God."

"That, too, takes time."

"Which of us can promise himself time? Is your span so certain? Or mine?"

Calitri was silent.

"Will you think about what I have said?"

"I will think about it."

"And not resent me?"

"I will try not to resent you, Holiness."

"Thank you. Before you go, I should like to tell you

that here, in this place three nights ago, I stood and suffered with a man who is as dear to me as life. I love him. I love him in the spirit and in the flesh. I am not ashamed of it because love is the noblest emotion of humankind. . . . Do you ever read the New Testament?"

"I haven't read it for a long time."

"Then you should read the description of the Last Supper, where John the Apostle sat on the right hand of the Master and leaned his head on His breast, so that all the others looked and wondered and said, 'See how he loves Him.'" He stood up and said briskly, "You are a busy man. I have taken up too much of your time. Please forgive me."

Calitri, too, stood up and felt himself dwarfed by the tall, commanding figure of the Pontiff. He said not without humor, "Your Holiness took a great risk calling me here."

"This is a risky office," said Kiril evenly. "But very few people understand it—besides, your own risk is much greater. Don't, I beg of you, underrate it."

He pressed the bell and handed his visitor back into the practiced hands of the Maestro di Camera.

When Corrado Calitri walked out of the bronze gate and into the pale sunshine of St. Peter's square, the Princess Maria-Rina was waiting for him in the car. She questioned him shrewdly and eagerly. "Well, boy, how did it go? No problems, I hope? You got along well together? Did he talk about the verdict? About politics? This sort of thing is most important, you know. You are going to live with this man for a long time."

"For Christ's sake, Aunt," said Corrado Calitri irritably, "will you shut up and let me think!"

:

At eleven o'clock the same evening, the telephone rang in Kiril's private apartment. Cardinal Rinaldi was on the line. He was in deep distress. Jean Télémond had suffered a heart attack, and the doctors expected another at any moment. There was no hope for his life. Rinaldi had already administered the last rites and summoned the Father General of the Jesuits. Kiril slammed down the phone and ordered his car to be ready in five minutes with an escort of Italian police.

As he dressed hurriedly for the road, childish, simple prayers leapt to his lips. It must not be. It could not be. God must be kinder to Jean Télémond, who had risked so much for so long. "Please, please hold him a little longer! Hold him at least till I get there and can set him at peace. I love him! I need him! Don't take him so abruptly!"

As the big car roared out through the nighttime city, with the Vatican pennant fluttering and the police sirens clearing the traffic, Kiril the Pontiff closed his eyes and fingered the beads of his rosary, concentrating all the resources of his spirit in a single petition for the life and the soul of Jean Télémond.

He offered himself as a hostage—a victim, if necessary —in his place. And even as he prayed, he wrestled with the guilty resentment that thus incontinently the man he loved should be snatched away from him. The darkness that Jean Télémond had endured seemed now to come down on him, so that even while he wrenched his will into submission his heart cried out bitterly for a stay of judgment.

But when Rinaldi met him at the door of the villa, gray-faced and shaken, he knew that his petition had been refused. Jean Télémond, the restless traveler, was already embarked on his last voyage.

"He's sinking, Holiness," said Valerio Rinaldi. "The doctor's with him. He will not last the night."

He led the pontiff into the antique room where the doctor stood, with the Father General of the Jesuits, looking down on Télémond, and the candles burned for a last light to the departing spirit. Télémond lay, slack and unconscious, his hands at rest on the white coverlet, his face shrunken, his eyes closed deep in their sockets.

Kiril knelt by the bedside and tried to summon him back into consciousness. "Jean! Can you hear me? It's I, Kiril. I came as soon as I could. I'm here with you, holding your hand. Jean, my brother, please speak to me if you can!"

There was no sign from Jean Télémond. His hands were still slack, his eyelids closed against the light of the candles. From his cyanosed lips there issued only the shallow, rattling breath of the dying.

Kiril the Pontiff leaned his head on the breast of his friend and wept as he had not wept since his nights of madness in the bunker. Rinaldi and Semmering stood watching him, moved, but helpless, and Semmering, unaware of the trick of circumstance, whispered the Gospel words " 'See how he loves him.' "

Then when the weeping had spent itself, Rinaldi laid his old hand on the sacred shoulder of the Pontiff and summoned him gently. "Let him go, Holiness! He is at peace. It is the best we can wish him. Let him go!"

Early the next morning, Cardinal Leone presented himself unannounced in the papal apartments. He was kept waiting for twenty minutes, and then was shown into the Pontiff's study. Kiril was sitting behind his desk, lean, withdrawn, weary of mouth and eye after the nightlong vigil. His manner was strained and distant. It seemed an effort for him to speak.

"We had asked to be left alone. Is there something special we can do for your Eminence?"

Leone's craggy face tightened at the snub, but he controlled himself and said quietly, "I came to offer my sympathy to your Holiness on the death of Father Télémond. I heard the news from my friend Rinaldi. I thought your Holiness would like to know that I offered a Mass this morning for the repose of his soul."

Kiril's eyes softened a little, but he still held to the formality of speech. "We are grateful to your Eminence. This is a great personal loss to us."

"I feel guilty about it," said Leone. "As if in some way I were responsible for his death."

"You have no cause to feel that, Eminence. Father Télémond had been ailing for some time, and the Holy Office verdict was a shock to him. But neither you nor the Eminent Fathers could have acted differently. You should dismiss the matter from your mind."

"I cannot dismiss it, Holiness," said Leone in his strong fashion. "I have a confession to make."

"Then you should make it to your confessor."

Leone shook his white mane and lifted his old head in answer to the challenge. "You are a priest, Holiness. I am a soul in distress. I elect to make my confession to you. Do you refuse me?"

For a moment it seemed as if the Pontiff would explode into anger. Then slowly his taut features relaxed and his mouth turned upwards into a tired smile. "You have me there, Eminence. What is your confession?"

"I was jealous of Jean Télémond, Holiness. I did what was right, but my intention was not right while I did it."

Kiril the Pontiff looked at the old man with puzzled eyes. "Why were you jealous of him?"

"Because of you, Holiness. Because I needed but could not have what you gave him at a first meeting—intimacy, trust, affection, a place in your private counsels. I am an old man. I have served the Church a long time. I felt I had deserved better. I was wrong. None of us deserves anything but the promised wage for a worker in the vineyard. . . . I'm sorry. Now will your Holiness absolve me?"

As the Pontiff moved toward him, he went down stiffly on his knees and bent his white head under the words of absolution. When they were finished, he asked, "And the penance, Holiness?"

"Tomorrow you will say a Mass for one who has lost a friend and is still only half resigned to God's will."

"I will do that."

Kiril's strong hands reached down and drew him to his feet, so that they stood facing each other, priest and penitent, Pope and Cardinal, caught in the momentary wonder of understanding.

"I, too, have sinned, Eminence," said Kiril. "I kept you at a distance from me because I could not tolerate your opposition in my projects. I was at fault with Jean Télémond, too, I think, because I clung to him too strongly; and when the moment came to let him go into the hands of God, I could not do it without bitterness. I am empty today, and very troubled. I am glad you came."

"May I tell you something, Holiness?"

"Of course."

"I have seen three men sit in this room; you are the last I shall see. Each of them came in his turn to the moment where you stand now—the moment of solitude. I have to tell you that there is no remedy for it, and no escape. You cannot retire from this place as Rinaldi has done, as I hope you will let me do very soon. You are here until the day you die. The longer you live the lonelier you will become. You will use this man and that for the work of the Church, but when the work is done, or when the man has proved unequal to it, then you will let him go and find another. You want love. You need it as I do, even though I am old. You may have it for a while, but then you will lose it because a noble man cannot commit himself to an unequal affection. And a gross man will not satisfy you. Like it or not, you are condemned to a solitary pilgrimage, from the day of your election until the day of your death. This is a Calvary, Holiness, and you have just begun the climb. Only God can walk with you all the way, because He took on flesh to make the same climb Himself. . . . I wish I could tell you differently. I cannot."

"I know it," said Kiril somberly. "I know it in the marrow of my bones. I think I have shrunk from it every day since my election. When Jean Télémond died last night, a part of me died with him."

"If we die to ourselves," said the old lion, "in the end we come to live in God. But it is a long, slow dying. Believe me, I know! You are a young man. You have yet to learn what it is to be old." He paused a moment, recovering himself, and then asked, "Now that we are at one, Holiness, may I ask you a favor?"

"What is it, Eminence?"

"I should like you to let me retire, like Rinaldi."

Kiril the Pontiff pondered on it for a moment, and then shook his head. "No. I cannot let you go yet."

"You ask a great deal, Holiness."

"I hope you will be generous with me. You were not made to rusticate or wither away in a convent garden. . . . There are lions abroad in the streets, and we need lions to fight them. Stay with me awhile longer."

"I can stay only in trust, Holiness."

"In trust, I promise you."

"You must not flatter me, Holiness."

"I do not flatter you, Eminence," said Kiril gravely. "You have much courage. I want to borrow it for a while. . . . Just now, you see, I am very much afraid."

The fear was tangible, familiar, and mightily threatening. It was the same which he had endured in the hands of Kamenev, and he had been brought to it by the same process. . . . Months of self-questioning. Recurrent crises of pain. Sudden and spectacular revelations of the complexities of existence, beside which the simple propositions of faith seemed pitifully inadequate.

If the pressure was kept on long enough, the delicate mechanism of reflection and decision seized up like an overdriven motor. All the processes of the personality seemed to fall into syncope, so that one was left confused and irresolute—even grateful to be swayed by a stronger will.

Every day during these first months of his Pontificate he had been forced to question his motives and his capacities. He had been forced to measure his private convictions against the accumulated experience of the bureaucracy and the hierarchy. He felt like a man pushing a stone uphill, only to have it roll back upon him at every third step.

Then, just when the progress seemed easier, he had been faced with a deep and long-hidden weakness in himself: the need for love that had driven him to cling so urgently to the friendship of Jean Télémond that his detachment as a religious man had been almost wholly destroyed. The foundations of his confidence had been weakened still further by his indulgence of resentment against Leone. It was not he who had taken the first step to reconciliation, but the old Cardinal. It was not he who had helped Jean Télémond to the conformity in which he needed to die, but Rinaldi and Rudolf Semmering.

If he had failed so dismally in these simple relationships, how could he trust himself and his convictions under the complex demands of leadership in the Universal Church?

So even after seventeen years of endurance for the Faith, everything was called in question again, and he saw how easy it would be to shift the burden of action. He had only to relax, to let the system of the Church take over. He did not have to decide anything. He had simply to propose and suggest, and work according to the opinions tendered to him by the Secretariat of State, by the Sacred Congregations, and by all the administrative bodies, little and great, within the Church.

It was a legitimate method of government. It was a safe one, too. It rested itself firmly upon the collective wisdom of the Church, and could be justified as an act of humility on the part of a leader who had found himself wanting. It would preserve the integrity of the Church, and the dignity of his office, against the consequences of his own incapacity. Yet deep inside him—deep as the roots of life itself—was the conviction that the work to which he had been called was far other. He had to show forth in himself the faculty for renewal which was one of the marks of the living Church. The problem now was that he could no longer reason out the conviction. The fear was now that he was living an illusion of self-love, and self-deception, and destructive pride.

Daily the evidence was mounting up against him. The question of his visit to France and of his involvement in the political discussion of the nations was already being canvassed among the Cardinals and Primates of the Church. Daily their opinions were being brought to his desk, and he was troubled by the extent to which they differed from his own.

Cardinal Carlin wrote from New York:

So far the President of the United States has professed himself happy with what your Holiness has done to assist the opening of negotiations with the Soviet Union. However, now that the talks have begun at diplomatic level, there is a fear that the Holy See may try to color them by using its influence in the European bloc of nations, whose interests diverge at certain important points from those of America. Under this aspect your Holiness' proposed visit to France may wear a far different look from that which is intended.

From Archbishop Ellison, who had not yet received the red hat, came the cool comment:

Your Holiness must be aware that the Republic of France was the bitterest opponent of the participation of England in the European community of nations. If your Holiness goes to France, inevitably you will be invited to Belgium and to Germany as well. It might seem to many Englishmen that France is trying to use the Holy See, as she used her before, to strengthen her own position in Europe at the cost of ours.

Platino, "the Red Pope," had another point of view:

I am convinced, as is your Holiness, that sooner or later the Vicar of Christ must take advantage of modern travel to present himself in person to the churches throughout the world. I ask myself, however, whether the first gesture should be one which is free from historic association. Might it not be better to plan much further ahead for a visit, say, to South America or to the Philippines, so that the missionary work of the Church would receive an impetus which it so badly needs at this moment?

From Poland, where Potocki was dying and where his successor had already been secretly named, came a warning even more blunt. It was delivered by word of mouth from the emissary who had carried the papal appointment to the new incumbent:

There is a feeling, strongly expressed, that Kamenev, who is known as a subtle and ruthless politician, may be trying to create a situation in which the Holy See can be named as a co-operator with the Kremlin. The effect of this among Catholics behind the iron curtain could well be disastrous.

On the other hand, there was Kamenev's last letter, which, if it meant anything at all, meant a startling change in the rigid Marxist thought, and a deeper change working in the man himself. Man was not a static animal. Society was not static, nor was the Church. Whether in the sense of Jean Télémond or in another, they were evolving, shedding historic accretions, developing new attitudes and new potentials, groping consciously or instinctively toward the promise of more light and fuller life. They all needed time—time and the leaven of divinity working in the human lump. Every moment saved was a deferment of chaos. Every hint of good was an evidence of God's ferment in His own creation. . . . Kamenev wrote:

. . . So, thanks to your good offices, we are enabled to begin at diplomatic level a negotiation with the United States which has at least some hope of success. There will be rough words and hard bargaining, but time is running out, and of this at least we are all convinced.

I am interested in your plan for a visit to France in the first part of February. I agree—though the Party would have my head if they heard it—that you may do much toward preparing a suitable climate for our discussions.

I shall be more than interested to read what you will say. Inevitably you must discuss the question of rights and duties between nations. How will you treat the rights of Russia, where you have suffered so much and whence your Church has been extirpated? How will you treat the rights of China, where your bishops and priests are in prison?

Forgive me. I am an incurable joker, but this time the joke is against myself. If any man could convince me that there is a God, you, Kiril Lakota, would be the one to do it. But for me there is still an empty heaven and I must plot and plan, and lie and bargain, and close my eyes on terror and violence, so that my son and a million other sons may grow and breed without a canker in the guts or a monster in the cradle because of atomic radiation.

The irony is that all I do may be proved a folly and a precipitant for what I am trying to avoid. You are more fortunate. You believe you rest in the providence of God. Sometimes I wish—how very much I wish—that I could believe with you. But a man carries his destiny written on the palm of his hand,

and mine is written differently from yours. I am often ashamed
of what I did to you—I should like to prove to you that you
have some reason to be proud of what you have done for me.
If we have peace for only a year, you will have earned a great
part of it.

Think of me gently sometimes.   Yours, Kamenev.

They were all separate voices. Yet in their diverse ac-
cents they expressed a common hope that man, living
under the shadow of the mushroom cloud, might yet survive in peace to fulfill a divine plan in his regard.

He had to listen to them all. He might hope that in the
end the conflict of their opinions would resolve itself into
a harmony. Yet for all his fears, he knew that this hope
was an illusion.

He could not, without a grim risk, step outside the
field of action set down for him by divine commission. But
inside that field of action he was supreme. The government was upon his shoulders and upon no other's. In
the end he must decide. . . . Yet knowing his own infirmities, he shrank away from the decision.

Only two things were guaranteed to him by divine
promise—that standing in the shoes of the Fisherman, he
would not err in doctrine and that whatever folly he
might commit, the Church would survive. . . . In all
else he was left to his own devices. He might augment the
Church gloriously, or inflict upon it a terrible diminish-
ment. And this was the prospect that terrified him.

He was free to act, but he had no promise of the consequences of his action. He was ordered to pray, but he had
to pray in darkness and could not demand to know the
form in which the answer might come. . . .

He was still wrestling with the dilemma when the Father General of the Jesuits telephoned and requested an audience with him. He had, he said, a mass of business to discuss with the Pontiff, but this could wait until the day set for normal audiences. This time, he wanted to convey to the Holy Father the substance of his last talk with Jean Télémond.

"When I went to see him, Holiness, I found him in deep confusion," Semmering began. "I have never known a man so shocked. It took me a long time to calm him. But of this I am convinced. The submission he had made to your Holiness was firm and true, and when he died he was at peace. . . ."

"I am glad to hear it, Father. I knew what he was suffering. I wanted so much to share it, but he felt he had to withdraw from me."

"He did not withdraw, Holiness," said Semmering earnestly. "The thought in his mind was that he had to carry his own cross and work out his own salvation. He gave me a message for you."

"What message?"

"He said that he did not believe he could have made this final and necessary Act of Faith without you. He said that when the moment came it presented itself to him as the greatest risk of his life. A risk of his integrity and of reason itself. It was almost—and I use his own words—as if he might be launching himself into insanity. He said that the only thing that gave him courage to make the leap was that your Holiness had already made it before him, and that you had not shirked a single risk of speculation or of authority. . . . I wish I could convey to your Holiness the intensity with which he expressed himself." He gave a grim, restrained smile. "I have learned to be very skeptical, Holiness, of displays of fervor and religious emotion, but I am convinced that in this struggle of Father Télémond, I was witnessing the very real battle of a soul with itself and with the powers of darkness. I felt myself ennobled by the victory."

Kiril was moved. "I am grateful, Father, that you have told me. I am myself facing a crisis. I am sure Jean would have understood it. I hope he is interceding for me now with the Almighty."

"I am sure he is, Holiness. In a way his death was a kind of martyrdom. He met it very bravely. . . ." He hesitated a moment, and then continued, "There is another thing, Holiness. Before he died, Father Télémond told me that you had promised that his work would not be lost or suppressed. This was, of course, before the Holy Office issued its opinion. All Father Télémond's manuscripts have now come into my possession. I should like an indication of how your Holiness would prefer us to deal with them."

Kiril nodded thoughtfully. "I've been thinking of that, too. I have to agree with the option of the Holy Office, that Jean's opinions require re-examination. Speaking privately, I believe that there is much of value in them. It would be my thought to submit them to new study, and possibly to publish them later with annotation and commentary. I should think the Society of Jesus admirably equipped to carry out this work."

"We should be happy to undertake it, Holiness."

"Good. Now I should like to ask you a question. . . . You are a theologian and a religious superior. How far was Jean Télémond justified in taking the risks he did?"

"I have thought about that a long time, Holiness," said Rudolf Semmering. "It is a question I have had to ask myself many times, not only with Father Télémond, but with many other brilliant men inside the Society."

"And your conclusion, Father?"

"If a man is centered upon himself, the smallest risk is too great for him, because both success and failure can destroy him. If he is centered upon God, then no risk is too great, because success is already guaranteed—the successful union of Creator and creature, beside which everything else is meaningless."

"I agree with you, Father," said Kiril the Pontiff. "But you ignore one risk—the one which I am facing now—that at any moment up to the moment of death man can separate himself from God. Even I, who am His Vicar."

"What do you want me to say, Holiness?" asked Rudolf Semmering. "I have to admit it. From the day we begin to reason until the day we die, we are at risk of damnation. All of us. This is the price of existence. Your Holiness has to pay it like the rest of us. I could judge Jean Télémond because he was my subject. But you I cannot judge, Holiness. . . ."

"Then pray, Father—and have all your brethren pray —for the Pope on a tightrope."

The meeting of the Roman Curia, which Kiril had called to discuss the international situation and his proposed visit to France, was set down for the first week in November. It was preceded by a week of private discussions in which each of the Cardinals was invited to explore with the Pontiff his private opinions.

He did not attempt to sway them, but only to expose to them his thinking and to give them the confidence which they deserved as his counsellors. They were still divided. There were the few who agreed, the many who doubted, those who were openly hostile. His own fears were no less, and he still hoped that when the Curia came together in assembly, they would find a common voice to counsel him.

To assist them in their deliberations he had called Cardinal Morand from Paris, Pallenberg from Germany, Ellison from London, Charles Corbet Carlin from New York. Cardinal Ragambwe was there by accident because he had flown from Africa to confer with the Congregation of Rites on the new liturgical proposals.

The place of their meeting was to be the Sistine Chapel. He had chosen it because it was numinous with memories of his own election and all the others which had taken place there. He himself spent the night of the vigil in prayer, hoping to prepare himself to interpret his thoughts to the Curia and to receive from them some clear and concerted expression of the mind of the Church.

He was no longer confused, but he was still afraid, knowing how much might hang upon the outcome. The proposition which Semmering had presented to him was devastatingly simple—that a man centered in God had nothing to fear. But he was still troubled by the knowledge that he had been all too easily separated from this center and led astray into egotism. It was not the enormity of the act that troubled him, but the knowledge that the small lapses might be symptomatic of greater and undiscovered weaknesses in himself.

So when the Cardinal Camerlengo led him into the Chapel and he knelt to intone the invocation to the Holy Spirit, he found himself praying with a vivid intensity that the moment would not find him wanting. When the prayer was done, he stood to address the Cardinals.

"We have called you here, our brethren and our counsellors, to share with you a moment of decision in the life
of the Church. You are all aware that in the spring of next
year there may well be a political crisis which will bring
the world closer to war than it has been since 1939. We
want to show you the shape of the crisis. We want to show
you also certain proposals that have been made to us
which may help to minimize it.

"We are not so naïve as to believe that anything we may
do in the material order will effectively change the dangerous military and political situation which exists today.
The temporal domain of the Holy See has been reduced
to a small plot of ground in Rome, and we believe that
this is a good thing because we shall not be tempted to
use man-made instruments of intervention when we should
be using those provided us by God Himself.

"We do believe, however, and believe with firmest
faith, that it is our commission to change the course of history by establishing the kingdom of Christ in the hearts
of men, so that they may establish for themselves a temporal order based firmly upon truth, justice, charity, and
the moral law.

"This is our charge from Christ. We cannot abrogate
it. We must not shrink from a single one of its consequences. We dare not neglect any, even the most dangerous,
opportunity to fulfill it.

"First let us show you the shape of the crisis."

With swift, decisive strokes he sketched it for them—
the world embattled as it looked to one man sitting on a
pinnacle, with the nations spread below and the atomic
threat hanging above. None of them disagreed with him.
How could they? Each from his own vantage point had
seen the same situation.

He read them Kamenev's letters and those from the President of the United States. He read them his own commentaries and his own assessment of the characters and the dispositions of both men. Then he went on:

"It may seem to you, my brethren, that in the intervention we have already made there is a great element of risk. We admit it. It is clearly defined even in the letters from Kamenev and the President of the United States. We as Supreme Pontiff recognize the risk, but we had to accept it or let slip out of our hands a possible opportunity to serve the cause of peace in this dangerous time.

"We are aware, as each of you is aware, that we cannot count wholly on the sincerity or the protestations of friendship of any man who holds public office, even if he be a member of the Church. Such men are always subject to the pressure of influence, and opinion, and the actions of others over whom they have no control. But so long as a light of hope flickers, we must try to keep it alight and shield it from the harsh winds of circumstance.

"We have always believed, as a matter of private conviction, that our connection with the Premier of Russia, which dates back seventeen years, to the time of our first imprisonment for the Faith, had in it an element of Divine Providence which might one day be used by God for Kamenev's good or ours, or for the good of the world. In spite of all risks and doubts this is still our conviction.

"You are all aware that we have received an invitation from the Cardinal Archbishop of Paris to visit the shrine of Our Lady of Lourdes on her feast day, February eleventh, next year. An invitation has also been added from the Government of France to make a state visit to Paris afterwards. We do not have to tell you the risks of one.

kind or another which such a historic step would entail. Nevertheless, we are disposed to make it. Immediately we do so, other invitations will no doubt be issued, to visit other countries of the world. We shall be disposed to accept these, also, as time and circumstances permit. We are still young enough, thank God, and transport is now swift enough to permit us to do so without too great or too disastrous an interruption to the work of the Holy See.

"We have said we are disposed to do it. Before making a final decision we are anxious to have your opinion as our brothers and counsellors. We point out that if we decide to make the visit an immense amount of work will have to be done in a short time to prepare the public mind and to secure, so far as is possible, a friendly attitude from our brethren of other communions in Christendom. We do not wish to make a barren spectacle of our office. We do not want to raise historic animosities. We wish to go forth in charity to show ourselves as a pastor and to proclaim the brotherhood of all men, without exception of nation, race, or creed, in the Fatherhood of one God.

"If we do decide to go out thus into the world—this new world, which is so different from the old—then we do not wish to insist on niceties of protocol and ceremony. These are affairs of court, and if we are a prince by protocol, we are still a priest and a pastor by the anointing and the laying on of hands.

"What more can we say to you? These first months of our Pontificate have been full of labor and full of problems. We have learned much more than we should ever have believed possible, about the nature of our office, the problems of our Holy Mother Church and Her constant battle to make Her human body a fit vessel for the

Divine Life which infuses Her. We have made mistakes. We shall no doubt make many others, but we ask you, our brethren in the pastoral office, to forgive us and pray for us. Last week we suffered a grievous personal loss by the death of our dear friend, Father Jean Télémond, of the Society of Jesus. We beg you to pray for him, and we beg you to pray for us, also, who stand on this stormy eminence between God and man.

"The question is before you, dear brethren. Shall we go out from Rome and travel like the first Apostles to confront the twentieth century, or shall we stay at home here in Rome and let our brother bishops take care of their own vineyards in their own fashion? Shall we let the world look after its own affairs, or shall we, as Supreme Pontiff, risk our worldly dignity to step down into the market place and proclaim the Unknown God . . . ?

"*Quid vobis videtur.* . . . How does it seem to you?"

He sat down on the throne prepared for him and waited. Silence hung over the assembly like a cloud. He saw the old men looking one at the other as if they were exchanging a thought that they had already discussed in private. Then slowly Cardinal Leone, senior among the seniors of the Church, stood up and confronted the assembly.

"I will not rehearse for you, brethren, the hundred and one reasons for or against this project. His Holiness knows them as well as we. I will not recount the risks because they are as vividly present in the mind of the Pontiff as they are in ours. There are those among us—and I say frankly that I am one of them—who have grave doubts about the wisdom of a papal visit to France, or anywhere else, for that matter. There are others, I know, who see such a visit as a gesture both timely and efficacious. Who is right and who is wrong? Only God can decide the outcome and history pass a verdict on it. I do not think that any of us here would wish to increase the burden of His Holiness by attempting to sway him this way or that.

"The position is very simple. The authority of the Holy Father is supreme in the matter. Now or later he must decide on what is to be done. Whether our votes are for or against, *he* must decide. . . ."

For a brief moment he stood doughty and challenging, and then flung the last words down like a gage in front of the Curia:

"*Placetne, fratres.* . . . What say you, my brothers? Does that please you or not?"

There was a moment of hesitation, and then one after the other the red caps came off, and the murmur of assent ran round the assembly!

"*Placet* . . . It pleases us. We are agreed."

This was something Kiril had not expected. It was more than a formality. It was a vote of confidence. It was a gesture, prepared by Leone and the Curia, to affirm their loyalty and to comfort him in his trial.

It was more yet—an irony like the handful of flax burned under his nose before they crowned him, so that he would always remember his mortality. It was a committal of the Church, not to him, but to the Holy Spirit, who, even in spite of him would keep Her whole and alive until Judgment Day.

Now everything that he had inherited, everything that he had secretly demanded in his office, was in his hands: authority, dignity, freedom of decision, the power to loose and bind. . . . And he had to begin paying for it. . . . So there was nothing to do but say the ritual words of dismissal and let his counsellors go.

One by one the Cardinals came and knelt before him and kissed his ring in token of fealty. One by one they left. And when the door closed upon the last of them, he rose from his throne and knelt on the altar step before the tabernacle.

Above him was the towering splendor of Michelangelo's *Judgment*. In front of him was the small golden door, behind which dwelt the hidden God. The weight of the Cross was on his shoulders. The long Calvary was about to begin. He was left, as he would be left henceforward for all the days of his life. . . .

Extract from
the Secret Memorials of
K I R I L I, Pont. Max.

. . . I am calm now because the moment of decision
has come and passed, and I cannot rescind the choice I
have made. But the calm is at best a truce: uncertain,
embattled, dangerous to him who rests in it too confidently.

The next day or the next, the clash of arms will begin
again: the battle of myself with myself, of man with his
ambient world—and with his God, whose call to love is
always and most strangely a call to bloody conflict.

The mystery of evil is the deepest one of all. It is the
mystery of the primal creative act, when God called into
existence the human soul, made in His own image, and
presented it with the terrifying choice: to center itself
upon itself, or to center itself upon Him, without Whom
it could not subsist at all. . . . The mystery renews itself
daily in me, as it does in every man born of woman.

Where do I go? Where do I turn? I am called like Moses to the mountaintop to intercede for my people. I cannot go down until they carry me down dead. I cannot go up until God elects to call me to Himself. The most I can expect of my brothers in the Church is that they will hold up my arms when I grow weary of this life-long intercession. . . . And here is the shape of another mystery: that I who am called to spend so much find myself so poor in the things that are of God. . . .

"Forgive us our trespasses, as we forgive those who trespass against us. And lead us not into temptation, but deliver us from evil. Amen."

New York, March 1961—Sydney, August 1962